TORNADO
ALLEY

Novels by Craig Nova

TORNADO ALLEY

CRAIG NOVA

Delta

A Delta Book
Published by
Dell Publishing
a division of
Bantam Doubleday Dell Publishing Group, Inc.
666 Fifth Avenue
New York, New York 10103

ISBN: 0-385-30078-6

Reprinted by arrangement with Delacorte Press

Printed in the United States of America

Published simultaneously in Canada

September 1990

10 9 8 7 6 5 4 3 2 1

BVG

For Carole

Who would not regret his youth?

Joseph Conrad

Did I tell you about the storm I saw lately?

Vincent Van Gogh

Book I

Marie Boule, Night Crawlers

Baxter, Pennsylvania, 197–

AT NIGHT, IN MY ROOM, I SAW FROM MY WINDOW THE DARK shapes of people fluttering around the fires in those oil drums and trash cans. There were times when the stray dogs howled. I heard my father down the hall, the springs of his bed squeaking as he turned from side to side, waiting to take the next pill. My mother slept in her own room now, opposite my father's.

My mother was different when my father first bought this place. She was the most beautiful woman this town had ever seen, and I'm told that's where I got my looks, although mine are thinner, a little harder. My mother was tallish and had definite, high cheeks, full lips, and a beautiful, straight nose. I loved to look at her when her head was turned to the side. She had blue eyes and dark reddish hair. There was about her, even when she had gained a little weight, a broad, definite beauty that made people stop when they first came into the store and say, "Say, weren't you in the movies about ten years ago?"

Our house was at the top of the hill, had two stories, was covered with white siding, had dark green trim and a roof of asphalt tile. The store, at the front of the building, was connected to the house by the kitchen, like an architectural version of the flesh that holds Siamese twins together. We sold cans of soup, beans, beets, potatoes, peas and rice, Spam and corned beef, jars of mayonnaise and mustard. These things were in small, almost miniature packages and cans, as though only midgets came to shop here. Next to the cash register there was a rack of candy that came in rolls. There was a glass counter filled with pistols, and on the left-hand side of the store there was a cooler for milk, and beyond it there were fishing rods and reels, targets and ammunition, Day-Glo sweaters and sweatshirts, hats, jumpsuits and jackets, and there was a rack of cheap rifles and shotguns, and a rack of compound bows and arrows, the tips of which were stuck into a block of Styrofoam. Some of the arrows were bleeders, ones with a point that kept a wound open.

Across the street there was a lake with bungalows around the shore. These were places where people came for the summer. When we first arrived here, the three of us stood in front of the store. There was a breeze from the lake and the strands of my mother's reddish hair blew around her face, the cheerful, carefree movement of them and the expression on her face suggesting some steadfast, vital, and even childish thing about her, since she then believed life had its own mysterious, although benevolent design, and if you were patient and did what you knew you were supposed to do, why, then, things would turn out the way you wanted.

My father was of medium height and had dark, almost black hair, and in the beginning, when we first arrived here, there wasn't one white strand in it. That came later. He had blue eyes, and a reddish, tanned face, and there was more than one woman who would have found him attractive and who would have been beguiled, or taken outright, by his everlasting hope, or his belief that some new idea or saleable thing was going to make us rich and maybe even famous, like Thomas Edison or Alexander Graham Bell. My father believed in great men and that you learned to become one. There was a trick to it, a knack, like learning how to work a yo-yo.

My father usually wore a white shirt and a bow tie, a pair of gray flannel or wool trousers, and a green cardigan sweater. He had been born in Chicago, his parents being a Polish barber and an Irish seamstress. My father left after finishing two years of an unaccredited engineering school, which is to say he left Chicago not even half educated. He began a series of jobs, laboring and otherwise, and as he went from oil fields to construction gangs, building logging roads in Washington state and Oregon, he brought with him the one small business that was always successful, but which my father disliked, or felt uneasy about, and that was lending money at rates computed weekly to the men who worked for and with him on those construction sites, at car washes, and in cafeterias, or in taxicab shape-ups, or at any other place that gave my father an anonymous living. These loans, or the accumulation of the profits from them, went into a bank, or "a real bank," as my father said.

My mother was part Russian and part French Canadian, and my father never forgave my mother for her ethnic heritage, just as she never forgave my father for his, and each saw the other's origins as a social tattoo or maybe even a social scar. And neither one forgave the other, either, for the thing that held them together, which was a long, smoldering attraction which at times humiliated both of them, although the attraction had its moments, too, and left them with a kind of sensual arrogance. When they moved up here, and my mother began to suspect that life's plans weren't so benign and not anywhere near as mysterious as she had supposed, that smoldering attachment deserted them, and my mother was left with an unencumbered look at the man she had married.

I was fourteen when my father bought this place, the money for it coming from those innumerable loans, and when we first moved in my father brought with him some wood, paint, and brushes, and even before we started to unpack our boxes, my father cleared a space on the kitchen floor, and then, after he made himself a drink from a bottle of Old Grand-Dad bought for the occasion, he sat down and made a sign, which he hung out front the first morning we were here, and which said, AL BOULE'S HILLTOP STORE. GASOLINE, GUNS, FOOD, WORMS AND NIGHT CRAWLERS. At the closing, when my mother and father sat in the basement of the bank with the lawyer for the people who had owned the store before us, my father took from his pocket a roll of one-hundred-dollar bills, and he counted them out, one, two, three, four, five, six, putting each one down with a thump on the imitation oak table before the uninterested eyes of the lawyer and the banker, my father then wetting his finger and peeling off yet another bill. Later, when I got away, I understood that there is nothing more bitter than a woman who has been seduced, or whose passion has taken up not only her energy and money, but a lot of time.

Across the street, in a small house with white siding and black trim, there lived a Russian woman. I called her Aunt Natalya. She must have been seventy years old, and she wore black clothes and black shoes and a black kerchief over her hair, which was gray, the color of steel wool. Her eyes were black, and her cheeks were still pink, even though her face was wrinkled. The woman came to see us in the evenings, and then she whispered stories to me, told me about her cousin who had been in the Russian army and who had marched into Germany and who, with a friend, had shot and then eaten a German soldier. Aunt Natalya told me about the famine in the Ukraine when people had died in the streets, and when she spoke this way, she picked things out of the trash basket and ate them or wrapped them up in a paper napkin. But then there were times when she stole candy from the front of the store and gave it to me, telling me I was pretty.

The first morning my father stood out front, dressed in his flannel pants, bow tie, and green cardigan sweater. He was obviously firmly in possession of the place, and with the paint slowly drying on that sign he had painted, he waited on those people who came in to buy gasoline. In the afternoon he thought about "new ideas" for twenty minutes. Then he came inside, took a black Magic Marker and a piece of cardboard, and made another sign, which said, FREE COFFEE AND DONUTS. In the morning he put a large electric urn outside

and filled it with water and three small jars of instant coffee.
Next to the urn, in a cardboard box, there was a pile of doughnuts my father had gotten for almost nothing in the bakery in
Baxter. The doughnuts were two days old. When the first
customer came in, my father pointed out the sign and the urn
and the doughnuts, and when the driver of the car took the
coffee and the doughnut, my father made a note of what the
driver had wanted. He had a little spiral notebook and a mechanical pencil for this, and he wrote, *Ford, bald tires, bald
man, mole, Coffee Light and Jelly.* Soon he didn't need the
notebook anymore, and when a customer drove into the station, my father was already walking toward the car, carrying a
cup of coffee ("Customized coffee," my father said) and a stale
doughnut wrapped in waxed paper. Sometimes I sat by the
urn before walking up to the bus stop, and when a car pulled
in, my father said, "Marie, a coffee black and see if you can find
a plain doughnut." My father kept clippings from *The Wall
Street Journal* in his pockets, and between cars he took one out
and read it, standing alone and turned toward the lake.

At dinner he said, "I've been thinking, you know, about
Edison."

"Have you, Al?" said my mother.

"Yes, Sherry, I have. And there is a secret to the man. And
do you know what it was?"

"No," said my mother.

"Marie," said my father, "do you know what it was?
Come, take a guess."

"He was lucky," I said.

"*Luck,*" said my father. "There is no such thing as luck.
Edison took three naps a day, each one for ten minutes. Got
his best ideas right after waking up. *Ten* minutes, *three* times a
day."

In the morning I went out the door, passing the urn and
my father, who was bent over the cardboard box. The bus stop
was beyond the store and downhill. It was springtime now,
and I waited in the cool air, seeing the lake, the bright green
trees around it, and the blacktop road with the white line on it.
Up above, a car stopped at the gasoline pump and my father

went toward it, carrying that Styrofoam cup and that doughnut wrapped in paper, and in a minute the car pulled away
from the store and went down the hill. It went fast, but it
didn't go very far. The car stopped at the bottom of the hill,
which was the first spot out of sight of the store. The driver
reached over and rolled down the window on the passenger's
side and threw the doughnut, still in its paper, and the coffee,
in that Styrofoam cup, into a gulley by the side of the road,
both of these things flying from the car in silent desperation.

Soon another car came up to the pump and then pulled
away, going down that hill and stopping in the same spot, next
to that gulley, where the coffee and doughnut were shot from
the window, the things moving with a kind of hasty expulsion,
the paper separating from the doughnut, the top coming off
the coffee, the mud-colored stuff splashing against the scrub
brush. After a while I didn't have to look. I stared at the lake
and heard the cars stop at the bottom of the hill, where the
engine idled for a moment.

At dinner, over fried chicken, peas, and mashed potatoes,
my father said, "Marie, you're not eating."

"Oh," I said. I began.

"I was thinking this afternoon about Henry Ford," said
my father. "Now, there was a man's man. A problem solver—
but you know, it wasn't such a large thing that got him started.
He wasn't a genius. He had just one small idea. *One.*"

"Dad," I said, "maybe people don't want to have a free
cup of coffee."

"What?" he said.

"Maybe not everyone wants that cup of coffee in the
morning."

He had his fork in one hand, tines up, gesturing with it,
but then he put it down, back onto his plate, and said, "You
don't understand merchandising, Marie." He looked down
when he said this, his face a little drawn, or tired.

So I went on, standing out there in the morning and
watching those two objects thrown through the open window
of each car that stopped first at the gasoline pump and then at
the gulley below the store, the haste of getting rid of these

things becoming a little less as the dumping of them became part of the everyday routine, so that soon, when the cars stopped at the bottom of the hill and the window was rolled down and the cup and doughnut flew from the window, it wasn't done with embarrassment so much as nonchalance or maybe even boredom.

The fire marshal put a stop to it. He made periodic tours of the county, looking into swales and gullies, into any likely spot where people knew they weren't suppose to dump things but did anyway, and when the fire marshal drove past the store, looking for piles of combustible things, he stopped at the bottom of the hill, next to the gulley, and there he found the clutter of Styrofoam cups, the soggy accumulation of waxed paper, and the rest. Each of the cups had stamped on it, in blue ink, AL'S HILLTOP STORE. My father had sat at the table in the evening with a rubber stamp he had ordered and with an ink pad, carefully rocking the stamp over the curve of the cups, almost as though he were taking someone's fingerprints.

The fire marshal came up to the store, and as he stood there, trying to explain about the gulley, he didn't look my father in the face. The fire marshal stared toward the lake, and then, after pointing in the direction of the bottom of the hill, he got back into his red four-wheel-drive car and drove away. My father and I went outside, where both of us felt the cool May breeze.

"Don't cry, Marie," said my father.

I looked at the lake.

"I said, don't cry," said my father.

"I'm not crying," I said.

"Oh?" said my father, now kneeling and facing me and taking his handkerchief from his pocket. "Oh? What's this?" He wiped my eyes with his handkerchief, and as he did so his fingers trembled. They made a soft tapping against my cheeks. "Well, Marie," he said, "if they don't want coffee and dough-nuts, why, then, they don't have to have them." We went into the store and got some black plastic bags off the shelf and walked down there, where we cleaned the gulley, my father's hands shaking again as he reached for the cups and wrappers.

In the morning, when I went out to wait for the bus, the urn, the box, and the sign were gone, although at school the girls behind me giggled and passed a note, and when I grabbed it and opened it up, I saw written on a piece of lined paper, FREE COFFEE AND DONUTS. In the evening my mother stood at the sink, looking out the window at the darkness, and my father sat at the table, one hand just touching his Old Grand-Dad and water, and while neither said much, it was clear to both of them we'd only lived there ten days.

"Well, Al," said my mother, "why don't you tell us about Thomas Edison."

"Sure, Sherry," said my father, looking up and trembling a little, "sure. Did you know he made kites? The most beautiful round kites you've ever seen. Big as a house."

In the evenings now I did my homework at the table and my father sat opposite me, having an extra drink in anticipation of going out in the morning and facing the people who had thrown the coffee away. My mother stood at the sink, looking over her shoulder and seeing that life was becoming a little less mysterious. But this didn't last long, and within a week we were playing a game my father loved, and one that I loved, too, at least until I got be a little older. The game didn't have a name, but if it did, it would have been called "When My Ship Comes In." Mostly we played after dinner, when my father put *The Wall Street Journal* away and sat with a bowl before him in which there were three scoops of ice cream, one chocolate, one vanilla, and one Mystery Delight, and as the sweetness melted on his tongue, he looked at me and said, "Marie, when our ship comes in, what are you going to get?" and in the beginning I said, a pony, and then a horse, and later, when I was fifteen, I wanted some clothes, a real Ralph Lauren dress, and a car, a red Corvette. My father asked my mother what she wanted, and she said, "Oh, Al, I don't know." Then she turned away from the sink, her eyes set on that empty spot in the middle of the kitchen. "Well, Sherry," said my father, "what's it going to be?" "Oh, Al, I guess if I wanted anything it would be a trip someplace, a trip to Florida, with all the trimmings." Then she smiled and shook her head. "Oh,

Al, what are you getting me to say?" My father smiled then and nodded and took a small spoonful of ice cream into his mouth. He closed his eyes with the cold sweetness of it.

In the morning my father went to face those people again, and my mother watched the store. I went to school, and stared straight ahead. The summer came, hot and dry and windy, and the dust blew around the lake, and the people from Jersey City or Scranton or Philadelphia came to the cabins on the shore, the women in housedresses staring through the small screened-in porches. The fall and winter came. Aunt Natalya told me about her cousin who had a job, during the revolution, of picking up dead people with a pitchfork. The seasons came and went, leaving behind the weight of promises not kept.

Now, on Saturday or Sunday evenings, when the store was closed and my parents went out, I bathed and stood in front of the mirror in the bathroom. As I grew, each new version of myself seemed to run together, the early, disproportionate features catching up with the others, the entire insistent growth appearing as a swelling and stretching, and when I think of those years, I see myself in my bed, the small creaking one in my room under the slanted ceiling, and there my legs got longer, the calves and thighs stretching, but having a shape now, thin at the ankle, curved at the calf, the new strength of them bringing a lack of clumsiness, and in that same rush there appeared strands of hair, the first filaments showing just above my ankles and then on my lower stomach, where they became thicker and formed a dark, straightish shape, and I can see my shoulders getting broader, the bones in them long and thin, my breasts appearing, too, the growth smooth and fluid: my figure appeared in that single bed like some young creature in a harsh, mysterious sleep, and I bloomed and stretched, my features becoming taut, or soft and private, and as I lay there, it seemed I grew with life's own indifference, its own lack of mercy for anyone who wants, even for a moment, to stand still, or to just stop and rest. And in this harsh (or at least fast) growth there were hints of secrets, of beguiling things that life sends just to take your breath away.

In the winters we spent the evenings in the kitchen. My father roasted peanuts in the oven, and we sat at the table, my father with his drink and *The Wall Street Journal,* both of us shelling the hot peanuts and burning our fingers as we tried to eat them before they had cooled enough. One winter, my father looked up from the paper and said, "Sherry, there's an inventor's trade show at the Coliseum in New York. How would you like to take it in?"

"Could we stay in a hotel?" said my mother.

"Well, I thought we'd make it round trip in a day," said my father. "I'd pack a lunch."

"Well, I don't know, Al."

"How about you, Marie, will you come along?"

In the morning, before we left, my father made two tuna sandwiches on bread that was out of date. He took some celery from the store, too, the stalks of it covered with brown spots. He chopped it up and put it in the tuna with mayonnaise from one of those miniature jars. Then he sliced the stale crusts off the sandwiches and wrapped them in white butcher paper, folding down the flaps so they looked like the back of an envelope. He tapped them shut. He took a can of ginger ale for me and a beer for himself, and put the picnic into a brown secondhand bag, and then we went out and got into the Chevrolet station wagon. My mother came outside to see us off, and as we pulled away, her features were set in an expression of wonder, or perhaps just mystification.

When we were almost to New York and crossing the marshes, my father pulled over, and as we looked through the windshield at the twin towers of the World Trade Center, my father passed over my sandwich. We ate, hearing the dry reeds rustle in the marsh, and in the distance the towers stood, the lights of the windows seeming divine. Then, before the car cooled off, we started again, and got through the tunnel. We parked on the West Side and walked east across Eighth Avenue, where my father said about the women there, "Those are whores, Marie."

We took the escalators into the Coliseum, feeling the hum and shove of the metal stairs. At the top there was a room as large as a football field, and in it there were long rows of booths, where the inventors stood, the things they had made on a table or on the floor next to them. There were robots and solar air-conditioners, circuitry made of gases, rail guns, engineered bacteria, and other things, too, the accumulation of them having the clutter of a dime-store counter. The inventors stood next to their machines or at their desks, all of them needing money, or a drink, or both. And when the show was over, we carried away piles of brochures and pamphlets, which we took home and went through carefully, or at least we did this until springtime, when my father was left to read them by himself. When we came out of the Coliseum, we found a hot-dog stand, or a counter, where we bought one hot dog apiece and then stood on the south side of the park and ate them in the cold, our fingers getting numb and the brochures and technical papers piled at our feet. There were times when an inventor mistook my father for an investor and listened politely and even with interest to my father's stories of Edison, Bell, Ford, Deere, and Whitney.

My father had dental theories, too, and he knew of a prison warden in Alabama who tried to eradicate crime by pulling his inmates' teeth. My father believed that teeth determined character, and after studying the dental records of great men, he said he could detect genius. My father told the inventors about the warden in Alabama, Henry Ford's bridgework, and Edison's constant toothache.

These trips had a practical application, too, since my father was looking for a "product." He saw his first Dynamo at the Coliseum. I was seventeen then, and the trip began like any other, and I supposed it would end like the others, too, with us coming into the store and then into the kitchen, both of us tired and cold and carrying those piles of schematics, brochures, and cost estimates. My father made sandwiches and put them into a brown sack, and we stopped in the marshland to have our lunch with the World Trade Center on the horizon, the towers looking like a monument and suggesting a

constant suspicion, if not outright disapproval, of us. Now I
had a can of beer, too, and we sat together, facing the towers
and eating, neither of us saying a word. We passed the whores
on Eighth Avenue, my father ignoring them (and probably
thinking they should have their teeth pulled), and then we
went into the Coliseum.

We rose on the escalator and heard above us, in that
enormous space, the hubbub of voices, the sound of cheerful
music, and the shuffle of papers as people moved up and down
before the booths where the inventions were displayed. My
father and I went down one row, picking up brochures as
always, my father asking a question here or there, and then we
turned the corner, into the next row.

We stopped at a largish booth. At the back of it there was a
heavy red curtain, which looked like velvet, and there were
signs on it and long ropes of tinsel. In front of the curtain, on
an elevated platform, there was a large, round, and shiny
cylinder. It was tall as a trash can, but it was smooth and
obviously made of stainless steel. There were wheels on the
cylinder, and piled next to it there was a coil of white tube,
which was big around as a coffee can and made with a long
spring inside so the tube could stretch back and forth: the
entire thing looked like a child's construction of an octopus,
say, made out of trash cans and the tubes used to vent a dryer.
There was a spotlight above the machine, and the stainless
steel was bright with it.

Next to the machine there was a woman who was dressed
in a one-piece bathing suit, only this one was covered with red
sequins. The woman wore black stockings and a pair of high-
heeled shoes, which were covered with red sequins, too, and
across her breasts and over her hip was a sash that said,
DYNAMO. She stood with one foot forward, the other back,
like a woman in a beauty contest. Her hair was piled up on her
head, and her smile came as a kind of commercial sultriness.
When I stopped and looked, I thought, *Mine are smaller, but
have a nicer shape. I've got better legs.* The woman smiled.
From a shelf she took a canvas bag like one used to feed horses,
and then she turned the bag upside down. The dust inside,

like charcoal-colored talcum, fell to the floor with a kind of powdery thump and left a filament of dust rising slowly into the air. The woman picked up one of those octopuslike tentacles, put a stainless steel attachment onto it, and touched a button on the machine. There was a rushing sound, like one made by a working model of a jet engine, as a gas moved through a blue, circular tube on top of the machine. The woman cleaned up the the dust, her hips swinging back and forth, her back straight, her long, thin fingers holding a metal tube.

The machine didn't clean so much as to make it seem the dust had disappeared. The light above the booth made the woman's sequins shine, and as she went back and forth, her arms coming and going, the shape of her breast became visible, and on the swell of it, which pushed out of the bathing suit, there was the tip of some small tattoo. It could have been almost anything, a wing, a talon, a flower, a stylized word, a name. It was done with blue-green ink, which looked almost like a vein. She stood up when she was done, and I couldn't see it anymore. My father didn't notice it. He stared at the machine and the clean place on the carpet.

The woman said, "Do you want to see it again?"

"Yes," said my father, keeping his eyes on the carpet.

The woman turned the bag of dust upside down again and the contents landed with a dusty thump, and I watched her side as she worked, seeing that blue line on the swell of her breast. She turned to look at me, and held the top of the suit with her thumb and forefinger and pulled it around herself, keeping her eyes on me all the time she did so. Neither one of us blushed. My father stepped up and looked more closely at the machine, and as he touched it, as he saw the shape of the thing and let his fingers linger on it, he said, "Marie, I think our ship has come in."

"How is that?" I said.

"I can sell these things like wildfire," said my father.

Then he stepped onto the platform, crossing it with three definite strides, and sat down at the table at the back, where there was a bald man in a pinstriped suit. On the table there were some brochures. I looked around the room, feeling the constant, infinitely slow pace of the people who walked by me, but I looked at the woman again, who now stood on the platform, one leg out, her back straight, the long metal tube in her hand. She winked at me and said, "Getting that tattoo is the best thing I ever did. Men die, I mean they *die*, to get a look at it."

"Is it a picture of something?" I asked.

The woman just winked again.

"Do you want to take another look at the machine?" she said.

"No. Thanks, though."

"I've got to clean the dust four times an hour." She looked around the room and squinted a little. "These egghead shows are the worst. Lot of brainy guys around here, but talk about tightfisted. And I'll bet they got it, too. Bundles." She sighed. "The auto show is better."

"Did it hurt?" I said.

"What?" she said.

"When you got the tattoo?"

"It was worth it," she said and winked again.

My father went on talking. The woman dumped the dust again and turned on the machine, the light going over the sequins in an endlessly repeated shimmer as she worked back and forth. The long muscles slithered in her legs. My father took out his checkbook. I turned from the bluish lines of the tattoo, from the swell of the woman's breast, and watched as my father took a fountain pen and started to write. The woman said, "Well, it was nice talking to you. It's my break now."

She put the coil and attachments neatly away and stepped down, and as she did so, my father came toward me, holding some completed forms and some brochures, which had a whitish sheen from the overhead light. I went down the aisle with my father, seeing ahead of us the broad, bare shoulders of the woman and the flash of sequins as she moved between the people who had stopped at a booth. My father didn't notice, though, since he was looking at his papers. We got onto the escalator, and in the gleam of it we fell away, leaving the noise of the show behind. Outside, there were the leafless shapes of the trees in the park, the dark stone of the buildings, which looked like dirty ice, and the sad flutter of the pigeons. I stopped in front of the counter where we usually ate, but my father took my hand and led me to a chophouse, which had linen tablecloths, heavy utensils and glasses, comfortable chairs, and a constant silver tinkle. I looked over the menu, trying to find something that wasn't expensive, and my father said, "Go on. You tell me what you'd like to have."

We got home after midnight, but even then my father went into the store and began to move the racks of compound bows and the Styrofoam blocks which held the bleeders, the counter on which there were piled the Day-Glo vests, sweaters, and hats, and to move the cheap gun cases and stands for the targets, and when he had finished there was, in the middle of the store, just back from the front door, a clear, clean spot. He stood for a moment, in the half-light, staring at it.

My mother came downstairs, and when she stood in the doorway of the kitchen, the light made her figure into a shadow in the whitish, almost transparent haze of her nightgown.

"What are you doing, Al?"

"Rearranging things," he said.

"Why do you want to do that?"

"I've found something I can sell."

"Did you, Al?" said my mother. She yawned and put the tips of the fingers of one hand to her lips and looked at the space on the floor. "What do you think you can sell?"

My father took a brochure from his back pocket and handed it over. My mother held it up to the light and then looked at my father.

"What is it?" said my mother, now wide awake.

"Aren't they the most beautiful things you've ever seen?" said my father. He stepped closer to her and looked at the picture in the brochure. "Look at the *engineering*. Why, it could have been made in Berlin."

"Berlin," said my mother. "What's going on, Al? What have you done?"

"I've bought three machines," said my father. "They came to fifteen hundred dollars."

My mother dropped her hands, the one holding the brochure making an abrupt fall into the light haze of her nightgown.

"Oh, Al, how could you?"

"You've got to break eggs to make an omelette," said my father.

"Is that right, Al?" said my mother. "And what are we going to pay the bills with?"

"I can sell these things, Sherry."

"Oh, Al, not fifteen hundred dollars. Couldn't we have talked about it?"

"Look at the design. Space age technology. *Computerized.* They've got an LCD display to tell you how they're cleaning. You know, how many cubic feet of air you're getting per second. And, Sherry, you should see the way they clean. Like magic. Tell her, Marie."

I described the woman in the bathing suit and the bag of dust.

"A *bathing suit?*" said my mother.

"I don't remember a bathing suit," said my father.

My mother and father stood opposite one another for a moment, looking into each other's eyes.

"Well, Al, maybe it will be all right," said my mother. "But fifteen hundred dollars? Are you in your right mind?" Then she turned and went upstairs, one hand trailing the brochure, the shadow of it on the floor looking like a long black handbag.

In the afternoons and on Saturdays and Sundays I helped my father, and either I watched the cash register in the store or I went out to the gasoline pumps when a car stopped next to them. When it was cold, I wore a duck-hunting coat that had been left in the cabin we had for rent, but sometimes I just went out in a pair of jeans and a T-shirt, feeling the cold. When I came back into the kitchen, my mother said, "Marie, you're being too revealing."

The cars came and went, the men in them watching me, their eyes behind the glass of the rolled-up windows. In one of the cars there was a man who had tattoos on his arms. The skin was almost entirely covered, the inky colors having a hairless sheen to them, like silk, and in the chaos of figures entwined together there were birds and snakes, women's hair, a setting sun, trees and plants with large leaves, flowers with a pink flush, and an endless number of small birds, hiding among the leaves and branches of the trees. On the seat next to the man was a magazine called *The American Tattooist.* He took a bill from his wallet, rolled down the window, and pushed it toward me. I was trying to see what was on the cover of the magazine.

"Are you interested in tattoos?" he said.

"I don't know."

"Look." He held up his arm. "The way it works is like this. If you get one, and then another, and then decide on a third tattoo, you're doomed. You'll end up completely covered." He shrugged. "Here," he said, passing the magazine through the window. "You want this? I've already read it."

In the evening, in my room, I turned the pages of it. Mostly it was printed on cheap paper, and the tattoos were hard to see, but there was one slick piece of paper in the middle of the magazine, and on it there was a full-color photograph. Sometimes I sat and looked at it, unaware even of the texture of the bedspread where I lay, the heels of my palms under my chin. A woman was shown sitting on a stool with a sheet draped across her lap, but otherwise she was nude. Her side was to the camera, and she held her hair on top of her head so it didn't cover any of the tattoo that went from the top of her buttock to her underarm. It was an Oriental painting, in which there were a pond, bamboo stalks with slender leaves, and a parrot, too, with a long, bright orange tail, which came as a splash of color against her side. The shape of her back, the tautness of the skin over her ribs, the narrowness of her hips, suggested a young woman. Her skin was pale and her eyes reminded me of winter, when someone is working in the snow, and you hear a metallic clang or the grating of a shovel.

In the back of the magazine there were advertisements
for patterns you could take to a tattoo parlor, and there were
other ones, too, temporary ones that went on like decals but
washed off. I sent away for some of these, and on a Saturday
night, when my mother and father were out, I'd take a bath
and shave my legs and stand in front of the mirror, holding up
one tattoo and then another. Or other times I wouldn't bathe
at all, and I'd stand there nude, with my hair dirty and hanging around me while I held up a logo from Harley-Davidson,
or a tattoo that said, OKINAWA. Finally I'd pick one, a screaming eagle, say, or a tiger (with long, bluish stripes), and put it
on, feeling the give of my skin. There was one that said, PAY AS
YOU ENTER, and I put it on my lower stomach, just below the
curls of light, brownish hair. When I put on a tattoo I stood and
looked at myself, holding my hair on top of my head.

While my father was waiting for the Dynamos to be delivered, my mother received a postcard in the mail. On one side
there was a photograph of a white beach, with palm trees and
milky blue water, and on the other side there was a typed
message, which said, *Congratulations. You have just won a
Free Trip to Florida! Call 800-555-6521.* My mother first read
the message as she stood by the mailbox. It was March now,
and beyond her there was the lake with dirty ice on it. The
wind blew her hair, which she touched in an abstracted, half-
hearted way while she looked at one side of the card and the
other and then turned it over again. She walked away from
the mailbox, still looking at the card, and when she came
through the store and into the kitchen, where my father was
reading the paper and where I was having breakfast, she said,
"Guess what? I've won a trip to Florida."

My mother hadn't latched the screen door outside, and it
swung back and forth in the cold March wind. My mother
pulled her green sweater together and stood there, one hand
at her throat, her eyes set on us.

My father looked at the front of the card, at the milky
sand and the whitish water, the palm trees. He read the back
and passed it to me.

"What do you think?" said my mother.

"Sherry," he said, "I'm not sure you've won anything."

"It says so right there," said my mother.

"I think it's a come-on."

"I've won a trip," said my mother. "There's an eight-hundred number."

"It's a come-on," said my father.

He looked at the card again.

"I'm sure of it," he said.

"I've won a trip," said my mother, looking directly at my father.

"That's not the way it works," said my father. "Probably they pay your way down there, but you have to rent a car, pay for your hotel room and food, and by the time you're done, you've more than paid for your ticket. People don't give away trips to Florida."

"I've *won a trip,*" said my mother.

"Okay. Fine," said my father. "Call."

My mother held the card and stood in the middle of the kitchen. Beyond her there was the counter, the draining board, the plates on it, the silverware as dull as bullets in the March light. My father looked back at her.

"You don't have to be smug," said my mother.

"Okay, it's your funeral," said my father.

"You're wrong about this, Al. I don't know why you can't understand."

My father went back to his paper and my mother picked up the receiver and then we heard the ratchet and stop, ratchet and stop, of her dialing. I held a spoon, halfway out of a bowl of cereal. My father stared at the paper. The screen door swung back and forth in the breeze, making that sound. My mother listened, and put down the phone, the hanging up of it not anything but a challenge.

"It's a recording. The place is closed until Monday."

It was Saturday. There was a small bulletin board next to the phone, and my mother pinned the card there, carefully putting a thumbtack through the crown of a palm tree. Every time I went outside, or when I came in to get a snack or for dinner, I saw it, the thing hanging there like some postcard on which there was a likeness of Jesus or Buddha. Because in those hours between Saturday and Monday it became a kind of emblem of faith, and with each passing hour my mother looked at it with more certainty, although with a little fear, or maybe just respect, since the card was evidence, to my mother, that life was made by luck. My father looked at the card but said nothing, although he obviously resisted anything as simple as luck, since he believed, or wanted to believe, that the world you lived in was formed by action, and that you just had to take the right one, and while this was difficult, it was not impossible.

My mother and father went through the hours, eating and sleeping and reading the paper, waiting on customers who came into the store to buy stale bread and small cans of tuna fish, and all the while that card sat there, appearing bigger, so that when you came into the room you had to look at it, almost as though the thing were a poster, the beach, the white sand and palm trees having about them the air of the supernatural. By Monday I recognized the sheen on that photograph of the beach, since it was the same malignant gleam as on the cylinders of those machines my father had bought with money that was supposed to go to pay bills.

On Sunday we had dinner together. Usually the store and the gasoline pumps were quiet, and on Sunday there was a kind of respite from the endless small purchases. We didn't have many friends, especially not since my father had given away coffee and doughnuts, although Aunt Natalya still visited, her figure in dark clothes rising from the other side of the road as she came toward the store. She dug through the trash and told me what young women had done to get something to eat in the Ukraine during the famine. Then she gave me cherry sweets. They were still warm from being carried in her hand, and I ate them, feeling her warmth on my tongue. This Sunday it was quiet, but not so peaceful.

My mother made meat loaf and baked potatoes and cabbage, and while the food was being cooked, my mother and father sat opposite one another, each of them holding a glass of bourbon. There was a *drip, drip, drip* as the last of the snow melted on the roof and fell from the eaves.

"Why don't you throw the card away?" I said to my mother.

"No," she said. She shook her head. "I'm not going to be cheated out of this because your father's afraid."

"Oh, Jesus," said my father, "Sherry, I'm not afraid."

After a while my mother went into the store, to the rack where we sold maps, and when she came back she spread one of Georgia and Florida on the table, and my father went on drinking, saying to the two-day-old copy of *The Wall Street Journal* he had laid out before him, "Look, it's just a come-on. Can't you see?" But my mother shook her head, probably knowing she was making things worse, but not giving a damn, if only because the worst thing in the world would be that my father was right. When she was finished with the maps, running her finger along the coast and silently repeating the names of the towns, she went back into the store and took from the magazine rack old copies of *Vogue* and *Cosmo,* turning the pages of them and looking for pictures of women who were shown on the beach in Florida, Mexico, or even Rio. They wore small bathing suits, and their long arms and legs glistened. Their skin gleamed, and the young women appeared, as they stretched out on that white sand, like luck incarnate.

We went to bed early, my mother and father going into their room and undressing in a formal, quiet way, and both of them probably lying down and staring at the ceiling and feeling around them the strong, definite eddy of what was wrong between them, or what had always been wrong between them, but neither one of them understanding a thing. I stretched out, too, down the hall, and every time the lights of a car filled the room with a slow pulse of light, I thought of those bodies glistening in the sunshine, and when the darkness came back in a flood, I remembered that card, pinned up on the bulletin board.

On Monday morning I got up and got dressed and ate my breakfast and then went to school. It was the spring of my last year, and I went through my classes, not really listening. I thought, *Well, she's probably called now. So, she knows now.* Then I went to the next class and thought the same thing, and then I came home, slowly walking up to the house with the white siding, the green trim and that big Gulf sign. I went into the store, hearing that long, definite *eeeeeah, eeeeeah* of the door.

My mother stood in the kitchen, holding the card, and by her face I knew she hadn't called yet. Maybe she had been afraid after all and had put it off, but now I had come, walking into the house and announcing, like some three-dimensional clock, that the time was getting short. My father came in, too, just as though he'd been waiting for me. My mother sighed and picked up the phone and dialed, making that ratcheting click and stop, that *a-tat-tat-tat-tat, a-tat-tat-tat-tat.*

"Hello," said my mother, "I received a card saying I'd won a trip to Florida."

My father stood there, watching her closely.

"Well, thank you. What? Why, yes, I'd be delighted to go. When? Well, I don't know. Pretty soon, I guess."

The bell from the pumps rang, but my father didn't move and I didn't either.

"Yes, that's what I've thought. Florida is nice this time of the year. Me? Well, I live in Pennsylvania. No, we don't have much snow on the ground, but it's still cold and spring hasn't really come yet. That sounds nice. Yes, I'd like to spend a little time on a deserted beach."

Outside, a man sat in his car and looked at the store.

"Yes," said my mother, "I'd like to feel a little sunshine. Well, what about next week? All right, I'd like to go then."

My mother stepped a little closer to the sink, so she could look out the window.

"Oh? What charges are those?" she said. "Uh-huh. Well, that's not much. Not really."

She closed her eyes now.

"Yes, I see. Well, of course. I can understand that," she said, "but the card says a *free* trip to Florida. Oh? I didn't know that. Well, of course, that makes it different. What will the complete charges come to? Well, I see." She still looked out the window and held the card in her hand. "Well, no. I guess you shouldn't send the ticket. I don't think I'll be able to go. Thank you."

Then she turned and put the receiver down and turned away from us. We didn't move, now, even when the driver of the car outside honked his horn. My mother looked out the window and said, "I'm going outside. If you come out while I'm there, Al, I'll leave this place flat."

She went into the cold air, the screen door making that lonely moan as she went through it. She crossed her arms and stared at the lake, or the sky, or nothing at all, and when the man in the car said something to her, she went over to the pump and turned the thing on, shoving the nozzle into the car with a kind of fury. The man paid her and left, and she held the ten-dollar bill he'd given her and stood with the wind pushing her clothes against her. She turned to the house and came toward the door, not walking so much as marching, and when she came back into the room, no less angry now, she said, "Well, Al, you were just as right as rain." She put the ten dollars into the cash register and snapped over it the wire that held the money down.

"I'll take you to Florida," said my father.

"No, you won't," she said. "Let's stop kidding ourselves." She slammed the cash drawer shut.

"No," she said again.

She went upstairs and stretched out on the bed, and every now and then the floorboards creaked with her quick tread as she went down the hall and sat in the bathroom and ran the water in the sink so we couldn't hear the sounds she made. After a while my father and I climbed the stairs. We went down the linoleum in the hall and stopped at the bathroom door.

"Stay out of here. Al, I warn you," she said.

"Sherry, Sherry," said my father.

My mother turned on the water again, and then we opened the door. She looked up, her face wet.

"Oh, Al, what's gone wrong?"

"I don't know," he said.

"What are we going to do?" she said.

"I'm going to try to make some money," he said.

" 'Try,' " she said, closing her eyes.

My father took one of her hands and I took the other, and she squeezed both of them, trembling as she did so. "All right," she said. "We'll go on. Let's all try. I just wish you'd thought I had a chance, Al. That would have made it so much easier."

A week later I stood outside, watching the lake, which had thawed out, but the weather had turned cold again, and now new membranes of ice formed on it. Down the road and beyond the gulley where the coffee and doughnuts had been thrown, there was a loud banging and rattling sound, as though a large trailer, filled with junk, were being pulled over the road's frost heaves: there was a pounding and jangling, and a noise obviously made by an engine. There was a line, too, beyond the trees down there, of dark smoke, which rose and thinned out and spread into the blue sky of springtime, and while the smoke rose and dispersed, a largish truck came around the turn by the gulley. The front fenders had rusted away, but they had been remade by someone using duct tape over a wooden frame, which in turn had been bolted to the metal beneath the sides of the hood. The windshield was new, although it did not fit into the space for it, and was taped, too, around the top so that the rain wouldn't get in. The cab was brownish and shiny, although the paint had been applied from a spray can over creases and dents and the chrome that was still on the truck's doors. The truck rattled and the noise became louder, not to mention that the black mist or exhaust became darker and that more of it came into the air, too, as the truck came up the hill, not going slower, and maybe even going faster as the driver saw the sign that said, AL BOULE'S HILLTOP STORE. The box of the truck had been crumpled when someone had tried to drive it under a bridge that was too low, and the aluminum had a regular, neatly folded quality, like the flexible part of an accordion. The entire aspect of the thing, the sound and taped fenders and new window, not to mention the partially collapsed box, came as bad tidings, or at least as evidence of a hard, desperate journey.

The driver wore dark glasses and a leather coat, and he turned into the gas station and pulled on the emergency brake, not looking at me or the store or anyone at all: he jumped out and went to the back of the truck and opened the door, doing so with the air of a man who has dreamed of performing this action for a long time. The doors had WASH ME and FUCK YOU written in the dust on them, and when they swung open, there stood three large and innocuous-looking boxes, each one of which had DYNAMO printed on it in new, clean, and large blue letters.

The driver dropped them onto the black asphalt of the apron, each one coming down with a kind of metallic crash, and then he turned to my father, who now stood with me in the cold. The driver held out a clipboard and a new blue grease-pencil and said, "Sign here."

My father signed. The driver got back into the truck and started the engine, the black clouds rising from under the cab rather than from behind, and the truck went downhill, the unrelenting sound disappearing with a suddenness that didn't suggest being in a hurry so much as being in a race.

My father and I carried the boxes into the store and put them in that blank, waiting space, and there we unpacked them, putting the domes onto the cylinders and attaching the long white tubes, so that, when all the machines were lined up, they looked like a family of mechanical octopi, triplets, say, and in front of each one there was a neat pile of stainless steel attachments, tubes and flattened cones and squarish things with a little black brush around the opening, which you could use to clean drapes, stairs, carpets, and dirt of varying coarseness, from fine dust to stuff made of pieces the size of marbles. The cylinders were shiny, bright as polished silver, and the gas tubes on top were bluish. The machines looked a little sinister and each one smelled of lubricant and new electric cord. Above them, hung from two new hooks in the ceiling, there was one of my father's signs, which said, with the

letters made by hand and bunched a little to the left side, THE
DYNAMO. THE BEST VACUUM CLEANER IN THE WORLD.

My mother came in and looked at the machines. She went
from one to the other, seeing her distorted reflection on the
surface of the cylinders. Then she took me with her down to
Baxter, where she bought her first copy of *Ms.*, not to mention
a copy of *Mechanix Illustrated*, as though the two formed
equal parts of her thinking, one half accusation, the other half
proof.

We sat at the counter at the coffee shop. My mother
bought a package of Salem cigarettes, and while we had our
coffee, she flipped through the *Mechanix Illustrated* and the
Ms., stopping from time to time to read something out loud,
balancing homemade computers against karate for women,
and saying, after having a long drag on the Salem, the words
coming out in large, definite puffs, "The thing is, you want to
make men sweat. Just look what they do if you don't." Her
finger tapped the *Mechanix Illustrated*, and then she gestured
over her shoulder, which I knew meant my father's machines,
now gleaming in the front of the store, their presence appearing like the first splash of paint, silver colored, say, on a previously clean piece of canvas. "It doesn't matter how you make
them sweat, so long as you do," she said, and then we went
out, my mother leaving the magazines on the counter and
driving home, the cigarette dangling from her lips, the tip of it
jumping as she spoke.

My mother was smoking a Salem when she came into the
store, where my father sat, looking through a manual for the
Dynamos. He had a chair next to the machines, and one of
them was half apart, the motor and wiring exposed. My
mother passed him and went into the kitchen, where there
were glasses and dishes in the draining rack. She began to put
them away.

"You see, Sherry," said my father, looking into the machine, "no one gives away a free trip to Florida."

My mother jerked around and looked at him. She held a
glass in her hand, and she brought it down in one smooth
motion, which appeared as a clear streak and a crash as the

pieces of it slid across the blue linoleum in a pattern that
suggested a star, or the rays that come from one, all the small,
sharp bits flying away from the center.

"Sherry," said my father. "Stop it."

She broke another glass and then went out of the room,
leaving my father and me. There was a lot of glass on the floor,
and you felt the presence of it like a swarm of bees or wasps.
My father looked at the manual again, holding it with both
hands, but soon he put it down and took one of the machines
by the handle on the cylinder and rolled it into the kitchen.
My father brought the tubes and attachments and connected
them, and after plugging the thing in, he went over the glass,
the machine making a steady, pumping throb as the gas
rushed through that blue thing on top of the cylinder. He
wore his white shirt, bow tie, green sweater, and gray trousers. His heavy hands held the metal tube, into which the bits
of glass disappeared with a jerk and a rattle, the stream of glass
there giving him not only pleasure, but vindication, too.

On Saturday mornings my father and I loaded the machines into the back of the station wagon. My father got behind the wheel. On the seat next to him there was a Geological
Survey Map, on which he had carefully marked the day's
route in Magic Marker, the red or blue or green line going
along roads which the map showed as having a lot of houses on
them. There was a lunch, too, in a paper sack. We went downhill, my father cheerful and maybe even happy, since he had
the machines and a plan, not to mention me, too, as though
our family didn't exist, or couldn't be really experienced, unless we were facing embarrassment.

My father went up to the houses and rang the bell or just
pounded on the door, and when someone came out, a woman
in a housecoat or a man in his pants and an undershirt, my
father started talking, showing brochures and looking at the
dusty rooms beyond the front door. If he thought someone
wanted to see a machine, he made an O with his fingers
behind his back, and when I saw it, I got out of the car and
opened the back and got things ready. Then my father and I
lifted the machine and carried it up to the house. Usually the

houses had the stale, cooped-up air of coffee, cigarettes, and broiled chops. In the living rooms there were lacy metal frames with pictures of children in them, or animals, dogs, say, and on the shelves there were small figurines and bowling trophies. There were rifles hung on the walls or displayed in glass cases. When we showed how a machine worked, I handed my father the attachments, and he used one and then another, demonstrating the machine with a gentle sway, a rhythmic two-step like slow dancing.

The first morning my father stopped in the driveway of a small house. It was built on cinder blocks, had a garage underneath, and was covered with asphalt siding. There was a front door but it had no steps, and the door hung there, three feet off the ground. My father went up to the side door and knocked, and when someone answered, he made his sign. I got the attachments ready, and when we carried the machine up to the door, I heard someone say, "Hey, Mary. It's Al, from the store. You know, the guy who gave away those stale dough-nuts. He's got a vacuum cleaner out here. He's got that little piece of jailbait with him."

In school the girls giggled behind me and passed notes. They were written on plain, unlined paper, and when I picked one up, I saw that it said, *Dynamo.* On Saturdays my father and I still carried those machines up to the houses, and the people in them looked at me like I was a Jehovah's Witness. I said to myself those looks didn't matter at all, or that they were nothing more than someone shooting a BB gun at a piece of tin, and I'd never feel more than that harmless *ping, ping, ping.*

The first Saturday we went up to a large white house. The porch had new screens, the color of nickels, and the floor was a newly painted gray. The ceiling of it was a pale blue. The house was off the road, on its own private drive, and on the map my father had traced a line toward it in red Magic Marker. He had put a little circle around it, too, which was his code for a "real possibility." We drove up the road, through a grove of pines, and then the house appeared, a field in front of it. It was two stories, clean and white, and in front of it there were big maple trees. It was just the beginning of spring, and the fields in front of the house were brown. The house was large and well kept, and in front of it there was a new four-wheel-drive station wagon.

My father went across the porch and up to the door. A man of about sixty answered, and he was of middle height, but with a straight posture. He had short, whitish hair, and a skin that fit him tightly, so much so you could see the bones in his face. He smiled and had blue eyes and he was drunk. He listened to my father and slapped him on the back and said, "Of course I'd like to see the damn thing."

My father came out to the car, and I said, "Dad, maybe this isn't a good idea. They don't want a machine."

"These are the Chesterfields, Marie," said my father. "They've got scads of money."

We carried the machine to the house, lifting it carefully up the steps. Then we took it inside, into a large room there, which had an Oriental carpet, chairs, and padded sofas, pictures in gilt frames, lamps and curtains. The fireplace had a kind of seat around it. The seat was covered with leather.

The man had a drink in his hand now. He was dressed in brown trousers and a shirt and a jacket with a tie. In the doorway there was a man of about twenty-three. He was tall and had sandy hair, and his face and arms were sunburned.

"Well, Robert," said the old man, "these people are going to demonstrate this thing for us. What do you think about that?"

"Fine," said Robert. But he stood there, keeping his distance.

My father demonstrated the machine, and the older man asked questions and filled his glass again. My father handed the tube over to me. "Just go over the carpet here, Marie," he said. I took the tube and went back and forth, trying not to swing my hips, and when I looked up, the young man was watching me. I looked down to hide the blush. Then I gave the tube back to my father and handed him the attachments, and my father went over the rug, the sofas and love seats, the

drapes. Finally Mr. Chesterfield said he'd think it over and my
father and I carried the machine out to the car. My father
couldn't see that the man was only drunk and amusing himself. He went back to get the attachments.

Robert came out of the house. It was a cool, clear day, and
the trees were running with sap and were turning a reddish
color. He stood next to the car and said, "I want to apologize
for my father. He's drunk."

"Oh, that's all right," I said.

I blushed and tried to push the machine farther into the
car.

"I'm sorry," said Robert.

He turned and went back up the steps and into the house.

Summer came. I finished school for good, and now, as
every year, people came to the lake and rented the cottages
around it. Mostly the cottages were small, two rooms at the
most. They had broad white siding, a screen porch with holes
that let the mosquitoes in, and on each porch there were two
folding lawn-chairs. Mostly men brought their families up
here in July and went back to Scranton or Philadelphia and
then returned in September. The wives who were left behind
sat on those lawn chairs, smoking cigarettes, drinking coffee,
and staring at the water.

We owned one of these cottages, and now it was rented to
a man from New Jersey. He was in his forties, was tall and thin,
and his hair was a mixture of blond and a metallic gray. He
wore pleated cotton pants from Brooks Brothers and cotton
shirts, nice ones with a blue or red stripe in them, the shirts
always fresh from the laundry. The man sat behind the screen,
which he had carefully patched with new pieces, sewing the
edges down as though he were fixing a sail. He smoked cigarettes, looked at the lake, and had beside him a small, inexpensive radio. He had come to work on his "proposals," which, in
the past anyway, had made him money, or so he said, although
they must have caused him trouble, too, since he wanted to
know if anyone ever came asking about him. He said he had
been "harassed" by the New Jersey attorney general and by

lawyers for the Securities and Exchange Commission. Mostly he was quiet, working in the afternoons and having a drink in the evening, listening to a soft rumba on that radio.

My father and I took the machines greater distances now. It was summer and I didn't have school. In the beginning my mother looked out the kitchen window and saw that cabin, one a little isolated from the rest, the lake beyond it dark with wind. In the middle of the second week she took a package of the kind of cigarettes the man smoked and went down and said hello and gave them to him, the squarish package in the cellophane wrapper being handed over with a vague, or maybe just undecided, overture. The man took them, and they talked through the screen. A week of so later, when my father and I were moving along those roads which had been marked in red on the Geological Survey Maps, my mother made two chicken sandwiches on new, fresh bread, with lettuce, and put them into a basket she had first lined with a linen towel. She took some sweet pickles and maybe even a piece of apple pie she had baked herself, not to mention two bottles of expensive beer, which she hesitated over at first but then went right ahead and put them in, beginning to discover as she did so, with all the certainty disaster or at least being human could muster, the implications of that time she had stood in the kitchen and said, "No," her voice rising in an unmistakable balk.

In the afternoon she put on a pair of white high-heeled shoes and her good white dress with the blue dots on it. She put up her hair and went across the road, swinging the basket and walking with her long neck straight up, her shoulders square, her high cheeks looking youthful, and maybe even a little flushed, her eyebrows still reddish, her entire aspect suggesting why people came into the store and said to her, "Say, weren't you in the movies about ten years ago?" In the basket with the lunch there were some cigarettes, too, the squarish package sitting on top, and when she stood on the screened-in porch she held the cigarettes out, frankly offering them.

In the evenings my father and I carried the machine in

from the car and put it in the store with the others, and then
we went into the kitchen, where my mother put food on the
table. She listened with a kind of remoteness as my father
recounted the things we had seen during the day, a man with
a wooden leg, an idiot child, a woman who played the accordion. When my father sold a machine and put the filled-out
order form and a check on the kitchen table, my mother only
glanced at them and said, "That's swell, Al." Then she served
the meat loaf or roast chicken or pork chops, her movements
suggesting not so much dishevelment as an air of having been
profoundly mussed, as though she had just gotten out of bed
and put her clothes back on, the quick dressing, or even the
languid dressing, somehow having carried with it that chaos
and heat of the afternoon, and as she walked across the
kitchen floor, putting those things on the table, there was in
her gait a liquid swaying which could only have been inspired
by one of those rumbas that had played quietly on that inexpensive radio down there by the bed.

My mother made a spare room upstairs into a place of her
own. It wasn't much bigger than a closet, and in it there were
a padded chair and a lamp, an ashtray and a small table. Now,
after dinner, when my father and I sat opposite one another
with bowls of ice cream, my mother went upstairs and into her
room, where she stuck her legs out in front of her and with a
Salem dangling from her lip she leafed through a magazine, or
read a book, or just stared.

In the morning my father and I loaded the car again. My
father packed a lunch in a brown bag, although now he
brought the bag out to the car and threw it onto the seat with a
backhanded jerk. Then we went downhill, my father gripping
the wheel and driving fast, as though he now believed if he
could just sell an extra machine, or maybe even two, why,
then, things would take a turn for the better. He went up to
the houses with a new insistence and charm, smiling and
laughing, but not being put off for a moment and even going
so far as to put his foot in the door, all the time talking his new
line and signaling to me to get the machine ready. When we
carried it in, my father kept right on talking, and when he

demonstrated a machine, he did so with a loud, no-nonsense description that made the thing appear to be a piece of clear, inspired engineering. And even though I was his assistant and maybe even his co-conspirator, I listened to my father and looked at the machine with a new interest, if not a new respect. My father sold three of them in two days and took deposits that were three times what he had been paid before.

In the afternoons we stopped as always to have lunch. Before, when we first started, we usually found a hill from which we saw into the valley below, the green fields divided into squares and rectangles by stone walls and barbed wire fences. Now, though, my father pulled to the side of the road and ate his sandwich, wolfing it down while he stared at the Geological Survey Map, drinking his beer while his mouth was full, and after swallowing hard he said to me, "Marie, the map shows a lot of houses up ahead. What's taking you so long?"

My father now spent longer hours at it, leaving in the morning and usually coming back late. Now he didn't insist on people buying machines so much as to argue with them, even when someone was pushing him out the door or threatening to call the police.

One afternoon he sold three machines. Usually, when he sold more than one, he turned to me and said, "Marie, we're working on the record day. You aren't tired, are you?" But now he sat in the car, the forms and checks in one hand and the Geological Survey Map in the other. Then he folded the map and turned the car toward home even though it wasn't very late. It took us an hour to get home, but it was still broad daylight, and as we stood in the kitchen and stared at the lake, we saw my mother emerge from that cabin. She walked across the road and came into the kitchen, the two expensive and now empty beer bottles rattling in the basket, her entire gait suggesting a kind of warm, pleasant tiredness, or liquidity and ease of motion.

"You're home early," she said.

"Yes," said my father. "Look."

He held out the signed order forms, each one of which had a check stapled to it.

"I sold three of them," he said.

"That's good, Al."

My mother put the empty beer bottles into the cardboard container for them, which she had put on the floor, and then she turned the basket upside down and knocked the crumbs out of it.

"We can go to Florida next winter," said my father.

"It's funny. I'm not so interested in Florida anymore."

My mother started dinner, and she went about it with a remote but still efficient air, her long fingers picking up the things she needed. Every now and then she put her hand to her hair, to push a strand back into it, the reddish pile of it having obviously been spread on a pillow or on just the bare sheets before she had put it up with a quick twist and a few bobby pins.

We sat down at the table, my father now eating with ironlike gestures, each movement of the silverware being identical to the last, the entire performance repetitive, silent. My mother ate nothing. She sat opposite him, lighting a cigarette before my father and I were finished. I cleared the table and then my mother took *The Wall Street Journal* (which she had never shown interest in before) and went into that small room upstairs, where she sat, that Salem dangling from her mouth while she tried to figure out what that man across the road was really up to, or at least how he had gotten into trouble or how he might get into it again. My father brought one of the machines into the living room and vacuumed the rug there, taking pleasure in how the dust and bits of dirt weren't cleaned up so much as made to disappear like magic.

My father and I went out each morning when the moisture rose from the asphalt and smelled a little like sand. We put the demonstrator into the back of the station wagon, as we did every morning, and then we went along the roads my father had marked in Magic Marker, although now my father drove fast, the tires squealing a little in the turns, and when he went up to a house, he did so with a kind of fury, or at least an obsession, and now he didn't wait for the door to be answered and sometimes he didn't knock at all. People came into the front room to find out what was wrong and found my father, already running a finger along a mantel or over the molding at the top of a door, his actions now coming not with the insistence of a salesman but with the authority of an inspector, and as the days went by, he became harsher, tougher, not taking no for an answer and not believing it or accepting it when someone slammed a door in his face, either, because then he stood there, rattling the doorknob or handle of a screen door, and said, "Listen! Listen! You're making a mistake!"

We came home a little later each night than the one before, since we were now going farther away, but even so, when we drove up to the house, my mother was still down there by the lake. When we arrived, she began that long, easy walk (with her stockings now in that basket she carried), emerging from the dim glimmering of the cabin's white siding and the slick glow of the lake itself, which looked as shiny as the cellophane on the packages of the cigarettes she still carried down there. Then she came into the house, not consciously more disheveled than the evening before, but nevertheless appearing so, at first having nothing more than her hair a little more out of place, but after a few days she had a button undone or a zipper not quite run all the way up, these details suggesting not her confusion, but her dedication. She walked across the road with an air of quiet exile, from which she would emerge as soon as she could get to her room with that copy of *The Wall Street Journal*.

Still, each evening she cooked a meal, each one the same as always, or maybe even better, her long hands picking up things with the certainty of a woman who is getting, or believing she is getting, what she wants. And while my mother went about the kitchen, my father took out those forms he had filled out during the day, since he was now selling four and five machines at a time. He put the orders and checks into the envelope with the manufacturer's name printed on it, my father licking the flap and sealing them and putting on a stamp, which he stuck on and then slapped, his hand coming down like a *whack*. By then my mother was finishing the dishes and was getting ready to go upstairs, already having *The Wall Street Journal* folded under her arm.

One night, when my mother tucked the paper under her arm and turned toward the stairs, my father said, "Wait a minute, Sherry. Sit down."

"What?"

"Sit down," said my father.

My mother shifted the *Journal* from one arm to the other, just standing there. Then she lighted a cigarette and flipped the match into the sink and said, "All right, Al."

My father put the envelopes and papers to one side and with his hands out before him, palms down, he said, "Sherry, I know what you're doing down there by the lake. I haven't said anything about it because I love you and hope you'll stop going down there."

My mother stared at him over her cigarette and said, "Oh, Al. You're such a jackass."

She stood up and went out of the room, going not with that easy, liquid sway, but just going, climbing the stairs, her feet making a *pat-pat-pat-pat* as she went. She closed the bathroom door and turned on the water in the tub and then swirled it around so we couldn't hear and then obviously she didn't care about that anymore and cried openly, the sound loud, unmistakable, repetitive, filled not only with grief but with dismay, too. In the kitchen the sound of the water was as loud as a torrent, and my father sat at the table, slapping it with the palm of his hand, the gesture just as insistent as when he had rattled some screen door and said, "Listen! Listen!"

I went upstairs and into my room, where I closed the door. There were tattoos on my desk, and I looked at the hearts and words, the snakes and tigers. All I wanted was to be able to hear that steady, harmless *ping, ping, ping,* as though nothing bothered me at all, but instead all I heard was my mother at the end of the hall, crying behind the door. Down below, in the kitchen, my father's hand hit the table again, the hard *whack* of it like the slap of a fish's tail in that sound of running water.

The next Saturday my father went to Baxter. It was September now, and the sky and lake were the same shimmery blue. Most of the people in the cottages began to move around, as though they had been drowsing all summer and the first cool weather had woken them up. In front of each cottage there were a couple of old, cheap suitcases and some bedding, tied together with string, the piles of these things neat and expectant, the women who had packed them smoking cigarettes in the cool air and waiting for their husbands, who would come just as surely as the equinox or the first migrations of geese.

I went into the house and found my mother dressed in a white blouse, her gray suit, and a new pair of stockings. She looked nice. She was carrying a new plastic grip, had a raincoat over her arm, and there was about her the sweet, fragile air of a grown woman who is going to take her first trip on an airplane. Her hair had been put up in a businesslike way, and as she turned toward me, her shoulders square and her head up, she didn't seem distracted by intimacy anymore so much as someone who has gone through all that and has emerged, not enlightened exactly, but certainly more alert, and having the desperation to go along with it.

A little red car pulled up and stopped by the door, and sitting behind the wheel was the man from the cottage, his silver-blond hair perfectly combed, his white shirt starched, the cuffs turned back. He was wearing a tie. Behind him, across the backseat, there was a rod like one in a closet, and his clothes were hung from it.

"Go upstairs, Marie, and pack a bag," said my mother.

"Where are we going?"

"Just go pack a bag, some things for a few days," said my mother.

"But—"

"Just go on!"

I climbed the stairs and went down the hall, but I stopped at the doorway of my mother's and father's room. The drawers of the bureau had been pulled open and from them hung stockings, an old brassiere, a cotton blouse with paint stains on it, and a silk scarf, which flowed from the drawer and collected in a pool on the floor. The mattress had been turned over and my father's drawers had been opened, too, a red sock hanging out like a dog's tongue. His clothes had been thrown on the floor, and the things in his closet had been gone through, the pants pulled away from the hangers and the white linings of the pockets turned inside out. The room appeared more blown up than cluttered, as though everything had been kept in the drawers by some domestic or even loving restraint, the first sign of the disappearance of which was the chaos of clothes and sheets and blankets and the evidence of the search for the roll of hundred-dollar bills my father was supposed to have hidden.

I went downstairs to the store. Outside, my mother stood next to the car and talked quickly, although the man in the car only shrugged and stared through the windshield. My mother looked toward Baxter. Then she came back inside and went over to the cash register, which she opened and cleaned out, leaving those wire flaps standing straight up. She cleaned out the quarters, too, and then said to me, "Come on."

We went outside. The man behind the wheel had lines around his mouth and at the corners of his eyes, but they made him look good, although accustomed to worry or bad luck. He turned toward us once, the movement of his head seeming a little tired or at least wary.

"Sherry," he said, "are you bringing the kid?"

"I can't leave her here," she said.

"Sherry," said the man, his voice not threatening, not complaining, flat. "You can send for her."

"I don't know," said my mother.

"I'll be all right here," I said.

"No, you won't," said my mother. "No one could be all right here."

"Sherry," said the man, "we haven't got time."

She looked at me for a moment and then glanced back at the man.

"Well, I don't know," she said.

"I'll be all right," I said.

"How come you haven't packed a bag?" she said. "Didn't I tell you to pack a bag?"

"Sherry."

"I'm coming." Then she turned to me and said, "Do you understand? I'm not going to be cheated out of my chance." Then she opened her handbag where she had put the bills from the cash register: it looked like a purse full of green leaves. My mother picked out two twenties and smoothed them flat.

"Here," she said.

The man in the car turned those greenish eyes on me and reached into his wallet and slid out a clean, ironed-looking ten-dollar bill. It was as smooth as the cuff of his shirt.

"Sherry," he said, "here's ten bucks from me, too."

"I'll send you a card with my address on it," said my mother. She stepped forward, put her arms around me, and then she went around to the other side of the car and got in, not looking at me or the house or anything else, although she did say to the man as she looked down at her feet, "Go on. Go on. Why don't you just go on?"

The car went downhill. A little breeze came from the lake and on the surface there were dark abrasions where the water seemed to shrivel in the wind. The screen door was open and it creaked a little, and then I went into the kitchen. After a while I went into the store and put down those wire flaps in the cash register. Then the place didn't look so looted or robbed. I took a bag of chips into the kitchen and sat at the table, eating them one at a time, just eating, the motions of it mechanical, repetitive.

My father's station wagon came up the hill and pulled in at the side of the house, and my father got out, dressed in that sweater, white shirt and tie, his head floating along the window like something in a shooting gallery. My knees wouldn't stop their shaking. I watched him come through the store and into the kitchen, and when he stopped opposite me I said, "She's gone."

For a moment my father only listened to the silence of the house, the damp, cool lack of sound that was not forlorn or sad or anything so much as a kind of disheveled emptiness. My father stood there like some kind of dog, a black lab, say, head tilted, listening. He looked around the kitchen, taking inventory, as though if the things my mother had left behind, or the things that had been worn down by her own hand were still here, like the kitchen knives with the wooden handles or the wooden spoons, why, then, she had to be here, too. Then with strides that were slow at first, but with increasing length and speed, he went up the stairs until he came to the door of his and his wife's room. He waited there, as he had in the kitchen, now standing with his head cocked to one side, his eyes slowly going over the chaos of the things there as he felt the lingering explosion, or maybe just seeing the end of it, those clothes spread over the floor, the gray scarf slowly running into a pool by the bureau, the mattress canted over, his own clothes with the pockets turned inside out with searching. So my father stared, carefully going over each object, and was left with the message, or maybe the import of what my mother had left behind, which was a room that needed, if nothing else, a good vacuuming.

He turned and went downstairs, not running, or really even seeming to hurry so much as going with the same heavy-footed, furious gait as when he went to the doors of those houses and opened them without bothering to knock. He went through the kitchen and into the store, with me following, and when my father opened the cash register he didn't notice or even care that it was empty. Instead he lifted the cash tray and took from underneath it the key to the glass case in which there were two rows of inexpensive pistols. My father stabbed the key into the lock with that same measured fury. Beyond him, on the other side of the case, there was the line of Dynamos, three of them in a row, the cylinders shiny, each surrounded by those enormous white tentacles.

The case had a glass door at the back, and my father didn't slide it open so much as he gave it a shove, as though elbowing someone out of the way, and then with that same abrupt motion, he picked up a chrome-plated .357. There were boxes of ammunition on a plank shelf behind the cabinet, and my father took one down and slid the Styrofoam packaging out and dropped the shells onto the glass, the bright, silvery cartridges splashing like a handful of coins, nickels, say. He loaded the thing, dropping each cartridge in and slapping the cylinder shut, and then scooping up the rest of the shells and putting them into his right front pocket.

"Come on. You point out their car. It was a little red one, wasn't it?"

"A Toyota," I said.

"That's just *perfect,*" said my father. "*A Toyota.*" He slammed the empty cash drawer shut. "Come on."

In the car my father put the pistol on the seat between us, in the same place where that lunch in a brown paper bag usually sat. He didn't say much as he drove, his hands gripping the wheel with a new sense of authority, or maybe only justification, and as we went I stared at the clutter at the side of the road, the bits of paper and cans and pieces of waxed paper and Styrofoam cups. The pistol sat on the seat, bright in the square of afternoon sunlight that came in through the window.

We went quickly now, stopping at each roadside hamburger stand, restaurant, or chain store, like Denny's or Howard Johnson's, and at the motels, too, the managers of which my father knew on a first-name basis, since at one time or another he had tried to sell them a vacuum cleaner. And now, when he parked the car and went up to a restaurant, it looked like he was still trying to sell the manager a machine, and that this time he might succeed. Then he came out, not closing the door of the place behind him, just coming straight out, walking back toward the car with a kind of insatiable haste and then saying, when he got back in and slid over, next to the pistol, "They haven't been here."

It got dark. We hadn't eaten, and now my father stopped at a combination gas station and store, and there he bought some fresh balloon bread, a package of sliced baloney, and a six-pack of half-quart cans of beer. We made sandwiches in the car, slapping the baloney on the dry bread, and both of us ate with the same mechanical gestures. Then we started looking again, going from restaurant to restaurant, and from motel to motel, our progress not being measured in the miles we had gone, or the people my father had talked to and dismissed, but by the repetitive *pffffft* when one of those cans was opened. I drank one, too. We went down the road with that pistol between us, both of us tasting the hops and holding a can of beer between our legs. Every now and then my father threw a can out the window, not with malice or anything aside from that ongoing, furious dismissal.

I turned toward him.

"Marie, what is it?" he said.

The pistol sat between us, the thing looking like humiliation itself.

"Why do we have to do things this way?" I said. "Can't we do something else? I'm so tired of being ashamed I could die."

"Take it up with your mother," said my father, "if she's got that much time."

We found them in a motel in New Jersey. It was one long whitish building, divided into rooms, each one of which had a door facing the parking lot. The motel was close to the marsh, where reeds grew, and where small rivers or backwaters meandered without any pattern or discoverable direction, although the dark surface of the water was touched by the lights of New York City, and each yellow point was smeared into rays. The small red car was parked at the end of the building. There was no one else staying at the motel, and from the one lighted window, opposite the car, a soft yellow pool collected in the parking lot. My father stared at the window, and the car, too, not even having to ask if that was it. He drank the last beer, and between sips he tapped the can against the steering wheel.

Beyond the motel, to the south, the twin towers of the World Trade Center rose from the flats, and they were lighted, too, the bright windows arranged in a random way, the collection of them seeming sidereal, as though the stars in the southern sky had been concentrated in two enormous rectangles. The marshes stretched before them, the reeds moving in the breeze, not seen so much as heard in their endless hiss. In the dark there was the sure, salty odor of tidelands. We saw the towers clearly, both of which were reflected in the meandering, directionless backwaters.

My father got out, not closing his door, but gently pushing it shut. He walked toward the room, his eyes on the door, but when he was halfway there he stopped and cocked his head: it seemed, over the sound of the reeds, there was a muted rumba or tango coming from that small, inexpensive radio. I got out of the car and walked to my father, making a whispering, desperate hiss as I came, a repeated, insistent, "Listen! Listen to me!" But he walked on, now going down the sidewalk that ran in front of the rooms, stepping around the aluminum lawn chair that was next to each door. I whispered, "Wait. Just Wait. Will you?"

My father didn't knock on this door, either, but went right in. My mother's friend stood at a suitcase that was open on a desk built against the wall. He was wearing a good plaid bathrobe, and his silver-blond hair had just been brushed: it shone in the light from a lamp. When the door opened, he just looked up, his hands holding a clean shirt and a neatly folded pair of socks, his eyes unerringly sweeping down my father's arm to the pistol, which was pointed at the floor. My mother wore some panty hose and a brassiere, and she stood in front of the bathroom mirror, her head held to one side while she brushed her hair, the sound of it coming as a slight, dry crackle. The air was damp from the shower and there was a stink, too, from someone having used the bathroom. The smell of it hung in the smallish motel room. My mother looked over her shoulder, and then she stopped the brush at the end of a stroke, her eyes moving now, too, in that same unerring path toward my father's hand.

"Oh, Jesus, Al. Oh, Jesus," she said.

"Get your things, Sherry. You're coming home."

"Now, just wait a minute," said the man in the bathrobe. "Let's not be hasty."

"Did you say *hasty*?" said my father. "Is that the word you used? Why, you poor, dumb bastard."

The man in the bathrobe still held his shirt and socks,

although he now stood straight up. My father wasn't quite as tall as he.

"Get your things, Sherry," said my father. "You can tell this bozo here that if he isn't quiet, I'm going to kill him."

My mother's friend put his shirt down, but then picked it up again. My mother stood straight up, her hair over one shoulder, her eyes still set on my father.

"Get your things, Sherry," said my father. "I'm not going to tell you again."

My mother stood there, holding the brush, her hair splayed out with static.

"You had to bring Marie along, too, didn't you?"

My mother still hesitated, standing in the bathroom door, the brush held out, her eyes set on my father.

"I'm going to go, Billy," said my mother to her friend.

"Billy," said my father. "That's perfect."

"Maybe that's best," said Bill.

Bill and my mother looked at each other, and then my mother closed her eyes for a moment.

"I didn't bank on all this," he said.

My mother looked at his sad, lined face. He shrugged.

"No, I guess you didn't," said my mother.

She began to go around the room, picking up her things and putting them into that inexpensive bag, and she didn't cover up or get dressed before doing so either. Her back was white and smooth, a line of small bumps, from the vertebrae, running down it as she bent over to pick up a shoe. So she went around the room, the weight she had gained showing around her waist, at the band of the panty hose. The two men stood there, not looking at one another, but somehow feeling that they should. They stood in that odor from the bathroom. My mother picked up her things and put them into that inexpensive bag, and then she got into that white blouse and gray skirt and jacket, not zipping her clothes up or buttoning them, either, but simply throwing the blouse over her shoulders and putting her arms through the holes and pulling the skirt over her hips. She stuck one hand into the sleeve of her jacket and swung it behind her and then got her other hand in, too. And while she slid the jacket over her shoulders, she stepped into her black high-heeled shoes.

"Have you got your toothbrush?" said my father. "I want you to get everything out of here. I don't want one trace of you here."

My father went into the bathroom, turning his back on the three of us, and stopped at the sink, where he found the toothbrush, just as he knew he would, if only because my mother had left it next to the cold water faucet every morning and every night they had lived together, and as my father came into the room again, carrying the toothbrush in one hand and the pistol in the other, he walked past Bill and said, "You're lucky I don't shove this up your ass," and then threw the brush into my mother's purse.

My mother carried that new bag and my father took her arm, not shoving her exactly, but adding a little speed as they went past the unmade bed, out the door, and into the cool, salty air from the marsh. My father threw the bag into the back of the car.

My mother got into the front seat. She was disheveled, but not in the same way as when she came back from the cottage. Now she looked disoriented and as though her clothes hadn't been put on quickly so much as half ripped off. You could feel the presence of her disorder in the dark and the terror of it, as though everything was wrong because she sat there like that.

We drove for a while, the marshes, the grass, the lights in the open water sliding past like discarded things. The towers of the World Trade Center stayed on the horizon, cool and impossibly remote, as though we were separated from them by a barrier made of all the weaknesses of the human heart. After a while my father parked the car and got out. He walked to the edge of the marsh and stood there, looking at the towers, his figure dark against the lights of the city and the sparkling surface of the water. He pointed the pistol at the towers, which were ten miles away. He fired once and then again, the sounds coming as relief, or as something my father and I had been straining to hear for hours: the harsh bang or whack of departure, the slammed door, or the long-lasting curse my father had been cheated out of, since my mother hadn't had the time to leave it behind. Now the pistol went *bang Bang BANG*, my mother and I flinching in the car, but both of us counting each shot, and when six had finally come, my father stood there while he stared at the unchanged, aloof, and knowledgeable buildings in the distance. We smelled the marshland, the sea breeze. Then my father threw the pistol onto the front seat and said, "I just didn't want to change my mind on the way home."

He got into the car.

"Well, Sherry, now do you want to go to Florida?"

She put a hand to her forehead and sighed.

"Oh, I don't know. . . ." she said.

"Just say you want to go to *Florida,*" said my father. Then he started to cry, putting his head down on the wheel. My mother reached out to touch him, but stopped, her hand suspended over the seat. We listened to that sound, and while we sat in the dark, my mother started to button her blouse and to rearrange her clothes.

"Just let this be a lesson to you, Marie," said my mother.

When we pulled up in front of the house, my father carried my mother's bag in, walking behind her and opening that screen door, the long, lonely screech of it coming as a welcome to us all. My father dropped the bag and went into the store, where he got a loaf of stale bread and a can of tuna. He poured a drink for my mother and one for himself, and then, without saying a word, he made three tuna sandwiches on stale bread. We ate them, my mother and father saying nothing, until we were done, and then my father said, "We're going to start again. That's what made this country great."

He went into the store and emptied the bullets from his pocket onto the top of the glass case with that same sound of spilled change, and then he put the pistol back, too, sliding the door shut and locking it. When he came into the kitchen, he said to my mother, "Why don't you go take a bath."

My mother went upstairs, now carrying the bag that was still leaking some stockings and part of a pink nightgown. Soon water ran into the tub and there was the quiet slosh as my mother got in, and in the watery plash of the house, my father wheeled a machine in from the store and carried it into the bedroom, where he shoved the clothes and scarves and undershirts back into the closets and the bureaus, and when the drawers were closed and the mattress was back on the bed, he turned on the machine and cleaned the room, doing a good job and leaving large, flowerlike shapes on the rug.

We all went to bed, and as I lay under the cool sheet in my room, I heard from down the hall the constant *buzz mumble buzz mumble* of my parents' muted talking, although once I heard my mother say, "Why, did you see his face when you walked in? I thought he was going to *die*. I mean right *there.*" Both of them laughed nervously, but just for a moment.

They made some other sounds at the end of the hall, and I stayed awake, listening, turning my pillow to keep the cool surface against my face. Even then I began to think things over, and if my father believed the world you lived in was formed by your own actions, and if my mother put stock in luck or in the benign progression of life, I now thought there was only one solution: If you got far enough away from nights like this and kept people at arm's length, then everything would be all right. It took a couple of years to do anything about this, though, and in the meantime I almost fell in love.

Marie Boule, Lotions
Baxter, Pennsylvania

CHARLES SEVETTE'S PARENTS WERE FRENCH CANADIANS who still spoke French and who lived in a small house outside of Baxter. It was a two-story house with blue asphalt tiles. Charles was twenty-four years old, tall and dark haired, and he had greenish eyes and skin that was pale, especially in the winter. He worked in a sawmill, although he drove a backhoe when there was work for one, and he dug graves with it, too, in the cemetery outside of Baxter, where most people did their burying. When he went down to the cemetery, he drove the five miles from his house, passing the store. At first I'd hear that noise and then I'd see the yellow backhoe emerge, going fast, in high gear, and jumping from side to side because of the speed. When the machine bucked like that, it reminded me of a horse in a rodeo, and when I first saw Charles, going by on that yellow machine, I was reminded of a cowboy.

When we moved here, Charles attended the Baxter School of Hair Design, and for a while I didn't see that yellow machine go by as often as Charles's black Pontiac, with him at the wheel, going to town, his expensive scissors and combs all tucked into a little cloth bag, which had a separate pouch for

each one and a string, too, so you could roll the bag up and tie
it closed.

Charles loved women's hair, the texture and odor of it,
the weight of it in his hands, the way the light hit the strands of
each color, whether blond, red, auburn, or black. He liked to
see the light, too, on tightly curled, platinum-colored hair, or
on hair that was wet and slicked back. The first thing he
noticed about a woman was her hair, and his earliest memories were of women he had seen in old movies on television,
especially actresses from the forties, who appeared in black-
and-white movies, their hair blond and tightly curled and
beautifully lighted. There was something intimate in being
able to touch a woman's hair, and the slither of it over
Charles's fingers always interested him. He had passed by the
School of Design every Saturday when he was growing up, but
it wasn't until he was nineteen that he turned into the door of
the place, still dressed in his mill hand's clothes, and said, "I'd
like to take a class. Who do I have to talk to?"

He was a good student, too, so much so that the woman
who ran the school began to look over her shoulder when she
thought about the possibility of Charles opening a shop, or
worse, a school in town, and at about the time she began to
offer him free lessons in exchange for signing an agreement
which, in effect, made it illegal for Charles to cut hair within
fifty miles of Baxter, Charles quit. The free lessons didn't matter, since Charles already knew more and had better taste
than the woman who ran the place. One day he came into the
school, dressed again in his mill hand's clothes, although now
he was carrying a large canvas bag, into which he put his
lotions, dyes, conditioners, and mousses, his hair dryers and
brushes, not to mention that cloth bag with the expensive
scissors and razor and comb. He carried his things out the
door, after saying good-bye to his fellow students, who all
stood in a line, giving shampoos at reduced rates.

So he put the white canvas bag in a closet in his parents'
house (the two old French Canadians watching this with a
barely disguised pleasure) and then he went back to digging
graves and working in the sawmill. Every now and then I

went to the mill with my father to get some lumber, and I saw Charles, his hand on the lever that ran the log cradle, his head turned toward me, his eyes set on my hair.

After a while Charles started to work for my father. In the fall, during the deer season, a man came into the store, dressed in new, clean hunting clothes, and after he looked around the shelves and picked up cans of beans or tuna or Day-Glo shirts he had no intention of buying, he stepped over to my father and said, "Say, can we talk?"

"Sure," said my father, "what can I do for you?"

"I mean can we talk privately?" said the man.

"You can say anything in front of Marie," said my father.

The man wrinkled his brow and then looked outside, at the empty gas station. He lowered his voice a little.

"Well, I was looking for a piece of venison to buy," said the man.

"A piece?"

"Maybe a whole deer," said the man.

"A whole deer?" said my father.

The man nodded.

"Not cut up or anything, just gutted," said the man.

"Why?" said my father, his eyes now showing a keen commercial interest. Then the man leaned over the counter, his new Day-Glo orange clothes smelling of sizing or the dusty store shelves they had been sitting on. He said he didn't actually go deer hunting in the fall so much as to tell his wife that's where he was going, and then he took his girlfriend to Florida, where they checked into a hotel and had a good time. He said he wanted to have insurance against the possibility of his wife wondering why, when he spent so much time in the woods, he never brought home a deer. The man spoke with a clear, cold voice.

In the past, when these men in new hunting clothes came into the store and asked to speak privately with my father, he showed them the things he had for sale, the cheap rifles, both bolt and lever action, the piles of ammunition, the bows, the arrows with bleeder heads, the Apple and Doe-in-Heat lures, and said, "If you want a deer, go out and kill one."

But that was before my father had gone to collect my mother from New Jersey. Now my father said to the men in new clothes, "It will cost you. Seven hundred and fifty dollars. Not a cent less. I'll take half right now."

The man tried to offer less, but my father had about him that same insistent fury as when he had gone up to the doors of those houses. The man in the hunting clothes took out his wallet and counted out the money, pushing the bills across the table with a gesture that was half sullenness and half hope he wasn't getting fleeced. He said he'd be back the next night for the deer.

Then my father got into his secondhand pickup truck and went around to the house trailers of the more obvious poachers, not to mention the deer camps of men whose wives had gotten hunting licenses, too. These men could then kill a deer on their own license, one on the extra license each man had from his wife, and then, of course, they put in for a doe permit. Anyway, my father went around to the trailers and camps and found a deer, for which he paid a hundred and fifty dollars. The next night he sat in the kitchen, with the deer hung out back, waiting for the man in the new clothes to show up with the rest of that seven hundred and fifty dollars.

My father knew this was illegal, but he didn't care, or he saw it as a kind of justice or maybe compensation for having had his wife run off. It wasn't just that he was vicariously settling old scores by helping men get away with what his wife hadn't been able to handle, although this was part of it, but he also believed he was doing some good, too, in that a man who can get away for a week with his girlfriend isn't so likely to run off with her for good. On the first night, after that man in new clothes had turned up with the rest of the money, and the bills were safely in my father's pocket, he looked a little bewildered, as though he had just discovered the facts of life and couldn't quite believe that these things were really so. And when he looked at my mother, it was with something like new respect, as though she had somehow been the one to teach him how to put that seven hundred and fifty dollars in his pocket, or that he wouldn't have it without her. Mostly, my father's expression was that of a man who is in the enviable position of having his morality (or better, his sense of justice) combine with enterprise to produce profits.

But even he knew he couldn't go around from deer camp to deer camp, advertising, so to speak, that he was willing to pay cash for deer, since this was a crime, and if he did go around from camp to camp advertising it, it wouldn't be long before the game warden showed up with the state police. Obvious violators of game laws in this state weren't fined. They went to prison. So my father drove out to that small, two-story house with the blue asphalt siding, and knocked on the door, and when Charles's father opened it, my father said, *"Bonjour, je voudrais parler à Charles, si'l vous plaît."* Then he asked Charles to come back to the store, where they sat around in the kitchen, drinking beer and just talking until my father put the question to him, and after haggling a little about the price (about which my father was just as insistent as always), Charles agreed. The next day my father went down to one of those wholesale houses in Scranton where he usually bought those cheap rifles for the store, although this time he didn't hesitate, at least as a matter of taste, not to mention expense, to buy a 7mm Ruger with a Leupold 3x–9x scope and a two-thousand-candlepower spotlight that could be plugged into an automobile cigarette lighter. The spotlight had a little stand with rubber tips on the feet of it so you could put it on the hood of your car.

My father had these things wrapped in plain brown paper and brought them home and gave them to Charles, who took the rifle into the woods and sighted it in and then played around with the spotlight, figuring out how it worked. Then, after dark, Charles dressed in black clothes and got into that black low-slung Pontiac (with the racing tires) and went down the back roads until he came to an out-of-the-way field or an abandoned orchard. There he stopped the car and plugged that two-thousand-candlepower spotlight into the cigarette lighter and turned it on. It made a column-like luminescence, through which there curled smoky filaments from Charles's breath, and at the end of it, in a circle the size of a dinner

plate, there was the head of a deer. The animal was still, its
head just above a half-frozen and half-rotten apple, its eyes as
bright as the foil a piece of chewing gum comes wrapped in.
Charles put the stand with the rubber-tipped legs onto the
hood of his car and carefully moved the spotlight to it, never
taking the end of that smoky column from the deer's head.
The animal stood there as though hypnotized, and Charles
took that expensive, heavy rifle out of the backseat and laid it
over a towel he had spread on the top of the open door. In the
explosion, in the bright silver-and-gray collapse of the deer,
Charles unplugged the spotlight and shoved it into the backseat, along with the rifle. He got behind the wheel and started
the engine, all of this done in one chaotic motion, and as the
echo rolled back to the orchard, Charles turned onto the road,
lights out, the car disappearing at the head of one long stream
of dust.

After a while he slowed down and turned on the lights
and came up to the store, where he waited to make sure no
one had heard a shot. He sat quietly in the kitchen, eating a
sandwich my father made for him.

Later, the two of us got into my father's pickup truck and
drove to those deserted orchards and fields and picked up the
deer, me grabbing the front legs and Charles grabbing the
hind ones and both of us swinging it into the bed of the truck
like a body in a blanket. We drove up a little wood road that
went through a half-grown-up field, the grass and whip-stage
popple scraping the floorboards. Through the windshield
there were the stars and the woods at the edge of the field, the
scraggle of trees not ominous so much as unfriendly. We came
to a barn. It was weathered and not too long for this world,
although the doors still opened. We backed in, under a beam,
from which there were hung steel cables, each one about as
big around as my little finger and each one having a noose. We
hung the deer there, the cable bright against the silver-gray
fur, the animal's hooves black and just as shiny as though
they'd been shined with shoe polish. In the truck there was
the scent of blood, and in the dark the odor was salty and
metal-like. Charles didn't speak when we did this, and I didn't

either: we just did it quickly and came home, as though we'd been dreaming. I came home and washed, glad to get the stains off my hands.

So the business went ahead. Word got around fast, and it didn't take long before postcards began to come from the Bahamas, Jamaica, and Florida, each one of them with a short message, a kind of reservation of an animal and the date it would be needed, or at least picked up. These cards almost always had pictures of hotels and palm trees, of white beaches and of milky blue and smoothly flowing waves, and when they arrived, my mother took them from the mailbox and said, "Here, Al. There are some more cards for you."

Now, on Saturday night my mother got into her new, good dress and my father put on a jacket to go with his tie, and the two of them went down to Baxter to see a movie.

When they were gone I went into the living room and turned on the TV, especially if I had looked in the paper and found a movie. I made myself a drink and turned the sound down and I watched William Powell or Cary Grant or one of those men who knew how to make a woman laugh. The movies were in black and white, and the women in them wore shiny dresses that were tight around the waist and back, and as they walked the material showed in a glimmery stride, the soft light of it suggesting a world that was clean and where there was charm, if not love and passion.

The rooms where these women and men lived seemed to be elegant and to have a view of the river, any river. And when I began to tremble with wonder or maybe with fear that the world of the movie might actually exist, I went into the store and opened the pistol case and took from it a .357 Magnum and loaded the thing and went back to the living room, where I sat down, the pistol in one hand, a short drink in the other. Then Cary Grant or William Powell charmed those women in those silver dresses, and after a while, when I couldn't tell which made me angrier, that this world did exist and that I was excluded from it, or that those women were being seduced by a lie, I pulled back the hammer of the pistol and pointed it at the screen, at the precise and even elegant figure of Grant or Powell, and as one of them went across a room, endlessly approaching one of those women with blond hair and a deep angel's kiss, I followed along with the pistol and thought, *Go on, just go on. If you kiss her, if you touch her with your lips, if you lie to her that way, if you seduce her, I will blow the living shit out of you and the television, too.* Then, with a kind of nightmarish smile, Grant or Powell leaned over and put on the woman's lips the sweetest, most perfect, romantic kiss you have ever seen. The empty house ached with it. I sat there with that loaded pistol and watched the light slide over the woman's satin dress, the quiet liquefaction of it suggesting the thrill of the kiss and an unstoppable gentleness moving through her back and legs. I let the hammer down and put the pistol next to the television, my hands still shaking.

When the movie was over, I put the pistol back into the case and washed out the glass and left it draining in the rack, the drops of water coming off of it, just as lonely as could be. I went upstairs and got into bed and looked out my window at the stars, which reminded me of the light running over the hair and clothes of those women in the movies. I looked out the window and thought, *Maybe that world does exist, but how do you find it? How?*

The deer season ended, and the cards from Jamaica or Florida stopped coming. Charles brought the rifle and the two-thousand-candlepower spotlight back, and my father put the rifle in the rack and the spotlight in the attic, hidden there under some blankets and old overcoats. And, as Charles stood in the cold store, he turned to me and said, "You know, Marie, I'd like to do your hair. What do you say?"

"I couldn't afford it," I said.

"I never said anything about charging you," he said. "What do you say?"

"I don't know," I said, "my hair has always been frizzy and too thick. Do you think you can do something with it?"

"It just needs a little conditioner, a little trim. . . ." he said. "Sure, I can do something with it."

"I just brush it," I said. "That's all I ever do to it."

He reached out and touched my hair, picked it up between his fingers, felt the weight of it.

"How about Saturday?" he said.

"Well, all right," I said with a little laugh. "I never had anyone ask me to do my hair before. You're not kidding me, are you?"

"No," he said. "Is Saturday night all right?"

"I guess so," I said, "Sure. Why not?"

So on Saturday, at about the time my parents were getting ready to go out, that black Pontiac stopped by the side of the store, and Charles got out, now carrying that white canvas sack in which there were lotions and creams, conditioners and shampoos, dyes, a hair dryer, rollers, clips (of four different sizes), not to mention that small cloth bag with the pouches for his straight razor with the ivory handle, his scissors from England, and his brush and comb. He came through the store and into the kitchen, where he dropped the bag as though it were a toolbox brought in by a plumber's assistant, the thing coming down with a rattle and a *clunk.*

My father was in the kitchen, waiting for my mother to come down, and when Charles dropped the canvas sack, my father rattled the ice in his glass with a kind of practical excitement, as though Thomas Edison were going to do my hair. Then my mother came down, and the two of them went out, my mother's high-heeled shoes hitting the cold asphalt outside.

"You've got a lot of split ends," said Charles, "and your hair is dry. You can tell just by looking at it."

"It gets that way in the winter," I said.

"What do you wash your hair with?" he said.

"Whatever is in the bathroom," I said. "When there's nothing I come down here and get the dish soap."

"Oh, Jesus, Marie, not *dish* soap," he said. "Your hair needs vitamins. It needs aloe."

He pulled up a chair with the back of it toward the sink, and I brought in two telephone books to sit on. Charles put a towel around my neck, barber style, and then I sat down and leaned my head into the sink, where he wet my hair with the nozzle for rinsing dishes. The water sunk in with a warm and spreading weight. It felt good. Charles squeezed the water out and put on some shampoo, a little from one bottle and a little from another. His fingers went over my scalp, the busy, certain movement of them making me want to close my eyes. The lather, under his fingers, made a small, repetitive sound, a little *quick, quick, quick.* Then he rinsed and toweled my hair and combed it out. The little bag was unrolled on the counter, the scissors and combs looking like instruments in a doctor's emergency kit, and when my hair was combed straight down, over my shoulders, Charles trimmed it, and when he cut the hair above my face, small bits fell in a cold, pleasant chill. He used the dryer and his little comb to make curls, and if in the beginning Charles had looked at me with a kind of disapproval, or maybe even a slight lack of interest, he now warmed up, touching my hair and fluffing it out. When he was finished he showed me how I looked in a mirror he took down from the wall in the living room, and from the first glance I blushed, not because of how good or even beautiful I looked so much as how sweet and innocent. I blushed again and put my hand to my cheek and laughed.

"It's nice," said Charles, and in his voice there was the fatigue of the weeks gone by and some satisfaction, too, as though doing this to my hair, and to me for that matter, took some of the sting out of the nights he had spent in those abandoned orchards, or of the memory of that barn where those animals had hung. "You could be in *Vogue,*" he said.

We got into that black Pontiac and went down to Baxter, and when we went into the new coffee shop and sat in one of those booths, all the heads in the place turned toward me.

At first Charles was trying to get away from the atmosphere of poaching, or of market hunting, and then we wanted to get through January and February, both of us agreeing without talking about it that the Saturday nights in the kitchen were a good way to kill time. In the middle of the week we looked through *Vogue* or *Cosmo* or *Mademoiselle* and picked out a style, or a color, and Charles thought about it

at work. On Saturday he came up to the house, carrying that
canvas sack and dropping it in the corner with that same
clunk. He brought some makeup, too, not a lot, but of good
quality: it never showed, just enough to make my eyes a little
bigger or darker, or to make the few freckles I had on my nose
harder to see. When we were done, we got into the car and
went down the hill and sat in the coffee shop. It was too cold to
do much else. Sometimes Charles reached across the table to
touch a strand of hair or a wave.

But with each new style, Charles seemed not so much
interested in the hobby of it as just interested, as though with
each Saturday he wasn't covering me up, or getting away from
something (like killing deer for money), but discovering something about me, if only through the pressure of each new style,
or the implications of it. And they did have power. When
Charles did things to me to make me look fresh and innocent,
I acted that way a little, or at least I felt the pressure of it. I
couldn't help it. It even made me angry, but there wasn't
much I could do about the hard shove of each new style.

Charles watched me closely. He said he'd like to spend
more time with me, and not just doing my hair, either, or
sitting around in a coffee shop, waiting for spring to finally get
here. I smiled at him, like the friend of his I had become, and
said, "You don't really want that. Not with me. Caring for me
would be the worst thing that ever happened to you. I guaran-
tee it."

"How can you be so sure?" said Charles.

"Listen to me," I said. "I'm trying to tell you something.
You don't want it."

We went ahead, if only because of the winter, or the
pleasure of those nights in the kitchen, where we both lost
ourselves a little. But now there was a slow, definite progression from one Saturday to the next, since each new style was a
little more daring or provocative than the one from the week
before, and if in the beginning, on the first night, I looked like
a bride in a New England wedding, why, soon I looked like a
college girl at her first nightclub, and then like a young
woman at a fashionable party, not quite sophisticated exactly,

but getting there. Each new style advanced with a kind of relentlessness, and an attraction, too, not to mention a kind of farewell.

Charles brought expensive makeup now, and he put it on me and then I did it myself, standing in front of the mirror, no longer blushing so much as raising an eyebrow in a slow, private acknowledgment, as though the image in front of me were saying, *So, you've discovered* that, *too?* Near the end I looked as though I never got out of bed before noon or one in the afternoon, that I was capable of asking a man with a kind of friendly smile how much he made a year, or that I'd lie down with you as easily as taking off a glove, and then I'd swallow a goldfish, just to watch your face. I wore a white cotton shirt, and a bleached denim jacket, my hair blondish and wet-looking, my lips bright red and glossy, and when Charles and I went to town now, people turned and looked, as though I had changed from a caterpillar to an expensive butterfly right before their eyes.

After Charles had washed and rinsed my hair, and was getting ready to trim it, he took a handful of it and tugged it, letting the hair slip through his fingers with a long, definite squeak. He pressed his lower stomach against my shoulder when he tugged my hair. He told me he loved me. I shook my head, but he told me to hold still, and then there was that steady, quiet squeak of his fingers pulling my hair. The dryer whined and he worked with his comb, his hands trembling a little now. My own hands were trembling now, too, if only because of the endless teasing we'd gone through, just to get closer to springtime. My hair was lightly curled, and when we got into the car and began to go to town, the light swept over me and made my hair and lips shine. I felt the accumulation of those styles, the relentless shove of them, and a kind of disorientation, too, from the number of them, or from the slightly different tug of each, although the direction they had unerringly taken was not so much a surprise as a discovery, although one that left a kind of fury at being teased. So with a sigh of exasperation I told Charles to pull over, and without saying a word he turned onto the wood road that led to that weathered barn, and when we got there I said, "Warning didn't do you any good at all, did it, you poor—"

"Hush, Marie," he said.

I was laughing then. We left the heater running. Out the window I saw those stars, each one purple and trembling beyond the scrabble of the treetops, the points of light quivering before they were obscured by the fogging window. The heater made a long, steady whirring. Then I stood outside, feeling the cold on the wet places, but I was able to get into my jeans easily. Charles said nothing. The heater sounded just like a hair dryer.

We went back to the store, where Charles gave me a peck, just as innocent as could be, and then I went upstairs and ran the water in the tub and stood next to it and washed myself completely, hearing the slight hush of the terry cloth over my skin. I stood next to the tub, seeing the curls of steam rise, and then I rinsed the cloth and spread it to dry and let the water out. I filled the tub again with clean hot water and got in, and all the while I thought about the things Charles had said in the car and all the while wishing, too, that he'd been quiet: those words just made me think about the look on my mother's face when we brought her back from that motel in New Jersey. Then I dried myself off and put on a tattoo, a tiger, and lay on my bed, feeling the dark, inky shape of it. I didn't cry, though, not for a moment. I just lay there, seeing those bluish-purple stars quiver while I thought, *So, I'm all grown up now.*

But I was wrong about that. It took a while yet. And if in the beginning, when Charles began to do my hair, there was a slow, definite progression in style, moving without one false step from innocence or even prudishness to sophistication and from there to jaded belief in impulse, so now there was a similar progression, but this time I was in charge and working with a fury, if only because Charles had tried to suggest something I wasn't (in the beginning) and had ended up by teasing me with what I was. Both cases demanded a kind of relief, or the keeping of a promise, the terms of which were, *So, you thought you wanted me, did you? Well, here it is. Every last bit.*

So we continued in the car, the innocence of it falling away, not only in what we did, but in what I said, and with each new Saturday the sense of innocence was adjusted, and soon we gave up the car and the stars disappearing in the fogged window and started waiting around for my parents to go out so we could go upstairs and into my room.

My trouble was that there was no school I could go to like the Baxter School of Hair Design, and so in the beginning I made my way with a kind of instinct or guessing, but this wasn't good enough. I found books listed in a mail-order catalogue, and I sent away for them, the packages arriving in the postman's red, white, and blue Jeep. I read them at night when my parents were asleep, and just as Charles had learned the use of lotions and creams, dyes, hair dryers, and brushes, so now I found a sexual correlative of the wet, slick styles Charles had picked out of the pages of *Vogue* and *Cosmo.* And in the beginning, Charles was pleased by what seemed innocent and safe enough (his expression something like that of a New England groom), but we went along from there, Charles learning things about himself, too, some of which were frightening. Now, when we climbed the stairs to my room and felt the silence of the house around us, he looked at me not with fear, although there was already a little of this, but more as though we had come into an old place, a church or monastery that had in it the hush of devotion. Then, with my face over him, I'd whisper, or tell him I was going to do . . . something, and as I watched his face, or felt him straining against me or under my fingertips, it seemed we had gone to a place from which you never come back quite the same: there was terror in this, and the sense of some enormous, powerful thing, and that was just fine.

In public I winked at Charles, or raised a brow, and he went a little pale and nervously licked his lips. Sometimes we shared the secret with a nervous, short laugh. I liked to walk around with those tight, wet curls around my face, my eyes turning now and then to Charles. Now, on a Saturday night, we used my bed and carefully made it again, knowing my parents would be home soon, and then we got into that black

Pontiac and Charles drove toward town fast, the car filled with our quiet amazement that these things could be done after all: our speechlessness had about it a centuries-old hush like in some sun-washed ruin.

Then Charles started fighting back. He said he wanted to do my hair again, and I said fine. He came up to the house on Saturday evenings, just as he used to do, dropping that bag next to the kitchen table. I sat on the telephone books with my head in the sink, my neck taut, held up toward him, and he washed my hair and rinsed it with the black-rubber sprayer that was usually used for washing the dishes. He was quiet now and I was, too, as I felt the gentle, warm sensation of his fingers and heard the sound of them in the lather. He leaned against me and tugged my hair, making it squeak between his fingers, and as he worked, I wondered what the new style would be, although after the second one I guessed easily enough, and at each new one I got angrier.

The anger was like having a dream in which you are driving a wagon behind a horse. It runs away and you pull on the reins, but all you feel is the power of the animal, the blind strength of it, and all you see is the tossing of the horse's head, the ragged splash of mane in the air, and the road flying along beneath you. If, in the beginning, the styles had started innocently enough, with me looking like a bride, and if from there they had made some stops along the way, those, for instance, for a housewife out on the town, a workingwoman who wants to be attractive, or a workingwoman who wants to be provocative, and then ending up, without one false step, at those for an expensive slut, why, now the progression went the other way.

Each new style now became a little less daring than before, each a little less lively, although this was difficult to do, since Charles still wanted me to look good. He tried hard, as though he believed he could control things with the steady click of those expensive scissors and the long, lonely moan of the hair dryer. Now that he had seen me on the seat of the Pontiac or in my bed he wanted to put everything back, since not only was the way I looked a reminder about me, but one

about himself, too, and those moments, or those hours, when
he had abandoned himself, or when I had seemed to hold his
life in my hands. He brooded about it. And about style, too,
since, as far as he was concerned, style for the sake of style, or
for the sake of some motive (like trying to get into someone's
pants), was fine, but style with substance was another matter.
And Charles wanted not only to deny us, or me, but the deer
he had shot in those abandoned orchards and hung in that cold
barn, or worse, to deny why those men needed to have those
deer: love gone haywire, or amuck, or maybe love just doing
business as usual.

But I let him do his work and sat through the combings
and dryings. At first I looked not sexless so much as restrained,
but soon that turned into a kind of severity, which in turn
became dullness, although there was one desperate attempt
at sweetness before the end, when he held up the mirror and I
saw my hair in a little flip, just above the shoulders, that made
me look like a librarian whose idea of a good time is to go
home and have a cup of Sleepytime tea while balancing her
checkbook and paying her bills. I looked in the mirror and
laughed, putting back my head and feeling the tears in the
corners of my eyes.

"Why, Marie," said Charles, "what's wrong?"

"I want it put back," I said.

"Back?" said Charles. "I don't understand."

"Put it back in loose, wet-looking curls that hang around
my face. Or make it a rooster cut, a slick one. Or bleach it."

"But what's wrong with this? Princess Di could wear her
hair this way."

"Princess *Di,*" I said. Then I started laughing harder than
before. It hurt in my stomach and the tears made my eyes wet.
"I want it harsh and slick."

I winked at him and raised a brow.

He picked up his things and said, "I'll see you next week."

"I'll be waiting. Right here," I said.

The days went by, and on the next Saturday Charles appeared at the door, carrying his white bag and dropping it
again just like a bucket of fittings, copper elbows, washers, and

bolts. My mother and father went through the kitchen and outside, both saying good night with a kind of ordinary cheerfulness. When their car pulled away, I looked at Charles and said, "Why don't you come upstairs?"

"All right," he said.

We went down the hall and into my room.

"Sit down. On the bed," I said.

I pulled up a chair and sat opposite him and looked him full in the face, and while I kept my eyes on his, I began telling him what I wanted to . . . do, and how, the words coming out in one long whisper. I leaned closer to him, still looking into his eyes, talking. He was a little pale now, since just the talk made him begin to feel he was floating a little, or that the ordinary world was beginning to fall away and that if he'd let me I'd soon bring him to that brink of disappearing, where the only thing to keep him from vanishing altogether, or so it seemed in that terrifying moment, was the touch of my fingers, the light pressure of my hair, or the odor of my skin. He sat back, watching me, nodding. "Maybe later," I said, and got up and went into my small bathroom, where I undressed and took a washcloth and made it damp and washed my breasts and under my arms, leaving the door open about a foot. I wet my legs with the washcloth and then shaved them, putting one on the rim of the tub and then the other, running the razor over the calf, knowing that he saw through the wide crack in the door the planes of a moving arm, thigh, or calf. So I came back and stood before him, my skin rough from the towel, and while I took my robe from the hook beyond him, I said, "Well, will you do my hair?"

We went downstairs and I sat on the telephone books and he washed my hair. I stared across the kitchen, into the store where the Dynamos sat with their gleam. I didn't say much, although once, when he looked at me, I winked. He went about his work as though all he wanted was to make the surface of things look good so he'd be able to enjoy himself in private, as though what happened behind closed doors was a dream that had nothing to do with the world. I felt him strain as he leaned against my shoulder and tugged the hair and put in a clip, and when he turned on the dryer, there was a slight, insistent change in the sound of it as his hands shook. Then he began to comb out the lank shape of that flip, and when he held up the mirror, he said, "There. Don't you think that's nice?"

"I'm not *nice.*" I said.

"Marie, Marie," he said.

"I suppose Princess Di could wear her hair like this, too?"

"Yes," said Charles, "and she'd look great."

I shook my head. Charles wrapped the cord around his dryer and picked up his creams and lotions and dropped each plastic bottle into his canvas sack with a practical, businesslike motion, each bottle coming down with a different *thump,* since no two of them were filled with the same amount. He shrugged and said, "Well, let's go upstairs."

"I want my hair harsh, wet," I said.

"It looks respectable now."

"No," I said, "you know what I want done with it."

"What's the big deal? It's just a damn hairdo."

"Oh? Is that the way it is?"

"Let's go upstairs," he said. "Your parents will be home soon."

So for the second week we stood there, the style coming between us as a delicate, sweet-scented lie.

"All right," he said, "I'll see you next week."

He picked up his bag with a sad, practical air, as though the thing had been reduced, that the magic had been taken out of it, and he was left with just some soapy bottles and a dryer. He went out, letting the cold air in and leaving behind the *screech* of the screen door. I sat down and looked out the window, at the surface of the lake, which was now thawed, dark.

But as I sat there, I thought about those silvery-and-black movies, and the decent, clean, and even passionate world of them, which I knew existed, if only by the golden light of the windows in the World Trade Center. I put my hand into my hair and pulled it a little, thinking, how could I find that world, and what would I do if I got there? If I got in, by some mistake, they'd kick me out. My father eats with his mouth open and sells vacuum cleaners. Don't they have cops for people like me? Or maybe just nasty waiters. I stood in front of the mirror, shaking out my hair, my eyes closed, and thinking, maybe there'd be a mistake. Maybe if I just got there they wouldn't kick me out. Oh, God, wouldn't that be something? Then I got angry again and jerked at my hair.

So it was late winter now and most of the snow had melted, aside from those patches on the north side of every building, which looked like ice left over from a fishmonger's. There was the wet, pinelike scent from the woods, and there was, too, that air of everything coming out of winter and being one winter shabbier for it. The paint on most buildings was cracked, and there was trash here and there, things that had been left in the snow, or there were piles of dirt and things the snowplow had piled up and which were now visible as small gray ridges.

I began to wait for Saturday, but by Tuesday I was already in my father's station wagon (which had DYNAMO written on the side) and on my way to the pharmacy in Baxter, the one that is almost as big as a supermarket and which has shopping carts you can roll up and down the aisles. I knew what I wanted and how much of it, too, and when I stood in the cosmetics section, smelling the vaguely medicinal odor of cotton and plastic bottles and new labels, I took from the shelf the conditioners and shampoos and mousses I had seen in Charles's bag, and as I drove to my parents' house, I thought, if nothing else, I had learned one hell of a lot about curling irons, hair dryers, conditioners, and shampoos.

In the morning I went into my bathroom and washed my hair and combed it out and used the curling iron and hair dryer, but this time I got precisely what I wanted, at least as far as the idea was concerned, although probably the execution left a little something to be desired. It's possible, though, that the roughness made it better, since now it was combed forward and slick, dark, almost glossy, and frankly suggesting not only what I had discovered about myself but the world, too. Then I brought in my box with the tattoos and looked through them, holding up one and then another, flirting with a Harley-Davidson logo I had been saving and then an Oriental tiger, blue-green and ugly, but finally I ripped them up and flushed them down the toilet, only wishing there were a tattoo parlor close by. I had a silk blouse and a short leather skirt I had bought with the money my father paid me for working in the store, and I put them on, the skirt making a squeak like a small sound from a saddle as I pulled it over a pair of black stockings and zipped it up. I wore nothing under the silk blouse. My lips were glossy and red. Then I got into my father's car and drove down the hill.

The sawmill sat back from the road. A long time ago it had been a one-man operation, and in those days there had been only a cradle that held the logs and a saw blade that was as bright as a nickel with the almost constant use. Simpson was the name of the man who had started the place, and he hadn't the money or even the inclination to buy a separate diesel engine for the mill so much as an idea about killing two birds with one stone: he had a bulldozer, an old one, not good for much, and he backed it up and used the power takeoff, through some elaborate connections, to run the saw. It worked fine. As a matter if fact, as the mill became more successful, Simpson put some studs, joists, and rafters (cut there, at the mill) over the saw and the cradle, and then covered the studs with rough planks to make walls and the rafters with tin to make a roof. I can remember the new pieces of tin in the bright August sunlight. After a while Simpson decided to give up all pretense of doing anything but running a mill, and this time when he expanded the building and put on a new roof, he enclosed and completely covered the bulldozer, and now it sat in a kind of pit, still hooked up with the same elaborate connections, but still having a blade and treads, too, and a black, good leather seat, where Charles sat as he started the thing every morning, being sure, just as Simpson had, that it was never in gear when the engine was turned over.

The sawmill was fairly large now, a building made of weathered wood and rusted tin, and around it there were

piles of saw logs, sorted by species. There was a long galvanized pipe, which brought sawdust away from the saw, and it
ran from the roof of the mill to a piece of flat ground, and
beneath the end of the pipe there were conical piles of sawdust, each one of them seven or eight feet tall. As one pile got
too high, the pipe was moved a little to make another, so they
were arranged by age and color, from gray to gray-yellow to
gold.

I turned off the road. The sawmill's drive went over a
ridge and came to the parking lot where there were the saw
logs and those piles of sawdust. In the spring, summer, and fall
you had to be careful about stepping into the piles, since the
wasps nested there, and the insects were easily disturbed.
They came out in one long, buzzing stream, just little flecks in
the air. Now, most of the snow in the parking lot had melted,
but at night it turned cold again, and when I got out of the car
there were frozen puddles with the sun on them. The sawmill
made a long tearing sound and the sawdust came out of the
pipe, the bits of it falling onto a golden cone.

The doors next to the saw were open, and Charles stood
with one hand on a lever. The blade spun, the surface of it
nickel-colored, the teeth of it disappearing into a transparent
blur. Beyond it, in the half-shadow of the mill, other men
stood in faded overalls and dark boots, their clothes only partly
visible in the shade and against the weathered planks of the
wall. The saw blade was a bright spot in the dimness of the
mill. The log had been cut once and the yellow wood showed.
The log moved again, the cradle carrying it back toward the
saw, and in the high screech of the cut, in the welderlike spray
of sawdust, Charles looked up, into the spring sunshine where
I stood. The men in the shadows stepped back, into the mill,
disappearing into the clutter of cant hooks and peaveys,
chains and sledgehammers. The saw shrieked, and the log
moved toward it with all the weight of some unstoppable
thing. The diesel engine made its popping noise and blew a
cloud of smoke into the air, the shadow of it coming across the
ground in a liquid swirl. Charles held the lever, his hands in
gray leather gloves, and stared into the parking lot where I

stood in the glare of the frozen puddles. The wind blew my hair and opened the panels of my coat, showing the black silk, which luffed against me, and in the clean golden sawdust, which flew like insects in summer, I gave Charles a wink, which came as the end of the argument, and maybe even the proof that all the lies in the world wouldn't help us. I stood there, the coat now wide open, some small glare coming off that tight, short skirt. The saw shrieked, and the log made a seemingly endless passage through it, until the slab of wood fell away and the saw changed pitch. Then I got into the car, already feeling tired, and backed it out of that half-muddy, half-frozen place, the bits of sawdust flying like the wasps that nested in the piles of it. I drove up to the house, thinking about the woman with the tattoo from her hip almost to her shoulder, the shape of those black lines against her skin, the blue-green ink of the trees and script, and that orange bird, the tail of it streaming over her.

But Charles didn't give up, not even then. In the evening, after work, that black Pontiac came uphill fast and stopped in front of the store, the loudness of the engine and the suddenness of the black car's arrival suggesting desperation, say, or panic. Charles got out of the car, still wearing his flannel shirt and overalls, and as he came into the store, he didn't look like a man trying to cover things up anymore so much as a man who is trying to do something about things before someone got hurt. He stood in the door of the kitchen, his hair still having bits of sawdust in it.

"We've got to talk," he said.

"I never said we couldn't talk," I said.

He stepped into the kitchen.

"What do you want to talk about?" I said.

"You and me," he said.

"I don't think there's a whole lot left anymore, do you?"

"Yes," he said. "Oh, yes. That's where you're wrong. I came up here to ask you to marry me."

He stood there, his faded overalls and flannel shirt against the doorway. Beyond him, through the store, there was a glint off the lake.

"Just listen," he said. "I've been thinking about it, lying awake at night, trying to find a way to arrange it." He looked at the store, where there were the Dynamos, in a row, and the miniature bottles and cans on the shelves. "I thought I could lease some of this space from your father and put in along the wall a couple of dryers and two sinks maybe and some outlets. I've got some money saved, and I'd make money here, with those women who come up to the lake in the summer time, and from Baxter, too, when word got around. We could stay upstairs until I got it making good money."

I looked down at the floor, at his boots there.

"You're just joking now," I said.

"No, I'm not," he said. "I love you."

I told him what I thought about love.

"You don't believe that," he said.

I closed my eyes and shook my head, thinking about the two of us living in the room next to my parents. I thought of those women coming out of the cabins around the lake, making toward the store with a hungry gait, their hair in bandanas.

"I'm sorry," I said.

"Marie, Marie," he said, "please."

"No," I said.

"Well," he said, "I want you to think about it. . . ."

I shook my head.

"Please," he said.

We stood there, feeling the cool, clean air of the kitchen. A car pulled up and my father went from the chair he'd been sitting on in the sunshine to the gasoline pumps.

Charles looked at my hair and said, "What conditioner did you use?"

"Protein Master," I said.

"Protein Master isn't ph balanced," he said. He touched my hair. "You're going to get split ends."

Outside, my father started to clean a window. We heard him whistle.

"Well," said Charles, "at least I could come and do your hair. Like before."

"I don't think that's a good idea," I said.

"Please," he said.

"I think you should go now," I said.

Then he went out the door, his figure tall and dark in his work clothes, and as he went there was about him, because of the golden sawdust, the hopeful, innocent odor of the sawmill.

He stopped coming on Saturday. Now I took my father's truck and went down to Baxter to see a movie or to buy a little something at the pharmacy, and when other young men in town came around, I said I was sorry, just sorry, but no. I stayed at home, watching those movies after my parents had gone to bed, and as I sat there, with the sound turned low, I thought about packing a bag and catching a bus, or just sticking out my thumb to get away, but I didn't. I had to almost fall in love before I could do that. So I went on, unable to resist, like having a loose tooth you shouldn't bite on, but doing it anyway to feel and taste the salty itch.

Then spring came in earnest. The sky was filled with white puffs, sparkling with moisture, and the ferns and wild-flowers began to show at the sides of the road. I went on working in the store, making a little money, which I put away, if only because I knew I'd need it. My mother and father and I ate the same meat loaf, breaded pork chops, or turkey roll we'd had for years, and on Saturday my mother and father went out, my mother's face a little brittle when she got into her gray suit.

At dinner my mother said, "What happened to Charles, Marie?"

"I guess it just didn't work out," I said.

She turned away, a little saddened.

"I guess so," she said.

Then she put her hand on my head, the way she did when I was young, and said, "Oh, Marie, aren't men something?"

The season began and those women and children came up from the city. The women sat on the small porches, smoking cigarettes and drinking coffee, and the children played around the shore, throwing bits of wood into the lake and standing in the water that lapped at the shore. Every now and then the sound of a radio came from one of those cabins. My mother and father went about their business, pretending they heard only the hush of the pines and the endless lapping of water against the sand of the beach. Sometimes the radio played a samba, or some quietly cheerful music from South America, but mostly the women listened to golden oldies.

In August the leaves became darker, as though they had stopped growing, and in the morning it was chilly. By September the trees began to lighten a little, some of them turning yellow and giving the woods a languid glow in the afternoon. Those women wore sweaters when they sat on those porches, but soon they began to pack and to watch the empty road for the return of their husbands. Then the leaves brightened, the maples having a shimmer to them, and at night I heard the geese flying, the endless *honk, honk, honk* coming as a kind of tug. The first of October came, and the cabins were empty now, their porches deserted, and the only sound that came from them was the occasional banging of a screen door that had come loose in the wind.

In the first week of October a Jeep station wagon stopped in front of the gasoline pumps. It was red and shiny, and the chrome was bright. In the back of the car there were two dogs, in crates, and beside the crates there were two bells, shotguns in leather cases, and some ammunition. Mr. Chesterfield sat at the wheel, his skin as tight as when I had last seen him, or even more so, as though age had somehow made him thinner and more angular. His whitish hair was cut short, and his eyes were a blue-gray that reminded me of bullets. Robert sat on the passenger's side, looking toward the store with those same gray-blue eyes.

When I started the pump, and the gasoline ran into the car, Mr. Chesterfield turned and said, "How's your father doing with those machines? They looked like the real thing."

"Oh," I said, "he sells one every now and then."

"I can tell he's a real go-getter," said Mr. Chesterfield,

turning those gray-blue eyes on me. Behind him the dogs put
their noses against the wire of their cages and sniffed. The
pump made a slow, steady ringing. Robert got out of the car
and opened the rear gate. He was wearing a clean, red-plaid
shirt and a pair of brown pants, and he had a whistle on a
string around his neck. He smiled in the pale sunshine and
said, "Hello. It's been a long time, hasn't it?"

"Yes," I said, "I guess it has."

"The winters are hard up here, I'll bet," he said.

"You could say that," I said.

There was a water bottle in the back, too, and he opened
it and poured some into the dog cages, the water splashing in
the small bowls for it. The dogs were setters, black, yellowish,
and white. One of them thumped his tail against the inside of
his box, and Robert put his fingers up to the wire, touching the
dog's nose.

"They're pretty," I said.

"Well, thank you," said Robert. "This one here is Misty.
That's Sam. Sometimes they can handle grouse a little."

"Oh, hell, Bob," said Mr. Chesterfield, "stop bragging
about the dogs."

The pump stopped and I took the nozzle away from the
car. My hair was in a bandana, and a strand of it had come
loose and was blowing around my face. I pushed it away.

"That's eleven dollars," I said.

"I left my wallet at the house," said Mr. Chesterfield.
"Will you get this, Bob?"

Robert took his wallet from his back pocket and took out
the money, the bills so clean they stuck together a little.

"Thanks," I said.

"You're welcome," said Robert, with a smile, and then he
got into the car and his father drove off, turning onto the dirt
road beyond the station that led to those ridges on the other
side of the lake. There were old orchards and abandoned fields
up there, half filled with berries and brush, which the grouse
liked, and there were damp places in the bottoms where the
woodcock billed for worms. I went into the store and opened
the cash register, snapping the wire flaps over the bills, and as

they came down with a *thap*, I was still aware of the tips of the fingers that had touched the money.

I went about my business, sometimes now watching the lake and hearing the creak and bang of an unlatched door down there, the sound of it now seeming a little forlorn. There were some nuthatches around the store, their markings making them look formal. My father was gone, now going door to door with his machines, not going up to the house with that furious insistence, but still selling a few. In the evening I thought about Robert getting out of the car in that clean plaid shirt, his fingers against the dog cage. My father sat at the table in the evening, reading *The Wall Street Journal,* checking on the one share he owned of IBM. When my parents were asleep, I watched an old movie with Marlene Dietrich in it. She turned toward a man and raised a brow, her hair shimmering, the light falling over her dress, and as I watched her I tapped my finger against the table, the quick, nervous gesture coming as recognition.

Now there were people who drove up here to look at the leaves. They pulled into the store and bought gas and film, and every now and then there was an accident, since they usually stopped in the middle of the road to take a picture. At night my father said, "Marie, is something wrong?"

I went on working, hearing the distant sound of a shotgun, but I didn't even turn in that direction. I never looked at a car until it had already stopped at the gasoline pumps, since I didn't want to be caught looking, or obviously waiting. The store was busy, and people bought postcards, small cans of tuna and Spam, stale bread. On the third day that red car pulled in, and when I looked toward it I blushed, and even then I told myself it meant nothing at all, or just that I was curious about Robert and maybe wondering if he was part of that bright, clean world I was sure existed. Mr. Chesterfield got out and said hello, and I put the nozzle into the gas tank and turned the pump on. Robert got out, too, and stood in a pair of pants with patches on the front that made it easier to walk through those old orchards.

"Well," I said, "how are you doing?"

"All right," he said.

He opened the gate and there were two grouse and four woodcock. The grouse looked gray and dusty, and the woodcock had long bills, a fine checked pattern over the backs, and breasts the color of apricots. Robert opened a cage and patted one of the dogs.

"Sure," he said to the dog, "sure, you're just a beauty."

The pump shut off with a jerk. Then Robert paid me, and the car went away, leaving me with the money. I stood in the warm sunlight and felt the heat of the blush, already beginning to explain it to myself, but then I stopped and just stared at the lake, past the slowly moving cars, which were filled with people who had come to see the leaves.

On Saturday, when my parents went out to the movies, I sat before my dinner of leftovers. I dumped them out, made a drink, and sat down again, hearing the lonely drip of the kitchen faucet. The lake had a cold, stonelike surface. I went into the store and looked at the rifles and ammunition, ran my finger across the counter, touched the glass case for the pistols, and stopped at the rack for the compound bows. The arrows had a tip of four sharp, triangular blades, and when I touched one I felt the whorled texture of my thumbprint. I stood there, feeling that unbelievable sharpness and thinking about Robert in his plaid shirt, his hair bright with sunshine as he showed me the sweet, dusty-smelling grouse.

Then I went upstairs and into my bathroom. It was a small room with a slanted ceiling. It had no window. I took from under the sink the bag in which I kept a curling iron, hair dryer, and those lotions and creams, conditioners and dyes. The things in it knocked against one another with a plastic rattle. The curling iron and dryer were wrapped in their own cords, and the bottles smelled of cosmetics. I looked at them and then shoved the bag back and slammed the cabinet door, the wooden slap of it coming as a surprise in the small room. In the mirror I watched the blush spread into my cheeks, but even so I kept shaking my head, and thinking, *No, absolutely not. No.*

In the morning I began to work outside. I swept up, put

out new paper towels, and stacked up the shiny cans of oil, but when the cars stopped they were always strange ones filled with people who had come to see the leaves. When I saw them I was vaguely disappointed. At night, after my parents went to bed, I went into that small bathroom and took the bag from the cabinet, and after a while I held up the bottles, looking to see how much there was in each one, and even as I did so I shook my head and then threw the things into the bag and gave it a kick back into the space under the sink, the half-empty bottles rattling together there in a sad, idle jumble. I reached down and shoved it farther back. I looked in the mirror and shook my head and told myself it was time to get the hell away from here.

But I didn't. I went on spending my time in front of the store, or someplace at least where I could see the cars come in. At night I saw the lights on the road and heard that high, insistent sound of the geese. I went to town, too, and when I was there I watched the street for that red car, and when I didn't see it, I felt worse. After a while I began to think they had gone home, back to New York or Philadelphia, or wherever they came from, and at first I sighed and said, *Well, good riddance,* but even so, and in spite of the names I called myself (fool, idiot), there was an infuriating sense of loss. In the evenings Aunt Natalya came over, her clothes black and vaguely monstrous as she rose from the other side of the road, her shape dark against the yellow leaves of fall. I said to her, "What did you do in the Ukraine when you were in love?" and she said there was no time for that, not when everyone was starving. It is a good thing to stay away from, she said, and then I sat there, nodding, holding her brownish hand until she got up and stole some cherry sweets for me.

The next day it was cloudy, and the lake was dark, rippled like an Indian arrowhead. I was outside, dressed in a flannel shirt and a pair of jeans, when the red car came up the hill. The dogs were in the back, each with a nose against the wire of a dog box. Mr. Chesterfield wasn't in the car. Robert got out and said, "Hi, Marie."

"Hi," I said, "Robert."

"I like that," he said. "I hate it when people call me Bob."

He put the nozzle into the gas tank and turned on the pump. We listened to the steady ringing of the bell.

"It must get a little dull up here for you after city life," I said.

"Maybe," he said, "but I like it. As a matter of fact, my father's going back, but I'm going to stay on until it snows. There are a lot of grouse this year."

"Are there?" I said.

"God, yes," he said, "the covers are just stiff with them."

I took the money into the store and slammed the drawer of the register shut. There was a calendar on the other side of the room, and I stood underneath it, holding up one of the pages, seeing the quotation from the Bible ("To every thing there is a season . . ."). I looked at those empty days, whispering, hissing to myself, "He usually comes in on Wednesday, so it will have to be the night before, Tuesday. All right. So it's come to that. I should have known it."

On Tuesday evening I went into my bathroom and jerked the bag with the lotions and creams from under the sink and then slammed it on the counter and took the curling iron, dryers, bottles, and creams out, the bottles and things standing around the sink in a kind of shameless clutter. I washed my hair, and used a highlighter, a conditioner, and a cream for body, and after I used the curling iron and the dryer, I had a nice, polite flip. In the morning I put on a clean, proper blouse, a pair of slacks, and good shoes. When he came in, I smiled and we talked, but even though he stayed a little longer than usual, he hadn't noticed a thing. I stood there, trembling a little and watching that car go down the hill.

In Baxter there was one good restaurant. It had white tablecloths, dark paneling, and waiters in black jackets and small black bow ties. There was an elk head on the wall, and the place served roast beef, mashed potatoes, buttered peas, Black Forest chocolate cake. Now that Robert was alone, he had his dinner there. I saw him in the evenings, sitting by the window, drinking a beer and eating smoked trout.

In the evenings I went back to the conditioners and hair

dryer, and with a fury like my father's when my mother was spending her afternoons in that cabin down there by the lake, I abandoned that proper, decent flip. I curled my hair a little, and then a little more, always becoming more daring. I used some makeup now, too. Three times in the first week I got into my father's secondhand truck and drove to town, parking the rusted thing on a side street and then walking past the window where Robert sat. Each night he smiled and waved, but no more. I got back in the truck and sat there, whispering to myself, the words coming out in a long sibilant curse.

The weather turned colder. So now I made the same desperate progression as before, going from what looked like a college girl at her first nightclub to a young wife out for a good time, and then to a woman who wanted to be provocative, each step now leaving me a furious, eye-opening wonder. But even then I didn't get into a short leather skirt and black stockings, although I certainly got into tight blue jeans and a cotton blouse, worn over nothing, and went to town with my hair hanging in wet curls around my face and with my lips bright and glossy.

The truck had almost no padding over the springs, so I brought newspaper out and spread it to sit on, and then went to town, parking on that same side street and walking past the restaurant, getting only that polite smile and wave. I started to hate him, if only because with each passing night, I abandoned a little more hope, and began to know, too, right where we were going.

Finally, though, on the night I looked not like an expensive slut so much as a small-town girl who is almost dangerous with frustration, Robert stood up and came into the street and said, "Marie, I was wondering if you'd have a drink with me? You know, I've been eating here alone. Will you join me?"

I went in and we sat down opposite one another, the heavy white tablecloth between us. Only one place had been set, but the waiter came and put silver and a heavy napkin in front of me. Outside, people went up and down the street in the half-light of dusk.

"Why don't we have some champagne?" said Robert.

"I'd like that," I said.

The waiter brought a bottle in a cooler that stood on three legs. We drank some of it and the lights in the restaurant looked bright.

"Do you still sell those machines with your father?" he said. "I mean from house to house?"

"No," I said.

I blushed then, but kept my eyes on his.

"I'm sorry," he said, "I didn't mean to upset you."

There were other people in the restaurant, eating and talking, but there weren't that many, and we were far away from them. I told him about the inventions I had seen at the shows in New York, what happened in the store, the coffee and doughnuts my father had tried to give away. Robert had gone to school in England, and soon he was going to start teaching.

"What are you going to teach?" I said.

"Renaissance history," he said.

"Oh," I said.

I sat there, feeling the champagne, and knowing it was no use. I tried to talk about the people who came to spend the summer at the lake, but in a minute I stopped.

"Would you mind if I left?"

"Is something wrong?" he said. "Have I upset you?"

"I'd just like to get out of here. Maybe we could get into your car and drive around."

"Why, sure," he said. "Let me get the check."

He got a bottle of champagne, too, and we went into the dark street. It was a little cold, and when we got to the car, he turned on the heater. Inside there was the sweet, dusty scent of grouse and woodcock. We drove through the streets of town, passing the deserted square, the church, and the new police station. It was quiet in the car now, and for a while neither one of us spoke, so I said, "Why don't we go see the dogs? How are they?" Then he turned around and drove up to that large house, where he parked the car, both of us getting out and walking across that gray porch and into the living room. We hesitated when we crossed the rug, and I thought how I had demonstrated one of the machines on it, trying then

to do so without moving much, and as we stood there, I raised
a brow and said, "Well, what are we waiting for?"

In the days afterward I met him at his father's house, and
after he'd hung the grouse and woodcock on the back porch
and fed the dogs, we went upstairs, into the room with the
beautiful furniture, the pale rug, and the windows that looked
over the field. I told myself I knew what I was doing, and that,
if nothing else, for the rest of his life he'd remember me with a
groan, especially after he'd married a pale woman who wore
her hair in a flip. So I took charge. . . . I was determined to
say nothing, and I shook my head and closed my eyes with the
effort, but even so, there came a moment when I put my lips
against his ear and said, "Oh, God, I love you. . . ." He told
me what he thought about love, and that made it worse: it was
just what I used to say.

In the evenings we drank champagne, sitting in the quiet
room downstairs, not talking really, but still getting across to
one another: we'd wink, or laugh, and then we'd . . . begin
to find out how far we could go. Everything else was beyond
me, European history, the bloodlines of the dogs, the furniture
of the house, the large pantry filled with food, the ceiling of
the porch that was painted blue: it was like walking endlessly
up and down in front of the restaurant, waiting to be invited
in. So I didn't know then whether I was in love or just trying to
leave that pale woman he'd marry wide eyed with wonder
about what had happened before her. Upstairs, in that polite
room with the old bed, the chests that smelled of lemon-
scented polish, and with the white muslin undercurtain billowing in the breeze that came through the slightly opened
window, I took a bootlace or . . . picked from the floor a pair
of my underwear and swept them across his face, if only so
he'd remember, his features passing under my finger in one
slick rush. . . . We *dared* one another, our hands shaking. In
that polite room, or anywhere in the house, I felt some terror,
some danger just beyond the line of sight, and it made these
hours seem more serious and more risky, too. So I was scared
when we sat opposite one another, drinking that cold, dry
champagne and talking about meeting the next day. We were

separated from the world, cut off from the ensnaring things
that were surely lying in wait for me, but I knew they were
there, almost rustling in the dark. I gave him a peck on the
cheek and left, letting the lacquered screen door slam as I
stepped from underneath the blue ceiling of the porch, and
when I got to my father's truck and sat on the newspaper-
covered seat, I felt like a bandit, although I thought, *How
much longer? Isn't it going to snow soon?*

There were afternoons when it rained, or when Robert
killed his limit early. He came by the store around noon and
looked at me, or just showed me three woodcock and four
grouse. I made an excuse to my mother or father and got into
the truck or the station wagon (with DYNAMO on the side) and
went down the back roads which previously had been where I
went to waste time or to collect those deer Charles had killed
or to help my father demonstrate a machine. Now I turned
into the house's long drive. Usually, when I arrived, Robert
was on the back porch, putting the birds up to hang, or pouring dog food into two bowls, since even though it was early to
feed the dogs, neither one of us wanted them barking later.

We went up to that room with the cherry-wood bureau,
the small, gray-blue sofa, and the secretary with rows of pi-
geonholes, and in the middle of the afternoon I saw the light
coming through the curtains. On the polished surfaces, on the
handful of coins on the bureau, or on the mirror, the brass
doorknobs, the white tile in the bathroom, across the thin
platinum watch on the nightstand, or in the drops of water on
the windows there was a silvery luminescence, the same as in
those movies when light spread over those women like a thrill.
I stared at those smears of light, not thinking anything at all. I
got up and went downstairs and walked through the house
with nothing on, and in the kitchen there were old, large
appliances, an icebox, stove, juicer, all white and chrome and
having about them that same silvery edge. I stood outside,
feeling on my legs the slight drops that came from the rain
splashing on the edge of the porch. The birds were hung from
the tenpenny nails driven into a beam, the grouse with a line

of black across the tail and the woodcock with their long bills sticking out. Once, one of the long bills was shattered.

I kept working on my hair and nails and face, not able to stop now and not able to do anything, either, about the effect these things had on me, and with each new "look" I appeared more haughty and impatient. And with each sure, unavoidable step, with each maddening change, I abandoned something, giving up, in each of those afternoons or evenings, even the little flirtation I had had with love. Sometimes, when I thought about it, I took Robert's hair in my hands, and he said, "Marie, that hurts."

"Does it?" I said.

But even then I clung to a superstitious hope, if only because, if I believed there wasn't any chance, why, then, there probably was, just to prove me wrong.

A friend of Robert's came to dinner now. The deer season was about to begin, and there was the cool, heavy pressure of snow in the air. The friend's name was Witter, and he was tall, thin, and had blue eyes and a little blond mustache. The two of them had known each other at school and had been together on a yacht race, which they'd almost won. I was quiet at dinner, although I listened politely, holding my knife and fork the way Robert and his friend did. At the end of the meal Robert said he had to run into town, but that Witter would keep me company.

I'd had some champagne and I wasn't too clear about this, and for a moment I was only sorry Robert hadn't asked me along. That superstitious hope was still there, and it made me edgy. But then, by the time I got into the living room with Witter, who had a bottle of champagne with him, I understood perfectly, and as I looked down I heard Witter's voice saying that Robert wouldn't mind, that the two of them had shared a lot, that we'd have a good time. Finally he was quiet. He poured the champagne and the foam made a rush in the glass. I looked at the rug where I had demonstrated that machine, and thought, *I'm going to make you feel so good.*

As we climbed the stairs I unbuttoned my dress and undid

the belt, all of it done with a kind of angry frankness, and when we got into that room, I gave him a slight shove onto the bed. When I was done I got up and turned my back without saying a word and went into the bathroom, where I rinsed out my mouth and washed my hands. I put my clothes on with the same silent fury, not stopping when he spoke and not saying a word myself, just getting into my dress, stepping into my shoes, and going out the door, pulling my belt tight with a jerk. Outside, the air was snow laden, damp, and cold. I slid across the seat of my father's car, putting the key in and starting the engine in one quick motion, and as I drove toward the store, I stopped on one of those back roads and stood at the edge of a field while it began to snow, the cold points of it coming as a chill. All I could think about was the fire marshal telling my father that the gulley at the bottom of the hill was full of stale doughnuts and Styrofoam cups, and as those cold flecks touched my face, I started nodding, unable to speak, but still agreeing with my father as he had said, his hands trembling with fury, "Marie, if they don't want coffee and doughnuts, they sure don't have to have them."

I went back to the store and took a bath, trying to soak, but not being able to sit still. The bathroom was small and filled with fog, and I was glad I didn't have to see my face in the mirror. I got into bed and lay there, seeing the light fill the room as the cars went by on the road. In the morning I dressed and went outside, my face scrubbed and my hair clean, but now as I went about my business in front of the store I paced back and forth, feeling like a tiger behind bars in a zoo, the movement of it one constant flow, even down to making turns with a quick slink. There hadn't been more than a dusting of snow, and in the warm afternoons I heard a shotgun on the ridge where there were abandoned orchards and old farms.

In the evening my mother said, "Oh, Marie, what a catch Robert Chesterfield would be."

I went out in the morning, watching the cars go by, and now even admitting to myself that I was waiting. And it didn't take long, either, for that red car to stop in front of the store. Robert got out and said, "Hello, Marie, can you fill it up?"

I put the nozzle into the car and turned on the pump.

"Where have you been?" he said.

"Oh, shut up," I said.

"What do you mean?"

"Shhhhh," I said, "just be quiet."

We stood opposite one another, hearing the steady lapping of the lake.

"There are no hard feelings, are there?" he said.

"No," I said. "I just don't want to hear your voice."

He blinked and opened his mouth once to speak, but didn't say anything. The pump turned off and I took the nozzle out of the car. He held out a bill and I took it and went inside to make change, jerking the cash drawer open and dropping his money, and when I had snatched up the amount I needed, I knocked the wire flaps down, each one landing with a *thwak.* He was in his car, and I shoved his change through the window.

"Well," he said, "I'll see you next year."

"Sure thing, you asshole."

"Nobody talks to me that way," he said.

I stepped closer to him and put my lips next to his ear and said, "You're the biggest asshole I've ever met."

"Nobody says that, especially not some cheap—"

He got out of the car now, leaving the door open. I put my lips next to his ear and whispered again. The wind moved his sandy hair, and he stood there, saying nothing, although he clinched one fist and lifted it about as high as his waist.

"Is that the way you behave?" I said. "What are you going to do, knock me down?"

"No one talks to me that way," he said.

"I do," I said.

He raised his fist a little more.

"You heard me," he said.

He got back into the car and rolled up the window, the sheen of the glass coming between us. Then he started the engine and put the car into gear. I leaned forward and spoke again, my breath making the glass mist a little. Then he pulled onto the road and went downhill fast, and even as I watched him go, I started moving back and forth in front of the store, feeling in my legs and arms that endless flow and stop of some animal, that tiger, say, slinking back and forth behind the bars of a zoo.

It was late fall now, and those postcards arrived from the Bahamas, Florida, and Jamaica. The beaches on them were white and haunting, and the ocean was a soft blue, like ink and milk mixed together. My father put them in a little manila file with alphabetical tabs. The trees had lost all their leaves and in the distance the hillsides seemed to be covered with a gray fuzz.

In the morning there was frost on everything, the windshields of the cars having a pattern that looked like white coral. My father said the cold hurt his back and asked me if I'd look after the front of the store in the morning. So now I went into the cold, and when the sun rose the frost looked like someone had spilled glitter on it. The cars were filled with men in Day-Glo shirts and jackets, and they asked if I had seen any deer.

A week after Robert left, I went upstairs and took out my suitcase and began to put my clothes into it. I folded everything neatly. The blouses had the buttons done up, and my stockings were rolled into neat balls. I put in the lotions, creams, brushes, and a hair dryer.

My father came into the room and said, "Marie, what's this?"

"I'm getting away," I said.

"But, Marie, where are you going?"

"I don't know," I said. "California. How about that? I'm going to California."

"Don't go yet, Marie," he said. "Wait a little. Just a few weeks. All right?"

He stood in the doorway, his face pale, and he was sweating a little. He had his hand against his hip.

"My back's killing me," he said. "I need some help in front in the morning."

"Why won't you go to a doctor?" I said.

"It'll be all right. It just needs a little rest."

"I'm getting out of here," I said.

"Oh, Marie . . ." he said. "Wait a little, huh? Just two weeks. That's not too much to ask, is it?"

"It depends on who you're asking," I said.

"I'm asking you," he said.

He was sweating there, his brow bright with it.

"Will you go to a doctor?" I said.

"Oh, sure, Marie," he said, "if that's what it takes to make you stay. Sure, I'll go tomorrow, first thing."

I sighed and took my things out of the suitcase and put them into a drawer just as I had packed them. Then I went down to the kitchen, where my mother said, "Marie, what's wrong? Can't you sit still?"

My father was too sick now to take care of the postcards he had in that manila file, so in the afternoon, after I'd worked in front of the store, I drove up to the sawmill. There were still logs piled in the parking lot and beyond them there were the battened walls, in which there was a barn door, opened now to the darkness inside, through which the men moved, their passage marked by the glint of the peaveys they carried. The roof was rusted to the color of paprika, and the sawdust blew out of that pipe in a yellow stream. Charles stood next to a log that slid toward the saw blade, and when I came up to the open door, I shouted over the shriek of the place, "Come over tonight. I've got something for you." In the evening, when he came into the store with the sawdust still in his hair, I climbed into the attic and brought down that two-thousand-candle-power spotlight. The rifle with the scope was already on the counter, so he picked that up, too, keeping his eyes away from mine.

At dinner I sat opposite my father and said, "Well, what did the doctor say?"

"He wants to do some tests, Marie."

"When?" I said.

"Soon. Tomorrow or day after," he said.

I nodded, thinking about the things that were ready to go into the suitcase. I waited while my parents ate, and then I cleared the table and went outside, into the cold air.

The next night Charles killed a deer. I made him a sandwich (just as my father always did), and he sat at the kitchen table, drinking the beer I had given him and only saying with a kind of surprise, "This bread isn't stale." I read a book, hearing the sink drip, and Charles just sat there, his forearms on his knees. When it was late we drove the truck down to an old orchard and picked the deer up, swinging it into the bed and hearing the rattle of its hooves against the tailgate.

"Well?" I said to my father.

"The hospital is working on it," he said. "Maybe I got a bone problem, or a joint problem. I go back tomorrow."

At night I got into bed and thought of the neatly folded blouses and sweaters I'd pack and of the quiltlike blocks of color my things would make in the open suitcase. Outside there was the wind and the creak of the pines on the other side of the road.

The next day was cold, and the sky was a bluish white. There were small birds around the store, streamlined and dipping when they flew. In the evening my father came into the house and said he had cancer. "In the bone," he said. His expression and his voice suggested that the thing was a kind of financial possibility, or business opportunity (not so different from the machines in the store), and he went on about gene splicing, monkey glands from Switzerland, laetrile, interferon, blood doping, his voice rising a little with the possibility of each, his eyes moving from my mother to me in his now almost cheerful insistence that he would succeed here in a way he had never been able to before.

Then I started moving around the house in that constant pacing. I heard my father's voice ebb and flow as I went up and down the hall, the turns made not with a stop and start so much as with the nervous bend and slink of an imprisoned creature who believes the bars of the cage are only the pickets in a long fence and that the way to get to the end of it is to keep moving.

Marie Boule, The Flood

Baxter, Pennsylvania

THERE IS A RIVER HERE, AND IT RUNS FROM THE HILLS ABOVE Baxter into the valley below the town. You can see the valley and the town, too, from the upstairs window. Near the end of the winter the ice in the river broke up and floated downstream to the narrows. The pieces of ice were as big as a house, clear, although each one was filled with a whitish puff, just like in a half-melted ice-cube. The ice made a dam at the narrows and behind it there formed a lake, which reflected the skies of dusk and dawn and looked like salmon-colored silk.

People who lived in the floodplain woke up to find a foot or more of water around their beds. They got into boats, canoes, or climbed onto anything that floated, and started the slow, steady paddling that brought them to the outskirts of Baxter. There, that icy lake lapped against the back side of town.

The first to arrive was Mrs. Sloan, in her Sears canoe, which was jerry-rigged so as to have a small Evinrude outboard motor on one side of it, and in it, ahead of Mrs. Sloan, there were three chickens, a calf, a goat, a chest of drawers, and two bottles of Jim Beam. The canoe was announced long in advance of its arrival, since Mrs. Sloan's swearing, which she had learned from her husband, a carnival man, came across the water when the canoe was just a speck.

After her there was a clutter of canoes, boats, uprooted trees with men and women holding on to the branches, telephone poles, a barn door floating on empty barrels, johnboats, and even inflatable, yellow canvas life rafts. All of them came with no sound at all, aside from the steady working of makeshift oars and paddles, the men and women and children not saying a thing or doing anything aside from paddling or holding on to a piece of furniture, or gunwale, their eyes set on the town hall and dry land.

They arrived and silently unloaded their furniture and Coleman stoves and extra clothes, each group making a pile in a place separate from the others. There were people who had tents with them, too, heavy canvas or bright nylon ones, and they pitched them close to the water, which was still rising, the tents being put there as though to prove that not only would the people in them go back to their houses and farms, they were fixing to get wiped out twice by the same flood, too. And when the tents were set up, the men, women, and their children went methodically around town, picking up scrap lumber and paper, and then they brought it back, where they lighted fires in barrels and trash cans and cooked over them, the steam from the pots of soup and stew mingling with the smoke from the fires, which drifted over the clutter of the shore, and the patient, dark shapes of the people.

That was the first day. On the morning of the second day the people stood at the cluttered shoreline among their piles and tents, the men and women instinctively separating into two camps, each standing around a barrel filled with burning scrapwood. The water went on rising.

Soon it was obvious even to the tightfisted town council that dynamiters were needed, and in an emergency meeting conducted in the scent of burning scrapwood, the council agreed to pay for them.

The Italian dynamiters came into the store, one behind the other, three of them all together, each of the young men tall and dark haired and having dark eyes, too. The cold air came into the room with them. They wore new denim coats with blanket lining, new jeans, and new, inexpensive boots, which didn't look quite like they were made out of leather. Each one of them wore a new orange watch cap, from which there came an identical lock of dark hair. They walked to the counter, and one of them said, "Do you have a cabin for rent?"

"Yes," I said, "across the road by the lake."

One of them paid, taking the new bills from his pocket and pushing them across the counter, and saying, too, as I picked them up, "We need a place to cook. Is that a kitchen behind you? Can we use it?"

They didn't look so much like brothers as triplets, all of them watching me now, all of them blinking in the same way.

"I'll ask my mother," I said. "Wait a minute."

I went back into the kitchen where my mother sat, one of her hands pushing up her auburn and still beautiful hair. The Italians waited, looking around the store at the things in small cans and bottles.

"I can't have any loud noises," said my mother. "I have a sick man upstairs. Is that clear?"

"Of course," said one of them.

All three of them nodded.

"All right," said my mother, "you can cook here. You wash your own dishes."

They turned and went out, passing their truck. It was green and had a metal box on the back, like an enormous dog kennel, and on it there was a diamond-shaped, green sign that said, DANGER. HIGH EXPLOSIVES. KEEP BACK FIVE HUNDRED FEET. IF YOU CAN READ THIS YOU ARE TOO CLOSE. On each side of the aluminum box there was a fire extinguisher, and the red color of them and the bands of stainless steel that held them looked festive, like a red package with a tinsel ribbon. The dynamiters filed past the truck, still in single file, each one of those orange hats rising and falling with the same steady gait.

In the evening they came back to cook, and while they waited for a large kettle to boil, one of them winked at me. He introduced himself as Beniamino and told me he had a cousin in Italy who made fireworks and who had put on a show attended by the pope. He told me he had an uncle who had been a dynamiter, too, and that the uncle had been buried in a cigar box. Beniamino smiled, and said he missed Italy, the olive oil, the tomatoes, the anchovies, the oranges, the taste of the food, but no one had a use for dynamiters there. America was where you came to blow things up. In Italy they weren't so ready to demolish old buildings, but here, right down in Scranton, the previous week the Italians had blown up a building that wasn't thirty years old.

At night, in town, the dogs were skittish and watchful, and they sat just beyond the light of the fires, their eyes filled with the yellow glint of the flames. There was a grandfather clock sitting in a canoe, the box of it looking like a coffin. Country and western music played from a radio, and every now and then a dog howled. The Red Cross gave out sandwiches and coffee and began to put up a tent where they'd be able to serve a hot meal. Children went around the streets picking up scraps that would burn, dead branches from the trees in town, twigs, a picket or two off a fence when no one was looking.

In the morning the Italian dynamiters crossed the road and came into the kitchen and made espresso and hard toast, which they ate at the table, taking sips from the small cups they had brought with them. And after they'd washed their small coffee maker and those cups, Beniamino asked me to take them to the dam.

We went in my father's station wagon, Beniamino in front and the other two in back. The water was blue like the sky, and emerging from the surface of it there were those partly submerged barns, houses, trucks and cars, leafless trees and telephone poles. We went along the ridges above the flood until we came to the dam. The Italians got out, each one of them putting a hand to his head, not so much in awe or surprise as in disbelief.

The narrows were about a hundred yards across. Mostly they were just a passage through grayish stone, a lot of which

was solid and grained, although here and there, where water
had gotten into the cracks and frozen each winter for millions
of years, there was a steep and loose slag of rocks. Now,
though, the narrows were filled with ice, some of the blocks of
which were as big as a barn, or bigger, the slabs having about
them an enormous scale, although even with their size, their
effect was still one of clutter: the pieces of ice, with their edges
snapped crisply like a piece of coconut, weren't stacked on top
of one another so much as shoved together, the chaos of them
rubblelike, but still enormous. The angular pieces had been
pushed partway through the narrows, scraping the trees from
both banks and leaving them in a pile, their trunks twisted and
split open, showing the fibers of wood. On the face of the dam,
or over the arctic clutter of it, there were places where the
river had run, but now the water had stopped altogether, and
instead of it there were icicles, most of them so large as to look
like church steeples turned upside down.

The Italians seemed diminutive as they approached the
first, enormous cubes. They had mountaineers' axes and they
used them as they climbed, the three of them slowly going
over the white shapes, looking into the crevices between the
blocks. As they swung their axes the ravine was filled with a
steady *chip, chip, chip*.

Then they climbed down and argued in Italian, and as we
drove back along the edge of the lake, passing the barns and
houses which sat on their own reflections, the Italians spoke in
louder voices, their hands shooting into the air, as though to
suggest the direction of the blast, and as each spoke the other
two shrugged, the gesture coming as a kind of fatalism. They
argued at night, too, while they cooked, each one of them
making a point while slicing scallions or onions or tomatoes,
the sharp knives coming down against the cutting board in a
kind of emphatic disagreement or insistence, and while they
ate they gestured with a knife or fork, one movement being
repeated over and over, which, like their hands in the car,
suggested an explosion. Then they washed the dishes and
went out, still arguing, their voices receding as they crossed
the road.

When they had gone I put some powder for an orange breakfast drink into a glass and added water and took it up to my father. It was what he ate now. Sometimes he could keep it down. He now believed bathing was unhealthy, or worse, that it took something away from him. The room had a fetid, outhouselike smell, but my father refused to let us help him bathe. He drank the orange juice, and I sat down on the chair next to the bed. He raised his eyebrows and said, "Marie, what do you want when our ship comes in?"

"A Corvette, or maybe a Porsche," I said. "You know, with a pigskin interior."

My father closed his eyes and nodded, saying, "Yes, the smell of pigskin. And the actual touch of it. But you know, Marie, a Porsche is a hard car to have serviced." His hair was almost white, but he still kept it combed straight back, in the style of a technical man in the early twentieth century. Now he spoke of possible cures and talked about altered viruses, protein envelopes, toxic synergy, all of which he read about in *The Wall Street Journal.* "What I need is Thomas Edison," said my father. "But where are the great men?"

"Who was greater," I said, "Bell or Ford?"

"Marie, that's a tough one. I'll give it some thought," he said, "but I'll tell you one thing. Soon IBM will be into artificial intelligence. Then the sky will be the limit. I give you my word on that score. The sky will be the limit."

Then my mother walked into the room. He asked her what she wanted when our ship came in and she said, "Why, Al, don't you know?"

He shook his head.

"I'd like a trip to Florida with you."

The dynamiters came out of the cabin in the morning, each one still wearing a Day-Glo cap. They came by the gasoline pumps, through the store and into the kitchen. Now they made coffee and toast in silence, no one saying a word, even when they sat down at the table with their small cups and saucers. They had come to a decision.

Beniamino said his uncle, the one who had been buried in

a cigar box, had gotten sloppy and had worked with short fuses and old dynamite. When Beniamino did a job, he liked to think about the vegetable gardens in Italy, or the fishing boats that came into Porto Salvo. You could get octopus there and make it with tomato sauce. And fresh parsley.

"Why are you pacing so much?" said Beniamino. "What are you waiting for?"

I stopped and shook my head and then started again.

They finished their coffee and washed up, putting the small saucers in one pile and the cups in another. Then they went out and got into that green truck with the quilted, shiny box on the back and the sign that said, "DANGER. HIGH EXPLOSIVES. KEEP BACK FIVE HUNDRED FEET." And as one and then another slipped into the front seat, I put on my coat and got into my father's car with the DYNAMO signs painted on each door.

When we got close to the dam there were pickup trucks and cars parked on both sides of the road, and farther up, on the bank of the river, there were the evacuees, men, women and children, most of them standing with blankets held Indian style as they stared at the jumble of enormous white blocks. There were stray dogs here, too, and they moved along the bank, although none of them went onto the ice. And when that green truck with the high-explosives sign on the back pulled up, the people who were below the dam turned and started climbing the sides of the narrows, quietly assembling at the top, the long line of them suggesting people who had assembled on a mountaintop to wait for the end of the world.

Here and there a man or woman unwrapped a Red Cross sandwich and began to eat, their jaws working in an unemphatic, constant motion. It was a cold day, and even up here there was a metal trash can with a fire in it. Between the banks of the narrows there stretched the angular and white pieces of ice, all of them pushed together, the accumulation of them suggesting a kind of arctic desert. Crows that had grown fat on carrion flew through the smoke.

The dynamiters filed out of the cab and went to the kennellike thing on the back of the truck and removed blocks of explosive, each one of which was wrapped in sticky, rust-colored paper. There were rolls of white and red wire and a detonator too. The Italians picked up their things and walked toward the dam, which was as white as salt, and which was now making an eerie creak. And as they went, planting their charges, and sometimes arranging them in a shape like a U, there was that *chip, chip, chip* of their axes. They played out the wire and climbed to the top of the narrows, and when they had attached the wires to the detonator, they stood on the bald stone and looked across the arctic floe, the pieces of it heaved up, incoherent, and suggesting the weight of Easter Island statues.

The dogs wandered along the river, and those dark birds flew back and forth, looking for dead things. The people stood in their blankets, some of them chewing slowly, their jaws moving in a steady repetition that suggested thinking more than eating.

At first, when the Italians set off their charges, there didn't seem to be noise so much as the movement of a vertical geyser, like steam under pressure, say. The bits of ice rose into the air, twisting around and around and trailing smaller flecks, which in turn seemed to form a white mist, and for a moment there was the illusion of a kind of transitory fog, or wall, which hung up in the air as though it were going to stay. And while we stared at it, the sound of the explosion hit us like a wind, the *boom, boom, boom*, numbing the skin. Now the dogs began to bark, and the black birds stopped wheeling in the smoke of the fires and flew straight away from the noise and commotion. In the sound of the howling dogs and in the involuntary *ahhhh* that came from the men and women who stood along the edge of the river, that wall of ice and mist fell back into the gorge, and if the pieces of it didn't fall exactly where they had come from, the overall impression was that they had, the chaos and jumble being indistinguishable from the one before the explosion, and just as the dam was indistinguishable from the previous one, so was its effect. The dogs went on barking, heads out, their sides heaving with the effort. The men who had been eating a Red Cross sandwich had stopped, but now, as the ice fell back into the gorge, they began again, their chewing a little quicker than before, as though in nervous consideration of the fact that their houses were still underwater and likely to stay that way for a while.

The Italians glanced only once at the flat expanse in front of them, the barn-sized pieces of ice still shoved one against the other, and then they went down the face of that gray stone, all of them in a file. They stood beneath the white jumble, one pointing at one side, one at the other, and the third one shrugging and looking at the frozen ground. There was the sound of the barking dogs, and the voice of a man who stood at the top of the hill, a half-eaten sandwich in one hand as he said, "That's it? That's all? I got fields to plant. How the hell am I goin' to get them dry?"

Now the Italians filed back to the truck and completely unloaded it, piling the wooden boxes of plastic explosives in the mud, the crates looking somehow commercial or exotic, as though they held tea from Ceylon or Tibet. Then two of them dragged the boxes into that wilderness of blocks while the other took from the truck a machine that looked something like a posthole digger, only it was run by a chain-saw engine, and while the first two unwrapped the squares of plastic explosive, the other used the bore, putting on one extension after another. The men and women stood along the bank above the dam, patiently waiting, eating those stale Red Cross sandwiches, burning scrap wood and huddling in blankets.

This time, when the Italians stood on the top of that egg-shaped rock, there wasn't only a *BOOM* and geyser of ice and bits so fine as to make a mist, but now there were pieces of earth and stone in it, too, which made the airy conglomeration look as though the Italians had somehow struck oil, and as that misty wall of fog hung up there, now marked by the dirt, those enormous pieces of ice began to move. At first there was a long creak, like stepping on frozen snow, but then it got louder and the dam appeared to have a bulge in it, or just a kind of irruption, or dilation. Then the clutter of those white chunks swung out as though hinged, and while that creaking continued, the river revealed itself. The dam opened like a barn door.

Upstream the creaking moved across the floe, which began to lurch with a kind of prehistoric motion, as though there were some enormous, extinct thing come to life there. The dogs yapped at the blocks of ice, which moved now with an elephantine bob and scrape. The men and women stood along the bank, their faces tired, the children not enjoying the movement of ice so much as being frightened by it, as though before them there were a parade of white dinosaurs. Where the dam had broken the water spilled out, the edges of it streaked by the ragged pieces of ice, and in the downward arc of the river there were the things the flood contained, bureaus and chairs, wooden doors and planks, fence posts, boxes and trash, and dead animals, too, pigs, cows, and dogs, their stiff-legged carcasses bobbing in that long, slick fall, and as these things smashed together in the white water below, I sat down on the bald stone, and with the river roaring like a high wind, I thought, *Oh, God, dear God, why did I say I loved him? Why?*

In the evening the fire marshal brought the Italians a check, and then they came across the street, two of them standing outside while Beniamino gave me the key. He thanked me for the use of the kitchen. He winked and said America was the land of opportunity, and that with any luck the three of them would live long enough to blow up half of Philadelphia. "Remember," he said, "squid in tomato sauce. Fresh parsley. It's very good."

The river went down. The floodplain dried, although the roads were covered with a layer of silt, which turned to dust and filled the air like smoke. Just outside of town, or downstream from it, there were boats and homemade rafts tied in the crowns of trees. It took a while, too, for people to collect their pigs, chickens, and dogs from the side streets of Baxter. Men and women came to town, their clothes so covered with dust as to look as though they had just emerged from it, and they carried ropes or a box, and with the dust coming out of their clothes in puffs, they chased the animals, the grunt and squeal, or the flapping of wings, coming as a reminder that the land was drying out. In the floodplain the sides of the houses and barns were half covered with yellowish dust, the pale tint of it sweeping up from the ground and stopping about midway in a perfectly straight line.

My father got out of bed and got dressed, sweating with the effort, and then he told me to get some machines into the car, and after I did, I helped him downstairs. He said the sky was the limit with machines we could sell. He'd been watching the dust from the upstairs window. He sat in the front seat, on the right, and I drove over those flat roads, along which there were telephone poles marked halfway up with that straight yellow line of the high-water mark. It was almost spring, but the trees really hadn't come into leaf. My father sat next to me, sweating now, looking at the dust on the sides of the barns.

I pulled into a farm, going up the long, straight lane, which was bordered by trees with the same high-water mark on them, and when we came up to the house, a dog ran from under the porch and barked at us. My father got out and stood, shielding his eyes from the bright sunshine, looking at the house. I got out, too, and both of us stood there in the dusty yard, but soon my father started walking, his gait not insistent so much as slowly fleeing something. The porch was a high one, and there were four or five steps to it, the paint flaking from them and from the wooden newel-posts. My father stood at the bottom, sweating a little, and when a woman came out of the house, wearing an apron, her face and hair covered with that dust, my father said, "Please. Could I have a drink of water?"

"Why, sure," said the woman. "I've got some in the ice-box. Nice and cold."

She brought a glass, and my father held it, leaning there on the newel and looking around the farm. He sat down on the step and petted the brown-and-white dog that came up to him.

"You want some more?" said the woman.

"No, that's fine. Much obliged," he said. "Dusty, isn't

it . . . ?" but the woman had turned and gone back inside, taking the glass with her. We walked back to the car, where my father said, "It's no use, Marie. We better go home."

In the evening my father sat in his room, and even downstairs I heard his quiet, unemphatic, but continuous swearing. It sounded like someone counting. He didn't want the juice I brought him now, and when I came into the room he was sweating and shaking his head, now damning just about everything and everyone in that same quiet, unemphatic voice, although once, when I stood there with that orange liquid in a glass, he said, "Marie! Marie! You remember, it's the money that counts!"

Sometimes Charles came into the store, and while that whispering, countinglike sound came from upstairs, he said, "I've missed you. Don't you know that?"

"Shhhh," I said, "shhhh. Quiet. Please."

"But I don't want you to go."

"Let's not worry about that," I said. "Not right now. Why don't I make you something to eat, and then you can go home? Or just a beer? Would you like that?"

He just sat there, looking at me.

"You know what I mean," he said. "I don't want you to go."

When I sat in my father's room I looked through the window that faced the hillside. The next afternoon I took my place opposite him. He stopped swearing and coughed, and then began again. Beyond the window, which had a yellowish tint from the dust, the hillside was almost coming into leaf. There were some pines, too, bright there against the first red-green clusters of maple leaves. There were some apple trees, too, and in the crowns of them there still hung a few apples from the fall. The floor of the woods was cinnamon colored with old leaves, and while I sat there I heard the steady *turc, turc, turc* of a wild turkey. Great puffs of clouds dragged by above the hillside, the white fluff of them sparkling with moisture. The shadows swung over us, making the greens darker, and in the change of light I noticed the ferns coming up in a hollow, their heads reddish green and curled like the scroll of a violin. My father seemed to be sleeping, but I knew better.

I brought my mother up from the store.

"Oh, no," she said. "Oh."

My mother turned back the covers. The smell was very bad, and then both of us looked out the window, seeing those old apples on the trees. I turned away and without saying anything I went into the bathroom and let the stopper into the tub, the fall of it coming as a metal *plunk*. I turned on the water and then went back into the bedroom, where my mother and I stripped off those pajamas, his body now dead and loose. We carried him into the bathroom and lowered him into the water, the slick clearness of it roiling around him. We were both crying as he lay in the tub, his head back, cradled in my mother's hands, and while she held him I put soap on a washcloth and ran it over his shoulders and chest, on which there was now gray hair, and over his stomach and sides, where the ribs showed, and around the sad penis and the sack on which it sat, too. All I wanted then, while I cried, was to make that cunning smell go away, which, as I washed him, seemed to come out of his skin and to cover me, my mother, the house, and everything else: the soap was good and strong, and I used it to make a thick, heavy lather. We rinsed and toweled him, his arms hanging out of the tub, the two of us still crying and my mother saying as the last of the water rattled down the drain, "Oh, Jesus, Al, why did you have to be such a jackass?" We changed the sheets and dressed my father again and put him back into bed, where he lay with his arms crossed over his chest, his face now slack but still showing anger and a puzzled, confused kind of hope.

But we didn't stop grieving or crying, either. I went back into the bathroom and sprinkled scouring powder in the tub and swirled the stuff around with the sponge, making bubbled and greenish smears, feeling the grit and somehow thinking that this would make me forget what I knew, and even though this was impossible, or even crazy, I scrubbed the tub until it shone, until it had a kind of glow or whiteness that was clean, pure, and innocent, like pearls. My mother came in and both of us cried for a while, with both of us thinking about what we were going to put into our suitcases and where we were going to go, my mother probably already composing a letter to her flimflam man in New Jersey. Even as we held hands, we receded from one another like fog disappearing under a strong sun.

My father was cremated. When it had been done my mother went to Baxter and brought back a small, galvanized canister, about the size of a can of Ajax. She came into the house and put the thing down on the windowsill above the sink, and when I saw it there, like a can of scouring powder, I went upstairs and packed, taking my suitcase from the closet and putting into it those things I had kept clean and waiting in the drawers of my bureau. I put the hair dryer and lotions in, too, and then came downstairs, where I said good-bye, and as my mother pulled me against her I saw, in the store, the shiny cylinders of the Dynamos.

The cylinders of them were surrounded by a chaos of white tentacles. The room was dirty, and a dim light came through the window, but even so there was a horrifying gleam repeated on every shiny surface, on the cash register, the metal edge of the cabinet for the pistols, and on the pistols themselves, on the small cans of tuna and corned beef and beans, and on those machines, too, the three smug things lined up as though waiting for the next dreamer to come along. The store was cold. I put down my bag and went to the cash register, springing open the drawer and taking the key for the glass cabinet. I put the key into the lock and shoved the door back and took a large chromed pistol, a .357. There was a box of ammunition on the shelf behind the case, and when I took it down and slid the Styrofoam out, the cartridges spilled, the collection of them making the same smack as someone dropping a handful of nickels onto the glass cabinet. I loaded the thing and pulled the hammer back and the bullets went through the Dynamos with a sound like someone hitting a galvanized trash can with a baseball bat, the holes on one side small, dark punctures, but on the other side there were irruptions which were the shape and size of a beer can that has been torn in half and which appeared as my mother said, "Marie! Marie!" Gas hissed out of the top of the cylinders and the whitish tubes were torn and showing skin as thin as a surgical glove. I put the pistol on the counter, but then turned and went to the shelf and picked up another box of ammunition, which I put in my bag, along with the pistol.

The cannister still sat on the windowsill, the new galvanized metal having shapes on it like frost on a window. I picked the cannister up, too, and put it in my suitcase, the thing being passed over in the stink and echo of the gunfire and with my mother's obvious blessing. It was one less thing she'd have to worry about. I went outside and stood there, waiting for the ten-thirty bus and hearing the long *eeeeeeeeeeee* of the door.

I had a few minutes to wait, and I stood there in that bright sunshine. It was Saturday, and the cars began to go by on their way to Baxter, and it wasn't long before that black Pontiac came up with Charles at the wheel. He stopped in front of the store and got out and said, "What are you doing? You're leaving, aren't you?"

"I'm going on the next bus," I said.

"Marie, I don't want you to," he said.

"I'm sorry," I said. "Right now I want to be alone."

"Look," he said. He stepped toward me, his arm out.

"I wouldn't touch me if I were you," I said. "It's about the worst mistake you could make."

"What do you mean?" he said.

"Please," I said, "I just want to be alone."

He sighed.

"Look," he said, "I want another chance."

"Another *chance*?" I said, facing him. "Listen, I'm getting on the next bus and I'm getting out of here."

Then I turned and began to wait.

He got back into his car and drove down the hill, but even though it was Saturday he turned into the sawmill's drive. His car went through the pines and then came out in the parking lot, which I could see from the store. There were those saw

logs there, now settling into the mud, and beyond them there
was the building with the rusted roof and that long pipe held
up by guy wires. Charles got out of the car and walked up the
muddy path and when he stood in front of the door he picked
up a peavey and used it to pry off the lock. Soon I heard the
sound of the bulldozer as it started, and saw, too, a puff of black
smoke come out of the stovepipe that ran from the engine
through the mill's roof.

From a distance the walls of the mill, the piles of sawdust,
the dirt of the parking lot were the color of rabbit fur. The
sound of the engine became louder and a bulge began to
appear in one of the mill's walls, and as that stovepipe toppled
onto the tin roof, making a kind of screech and clash, the bulge
got bigger, bowing outward, and finally snapped open, the
planks shattering and showing their white insides. Now the
sound of the diesel became louder yet, and in the hole in the
side of the mill there was the sight of the bulldozer, its rusted
blade raised and those treads, which had so long been without
use, now surely turning. Then the roof began to sway a little,
and even at the distance I heard the long, definite *eeeeeeee* as
the building began to come apart. The mill lurched, the
planks snapping, the entire thing quickly settling into a pile of
kindling, or just trash, but nevertheless one that was still quaking as the bulldozer emerged, the timbers, pieces of tin, and
the gray planks teetering on the engine housing and then
falling to the side with a kind of capitulation. The machine
came out of the pile of sticks and tin and went toward the
parking lot. When the treads turned up the sawdust, there
appeared some small flecks, which at first seemed to be em-
bers from a fire, but in fact were the wasps that had been
nesting in the piles. The insects came in one long speckled
cloud. They followed the bulldozer, which now moved along
the mill's drive, the blade not all the way down yet, but it
would be soon: you could see what was happening now, almost
as though you'd heard Charles talking about it, or planning to
tear up the road out of town.

The bus stopped in front of the store, the enormous dog
on the side of it pale and silvery. The driver got out and

opened the bay, and I handed my bag over, all the while hearing the sound of the bulldozer on the mill's drive. Then the driver closed the bay and I got into the bus, holding out the money for my fare, I said, "I think you should make change later. Look."

The machine approached the road, the blade down now and pushing dirt. The bus driver kept his eyes on that rusted and half-yellow thing, beyond which there was a heap that had once been a sawmill but now looked like what was left after an earthquake in India. In the gray chaos of it planks and pieces of tin still rocked back and forth. And rising out of the pile, or at least from the disturbed sawdust in front of it, there came that long cloud of wasps, one end of which surely reached Charles, who even from a distance could be seen flinching with the countless number of hard, bright stings.

"Yes. Maybe later. . . ." said the bus driver, already pulling the door shut and letting the clutch in. The bus went down the hill fast, passing the entrance to the mill, where, through the tinted glass, I saw the last of that now Egyptianlike cloud of insects and that half-yellow machine still pushing dirt toward the road.

The bus went along for a while. I was sitting just behind the driver, next to a young man who looked like a college student. The driver said he'd take my fare at the next stop. I watched the road over the driver's shoulder, seeing the flashes of white lines and feeling the shove of the bus as it changed lanes. The man next to me wanted to know where I was going, and where I'd come from, and I looked ahead, not really answering, at least until he asked my name, and then I turned to him and said, "Christine. Christine Taylor. That's a name you could fall in love with, isn't it?"

Book II

BOOK II

Tubby Mars

Marlowe, Northern California, 196–

EVEN NOW IT IS HARD TO BELIEVE THAT THE TORNADO, AND all the other trouble, didn't begin on a hot summer afternoon, years ago, when Ben Lunn came walking down the main street of Marlowe. We had been without rain for a month. Ben Lunn was fourteen then, his face a little freckled, his shirt and jeans bleached by washing and by being dried in the sun. He came along in the heat, squinting, his entire aspect one of concentration.

In summer Marlowe looks like this: one long street with buildings on each side, their fronts a pale brown or blue, the windows of them a little whitish from the scalding heat, the cars parked head-in against the curb, their fenders and hoods blistered or just blasted to a pale blue or green or red, and when you stand out there and look into the distance, the cars, the street, the buildings seem drawn together and everything runs toward one shimmering spot out there in the flats. The eyes ache.

In front of my building there is a sign that says, "TUBBY MARS'S POOL HALL." It's a red neon sign, the rust on the metal of it bright as an orange, and at night it makes a buzzing sound and the moths flit around it, emberlike. There is a Coke cooler against the wall there, at the back of the sidewalk. The cooler sits beneath the window. On the road leaving town there are signs, too, and on each one there are some tall, faded letters that say, YOU'VE MISSED THE INDIAN WARRIOR'S BONES AT TUBBY MARS'S POOL HALL IN MARLOWE. SEE THE INDIAN WARRIOR NEXT TRIP. On the other side it says, SEE THE IN-DIAN WARRIOR'S BONES AT TUBBY MARS'S POOL HALL IN MAR-LOWE. BEER. CIGARETTES. CANDY. NO ADMISSION. GET A LIT-TLE DESERT HOSPITALITY.

I have the bones in a glass box made out of some long, narrow windows. There's a little door in one end with hinges. The window frames are painted a shiny red, and inside the bones have a porous texture. There are two long, clublike femurs, some ribs, but no breastbone, a curved spine made of identically shaped vertebrae, and a skull that looks like a bro-ken helmet. I have some Indian things on the wall above the case, a bonnet with eagle feathers, some clubs and spears, and some pictures of a buffalo hunt. The display is sad as a mu-seum. I've had the bones here for forty years, but there are times when I wish I had a nice small alligator in a pit. He'd eat garbage and hiss when some kid poked him with a stick.

Ben Lunn came right down the middle of the street, in the sunlight, and then over the curb, where he stood in those sun-bleached clothes, in front of my building, his eyes set on the barometer I have screwed to the wall there. Next to it there is a large thermometer, too, a long glass tube set into a metal sign that advertises Pepsi-Cola. Ben came out of the heat with a steady, businesslike insistence, and with his face intent on the dial he gave the barometer three quick taps to make the needle give a true reading.

On the other side of the street in a little line of shade about a foot wide there stood two Indians, each wearing blue jeans, a white T-shirt, cowboy boots, and hat, the brims turned up and the hats worn tipped forward over the eyes. They just stand in that bit of shade until they think it's time to cross the street and buy a beer, taking it back with them and turning the brown bottle up, puckering their lips in a kind of wet smooch. Then they go back to watching, keeping their eyes away from that reservation out there on the flats.

From the end of town and emerging from the heat there came Mary Sinclair and her friend, Cathy Dennison. Mary was blond and walked with a fluid, sleepy gait, and Cathy was as tall, a little heavier, but they both were thin and youthful. They wore print dresses, the cotton of which had been washed so many times it hung as delicately as silk. As they came up the street, the full force of the sun pushed their shadows into black pools at their feet. They were sixteen or seventeen, but not older: after that they go away or get married and don't take so many slow, hard walks in the heat to get a Coke. As they struggled against the sunlight, their legs swung out and the light, fuzzy down on them shone. Mary Sinclair fanned herself with a copy of the local paper, *The Democrat*, and said, "My, but it's hot, isn't it?" Then she moved from one leg to another, feeling the heat from the sidewalk, shifting her weight in the airy pressure of it.

Ben Lunn looked down at them from the box.

"What are you doing on that box, Ben?" said Mary. "It's hot enough right down here."

Ben got down and stood next to the young women, being about their size since he was a few years younger. He looked at the sky. In the shade on the other side of the street one of the Indians lifted one of his cowboy boots and leaned the heel of it against the wall behind him.

"Mary, I need a little bit of your hair. Just a strand or two. Mary?" said Ben. "May I have a little bit?"

"Why do you want it, Ben?" Mary said.

"I just do," he said. "I need it for something."

Cathy reached into the Coke cooler against the wall and put her hands down into the slick water, making the ice cubes on the surface give and clink. Her hands ached as she pulled up a bottle of Coke, the green glass running with moisture. There was a little metal box for people to put money in, and she put the right change into it, the coins of which were warm and moist from having been carried all the way from one of those wooden houses behind the main street.

Now Mary reached into the cooler and brought a bottle up and opened it, and after she had taken a long drink she said, "Well, if it means that much . . ." and then reached to her head, where her blond hair had been tied away from her neck, and pulled out two strands and handed them over.

Ben took the strands of blond hair and wrapped them around his finger, making a band like a wedding ring. Then he knelt down behind the Coke cooler where the water condenses, the beads of ice colored on the red metal. The girls looked over their shoulders.

"What are you doing, Ben?" said Mary.

"I'm just trying to find something out," said Ben.

Now Ben stood up and let that ring of hair unravel, and the strands hung there, curled like a thin corkscrew. The girls shifted their weight. The Indians watched.

"Mary always had the prettiest hair," said Cathy.

"But, Ben," said Mary, "you know I was never vain. You wanted it."

"Why, it *is* pretty," said Ben, "just as pretty as can be."

He took a tin matchbox from his pocket and unscrewed the thing and took out a match, which he struck on the wall behind the Coke machine. The flame flared up as bright as that hot summer sky. Ben burned that corkscrew of hair, the golden strands crinkling and disappearing, vanishing into filaments so fine as to be invisible.

"Well, Ben, what did you find out?" said Mary.

"It's going to rain, Mary."

"God knows we need it, Ben. I don't think the house has ever been so hot. I can hardly sleep at night, just lying there, praying for a breath of air."

The Indians stayed in the shade, watching the girls in front of the pool hall. Mary drank again, holding the bottle up, her head thrown back.

Ben looked at the barometer again and opened the door, making a screech. The men at the far pool table looked up, away from Charley Shears, who was making that funny bridge of his. Thumb stuck up like a turtle's head. Ben walked up to the cash register, his face looking dark against the windows. I

leaned in his direction a little and made a kind of friendly
squeak with my chair, just to let him know he had my ear. In
the back a ball fell into a pocket with a leathery *thunk.*

"It's going to rain, Tubby," he said.

"No, it ain't," I said. "Just look out there."

Ben turned toward the windows, through which there
were the mountains, the flat land before them so hot the
mountains moved as though they were painted on some sheet
that was slowly moving in a breeze.

"I think the heat's finally gotten to you, Ben," I said.
"Maybe you should go home and take a nap or something."

He just went to the other side of the room, walking with a
calm, quiet certainty, and took one of those hunting-and-fish-
ing magazines from the rack. He sat down in a chair that had
chrome legs and a padded seat and back. I looked away from
him, half thinking it wouldn't be a bad idea to call his father,
Dr. Lunn, as a kind of first aid or preventive medicine, but I
just sighed a little, feeling the tickle of the sweat on my side.
Mary and Cathy walked away from the front window and
disappeared into the heat.

Ben sat in that chair and read an article about shooting
deer. There were pictures of rifles and scopes and insulated
pants and jackets, and I looked away, knowing we got hunting
and fishing here only out of a magazine. On the flats there
were only snakes and rabbits and some nervous dogs and
coyotes. Beyond Ben the men played a new game of pool, and
when I looked back, Ben was still reading that magazine. The
glass of the front window was pitted from the dust storms, and
as I stared through it I realized, with a certain horror, that the
boy wasn't just killing time so much as *waiting* for the rain to
begin.

We hadn't had rain in more than a month, and there were
farmers here who were watching what they had planted and
what had come up in the early spring turn brown, but then
these months are always hard and hot, dry, and the dust rises
and covers everything. The farmers know better than to put a
seed in the ground, but they do it anyway. The Indians don't
complain about the dry weather, although you can see their

straight lips and the longing in their eyes. The boy went on reading, and I heard one of those big flies go *buzz zzzz* against the window.

But after a while there was a kind of mist or haze in the northwest. I had seen it before and it meant nothing, since there were days in August when it was already a hundred or more in the morning, when just getting out of my Mercury and walking to the pool hall was a struggle. On those days I stood in front of the door, the key trembling in my hand and my heart going *thump, thump, thump,* and then I saw that mist or haze come out of the northwest. It hung there the entire day, and I got up and looked at it and thought of the Pacific, the blueness of it, and of those fish in it, the salmon moving like long lines of silver. Cool.

So I wasn't worried. That kid sat there and went on to another fishing book. The pool balls clicked and the Indians stood in the empty street. But after a while I thought, *Well, goddamn it, those Indians are waiting, too.* Then the hazy smudge in the sky got a little bigger and darker, not so completely white anymore but a little gray, as though something over there had caught on fire.

After a while it got too hot to play pool, and Squeaky Hoskins took down his cue and put it into an aluminum case. Then he went out the door, saying, "I'll see you boys next week. Maybe it will cool off by then." His face had grease on it from the engines he worked on at the airfield, up in the mountains. At least he spent time where it was cool.

On his way out he looked over Ben's shoulder to see what was in the magazine, and then went on without saying a thing, having seen a picture of the wilderness, in which there were no airplanes and no pool halls and as such being without interest. The Indians were still in the shade, and they followed Squeaky with their eyes as he went into the sunlight. Squeaky owned a Corvette, and it was parked head-in against the curb, the front end of the thing patched and pink, looking like new skin after a burn. Squeaky started the engine, letting the entire town hear that noise, and when the front end of that car was pointed straight out of town, toward the flats and the mountains, Squeaky let the thing go, the momentum of it seeming to come so fast as to give you the idea that the machine had disappeared with a kind of mechanical legerdemain: it was just gone, and Squeaky and the car seemed to have departed in a long stream of fiberglass and noise.

The compressor in the cooler went on for a while, and there was the buzzing of the fly. Ben still sat there, turning those pages. I had on my half-glasses, since I was pretending to go over the bills from those lying beer and soda salesmen, and now I looked over the rims at him. Outside that smudge turned a little darker and slowly moved out of the hills, the color of it looking purple now: I had never seen such a thing in August, and I have spent every August of my life in Marlowe. For a moment it seemed that Ben hadn't predicted the change over the flat land so much as *caused* it. But it would only get darker out there and inspire a little more than the usual false hope. That would be the end of it.

Those two girls came back, since even though they had found it hot in front of the pool hall, it couldn't have been as bad there as in the front rooms or even on the porches of the houses they lived in behind Main Street. The houses back there are made of wood and covered with siding that is now the color of steel wool. The sun beats down and there are no trees there, either. The young women came up the street again, glad to be out in the air, although this time they didn't have a dime for a Coke.

By the time they were standing in front of my window the smudge in the northwest had turned into a dark, moving, and purple cloud, and as it came in this direction, you could see the shadow of it move quickly up the highway. The shimmer out there on the flats retreated before the shadow, and while the entire landscape wasn't soothing exactly, at least it looked blue-gray with shade.

The girls stood with their arms crossed, the first quick puffs of breeze making their dresses luff. The Indians turned toward the northwest, their eyes narrowing a little. There was a moist scent on the air. Ben Lunn went on reading, something now about killing bears.

After a few minutes, though, he got up and stretched and put the magazine neatly back on the rack, smoothing back the cover of it and tucking it in. Outside Mary brushed some hair out of her face and said, "Why, I guess Ben was right."

Mary looked over her shoulder, her face turned now toward the window.

"Ben, Ben, come outside," she said. "I want you to see something."

Ben stood in front of me, his entire air not one of gloating so much as a kind of bland, calm certainty. And there was a slight accusation in his eyes, too, for all those times I had refused to sell him cigarettes or had rounded off the time for a pool table in my favor.

"It ain't happened yet," I said.

But I was wrong. From the underside of those clouds there were lines of rain, which looked like Christmas tinsel arranged carefully, one straight strand of it next to another. The clouds were over the flat land and then the shadow of them raced up the road and went over the town, the light here going out exactly as if someone had pulled down all the green shades along the front windows, and as the light went out, the large drops hit the dust in the street, making it puff up and blow away. This lasted only for a second, because then the rain began with a pattering so loud as to sound like escaping steam. The dust turned to mud and the first purple and glowing tube of lightning rose from the flats to the clouds. The girls looked at Ben, who still stood in front of the cash register.

"All right," I said. "So what? It's raining."

"Why, I guess it is, Tubby."

"Here." I took a package of Lucky Strikes from under the glass counter and pushed them across to him. "On the house. How's that?"

He put the cigarettes in his pocket, not as though he were taking a handout but more like he had earned them, and stepped outside, his black, high-top tennis shoes turning a brownish color as the muddy water on the sidewalk splashed over his feet. A minute later they were washed clean as he walked out into the rain, the straight, tinselly lines hitting him on the head and shoulders, bouncing there and making splashes that were shaped like arrowheads. Mary and Cathy stepped out, too, letting the rain hit their upturned faces and those gauzy dresses, which were so thin as to take the water quickly and which soon clung to those thin, youthful figures. But the young women laughed there with the water splashing up waist high from the pavement, the rain sinking through their clothes and into their hair. They laughed with a kind of contagious disbelief, and then each of them put her head back to taste the rain. And even the Indians stepped out, putting their faces up while they stood in the middle of the street. The rain splashed up from the pavement and made a mist.

Then all of them walked to the shelter of the awning in front of the pool hall, where Ben took the package of Luckies out of his pocket. The Indians took two apiece (each putting one of them behind an ear) and then went back across the street, where each lighted a cigarette and stood in that one foot of what had been shade but was now shelter from those straight lines of rain. They smoked slowly and blew long plumes of white smoke into the air. Ben and the young women lighted their Luckies and stood under the awning, the young women now shifting their weight while the sidewalk, which was still hot, steamed like a jungle.

So they stood there, the girls warm and wet and happy, and Ben feeling each drop on his skin as a kind of vindication. I sat in my chair, making it creak, and hearing the lonely sound of it over the rain. So, in a manner of speaking, you could say the tornado began right there.

The Indians watched as they smoked, and their faces were wet, but their expressions weren't that much improved, since it was obvious that their problems weren't going to be solved by just a little water. My father, now departed for a world that couldn't be much worse than this one, used to say that the only good Indian was an Indian with money, although that has its drawbacks, too, you might say. There was a kind of heyday here, short-lived and a little chaotic, and that was when the tribe sold some land and every man, woman, and child got twenty-two hundred and some odd dollars, and for a while there were Indians, both male and female, who came in here and paid ten dollars apiece for cue balls they threw through my plate glass windows, which windows they paid for almost immediately after they had sung and danced in tribal celebration of a war victoriously conducted. Take it all around, it wasn't so bad, but then, as I've said, it didn't last long.

Of course word got around pretty fast. No one came right out and admitted he went to see Ben about the weather before planning anything, but nevertheless, when the school had an outing or the fire department was getting ready to kill and cook a hundred chickens, or if anybody was going to do something outside (like the time Bill Harold and I were going up over the border to hunt ducks), why, sure enough, someone went over to Dr. Lunn's house and hung around by the waiting room until Ben came out of the house. At that point the one who was worried about having the duck hunting ruined would say, "How are you, Ben?"

"Just fine."

"What you been up to?"

"Oh, I guess I been doing the usual."

"Yeah, well, that's good. What do you suppose the weather's going to be like this weekend?" and then Ben would say he'd think about it. At these times he went upstairs and looked at the things he had there, a recording barometer, a gizmo that told him about dampness in the air, and an instrument connected to a kind of ugly thing on the roof which told him how fast and in which direction the wind was blowing. There were times when he collected some June bugs or some dust, but mostly he used the instruments and then he came into the pool hall or stopped one of us in the seed store and said, "It's okay to go duck hunting."

Then there was the high school's fall picnic. The newspaper called for a clear, warm day for it. The principal of the high school had gotten the lieutenant governor to agree to come, and since the principal was a kind of closet handwringer and worrywart, he came to see Ben, who said the thing should be called off. So then there were some secret meetings behind closed doors, in basements, and in backyards and garages, not to mention a number of random but nonetheless casually hysterical occasions where people more or less bumped into one another, at which times all you heard was a kind of long, intense hiss of conspiratorial, if not outright panicky, whispering. There was a fair amount of quiet hemming and hawing, too, since the principal didn't want to admit, number one, he had been soliciting Ben's advice and, number two, he was taking it seriously even when the newspaper and the National Weather Service had said the day was going to be fair. Anyway, the principal decided to go ahead with the picnic, although there were a lot of duck hunters and fishermen, not to mention farmers and gardeners, who were less than comfortable when they heard about it. On the day of the picnic it began to rain and by noon we'd had over an inch.

That tornado got a boost, too, when Ben met Sally Cooke. He was eighteen then, just finished with school, and he met her at the airfield in the mountains. The soaring was good there because of the updrafts from the flats, and we'd see the sailplanes from Marlowe as they hung in the sky, their wings catching the sun.

That June, when Ben was eighteen, he asked Squeaky Hoskins for a ride to the airfield, which wasn't really a lot more than two long pieces of macadam, one crossing another to make a kind of big X on the ground. There were some hangars, a parking lot, a small terminal, and there were the sailplanes themselves, a row of them with short, narrow fuselages and long wings, a Plexiglas bubble over the cockpit, and a large hook, beneath the nose, for a towrope. The Corvette came up the drive of the airfield and stopped near one of the hangars, and Squeaky said, his deep voice filled with the certainty of a man who knows what the business of life is or at least ought to be, "Go on. Look around. They got a new Cessna over there. You can touch it if you want."

It was hot at the field, but not so bad as on the flats, although even up there the macadam airstrip was mirrorlike and there was the reflection in it of the planes as they came in to land. Ben looked at the new Cessna, which had paint so fresh as to have a faint odor of ether. Next to it, in a row, there were the platinum-colored sailplanes, each one tilted over on one wingtip.

On the hot macadam road something seemed to be moving, whatever it was appearing filamentlike and quavering, and as Ben squinted, he was able to make out a kind of wake as whatever it was came in his direction, the thing slowly becoming less inconstant, but still thin, and finally revealing itself to be a bicycle.

It glided out of the worst distortion, ridden by a young woman. She was about Ben's age, and she was dressed in a white shirt and a small pair of white shorts, and as she glided toward him she bent over the handlebars, her back parallel to the ground, her hair blowing away from her tanned face in a kind of sensual and animated tangle. She glided up to Ben and stopped, propping the bike up with one leg, keeping the other on a pedal, and as she stood there, with one hand over her eyes, she looked at the sailplanes in the sky and said, "Just look at those suckers, will you? I'm going to fly one of those one day. You just watch."

Ben shaded his eyes and put his head back.

"Look at 'em climb, would you?" she said.

She turned and looked him full in the face, her bluish eyes stopping on his for a moment and her lips breaking into a frank, friendly smile. Then she went back to looking at that pale sky and those sailplanes rising into it.

"I haven't seen you around here before," she said. "Are you from around here?"

"No," he said, "from down in Marlowe."

"Oh," she said. "What are you doing down there? What's your dad do?"

"He's a doctor," said Ben.

"Dr. Lunn?" she said.

"Yes," said Ben, "that's him."

"Oh, sure. . . . I heard . . . about . . ." but then she stopped and looked up at the airplanes.

"About what?" he said.

She blushed and said, "Well, you know, there's lots of talk and gossip. I don't take any of it seriously."

He stood there, looking at her.

"Who cares for gossip anyway?" she said.

"I don't know," he said. "People seem to like gossip. What did you hear?"

"Just some story. . . ." she said, looking back to the sail-planes. "I guess I put my foot in my mouth again. I'm always doing that. You know what? They're going to send me east to school. They're going to make a lady out of me, that's what my dad says. Then I won't ask about things I shouldn't. And my dad says that when they're done with me I won't say 'suckers' anymore, either. Do you think they can do it?"

She turned back to him, her face serious.

"I don't know," he said.

"Well, they've got a job cut out for themselves," she said, and then she put back her head and laughed. She still sat on the bike, leaning it over a little and supporting herself with one leg.

"Do you get up this way much?" she said.

"No," he said, "not often."

"Would you like to have a Coke?" she said.

"Why, yes," he said. "Yes, I'd like that."

She stepped off the bike and leaned it against that rustic split-rail fence in front of the terminal, and then they went inside. In a corner there was a radio, an old one which was housed in a black box and had dials and needles. On the walls there were clipboards which held flight plans and engine-maintenance sheets. The ceiling was painted blue and hanging from it there were models of biplanes with large wooden propellers. The young woman went up to the Coke machine and bought two bottles. Then they sat down at a table by the window.

"What do you like to do," she said, "down there in Mar-lowe?"

"Well," he said, "there's the pool hall. . . ."

"Pool," she said. "I play pool. . . ."

She wrinkled her nose.

"Are you any good?" he said.

"I can hold my own," she said. "I like riding my bike. And opera, too. I like to get up on the top of that ridge." She pointed with the mouth of her Coke bottle to the top of the purplish-black mountain above which the sailplanes were flying. "There's a road up there, a steep one. I've got a little tape recorder with a set of headphones and I get up to the top and then start coasting. Then I put *Madame Butterfly* into the machine and put my headphones on and turn up the volume about as loud as it will go and by the time I get to the bottom . . . that sucker bike of mine is getting ready to *fly*. . . ."

She took another drink.

He held his bottle in his hand and looked at the moisture condensing on it. Then he said, "I'm interested in the weather."

"The *weather*," she said, putting a hand over her mouth. She blushed and her eyes watered a little.

"Yeah," he said, "you know, predicting it."

"I'll even bet you got one of those . . ." She made a gesture like a man playing a trombone.

"A slide rule," he said. "Yeah, I got one of those. And some other stuff. A recording barometer."

"You mean one of those things that makes a little squiggle on graph paper?"

"Yes," he said, "and an aneroid."

"Uh-huh," she said, but she was looking out the window. There, near the top of the mountain, a sailplane rose on a current of air. The young woman turned her Coke up, her lips making a round shape at the mouth of the bottle.

"The *weather*," she said again, now looking at him, holding the empty bottle so the top of it pointed to the side. She drank the last of the foam and put the bottle down.

"Can you really tell when a cyclone is coming?" she said. He nodded.

"You're kidding me now," she said.

"No," he said.

"Well, I'll tell you what. When one is going to come, you give me a call," she said.

"All right," he said. "If that's what you want. What's your phone number?"

There was a little black-and-chrome box on the table with paper napkins in it so people could help themselves. Sally took one of the napkins and spread it out and on it she wrote her telephone number in large, open numerals. Then she pushed the piece of white paper across the table, the gentle shove coming as a slight, romantic dare.

"I'm not lying," he said. "I'll call you."

"Okay," she said. "I'll be waiting." She blushed. "Well, it's been nice talking to you. I got to go."

"Thanks for the Coke," he said.

"Sure," she said. "Have you seen the new Cessna? That's something. One day I'm going to get my hands on it, too. You watch."

She stepped outside, into that heat again, the force of it coming off the pavement. Ben came out now, still touching the pocket where he had put that napkin, and as she began to move away, standing on the pedals, he said, "Hey, what's your name?" She looked over her shoulder and said, "Sally Cooke," and then went off, pedaling toward one of those distant hangars, her hair falling over her back again.

Of course I wasn't there, didn't see this with my own eyes, but I can imagine how it was, especially after bits and pieces came out over the years, not to mention actually meeting the girl myself. But now Ben just waited until Squeaky Hoskins drove him home, and then he came in here and said, "Tubby, when was the last time we had a tornado?"

"Oh, it must have been twelve or fourteen years ago. It got some house trailers and knocked the lids off some houses. We were picking up glass for a month. Those house trailers just turned into a kind of metal dust."

The next week there was a wedding that took place in a dust storm, which Ben hadn't mentioned, even though he'd been asked. Actually, he hadn't said anything at all, aside from

suggesting the bride's family look in the paper, and he wasn't
around for the wedding, either, since by then he had gotten
on a bus and gone down to San Francisco, where he had spent
a day going through the music stores until he found a tape
recorder with headphones and a lot of tapes, too, of Gigli and
Caruso and some other foreigners singing *Madame Butterfly,
Otello, La Bohème,* and the rest. And then, when the bus
brought Ben back to town, he walked up the street as though
he had always carried a tape recorder and headphones, not to
mention a brown paper sack filled with tapes. He turned in
here and sat in one of those chairs with the chrome legs, a tape
in the machine and the headphones over his ears while he
watched the sailplanes over the mountains.

It wasn't, by the way, just stories and gossip Sally Cooke
had heard about. It was a scandal.

Ben's father, Dr. Lunn, was a tall, thin man with dark
brown eyes who wore gray trousers and white shirts and bow
ties seven days a week. He was divorced from Ben Lunn's
mother. Dr. Lunn had been a young doctor, just beginning to
practice in this town, when he married Ben's mother, who at
the time had been seventeen. She was pregnant by the time
she was eighteen, and I remember her before she left as a
pretty, brown-eyed woman in her twenties who spent hours in
that large house trying on new clothes and looking in the
mirror and coming down Main Street in summer wearing a
large straw hat that made a kind of pool of shade she walked
in. She came in here to get the magazines I ordered for her
and which I kept under the counter so they'd be fresh and
new smelling and cool. When she picked them up her eyes
went slowly over the covers of *Movie Screen, Glamour,* and
Hollywood Insider.

They lived in Dr. Lunn's house, which was just off Main
Street. It had trees in front of it, large elms that hadn't died
yet, and the house was a big, three-storied thing with white
siding and a big screened-in front porch. In the yard there was
a lawn that somehow stayed a little green in the summer and
there were tulips planted in the bed by the porch. On the left

side, when you faced the place from the street, there was a separate entrance, a few narrow steps, and a long covered porch that led to Dr. Lunn's waiting room, where he saw the women who came in their pale dresses and with their sun-bleached hair, and the dairy farmers who climbed the steps and sat down in the waiting room with a sound about twice as loud as the loudest cracking of knuckles, since they had what was known in the medical literature, especially in a paper written by Dr. Lunn, as "milker's knee."

When Dr. Lunn's wife came in here, her face always showed those same curious and disturbing lips, which were full and turned up at the corners. The Indians leaned on their pool cues, as did some of the boys and young men from town, each one of them watching her, their faces blank or just mystified as she came in here smelling sweetly of the bath and her skin looking translucent as she smiled. She took the movie magazines and went out into the heat, the door creaking and slamming shut behind her. At least, this went on until one day Charley Wolf, an Indian, had more beer than usual, and when Dr. Lunn's wife had picked up the magazines and smiled and gone out, he said, "She's still got hope. That's what confuses you, Tubby. God knows you don't see much of it here, do you?"

Her name was Gloria. She just refused to become another one of those pale creatures who drift up and down the street until one day they are nothing but coffin dust, and Gloria's resistance or hope didn't come out of defiance or even anger so much as from an oblivious cheerfulness: she continued to come in here with a kind of easy slink in those new clothes, her shoulders moving a little from side to side, and the air around her seeming as fresh and cool as in a florist's cold case. Then she went back to her house, or Dr. Lunn's house, leaving all of us blinking and gaping in cheerful admiration. And years later her son, Ben Lunn, had that same hope, although with him it was more serious and took the form of tapping the barometer out there under the awning, since he obviously believed that in the jerky rise and fall of the needle there was something worth knowing and even useful enough to keep him from getting hurt.

Gloria's cheerfulness had its insane quality, too, because it was clear that not only did she hope, she believed, as well, that places like Hollywood and Vine or Schwab's Drugstore existed, and that if she just went to them she would be pulled up into the world of the gods, which was so painstakingly delineated in the magazines I kept nice and neat under the counter. And it's true, too, that she did have some quality, some glittery aura and brightness, that made us think she wasn't totally crazy, and so we were all both sad and somehow pleased when she left on that Greyhound bus, taking with her a suitcase and two cardboard boxes in which she had packed her best clothes. We all stood at the windows of the pool hall, looking through that pitted, dusty glass. The last thing she saw as she left town was the line of faces of the pool players, the men and boys from town, the farmhands and Indians, their features close to the glass.

All of us waited until the bus made that turn into the flats, and we were still there when Ben Lunn escaped from wherever it was he had been kept and came running down the street. He was nine years old then, and his legs moved so quickly and stretched out so far as to seem for a moment that they weren't going back and forth, but around in a circle. The bus was already at the corner when he first ran into the street, but he didn't stop until he came to the pool hall. There he stood with his hands on his waist, grimacing as he breathed. The bus was on the road out of town, the slow disappearance of it seeming to make the landscape change, the brush and dust and the mountains now not so much harsh as indifferent, and as he stood there, watching not only the bus leave but the landscape change, his expression wasn't one of grief, or even surprise, so much as defiance. Then he turned toward the window. In the air there lingered the rank exhaust of the bus, and in the distance there was the diminishing whine of the engine as it went into high gear. After a moment Ben reached up to the barometer, and we stood there, each one of us blinking as we heard that *tap, tap, tap.*

Dr. Lunn walked up the street in his gray pants, white shirt, and blue bow tie, and he stopped under the awning, too, taking his son's hand as both of them stared into that white, dusty, and heated distance. Then the two of them turned around and walked back up the street, Dr. Lunn's long, thin hand still holding his son's. They went in and out of the squares and rectangles of shadow, Dr. Lunn turning his head toward the boy every now and then as he spoke. The two of them went on until they ran out of shadow and stepped into the bright, dusty street.

Dr. Lunn divorced Gloria, but, about a year and a half after the divorce was final, she came back. She got off one of those Greyhound buses and stepped into the street, this time not carrying cardboard boxes but newish suitcases, covered not with leather but crocodile skin, the surface of them brown and shiny and marked with irregular squares. She was wearing a blue suit with a small blue jacket that was cut high and moved from side to side as she left the suitcases under the awning of the seed store and walked toward Dr. Lunn's house. She was a little thinner and wore shoes with a heel so high there was a hitch in her walk.

She didn't smile. And she didn't wave, either, and more than anything else there was about her a businesslike air. One of the Indians at the end of the window said, "Well, she don't hope anymore." The rest of us watched as she went down the street with an angry matter-of-factness, her blue skirt and jacket going with a mechanical quality. Although she wasn't any less ambitious, since I saw, on top of those suitcases covered with crocodile, a newspaper called *Variety*.

In about twenty-five minutes Dr. Lunn came down the street, now driving that Willys of his, which he stopped in front of Bompasino's seed store. He got out and picked up the luggage and put it into the trunk. He didn't look up, but he knew we were there, all of us not knowing whether we were glad or infuriated. Or just sad she had been defeated.

We heard from the neighbors that at night the two of them sat in the kitchen, Gloria on one side of that small domestic table and Dr. Lunn on the other, a bottle of gin and some ice and two glasses between them. They talked and drank the gin, only getting up for more ice and even stopping that after three or four in the morning and taking the rest of the bottle at room temperature. Then it was time for Ben to go to school.

She only stayed a week. Perhaps it was because no matter what, she had married Dr. Lunn too early. As we all knew, she had learned some damned unpleasant and outright frightening things in Los Angeles, but she still wanted, or worse, needed, to go back there. Because she wasn't so much defeated yet as angry at the indignities she had gone through. And no matter what, Dr. Lunn was a small-town doctor who had published a paper (and one that was well received at that) on "milker's knee," and the farther she got away from that waiting room where the farmers came and sat down, their knees making that distinct, undeniable pop, like a cork coming out of a wine bottle, the better she felt. So the first night they stayed up, drinking gin until the sun rose. And after Ben went to school and the house was quiet and empty, Dr. Lunn went out to his office where there was a sign that said, MEDICAL EMERGENCY, BE BACK AT and set the little clock there for noon. So then the two of them were left alone, the house cool in the morning, the two of them going quietly and with a little fear up to the bed where they had made their only child.

So it was quiet the first night, and the following night, too, since they probably didn't even know what had happened to them, aside from the onset of a hangover that made itself apparent about the time most people are getting a drink to face watching the news on TV. But the second night just about every snoopy woman or man in a car or pickup truck who drove by the house saw Ben sitting on the front porch in the yellowish half-light there while he waited for the two of them to stop arguing so he could go back inside.

But they didn't stop, and after a while Ben left the porch and pretended to go to bed, but in fact he sat in his dark room and listened to the loud voices and the sound of a glass or two being thrown against the floor. Then there was a squeak and a slap or slam from the screen door. Gloria stood there, her arms across her chest. After a minute or two she came off the porch and stood in the yard, her arms still crossed, and when she was in the middle of that square lawn, which was still green even in July, she turned and faced the house. There were some lights on here and there in a way that wasn't usual and the place had a disheveled quality, what with the front door hanging open and those lights on and the atmosphere that comes from the sound of breaking glass, all of which added up to the inescapable presence of an argument, or worse: final, last accusations. Gloria stared at the house, the height of it against the purple sky, which was dusty with starlight. The moon was surrounded by dry, fuzzy light, and she stood there with her head tipped back, her features composed so as to make it seem it wasn't the expert on milker's knee who bothered her so much as that house, the heavy undeniability of it. So she stood there, knowing that life here, if nothing else, would turn her into one of those women who were bleached and tired and dry and who, in the bitterness of their hearts, were waiting to blow away.

She left on the Saturday bus. It hadn't been a complete week yet, although this time she didn't have to carry the cardboard boxes or those two crocodile suitcases. Dr. Lunn drove his Willys down the street and parked in front of Bompasino's seed store and then took those bags out of the back and put them on the sidewalk next to the racks for envelopes of seeds, which had on them bright pictures of carrots, tomatoes, pole beans, or yellow wax beans. The rack was only half full, some of the packages obviously having been in it not only for this season, but the last, and the weathered envelopes were the picture of hopes come to nothing. Gloria waited in her tailored skirt and jacket, Dr. Lunn with her, the two of them standing in the shade and mutually staring into the distance where the bus came from, this time not seeing what had happened so much as what was going to. When the bus came, they shook hands.

We had already seen what two years in Los Angeles had done (breaking her from hope to anger, which is to say defeating her without sending her the formal announcement). So there was that much anyway: the men at the window at least knew they wanted her never to come back, since that way they wouldn't have to see her eyes after she'd been sent, as you might say, that formal announcement.

Dr. Lunn and Gloria shook hands, and Charley Wolf said, "Oh, Doc, don't be such a gentleman. Kiss her, at least mess up her goddamn makeup. Don't you understand, she's saying good-bye?"

When the bus began to pull out, Ben escaped from whatever neighbor had been put in charge of him for the leave-taking, and he came around the corner, his legs going fast enough again to suggest a circular motion, but this time he stopped as soon as he saw the bus. He stood with his hands on his hips, his eyes set on the now harsh landscape, his expression just as defiant as the last time he'd watched the bus leave. It went around the corner, into the flats. Dr. Lunn walked from the front of the seed store, crossing that dusty street in his gray pants, white shirt, and bow tie and put down his long, thin hand for his son, but Ben looked at it and shook his head, not wanting it and probably not needing it now. Then they got back into that Willys and went toward that large house, shaded by the elms, neither one of them saying a thing this time.

It was Jack, a cousin of Charley Wolf's, who came back from Los Angeles where he had been working and said he had seen her after the worst had been done. She was working in a kind of bar in San Pedro where they have a big tank in which women swam without much on. You sat at the bar and watched the women, and they floated around underwater, getting air through a tube like a garden hose and then exhaling, the bubbles rising from their mouths and nostrils, their hair floating in the water. Her part of swimming included singing while a guy made underwater music. She sang in the tank, and she didn't appear angry anymore or anything, really. She kept her eyes on the thick glass beyond which Jack and some other men sat at the bar. She looked old.

When Jack told us about the bar he said, "Do you want to hear what she sounded like?"

The boys were leaning on their pool cues or against the wall. None of them said they wanted to hear what she sounded like. But Jack took a drink of his beer, put back his head, and began to gargle, the sound of it having an almost cheerful quality in that large room. When he was done, we turned and saw Ben, standing in the doorway.

Then someone broke a rack and started playing pool.

So the years passed, and Ben went up to the airfield and met Sally Cooke. And while you couldn't exactly say Dr. Lunn put much stock or faith in love anymore, he still was a medical man or at least still a man, and he believed in desire, in lust, or (when he was most sour) just hormones. One night Ben and Dr. Lunn stood on Main Street. It was Saturday, and those candy-apple-red cars were going up and down in front of Bompasino's seed store, and as Dr. Lunn watched the cars and the young men and women in them, he turned to Ben and said, "Don't ever forget lust. It's a good friend and a hard enemy."

"What about love?" said Ben.

"Love," said his father, "—why do you want to know about love?"

"Life could be pretty grim without it," said Ben.

"Stick with lust," said Dr. Lunn.

They walked along the street and up to Dr. Lunn's house. They sat in the kitchen, at that same domestic table where Dr. Lunn had sat with Gloria, and as Dr. Lunn drank his nightly gin-and-tonic, Ben changed a roll of graph paper for his recording barometer, and when Dr. Lunn was rattling the ice in the bottom of the glass, he said, "All right. Maybe you have to know about love, too. You'll come back to lust, though."

So it was scandal, or at least Gloria, that Sally had been referring to when she had said, after learning who Ben's father was, "Oh, yes, I heard . . ." and then had the good manners to change the subject. Now, Ben sat in the pool hall with those headphones on, listening to *Madame Butterfly*, or *La*

Bohème, or *Martha,* or to Gigli sing Puccini, or Caruso sing Verdi.

"Well," said Charley Wolf, "isn't that cyclone the first order of business? Isn't Ben supposed to call her when he knows one is coming?"

"We don't get cyclones. We get tornadoes," I said. "Ben told me."

"Call them what you want," said Charley. "It's a killer. A big flat cloud. The light looks kind of purplish. And then that long thing comes down from the cloud and makes some black fuzz at the ground. That time it got White Horse's trailer, bits of it came down for twenty-four hours."

Tubby Mars, The Tornado

Marlowe, Northern California

FOR A WHILE NOTHING CHANGED. THE WEATHER WAS DRY and hot. Every now and then Ben went out to the flats and came back with some dirt which he rubbed between his fingers, the dry dust trailing away, just as fine as flour. Then we saw him drive down the main street of town in his father's Willys, going south to Sacramento, taking with him a card from his father so he could use the scientific library there. And when he returned and parked out front, there was nothing but a bunch of books on the front seat of the Willys, and as if this needed verification, the men in the pool hall, even those who couldn't read, went up to the window and stared at the pile of them, which were large and heavily bound and had titles on the spine in worn-down gold. The men nodded at the books with a kind of approval, like some committee of ancient Europeans blinking at a keg of Chinese gunpowder.

Ben brought them in, the titles of them clearly going by my platform and chair: *Cyclone and Anticyclone,* Burke's *Heat and Meteorology, The Weathercaster's Physics, Mathematics for Meteorology, Methodology of Low Pressure Storms,* and one called *Disturbances of Air: Extreme Low Pressure and Wind.*

Ben started to read, having next to his right hand one of those little spiral notebooks with a brown cover. The players went back to their games, some of them now beginning to gamble a little, even though it was against the rules. I watched Ben turn the pages, seeing his hand make a note every now and then in that little book, and hearing him say, "Uh-hmmm, Uh-hmmm."

Then I closed the place. Ben took the books home. From the street you could plainly see his window, which was lighted, his shadow against the pulled-down shade as he sat Indian-style on his bed with one of those books in his lap. Every now and then, as he turned a page, a shadow rose and fell.

He spent a lot of time in his room, only going downstairs and getting something to eat in the kitchen with his father, who sat opposite him, talking quietly and not asking questions (aside from wanting to know if Ben was going to get the books back on time to the Scientific Library, since Dr. Lunn didn't want any fines levied against his card). Although once, in exasperation at the clutter of books, which Ben read at the table, still saying "Uh-hmm, Uh-hmmm," Dr. Lunn said, "You poor son of a bitch. Can't you see what's happening to you?"

Soon Ben was out on the flats again, taking samples of dirt, or looking at the bits of brush and weed he'd sliced off with a pocketknife, or leaving on the flats a small instrument he carried with him and which told him how much water vapor there was in the air, and as he went about these things there was an insistence that implied not so much waiting (as before, when he had told me it was going to rain) as *making.*

His making, though, wasn't at all like that time we had a rainmaker here. That was ten years or so ago when there was a drought. One day a pickup truck showed up with a man driving it and pulling behind it a kind of flat trailer with a piece of boiler on it that looked like (and I would swear until recently had been) the cooker for a still. And scattered around the boiler there were some dry plastic bags of dust ("crystals" is

what the rainmaker called them) and underneath the boiler
there was a kind of butane cooker. The rainmaker didn't have
any teeth and he was short and old, his skin marked with some
cancerous-looking splotches which peeled on his sunburned
and bald head. His clothes had holes in them, or were torn,
and if anything, he looked like he'd been mauled by a large
dog, and around him there was a definite, harsh malevolence,
right from the first moment he stopped his truck and stepped
out in front of the pool hall and said, "Dry weather, ain't it?"

We all stood around the truck, and it finally came out that
he wanted fifteen dollars a day and two meals and a bed in
someone's house to make it rain. We made the deal, too, although Mary Parker didn't look too happy about boarding him
and after the first two meals she looked even worse, saying,
"He eats without his hands, like something at a trough. I'd
turn him out if I wasn't hoping for rain." So he stayed out
there on the flats, burning his butane and putting crystals into
the air through some kind of smelly combustion, and sending
into town every now and then for a cold beer. He stayed at it,
always having that malevolent stench or air about him, which
was even reassuring, since as far as we were concerned, it
didn't matter who the hell he was or where he came from so
long as we got a little rain. He kept burning that smelly,
sulfurous stuff and drinking beer until Charley Wolf's cousin
got drunk and took a shotgun down there and blasted a hole
the size of a watermelon in the man's cooker with that old ten-
gauge Charley Wolf's cousin always carried around in the back
of his pickup truck. The rainmaker was sitting in the cab of his
own truck, his yellowish, reptilian eyes set on the dry flats
before him, his claw or hand clutching that long, tall bottle of
beer which had been cold when it left town but was warm by
the time it got to him. Charley Wolf's cousin didn't drive right
up to where the rainmaker could hear him. He parked about
two miles away and then worked his way through the tumble-
weed and scrub out there until he was close enough to stand
up and touch off the first barrel.

That's when the rainmaker came out of the cab, seeing
the smoke and mist boil out of both sides of the cooker, the last

strands of damp exhaust curling at the sides of the smokestack.
Then the rainmaker stood there, stink and clouds of mist suggesting they had just oozed up from some sulfured hot-spring.
The rainmaker kept his yellow-green eyes on Charley Wolf's
cousin, and as he did so his peeling hand held that beer bottle,
the scaled rash or cancer on his head getting darker with each
passing second.

"Not another fifteen dollars and no more free meals," said
Charley Wolf's cousin. "Get this stinking piece of shit out of
here."

The rainmaker looked down the one still-loaded barrel of
the shotgun, but even so he screwed up his face and hissed at
Charley Wolf's cousin, the sound coming out wet and malicious, as though there wasn't enough trouble in the world to
be called down on the Indian with the shotgun. Then they
both stood there for a while in that rotten-egg stink coming
from what was left of the boiler, and then, with the clouds
billowing around the truck and trailer, the rainmaker started
walking, his hand still clutching that beer bottle, and went to
the driver's side of the truck, where he opened the door,
making a harsh, deep creak, and got in, throwing the beer
bottle on the floor there with the others, the collection being
guarded because there was a deposit on each one and the
rainmaker fully intended to cash them in before leaving town.
And when the rainmaker had started the truck and turned the
thing around, he said, as he passed Charley Wolf's cousin, "It
ain't going to rain here. And when it don't, you just tell them
who came out here and hurt my machine. You tell them!"
Then he drove off, the trailer bumping over the land and
leaving the tall, hatless Indian against the shimmering heat,
those purple mountains, and the cloudless sky.

The boiler had about stopped smoking by the time the
rainmaker got to town, and there he left the blown-up thing in
the street (a few sad wisps rising from it) and went into Mary
Parker's house, his gait one of niggardly hurry. He opened the
door and let the screen slam behind him and went into his
room, or the bedroom Mary had always planned on sharing
with a husband, which is to say the room of hope or maybe

even desire, but which over the years had been downgraded
to the room of resignation and finally became the place where
she put her few guests. There the rainmaker gathered his
clothes, which he had taken out of a brown paper sack, the
shirts and pants and indistinguishable articles of clothing being rumpled and smelling of sulfur. Now he put them into the
paper bag again, throwing on top a handful of broken wrist-
watches and timepieces.

But before he walked across the porch again he went into
the house's one bathroom and opened the cabinet, in which
there were medicines and salves that Mary Parker had been
collecting almost from her first visit to a doctor. The rainmaker reached in there with those burned hands of his and
took the tubes and squirted the contents onto his scaled forehead and bald crown and swirled the greasy muck around,
making the crimson patches even brighter than before. And
while he did this his expression was one of cunning celebration, in that he had seen those tubes the first night he was here
and had planned on getting some use out of them before
leaving. Then he went out into the sunshine, walking across
the dead lawn and through the gate of the weathered fence
and got into his truck, sliding into it before him that brown
bag of clothes and watches, his movement in doing this being
one of careful precision, as though the bag were filled with
dynamite. Then he started up again and turned south, the
busted still leaving a white trail in the air. The rainmaker
drove with his head to one side, like a dog hanging out a car
window, the crown of his head as shiny as a lollipop, the sheen
having a medicinal quality so strong as to be smelled above the
lingering odor of sulfur, and as the rainmaker went, his mouth
opening and closing on the air like that of some animal caught
in a trap, his hand moved up and down and across, the gesture
so harsh and rich in ill will as to appear like a curse.

We watched him go, his eyes passing over us once as he
made that jerky sign of damnation. So the truck went away,
into the heat, leaving Mary Parker crying tears of rage over
the violation of that medicine which had been prescribed to
take care of an everlasting, private itch. She came out on her

porch, carrying what was left of the medicine, the ancient, typed directions on the labels now all but unreadable, and as she stood there, her hair coming down, her face red and a little splotchy (almost as though the rainmaker's disease had been catching), she said, her hair around her face, "Look! Look! He got into my tubes!"

Then she went into her house and lay down on her single bed, putting a cold, wet towel over her eyes. She turned on the fan that went back and forth in the dim room, and after a while she turned on the big brown radio and listened to a preacher from Eureka.

After this we saw the rainmaker driving slowly through town on one of his circuits of places that needed water or at least someone who, for a price, would give hope that water was on the way. Every now and then the truck had a couple of new tires, mismatched recaps, some of which had white sidewalls, and the machinery on the back of the trailer was about the same, although there were two large patches, like two bullet-colored welts, on each side of that enormous copper cooker. The rainmaker sat at the wheel of the truck, driving slowly and obviously taking enjoyment in each new flake of peeling paint here, or in a new broken window in the greenhouse of the seed store, or in the obvious closing of yet another business, and as the rainmaker looked at these things, his eyes were unblinking and yellow and his hand rose in a kind of continued curse on the town and everyone in it. He drove with his mouth open like a dog, sometimes biting the wind, his head out the window in the sunlight, the red blotches and the scales not noticeably affected by Mary Parker's medicine. He arrived here at the beginning of summer not to herald the beginning of dry weather so much as to suggest that he had killed the springtime himself. Sometimes he got out of the truck and came into the pool hall, his entire air like that of a man who kept a dog to beat it, and when he stood inside, blinking in the shade, he turned his yellow-green eyes on the bones in my display case, and as the rainmaker looked at them, he nodded, obviously taking satisfaction in them while thinking about the Indian who had damaged the cooker.

Ben Lunn's storm-making was different: his took the form of scientific certainty. You felt it when you saw him in the street or when he came in to pass the time of day after he had stood outside, looking at the white sky and touching the barometer, his finger making that steady *tap, tap, tap.*

About this time two Indians went up to the ridge beyond the flats. No one goes up there aside from the Indians, not even adolescent boys bent on proving something. The ridge is long and looks like some enormous sleeping thing. There is some scrub brush on the sides of it and some stunted pines, too, and that's about all you can see with field glasses. Sometimes the Indians go up there to have visions and are gone for days.

It was Charley and Harold Wolf who disappeared. Harold was about Ben's age. Charley was forty or so. Mostly, if they weren't working, or in here, you'd see them standing in the line of shade across the street, each of them wearing bleached jeans, a white T-shirt, a cowboy hat, and boots, Charley forty years old, Harold twenty, although in all other ways identical.

They came back at sunset of the fourth day. It was just twilight, and in the distance I saw two men, each wearing a T-shirt that glowed with a blue color, like the center part of a flame from a wooden match. Charley and Harold walked down the middle of the street, kicking up little puffs of dust. They came into the pool hall, their movements precisely alike, their appearance identical, their eyes having the same far-away expression and their hands hanging at their sides with an exactly similar fatigue as they stood before me in the twilight.

"We saw some high wind, Tubby. Dark clouds. Then thunder and lightning and a long, dark funnel. It got White Horse's trailer, just like last time. I'd like a beer," said Charley. "Harold wants one, too."

Then they each took one of those sweating brown bottles and went outside, where they stood against the wall, one leg up, hat brim down, their eyes now set on the empty space in the middle of the street.

The next day someone went out to White Horse to tell

him about the vision and to suggest he get some insurance or to move the trailer. White Horse stood in front of it, the door pressing against him in the hot, dry wind. He is tall and gray haired and he wears an L.A. Dodgers cap and a Hawaiian shirt. "I'm finished with crazy Indians now," he said. "They can sit up there until they turn into ice cubes. It ain't going to help. It ain't going to help me get a credit card or a loan from the bank. No, I'm finished with that stuff now. You tell them so." Then he went back inside and closed the door, the trailer seeming forlorn there on the flats, especially among the stumps of the trees, which were all that was left after the last tornado had come through and blown the trees and White Horse's previous trailer into shreds of wood and torn metal.

It got hotter. It was the season for thunderstorms, but they wouldn't come.

Early in the morning, just after I'd opened up, the men came in here in twos and threes or even alone and went over to the cue rack and took a stick and moved toward a table. But by noontime it was too hot to play, and then the men sat on the bench along the wall, fanning themselves with old magazines. About dusk Ben stood out there under the awning and made that *tap, tap, tap.*

Not only did it get hot, it began to get damp, too, and in the afternoons there was a hazy mist in the north, but it wouldn't build, and we were left fanning ourselves with the paper. The Indians and farmers (or ex-farmers, the ones who had sold their land) stood now, close to the window, their faces showing irritated expectation, since without realizing it they'd started to believe the mumbo-jumbo, whether Indian or scientific, and since this was so they'd begun to suspect they'd been cheated.

The heat was oppressive. There was a moistness, too, that clung to your skin and left you with the sensation of being touched by some damp, slowly moving membrane. The men raised their voices now and then, but it was too hot to argue, and they gasped at one another like fish out of water.

Bob Hartlund was a dairy farmer, about sixty years old,

hard, his chin speckled white with a half week's growth of beard: he wore his rubber boots and his faded red cap, and there was about him the everlasting aroma of cows. After a week of that heat he came in, wearing his rubber boots (even when it was a hundred degrees), and when Ben came in from the barometer, Hartlund said, "Why don't you just call her up and ask her to a goddamned movie? There's a double bill. I saw it in *The Democrat.*"

"Mr. Hartlund," he said, "I'd just as soon wait for a little."

Hartlund winced and made an angry, dismissing gesture.

Ben stood there, looking at the north, and then he turned to Hartlund and said, "Mr. Hartlund, have you seen the barometer this afternoon?"

"No," said Hartlund, "why should I?"

"Tubby," said Ben, "have you taken a look?"

"No," I said, "not recently."

Outside, in the north, those clouds had begun to get a little thicker, and there was a darkness to them that suggested rain.

"It's hot," said Hartlund. "Frankly, that's all I care about. I'm having trouble keeping my stock watered. You'd think I'd be making some hay in those upper pastures, but the grass won't grow. Now, that's what I'm worrying about. My damn feed bill. I don't know why I came in here at all. I got chores."

"It's hot, Ben," I said.

"I know," Ben said. "There's some cold air coming from Canada. It was getting ready to freeze in Idaho last night. That's what the radio said."

"It would be nice for the weather to break," I said. "I'm tired of the heat."

"Uh-huh," said Ben. He looked around at the windows. "Can you open those, Tubby? In a tornado buildings blow up because the barometric pressure drops fast. It's a good idea to leave the windows open."

"What do you mean?" said Hartlund.

"I mean the pressure drops so fast outside the windows and walls of a building just blow out."

"Well, well," said Hartlund, "you don't mean to tell me . . ."

Ben looked out the window again. Then he reached into his pocket and took out a piece of napkin on which there was a number written in a large scrawl. The telephone is on the wall and next to it, in the plaster, I've driven a nail so I can hang the invoices and shipping orders I receive from the beer and soda distributors. Ben walked up to the nail and put the napkin over it.

"Listen," said Hartlund, turning to the men in the room. "If you got stock, you better get it in. Or you better tell your families to get into the cellar." Then he turned to Ben. "Well, tell me. Is it coming?"

"I don't know," he said.

"When are you going to know?" said Hartlund.

"Not long," said Ben. "Burke's *Methodology* says—"

"The hell with that," said Hartlund, "I just want a straight answer. . . ."

Ben turned toward him now, blinking a little.

"In a minute," said Ben.

"I'm not in the mood to wait," said Hartlund, "not with—"

"In a minute," Ben said.

The men stood around the tables, some of them still holding cues. Their faces were a little drawn and yellowish or greasy in the heat and from the slight, nervous fear now, too.

Outside, in the north, that cloud moved and darkened, the underside of it purple and black and bearded, although it was still a good ways off. In the distance there was the sound of thunder.

Some of the men went out now, toward their farms or houses and to be with their families, but there were ten or so who stayed, watching Ben and that cloud and obviously thinking it would be better to take their chances here than in a trailer or a wooden house built without a cellar.

"Ben," said Hartlund, "now, let's get something straight between us. Now, I have a herd of cattle. Do you know what a

good dairy cow is worth these days? I mean delivered, truck-
ing, and everything?"

Ben stood by the window, blinking, patiently watching
that thing out there.

"I've got a good idea," said Ben.

"I'm glad to hear it," said Hartlund. "Now we understand
one another."

"I guess we do," said Ben. "Will you go over to the firehouse and turn on the siren? I think we're going to have a
tornado."

Hartlund swallowed and ran a hand over his forehead.

"Well, all right," he said, and he went out the door.

The rest of us lined up at the window and opened the
sashes. Outside the light began to look as though it had been
filtered through yellowish smoke.

In the distance, about two or three miles away, there was
the main cloud. There was about it a sense of turmoil, or of
movement, and the thing seemed circular, at the top anyway,
and around the edge of that circular shape there was a deep
groove where the wind moved. On top the cloud was whitish,
misty, like any other cloud, but underneath it was almost
purple, and here and there you saw the long, straggled beards.
The closer the cloud was to the ground, the blacker the thing
became.

The rain started with a rush of hot wind, and as it came up
the street the first drops hit the dust and made puffs like
someone shooting at it with a BB gun. The men stood at the
window, all of them except Charley and Harold Wolf, who
waited silently at the back of the room, near the cellar door.
Outside, the strands of the cloud lolled in the wind and along
the bottom of it there were sacklike, inky bulbs. It started to
hail, some of the stones as large as baseballs, and when they hit
the pavement it sounded like someone was throwing ice cubes
from the roof. Soon the cloud was closer to the ground, the
color of it having the unmistakable aura of ill will.

There was some lightning, but the flashes were blue, just
as blue as a gas flame, and they didn't come in the usual long
up-and-down column, but from side to side, in big zigzags.

The hail and rain stopped suddenly, and Ben said to the men along the window, "I know you haven't asked for my advice, but the cellar wouldn't be a bad place to be for the next few minutes."

None of them moved. They looked at the telephone. Ben's dime fell into it and there was the grind and stop, grind and stop of him working the dial. When the operator told him how much the call was, he reached into his pocket and took out the precise amount of change.

"Hello?" said Ben. "Is this Mr. Cooke? This is Ben Lunn. I'm calling from down in Marlowe. Is Sally home? Hello? Sally? It's Ben Lunn. Well, I'm fine, how about you? Uh-huh. Well, you remember that time we talked up at the air-port . . . ?"

For a moment he stared at the wall in front of him, still holding that receiver and saying nothing at all, not flinching exactly but still obviously shocked. Outside there was a little more hail, the ice shattering in the street. Then he said, "The phone's dead." He took a deep breath and put the receiver back on the hook. You could see that black mist through the window, the men with their backs to it.

"Goddamn phone company," said one. "My brother worked for them all his life, and you know what he got?"

The men went on looking at Ben.

"A gold watch and a pat on the back," said the man who had spoken before, "and now a man has to make a phone call and what the hell happens?"

"The phone company," said another, in short, precise agreement.

"And how they squawk if you don't pay them right on time, too," said another man.

"Well," said the first, "I guess if we're going . . ."

The men went quickly now to the back of the room, jostling at the top of the stairs, their heads bobbing into the cellar, Harold Wolf's cowboy hat floating into the darkness. Someone's hand came up, out of that dim place, and pulled the door shut.

The bottom edge of the cloud was as straight and flat as

the horizon, and from it there now came three funnels, each one taut, materializing quickly and having a black, ropy texture. When they touched the earth, they did so with a swaying motion, and around the bottom of each tube there was a smoky darkness through which even the mountains in the background disappeared.

"Have you ever seen one of those before, Tubby?" he said.

"No, the last time I was in the cellar."

"Don't you want to go down?" he said.

"No," I said, "I'd just as soon stay up here."

"There's no way of telling which way they're going to go," said Ben.

"I'd just as soon stay."

Ben went outside and leaned on that red cooler, holding on to it with both hands. The barometer was above him and he glanced at it as the pressure dropped, the air blowing out the door and through the windows with a *fizzt* like someone opening a bottle of seltzer. On the flats the tubes ran parallel to the ground, the thick ends of them rising and merging with the cloud. The funnels looked like enormous ear trumpets, although they were black, or worse than black, a color like the clothes you'd wear to a funeral. The wind was loud, too, not so much like a locomotive as a sawmill just before the blade hits a nail.

The funnels had at the bottom a kind of ragged arrowhead of debris. Sometimes in the black dust you saw an identifiable thing, but then it flinched and disappeared: a wheelbarrow, an automobile door, a lawn chair, a screen door, a pair of trousers, a lifetime's collection of the *National Geographic,* the yellow covers of them flickering in the wind.

One of the funnels went through the flats beyond Bompasino's seed store, the tubalike shape as gigantic as the biggest building you have ever seen, the speed of it surprising, too, considering its size. Now there was a puff of silver flecks. They rose and flickered and disappeared into the blackness, into a mess that seemed to be an airy claustrophobia of ordinary things, garden hoses, rakes, wheelbarrows, scrap wood, scrap metal, scrap. The silver pieces rose together and made the blackness shimmer, like a school of fish in dark water.

"That's White Horse's trailer," I said.

Now the funnels moved away, the bottom of them squiggling over the ground, the air above which seemed thick as egg white. The funnels went south, taking with them the ropy, dark twists of the wind, and as they went pieces of junk were still rising into them, wood and metal, the doors of cars and sheds, the vanes of a windmill and a black-and-white object, too, which looked like a cow, turning end over end, its legs rigid.

The windows were trembling and bowing, the glass in them pressing outward like a soap bubble. Ben held on to the door handle of a car in the street as dust and bits of paper and wood streamed by, going so fast as to seem blurred. I stepped back from the plate glass, still not going toward the cellar if only because I had spent too many years sitting in my chair, handing out racks of pool balls and cubes of blue chalk and probably even beginning to love the place, and if it was going to go, why, then, I wanted to have a glimpse of it turning into shattered glass and slivers of wood, not to mention the numbered balls disappearing into chaos.

The Klaxon on the firehouse roof came as just another shriek. Ben held on to that door handle, his clothes rippling in the wind, his hair blown straight back so that his forehead seemed high, and his voice came out of the wind and the dust and debris and the endless, repeated and useless sound of that enormous Klaxon, "Tubby . . . Tubby . . . look . . . just look . . . at . . . that . . . sucker. . . . Do you think . . . she . . . saw it?"

Charley and Harold came up first from the green-brown gloom of the cellar, emerging from it identically in their cowboy hats and boots, jeans, and white T-shirts. They walked across the poolroom and out the door, where they stood and faced the south.

The other men came up, too, and stood behind the windows. After a minute three of them went down the street,

toward the fire station, and soon the Klaxon stopped. Then the
men came back, stepping over the mismatched debris, the
three of them walking in single file, picking their way through
the screens, cardboard boxes, bits of timber, and sheets of
aluminum that had been dumped in the street. There were
chickens pecking in the junk. The men blinked at the birds,
and when they came up, one of them said, "Tubby, do you see
that? Those chickens haven't got any feathers left."

We looked south. The street was still damp and black with
moisture, not shimmering with the heat, and at the end of it,
in the distance, something moved. The road out of town dips
into a slight hollow, and when cars leave town they seem, for a
moment, to sink into the ground and disappear. Now there
was a short, up-and-down motion in that hollow, the repeated
quality of it suggesting the awkward, serial movement of a
limping man. All we saw was the top of whatever it was that
moved there. But the size of the thing increased, and when it
rose on the upslope of the road, the motion still insistent,
jerking from side to side, we saw that it was a man, now slowly
rising from that paved hollow. He was barechested (which is
all we saw), and was an Indian, too. His arms swung from side
to side in the gait that was not wholly healthy, but not completely injured, either: he came along, rising from the depres-
sion, revealing himself not to be completely naked, but
dressed in a pair of boxer underwear, the long kind that come
down to the knee. He was barefoot. We stood there, in a group,
with the featherless chickens pecking in the street. The man
approached, his gait steady, arm up, arm down, limping, finally revealing himself to be Petey White Horse, who came
directly up to Charley and Harold, and said, "There's nothing
left."

"We warned you," said Harold.

"Yeah, yeah," said Petey White Horse. "I was sitting there
drinking a Coke. Then that cloud came along and the next I
knew there was something trying to turn the trailer over. . . .
All that's left are some live wires, snapping at the ground."

White Horse's feet had been bleeding and were now cov-

ered with broken glass, bits of metal, and dust. The clotted
blood in the dust looked like raisins.

Now there was work to do, and soon the men were out in
the street, raking up the glass and wood and tin into neat piles,
pushed against the curb. They sorted out the signs that were
still legible and piled up the ones that were just unintelligible
pieces. It got hotter again, and the men went about their
raking, stacking, and sorting slowly, heads down, looking
through the debris, each impeccable in his fatalism.

There was a greenhouse next to the seed store, and for
years it had been run down and needing paint and new glass,
but now it looked even worse, since a lot of the cracked panes
had been blown away, and the place appeared not so much
run down as half demolished. In front of it, on the sidewalk,
there were two red geraniums, each in a cracked terra-cotta
pot. The geraniums were bright red, the color so strong as to
be like the ache you feel between your eyes after a cold drink.

In the flat stretch of road out of town there seemed to be a
film, as thin as foil, and in it there was a steady, gliding movement. It swayed from side to side, but was absolutely unlike
the wavering of heat. Ben was on the sidewalk, bringing his
father some black surgical thread from the pharmacy, the
neat coils of it wrapped in waxed paper. He had a good pile of
them. Now, though, he stared into that film, from out of which
a bicycle appeared, the thing ridden by a young woman.

She had a kind of blond-silver hair and was dressed in
white shorts, a white shirt, and a cap, her hair flying out behind her as she pedaled. She coasted into town, her face sunburned and set in a cheerful but determined expression. She
passed the seed store and those empty, overturned racks, the
bits of wood, glass and metal that had been collected into
heaps.

Ben stepped into the sunshine, the shadow of the awning
sliding off him, like a piece of black silk.

"Hi, Ben," she said.

"Hi," he said. "Did you hear me on the phone?"

She nodded, swinging a leg over the bicycle and standing
there in the sunshine.

"Yeah," she said, "I heard."

The chrome on the bike seemed to be pointed and sharp in the sunlight. She lifted the bike with a quick heft and put it down against the wall next to the cooler.

"Would you like a cold drink?" said Ben.

"Yes," she said, pressing her lips together. "You can't imagine how hot it is out there."

Ben opened the cooler, which was filled with ice, the cubes partly melted and smooth. He began to reach in, but she said, "Wait. Let me," and then leaned over the cooler, the color of her hair and the light coming off her shirt making the ice bright rather than clear. She pushed one of those longish hands to the bottom, the cubes making a soft, repeated click. She waited for a minute and brought some ice up and rubbed it on her face. Then she pulled up a soda, opened it, and drank, her lips against the brown bottle as she swallowed hard and then said, "Oh, my, that burns."

She looked at him, her eyes watering.

"What have you got there?" she said.

"Surgical thread," he said. "My dad's already running out. Come on, why don't you walk up to my dad's office."

"I'd just be in the way," she said, looking at those piles of broken glass, old signs, and unidentifiable stuff, all broken.

"No, you wouldn't," he said.

"Are you sure?" she said, looking right at him. "Because I could just ride right back . . ."

"I'm sure," said Ben. "Come on."

They turned and walked up the street, the shadows of the awnings sliding over them as they went, Sally making a gesture with one hand that suggested the size and speed of the funnels.

That afternoon Ben drove his father's Willys, picking up from the farms and houses around here people who needed to have a wound cleaned or bandaged or stitched, the men and women and children riding patiently in the backseat and looking at the things that had been destroyed. Mostly they had head wounds. And as he went, Sally sat with him in the front seat, far to the right on the first trip, but on each one after that she sat a little closer, at first blushing a little, but by the time she was right next to him and the backseat was filled with people talking about the wind, she stared straight ahead, her hand touching his.

They stopped in front of my building and went out to the cooler to get something cold to drink, and after they took a bottle from the ice and put change into the box, Sally drank and looked away from him. Her voice was a little deep and there was a catch in it, and when she looked up and down the street there was about her a frank considering of things.

"I haven't got much time, you know," she said.

"Why is that?" said Ben, trembling a little in the shade.

"I'm going east now to one of those schools they picked out for me," she said. "They're going to work on me. Do you understand? I'm going right away. I'm going to stay with relatives in New York and then I'm going to *orientation.*" She looked away. "Can you imagine an *orientation*?"

"No," he said.

"Neither can I." She stuck her jaw out a little. "Let them try. That's going to be a job."

They loaded Sally's bike into the back of the Willys, the thing light and umbrellalike as they put it in, Sally's hair swinging around her shoulders when she did so, her gait a kind of quick, nervous jerking. On the front seat there was an army blanket, green and neatly folded.

"Well, I can tell you one thing," she said, "I'm going to enjoy myself before I go. You understand me?"

When they stood next to the door of the Willys, Sally said, looking at the blanket, "I don't want anything pushing me around, not even this." Then she watched Ben as he went around and got in on the other side.

They drove for a while, and then Ben said, gesturing to a side road that ran into the flats, "All right, what about this?"

She nodded and looked into the distance where those funnels had moved over the land. The road was just two long ruts, running through the flats, and around it there was the smell of sage and dirt that had dried after a rain. The road was smooth, no longer muddy, and even though it had only been a few hours, the hillsides already looked a little greener. They drove until they came to some shade, and there, by some scrub trees now in bloom, Sally spread that blanket and stepped out of her clothes, the sun hitting her shoulders with a bright sheen, her hair coming as a splash against those purple mountains. The ground was faintly damp but warm, and as they sat down on the blanket, the flats and the scrub trees evaporated into that shimmering air.

Now, in the last week in August, a red car came across the flats, going fast. The newness of it, the bright paint, the shine on the tires came as a relief to the eye, and over the sound of the engine, which resisted the weight of the car as the driver shifted down, there was the faint, but still definite sound of *Madame Butterfly.* Then the red car came into town, bringing behind it a trail of dust and the music, too. Sally was at the wheel, her hair blowing in the wind that came in the windows, her shoulders against the seat as she drove in a straight-armed style. Then she stopped and got out, emerging from the car in an easy locomotion and having a smear of the sunlight on her legs. Then Ben got up from that chair where he'd been reading a copy of *Field and Stream* while he had waited.

The car was her father's, a good Republican Oldsmobile, lent to her, I suppose, as a bribe for going east without making more trouble than necessary.

That's the way it began, and now three or more times a week the red car came along the road from the mountains, approaching with a speed that was so palpable as to make you think the car wasn't metal and rubber, but long streaks of red and chrome mist or smoke. When the car arrived, the windows of it were rolled down and that young woman sat at the wheel, the tape recorder beside her filling the street with opera, the arias as recognizable to us as a horn that went *ou-ah ou-ah.*

Then there were only five days left, and three, and finally she dropped Ben off for the last time, saying to him, "Listen, I can't promise you anything. That school may turn me into a lady yet."

"But you're coming back," said Ben.

"Yes," she said. "Next spring. Will you wait?"

"Yes," he said.

"That's good," she ·said, wiping the side of her face. "That's just fine. Sugar. Maybe that school won't do that much anyway."

"Will you write?" he said.

"Sure I will," she said. "I'll tell every girl at that school about you and make them jealous."

"Will you?" he said.

"You bet," she said. Then she closed her eyes. "I'm going now. Okay?"

"Listen . . ." he said, reaching out to touch her arm on the side of the window.

"No," she said. "No. I'm going now. All right? I mean right now."

Ben reached to take her, but she just shook her head. Then she backed out, keeping her eyes on the parked cars in the street, the peeling paint of the buildings, and the white lines on the road, and as she went north now, the car dissolving into that unsteady heat, she passed the signs that said, YOU'VE JUST MISSED THE WARRIOR'S BONES AT TUBBY MARS'S IN MARLOWE. CATCH THEM NEXT TRIP. The sound of the opera disappeared out there, too, leaving behind the evening breeze, the smell of sage, and those distant, bluish mountains.

As far as the tornado was concerned, men and women compared notes for weeks, if not months, afterward, especially when it came to settling with the insurance companies. The funnels had passed to the east and the damage had been, so to speak, irregular. A funnel had come down on a dairy barn and left only a confusion of timber and planks, milking machines, stainless steel tubs and hay: the barn had exploded in an instant, leaving behind a mismatched and bewildering clutter. The cows had disappeared, at least for a while, and when they were found, some as much as a mile away, they were lying on their sides, and when you touched them, their bones were soft as jelly. One of them was found in a tree, its mouth open, its head hanging down. The storm had come after milking, and the stainless steel containers had blown up, too, into ivory-colored sheets.

A mattress had been found in a tree, and a dog had been blown through the wall of a house into a closet filled with canned goods. Two house trailers had disappeared, leaving only a kind of shadow on the ground. The people who had lived in them hadn't been hurt, since they'd seen the storm and gone to stay with friends who had houses with cellars. A car had been left with its door open, and the door had been blown off. Dr. Lunn's waiting room had been filled, and there were people sitting on his lawn, too, patiently waiting to have their wounds stitched. They sat in the yard, on boxes and chairs, blinking in the sunlight, their faces weathered, watching as each new pickup or car stopped and someone new limped out, holding a bloody rag. No one had been killed. What you heard there was "It stormed some, didn't it? We were due, I guess." Then the people nodded and went back to the thing they had done from the first moment of their lives, that patient, insistent waiting.

In town a large collection of pornographic magazines was found, the pages blown around like leaves in the fall. They were everywhere, mixed in with the rest of the things the storm left, and we saw the frank, full-color poses. The men and women looked foreign, German maybe or Swedish. The women had hair bleached white as sunlight, and a few had large tattoos.

Now we saw Ben going about town, his gait having about it a kind of certainty. Sometimes we'd see him looking at those mountains, or he'd tell someone that Sally was coming back in the spring.

"Well," said Harold Wolf, seeing Ben walk by the front window, "do you think that girl is coming back?"

"I don't know," said Charley, "but I'll tell you this. He does."

"Well," Harold said, "there it is."

"There's what?" said Charley.

"He's as goofy as Gloria," said Harold.

"Well, yes, I guess that's right," said Charley. "But you got to remember. Gloria was harmless."

Tubby Mars, Bompasino

Marlowe, Northern California

Now Ben went away, too, to the University of California in Berkeley, just as he had planned, but obviously going
now not because he wanted to so much as because the plans
had already been made. Dr. Lunn had pointed out to him that
even if he stayed the entire year, he'd still have some time,
next June, to wait for Sally Cooke. So, when the weather had
cooled off and the sky was as blue as painted tin, Dr. Lunn's
Willys came around the corner and stopped in front of
Bompasino's seed store, where Ben and Dr. Lunn got out. Dr.
Lunn was wearing a clean white shirt with a bow tie, his usual
flannel trousers, and Ben was dressed in a pair of jeans, but he
was wearing a white shirt, a sport coat, and one of his father's
cast-off bow ties. His hair was cut and combed and in his hand
he had a paperback book with a place marked by a Greyhound
bus ticket. On the sidewalk there was a big brass-trimmed
leather suitcase. Dr. Lunn had put it down with a kind of
rough salute, since it was the same bag he had taken to medical school and the same one he had dragged up here when he
had started to practice.

The bus came and the driver got out picked up that

scratched leather suitcase, the thing held together with a belt, and as the driver closed the bay, Ben turned to his father and put out his hand. Harold Wolf was standing in the poolroom, looking out the window, and when Dr. Lunn took his son's hand, Harold said, "Doc, what's wrong with you? Give him a hug, put your arms around him. He's your son." And as Harold spoke, Dr. Lunn dropped Ben's hand and gave him a quick, hard embrace, slapping him once in the middle of the back before turning away. Then the bus eased out of town, groaning and picking up speed on the south road, passing those signs that said, YOU'VE MISSED THE WARRIOR'S BONES AT TUBBY MARS'S POOL HALL. Dr. Lunn stood on the curb, watching the bus disappear.

So we went ahead, now depending on the newspaper for the weather. Otherwise, things here went on as usual. Indians kept running off to Los Angeles or San Diego or someplace and then came back, sad and angry and hung over, not able to stay here, but not able to get away, either. The flats sat out there in the hazy weather of fall. There were some automobile accidents. Every now and then Dr. Lunn came in and told us a little news: Ben was down there studying, even though Berkeley had gone crazy.

We watched it on the TV I have mounted on the wall. Berkeley was filled with a lot of angry young men and women, and at night their faces filled the screen as they told just about everything and everyone to go to hell. Sometimes I didn't even bother to look, since just hearing what was going on was enough to make me think it was time to send a contingent of hardworking dairy farmers down there to let those kids know which end was up. But even so, seeing those young men and women together, so young and unencumbered, we each pursued our private thoughts, each approaching in a somewhat different way what we all believed to be true: if nothing else, in an atmosphere like that, Ben was probably meeting some young women who lived along Telegraph, Channing Way, Shattuck, or Haste, and that in the rooms of their apartment houses he was probably getting a good chance to understand the first part of his father's comment that "Lust is a good friend," although, under the circumstances, Ben probably hadn't the experience, in a kind of plethora of opportunity, to understand Dr. Lunn's warning.

So we watched TV with a different perspective now, and on most evenings when there was a story about Berkeley we'd see a young woman, taking a sunbath, for instance, in that plaza beneath the Joshua trees, her hair thrown back in a pleasure of youth and sunshine, and as we watched, one farmer gently put an arm into the ribs of another, his knobby elbow showing the effect of forty years in the milking barn.

It didn't last. On a rainy evening in February the north-bound bus stopped in front of Bompasino's seed store and Ben got off. Just like that. He put the large leather suitcase with the brass snaps under the seed store's loading platform, where it was dry. Then he came in here and used the phone to call his father.

When Dr. Lunn drove up in the rain, Ben went out to meet him, and in the pittering sound of it Ben walked over to the loading dock where he'd left the bag. Dr. Lunn stepped out of the Willys, the rain hitting his coat and making a speckled pattern there, and as he got wet, he stared at his son, his eyes wide with disbelief.

"Well, have they sent you home?" said Dr. Lunn. "Have they kicked you out already? It seems to me that would be a pretty damn good trick, given the circumstances."

"No," said Ben, "they didn't kick me out. I've come home. Here."

He handed his father a thin piece of paper which showed Ben had received straight A's for the first half of the year. Dr. Lunn held the piece of paper, the small sheet trembling in his fingers. Then he said, "All right. I never said you weren't smart. I said you lacked good judgment. Why have you come back?"

"I've come to wait," said Ben.

"*Wait?*" said Dr. Lunn. "What the hell for?"

"I've come to wait," said Ben, looking at his father.

"And you've withdrawn from school?" said Dr. Lunn.

"I'd rather wait here," said Ben.

Dr. Lunn held the piece of paper, which slowly wilted in the rain.

"All right," said Dr. Lunn, "get in the car."

Ben climbed into the car with that leather bag sitting on the seat behind him like some stoic, humorless human being, and Dr. Lunn turned the Willys around and drove back to that large empty house with the elm trees in front.

Now Ben needed something with which to kill time, not to mention making money, since this certainly wasn't coming from Dr. Lunn anymore. Soon we saw him with the local paper, drawing a circle around a classified ad. After that we saw him driving an old Ford or Chevrolet, the thing smoking, steaming, and suggesting a kind of automotive futility. Then he'd go to work in the driveway next to his father's office, stripping the engines down while he read from a manual, holding a wrench in one hand and a rod or carburetor or gasket in the other. The patients came and went, soon not getting only good advice from Dr. Lunn inside the house about their physical ailments, but sound information about cars from Ben, too. Dr. Lunn looked out the window, over his half-glasses, while Ben patiently slipped new rings over a piston. Soon, we'd see ads in the papers for "Reconditioned Cars," and it wasn't long before people drove twenty and thirty miles to take a look, a few of them paying good money.

There was a morning, too, when Dr. Lunn's Willys wouldn't start, and he stood there in the rain while Ben came out and opened the hood and tinkered there for a while, and when the engine finally turned over, the two of them stood there, getting wet, not saying a thing and acknowledging each other as an adversary.

It wasn't long after this that Ben's car, or the one he was driving until he sold it, a 1957 Ford, for instance, was parked on the highway out of town beneath a sign, made by hand with a large brush, that said, JOE BEAUCLERK. CARS, HOUSE TRAILERS, RECLAIMED OIL. CREDIT TERMS AVAILABLE. BEWARE OF THE DOG.

Behind it there was a collection of trailers and cars, ar-

ranged in such a way as to suggest they hadn't been put there
so much as thrown. The trailers looked like the cars of a de-
railed train, some of them now having the grass grow up
around them, their doors unlatched and squeaking in the
wind. The cars were left here and there, hoods and doors
open, too, which made it easier for Beauclerk and his boys to
get a part when they needed a carburetor, a radiator, a differ-
ential, or an alternator.

Joe Beauclerk did business from the steps of a trailer. He
wore a pair of dark pants, a green shirt with a string-style,
western tie, and cowboy boots. His teeth were beautiful and
white. His boys, three of them between the ages of nineteen
and twenty-five, wore overalls and T-shirts.

It was from Beauclerk and the boys that Ben learned
things not mentioned in the repair manuals. It probably cost
him something, too, since Beauclerk and his sons didn't just
come right out and explain about banana peels or floor-sweep-
ing compound in the rear end of a car, radiators patched with
fiberglass rosin, engine blocks that were cracked and kept
from leaking with a couple dozen eggs, not to mention valves
that were kept from sticking by a judicious application of
transmission fluid, or old batteries that were given a quick
charge just before the new owner of a car came to pick it up.
These and a lot of other things Ben learned by going out there
and trading with Beauclerk and his sons, watching them as
carefully as though they were cheating at cards.

When he bought a car from them, he took it home and
parked it in the driveway next to his father's house, and then
stripped it down, finding strange substances, cheese, brake
fluid, sawdust, and vinegar in places none of it should have
been, and while he smelled or rubbed or just looked at these
things, he nodded and said, "Uh-huh, uh-huh," not to mention
those times when he looked into a radiator or a crankcase and
just burst out laughing.

Sometimes Harold Wolf helped him, and the two of them
stretched out there in the drive by Dr. Lunn's examination
room. In the evening, when Harold and Ben and Dr. Lunn
had dinner together, there were still some stains on Ben's

hands, even though he had washed with surgical soap. Dr. Lunn looked at the grease stains and nodded, as though he had before him, in those dark smears, the evidence of everything that was wrong.

It was on one of these evenings, when Ben and Harold sat in the dining room, that Ben and Dr. Lunn argued. The three of them sat around a large oak table in the dining room, which was lighted by a Tiffany lamp Gloria had installed before she left. They ate the broccoli, mashed potatoes, and brisket with horseradish sauce the housekeeper put before each of them. Beyond the lighted table there was the sense of the room's dark, paneled walls. They had raspberries and cream for dessert, and when the boys were finished, Dr. Lunn said to Ben, "Well, I've had just about enough. Why don't you leave? Why don't you go down to that school where you should be? Do you think that girl is going to come back? Do you?"

Ben sat there, opposite his father.

"Well, do you?" said Dr. Lunn.

"That's not your business," said Ben.

"Not my business," said Dr. Lunn. "Young man, you are going to make a fool of yourself. That girl is no more going to come back here than you are going to fly. She was just growing up, just enjoying herself, just flirting, just playing, can't you see? The worst thing in the world is a woman who hasn't grown up yet. The worst. Can't you see?"

"I said I'd wait," said Ben. "I'd rather do it here."

"Here?" said Dr. Lunn. "Well, I'll be damned. She's not coming back. Don't you see?"

"I said I'd wait," said Ben.

Dr. Lunn sat there, looking at his son. Then he got up and poured some gin into a glass, putting the ice cubes in later, as a kind of afterthought.

Then spring came. For a few weeks the flats have a bright, lime-colored haze. For a while the land looks like it will bloom. The air has a wonderful odor of new, pungent things, grass and young flowers, and the breeze that blows through town has the scent of drying earth and new leaves. People walk on the flats, seeing the snakes glide through the grass, and feeling that spring sun on the back of a shirt. Then the weather warms up and that green fuzz disappears, leaving behind some brown, lichen-colored stuff. The wind starts to blow and soon there are arguments in the street. More than anything else, when the flats turn brown again, you feel as though you had been shown something or at least promised something, some precious thing that makes life easy, and just when you've got used to it, the thing goes away and leaves you stranded, so to speak, and gasping: we all grew up with this. That scent and promise comes. It disappears. Again. Soon we are comforted by the vultures which totter in the air, their black wings unsteady as they land. There are dust devils, too, streaming across the flats.

Now Ben was finally old enough, and just experienced enough, to speak to Anthony Bompasino. Bompasino owned the seed store. He had come here thirty-five years ago with a load of flowers and some seeds, which he worked into a once flourishing seed supply, although it had collapsed into the weathered, peeling thing across the street.

In the beginning Bompasino had been tall and thin, and on Sundays he wore a dark suit with a carnation in the lapel, and his hair was so slicked down the part in it looked like a white line. He had a mustache, too, a small thin one, and at first people came into the seed store just to look at it, since before Bompasino came to town, they had thought such a mustache only existed in the newspapers, magazines, or on the face of a villain in the movies. In the beginning, on Sunday, he walked alone on Main Street, smoking a small cigar and smiling and lifting his straw boater to everyone he passed, for all the world appearing in this like a man taking an afternap stroll on some shaded Mediterranean piazza. Soon other people here began dressing up a little on Sundays, especially young women, who contrived a hat to go with those pale, faded dresses, which now were shortened, according to the pictures in the latest fashion magazines. And with a sour (and in some cases outright hostile) air the men got out their ties

and white shirts and summer-weight suits and they started
parading around on the long (and then by no means forlorn)
street in the afternoons of late June and July and even into
August (although, to be honest, this was the province of young
people who had the stamina). It didn't take long, either, for a
young woman to appear on Bompasino's arm, strolling while
he went in that fluid gait, swinging out his legs like some
boulevardier. Then he went back to his seed store, which in
those days was painted the soft color of Mediterranean terra-
cotta. The greenhouse was in good shape, and next to it, in
front of the store, there was a green canvas awning that made
a cool green shade. On Sundays, Bompasino put out a small
table and on it he served coffee and a sweet for himself and the
woman he was escorting, who was dressed in that cotton so
flimsy as to seem elegant and who wore a hat, a straw one,
decorated with flowers fresh from Bompasino's greenhouse.
So they sat there, drinking strong coffee out of small porcelain
cups, and while they did so they nodded to the people who
were out for a stroll. The young women who passed by in the
heat showed plainly on their faces, and in their frank swagger,
what they'd do for a chance to sit in the cool green shade of
that awning and to have some fresh flowers to put onto their
hats, not to mention being able to walk on the arm of that
boulevardier with his thin mustache, his dark suit, and boater.

This happened when I was young and my father had the
pool hall. There were some tense moments, too, in the heyday
of Bompasino, who was called "Three Finger Bompasino,"
like some hoodlum, by the young men who had been content
to do nothing on Sundays, but who now found themselves
smiling and nodding in the heat. The tense moments took
place at night. Then automobiles and trucks came down the
street fast and stopped in front of the seed store. There were
shouts and loud talking and even some guns were seen, the
blued metal of the barrels gleaming in the headlights.
Bompasino stood under the green awning of his store, dressed
in dark pants and a shirt without a collar, needing a shave and
talking fast, explaining everything, maintaining that the difficulty was, as they say, the difference between a hope and a

promise, at least as far as the last outraged young woman was concerned.

Then things settled down, or Bompasino settled down, since he was, if nothing else, smart enough to know there was a limit to the amount of outrage (no matter in what style it was done) the people here could take without doing more than just showing those pistols when they came for a late-night visit.

One day the seed store seemed not only closed, but deserted: the awning was rolled up, against the roof, and the sun beat down with a steady, silent pressure. No one came or went, although soon we saw Mary Parker, who was then just out of high school, going in and out of the greenhouse to water the plants. She went about this with a certain amorous quality, as though she had at least gotten into a man's private garden. And we noticed, too, that Bompasino's black Model T pickup was gone, its usual space empty, the oil and sand beneath it glittering in the heat.

The next Sunday evening, though, Bompasino drove out of the flats, that black truck having a kind of Mediterranean rake, if only because Bompasino was at the wheel, wearing his boater hat and smoking a thin cigar, which was pointed upward and reminded you of FDR with a cigarette holder between his teeth. In his absence the town was still taking the Sunday promenade, although the people went about it with a sense of lost direction, since the awning wasn't rolled down and Bompasino wasn't sitting under it with his current favorite: even the men who had called him "Three Finger Bompasino" had to admit that the heart had gone out of the parade, and while the strollers went around in the heat like sleepwalkers, not quite certain what they were doing or why, that black truck arrived.

On the passenger side there was a thin, tallish, dark-haired woman with black eyes and pale white skin: she was dressed in black and she had with her two small suitcases, made of wicker, which Bompasino carried for her, and as they left the hot, stinking truck, Bompasino made a show of the front of the store, the awning, the space for the small table, and the large sign that said BOMPASINO'S. Mary Parker came to the door with a watering can, and when she saw the young woman, whose name was Constantina, there was on Mary's face a look of angry betrayal, as though she hadn't been watering those flowers in the greenhouse so much as her hope. Now, even though Mary didn't know that Bompasino had driven to Sacramento, to the marriage broker there, and had come home with a bride, Mary certainly recognized the result. Mary passed the can to Constantina and said, "Welcome to Marlowe. Here."

The women on the street quietly paused to watch Constantina climb the steps of the seed store, and as they did so, each of the women knew right then that the Sunday-afternoon walk or parade was going to lose a little of its tension, and there was more than one who realized with a start just exactly how much more outrage she had wanted the town to take (and who probably thought, too, that this was by no means a settled issue, bride or not). Constantina took the watering can and smiled, obviously pleased to see so many people parading around in such a homelike, Mediterranean way.

The Sunday promenades weren't so thoroughly attended now, but for Constantina and Bompasino it didn't seem to matter. Bompasino walked up and down the street in his dark suit and boater, Constantina on his arm, and although Bompasino probably would have enjoyed Sundays more if the crowds had returned, he was still satisfied with that long walk taken after the nap, which was had not only in the heat of the flats but in the presence of Constantina.

Soon Bompasino began to put on weight, carrying it well, and having a new suit made every six months or so when he could no longer get into the previous one. Constantina kept up with him, remaking her clothes, the two of them still going up and down the street on Sundays, always becoming larger and strangely more peaceful as time went on, and after a while it was impossible for those women who had wanted to outrage the town with Bompasino to remember what the fuss had been about in the first place. They sighed with what they now saw as the foolishness of their early years.

There were children in town when Bompasino first began the Sunday promenades, and when they were of an age and predisposition, too, to begin a slow, hot courtship, they were amazed to find that Bompasino was no longer the boulevardier he had been, but a heavy man sweating in the heat next to Constantina, whose face was marked by perspiration running through her powder. The young people didn't understand that when Bompasino had been dashing he had outraged those young women as a kind of style or insistence of youth, and now that he was a married, prosperous man, he took pleasure in the weight which so obviously suited his position of heavy respectability.

In the days when Bompasino had been thin, the town wasn't exactly prosperous, but it had been moving in that direction. Across the street from the pool hall there was Bompasino's store with the canvas awning, the new asphalt loading platform, and a polished walnut door with a brass handle and a bell that Bompasino always kept shiny. The greenhouse was painted and had new panes of glass. Next to the seed store there had been a grocery with a big glass window and an awning, too, an orange one, and when this one and Bompasino's were rolled down at the same time, they gave a fruitful air to the street, as though the green and orange colors came from an enormous, horizontal carrot. Beyond the grocery there was the café, which had a window with a blue shade. It opened in the dark, at three-thirty in the morning, and the farmers (a fair number of whom were then trying to scratch a living out of the dirt around here) came in to have fried ham and potatoes and coffee before it got too hot to eat. The café had three rectangular windows set into white frames, and above them there was a white space with a sign in blue letters that said, BARSTOW'S HOME COOKING. PIES A SPECIALTY. At the end of town there was a white gas station with red pumps, and new black hoses. Above it on a sign there was an enormous painting of a winged red horse, rearing there, its front legs bent at the knees.

So you could say the place was comfortable and an ordinary, half-cheerful place to live, but soon people began to

leave. There was no one thing that made it necessary to go, no
large factory that folded, no mine that produced a suddenly
worthless metal, no railroad that went bankrupt, nothing like
that at all, and if it was any one thing, it was what didn't
happen. The early arrivals had a kind of half-assed belief in the
future and definite expectations for what the town was going
to become. As Bompasino began to put on weight and went
out walking on those warm afternoons, the town seemed to
slip, at first just a little (the civic correlative of that first bulge
around Bompasino's waist), but then more noticeably, and as
Bompasino changed his suits and as Constantina remade her
dresses, the result always a little less pleasing than before,
their mutual efforts going without one false step toward a
heavy dowdiness, so the town began to show the loss of people
who had expected so much: the restaurant's windows became
cracked, and when a pane of glass fell out a piece of cardboard
was used to cover the hole and was left there, too, even to the
time when the restaurant turned into a fix-it shop, which in
turn departed to leave behind an empty building, a piece of
cardboard still over the hole where the window had been. The
grocery's orange awning became bleached, appearing first
like a barely ripened pumpkin, but as time went on even the
traces of color faded, and the sun left the cloth bleached and
ripped. The awning was rolled up and held above the door,
but the tatters hung from it, the last of them serving as a kind
of warning.

Bompasino's seed store began to go without paint. The
windows became cracked, and the wood along the front of the
loading platform was smashed by the trucks that came more
rarely and with fewer supplies. Right along, though,
Bompasino kept the brass door-handle shined. It was curved
and looked like the trigger guard for an enormous shotgun,
and once a week, Bompasino stood before it with that small
gold can of paste wax and a piece of rag. But in the end he
gave that up, too, and no longer walked up and down the
street on those Sundays in June, July, and August. Instead,
Bompasino sat in his ill-fitting clothes at the small table with
Constantina, where, beneath the awning that was now a pale

mint color, they drank strong coffee and panted in the heat. But now he brought from the seed store a Victrola, along with some Caruso and Gigli records, that must have been a wedding present from Europe. He put the Victrola on a cantaloupe crate and while it sat there, he turned the crank. There was a bullet-shaped guide around which the records turned, and Bompasino found it by putting an enormous finger over the hole in the record. Then he painstakingly lifted the metal needle, which was on an arm like some strange foreign telephone, and after Bompasino found the right groove, the street was filled with Puccini or Verdi, the music coming as a general greeting and always ending in a steady *skitch, skitch, skitch.*

Even into the fifties Bompasino and Constantina spent Sundays under what was left of the awning. They sat at the flaking table and drank strong coffee, although their fingers were almost too big to pick up a demitasse cup by the handle. But even then there were people who took a walk and heard that *scratch, scratch, scratch,* of *Madame Butterfly* and *La Bohème.* But there were young people now, too, in their customized Fords and Chevrolets, who complained outright, and after they complained they drove onto the flats, where they sat with the car doors open so they could blare Fats Domino, Buddy Holly, the Platters, and Bill Hailey toward that ridge where the Indians went looking for inspiration or just practical information, like when a tornado was coming.

It was after drinking coffee and listening to opera that Constantina died. Bompasino called Dr. Lunn, who came through the heat of that August afternoon, carrying his black bag, although his haste didn't suggest urgency for something to be done so much as politeness for the business at hand. I imagine the two of them stood opposite one another with the enormous, swollen body on the bed between them, the sheet neatly pulled up to Constantina's chin, her powder marked by perspiration running from her dyed hair, and as they stood there, the entire aspect of the woman, even in this moment, must have been one of cheerful enjoyment of what life had brought her. Bompasino stood in the clutter of the dark knickknack shelves, the bureau covered with photographs in

frames, and the open wardrobe in which there was a carefully
ordered arrangement of suits, each one larger than the last
and suggesting the existence of a family, made up of men of
the same height, but of vastly differing weights. Dr. Lunn
agreed that Constantina was dead.

Dr. Lunn tried to call an ambulance, but Bompasino
stopped him. Then we saw Bompasino emerge from the glass
door of the seed shop, the frame of it cracked and peeling. He
stood there, next to the small table, and then walked into the
heat, his shadow the size and color of an inner tube a child
takes to the beach. Bompasino walked directly across the
street and into the pool hall and asked for ice, and I gave him
what I had. There was some in the cooler and some bags of it
in the back, stored there in the freezer I had bought when the
grocery went out of business. It was a lot of ice. Bompasino
wanted to pay me, and when I told him it was all right, he
looked at me and narrowed his eyes and said, "I want to pay
for the ice." Then he went out, walking over that large, round
shadow of his.

He backed that black Model T Ford up to the pool hall,
and then the Indians and farmers helped carry the ice out,
moving it in some galvanized washtubs I had in the back.
When they got outside with it, they looked at Bompasino,
who, with a gesture of his hands and a quick movement of his
head, let it be known he wanted the ice in the bed of the truck.
The cubes tumbled in and made a hard, dry rattle. The men
from the pool hall brought the last of it and poured that in, too,
and then we stood around, staring at the ice and being amazed
that what had looked like so much in the freezer appeared, in
the bed of the truck, like so little.

"Is there any more ice?" said Bompasino.

"No," I said.

"Are you certain?" he said.

"That's all I had."

He looked at the faded seed store, the table in front of it
peeling a little, too. He closed his eyes.

"I need more ice," he said.

So we stood there. The sky was blue and clear, and there

was almost no breeze. The cubes in the bed of the truck had a blue sheen from the sky.

"I don't want those birds following me," said Bompasino. "The black ones. The vultures. If I break down they'll be around the truck. I need more ice."

"We can keep her here," I said. "We can wait for an ambulance."

"I'm not taking my wife in a rented car," said Bompasino.

In the street there was a kind of wet rustle, like pebbles rolling in the surf, and something moved in the glare. The men stepped away from the truck. From those hot back streets and out of those gray houses there came women of all ages, wearing those pale dresses and carrying wastebaskets or just ice trays which were filled with ice, and when they came to the truck, they dumped the cubes in, the ice given as a kind of thanks or just a salute to those days when Bompasino and Constantina had walked the streets, the two of them going as tamed boulevardier and tamer, the hat worn by Constantina draped with old brown lace and Bompasino holding a cigar at a rakish angle.

The men went single file into the seed store, where there was the counter, worn down and smooth, the edge of it looking almost like a board gnawed by a horse. There were some faded envelopes in the seed racks. Bompasino led the men, still in a single file, into the bedroom, which they had never seen before, and which now was exposed in all the intimacy of its clutter. There were nightgowns and a sleeping mask of Constantina's, cold creams and powder boxes, a boa, and a fan made of palm leaves, not to mention the smoldering air of those Mediterranean afternoons. Now, though, the men stood on each side of the bed and lifted Constantina, who had been wrapped in a sheet. They flushed and their arms trembled with effort as they brought her out to the truck, where they put her onto the melting cubes. Bompasino was still wearing the last of those dark suits, the neck of his shirt tight and the tips of the collar standing out like small wings. He stood next to the truck bed, raking the cubes over his wife. The Indians stood back, but when one of the men from town began to help,

Bompasino said, his voice trembling a little, "I can manage."
Then he got into the cab and drove out of town, going south,
the noise from that black truck suggesting the emptiness of
the flats. Bompasino probably lighted a cigar out there, not
from disrespect so much as habit, appearing for all the world
as though he were going back to the marriage broker to ask for
some compensation, but in fact driving to the closest funeral
parlor. We didn't have one, if only because even in the town's
heyday no one here believed in the place enough to start a
mortuary.

Bompasino returned in the evening, the black truck hammering out there in the flats and announcing his coming.
Everyone in town stepped into the shadow of a doorway or up
to a dark window so as to be able to see, without intruding, as
Bompasino drove up to the front of his seed store, the last of
the ice melting and falling into the street with a dusty splash.
Bompasino turned off the engine and sat in the cab, now
hearing silence in place of the cheerful greetings and light
footsteps of the town's early blooming. Bompasino sat there
for a few moments smoking the last, short stump of his cigar.
He blew at the tip to keep it going, his full lips pursed to do so,
and then got out of the truck and looked around the street. He
climbed the stairs of the seed store and sat at the table on the
loading platform, the chair opposite him empty now. The
water from the last of the ice dripped from the bed of the
truck, and Bompasino sat there, listening to it and holding the
dead stump of the cigar between his fingers.

He became solitary. If you wanted to see him you had to
go in to buy the last of his seeds or even the plastic flowers he
sold instead of the fresh carnations and roses he used to get
from his greenhouse. Now, opposite the counter, there was
some chicken wire in which Bompasino displayed plastic flowers, the greens and reds of them appearing waxy and having
ridges that were left from the molding of them. Mostly he
stayed inside.

And the truth of the matter is that those pornographic
magazines, which had been found blowing in the street after
the tornado, belonged to Bompasino: with his age and disap-

pointment, his flirtatiousness and the chivalrous lovemaking and frank woman-chasing had been reduced, just as the town had been, and so Bompasino was left with the magazines, as though the brightly lighted photographs took the place of the expression in the eyes of young women who had smiled at him, or who had turned to look at him, their hair swinging across their faces in a tick of excitement. At night there was a light on in the apartment behind the seed store, and we knew that Bompasino sat there with a gallon of wine, drinking out of a water glass, smoking a cigar and looking at the magazines from time to time, screwing up his eyes in the smoke and remembering young women who had combed their hair and pinched color into their cheeks and who had taken Bompasino's arm for one of those cheerful, sultry walks.

And as his weight had suited his prosperous respectability, he now accepted this solitariness as being appropriate to a man whose wife had died, whose fortunes had declined, and whose influence, as exercised by thin cigars and straw boaters, had been reduced to a hazy memory. He went about his business with a remote, stylized shame, accepting his position as a crank just as he had gladly gone, each year, to have a new suit made. And if you asked him out for a cup of coffee, for a walk, or (as Mary Parker did) to a dinner of meat loaf, mashed potatoes, and salad with dressing out of a bottle, Bompasino thanked you, but said he was repairing the greenhouse, or writing to his uncle in Rome, a respectable man. Everyone waited, with all the pent-up fury of being resisted, for the day when one of Bompasino's excuses fell through.

Bompasino wasn't totally isolated, though.

When Ben had first appeared on the streets of Marlowe, wearing the headphones of the tape recorder he had bought after meeting Sally Cooke, Bompasino saw him and then came out of his seed store, if only because he had never seen such a thing before. Even then, in his sixties, Bompasino still was interested in novelty. Ben had stopped on the sidewalk in front of the loading platform, anchored there by the shadow at his feet, one of those black phones pressing against each ear. Bompasino stood under what was left of the awning.

"What have you got there?" he said.

"Headphones and a tape recorder," said Ben.

Ben handed them over. What was left of Bompasino's hair was combed in the style of the boulevardier. He put the headphones on, and then sat down, his eyes closed, his breathing a little blubbery, and his stillness suggesting concentration. After a few minutes Bompasino opened his eyes and said, "Ah, Gigli. Not as good as Caruso. More like a good mild cigar. Still excellent, but not so sharp. Come in. I'll give you coffee."

Ben went in and Bompasino gave him one of those small, heavy white cups, filled with coffee. Bompasino brought out one for himself, and the two of them sat on cane-backed chairs, among the last half-filled seed racks, and listened to the almost undecipherable sound of Caruso and Gigli, Bompasino's recordings of them so worn as to be heard mostly as a *scratch, scratch, scratch.* Ben listened while Bompasino smoked the stump of a cigar and reached out to dust the plastic flowers.

The flats were still green, even though it was late spring. Now, when Ben wasn't finding sawdust or banana peels in the rear end of a car he had bought from Beauclerk, he stopped by to see Bompasino. One afternoon, when Ben came in, Bompasino said, "So? Are you coming to listen to opera?"

"No," said Ben, "not today."

"What then?" said Bompasino. "Do you want some seeds? Spring is almost over. You should have some tomatoes started for your father. And some spinach, too. Can you cook, or can you just listen to opera?"

"My father has a housekeeper," said Ben.

"Irish? Indian?" said Bompasino. "What can she know about cooking? How does she make eggplant?"

"We don't eat eggplant," said Ben.

"No *eggplant?*"

"No," said Ben.

"I will teach you how to make eggplant," said Bompasino. "You peel it, slice it, and fry it. It should be crisp. You serve it warm with a paste made of garlic. What about arugula? Or zucchini?"

"We have zucchini sometimes," said Ben.

"I bet you don't stuff it," said Bompasino.

"No," said Ben.

"You must stuff zucchini. You must learn to cook. There is no better way to make love to a woman than to cook for her. Why have you come?"

"I've come to ask you for a game of pool," said Ben.

"Pool?" said Bompasino. "You mean in the café across the street?"

Bompasino shook his head.

"Come and play a game. My treat," said Ben.

"I don't get out so much."

"What is there to keep you here?" said Ben.

"I have my music," said Bompasino. "I read magazines. You can't read magazines in a pool hall."

"Of course you can," said Ben. "I used to read *Field and Stream* there all the time."

Bompasino stared for a moment at Ben. Then he said, "You are grown up now. I have heard. Here. You can't read one of these in the pool hall."

Bompasino took two magazines from the shelf beneath the counter. The pages were filled with those Swedish or German women. Ben looked through the wet, glistening photography of the magazines.

"Well?" said Bompasino. "As you can see, you can't take these into the pool hall. It's better for me to stay away from people, don't you think? I'm an old man now, waiting to die."

Ben closed up the magazines and pushed them back across the counter.

"I'd like you to come to the pool hall," said Ben. "If you don't like it, I won't bother you again."

"But the magazines," said Bompasino.

"I'll fix it so you can take them."

"Then I'll accept your invitation. With pleasure," said Bompasino, his eyes already looking a little uneasy. Then the two of them stood there, one on each side of the counter,

Bompasino now lighting the stump of a cigar and Ben looking back at him. Bompasino struck a match and drew on the stump of the cigar and smiled, his air as cheerfully insistent as when he had first started the walks in town, and Ben stood opposite him, his expression the same as when, years ago, he had told me it was going to rain. It was obvious to both of them that the magazines weren't the substance of their argument, but the ground rules of it.

"May I?" said Ben, gesturing to the magazines.

"With my pleasure," said Bompasino, watching closely now and putting another match to the stump of his cigar.

Ben picked up the magazines and went out the door, into the street. He disappeared around the corner and walked up to his father's waiting room, where he picked up two old *Time*s. Then he went to the stationer's, which still hangs on, selling paper and pens and ink, not to mention cards for birthdays, weddings, and the other human occasions, the number of which seemed to be increasing. At the back of the stationer's there was a paper cutter, and Ben stood next to it, stripping the guts out of the *Time* as though he were cleaning a fish. He put one of Bompasino's magazines into each of the *Time* covers and then, since Bompasino's magazines were bigger and leaked out a little, Ben put them under the paper cutter and trimmed them to fit exactly. There was a stapler, and he used it to fasten together the new editions, as you might say. Then he thanked Mary Parker, who owned the place, and went back into the street.

"Ah," said Bompasino, *"Time."* He held the magazines in his fingers, his face looking uneasy. He blinked at Ben. "Wasn't Luce an early supporter of Mussolini?"

Ben threw up his hands.

"Does it make any difference?" he said.

"Why, yes," said Bompasino. "I wouldn't want to be seen with the magazine of such a man. After all, Mussolini—"

"Mr. Bompasino," said Ben, "are we going to talk politics or are we going to play pool?"

"Listen. The reds are almost as bad. You know what it takes to make a phone call in Rome these days?" Bompasino blinked and swallowed. After a moment he said, "We are going across the street. I gave my word, didn't I?"

Bompasino went into the bedroom for a moment, and then reappeared, dressed in black trousers, a white shirt, and a white cotton jacket. He put the copies of *Time* under his arm and went out the door and into the heat. He came toward the pool hall, his thin hair shiny in the sunlight, but as he approached, his feet swung out with the air of an old boulevardier, and his face was raised in a smile of greeting. There was a cigar in the pocket of his jacket.

"Hello, Tony," I said. "It's been a long time."

Bompasino smiled.

"Ah, Tubby, it's great to see you," he said.

I gave him a beer and he took it and the magazines and went to the table in the corner, where he sat down. He could look into the pool room and into the street, too, and he sat there, drinking that cold beer and hearing the sociable click of the pool balls. He lighted the cigar he'd had in his pocket, blew streams of bluish smoke into the air, and when the place had been quiet for a while and the smoke had formed islands above the pool tables, he sighed.

So that was all right. He came back regularly, sitting at the same table, putting the magazines on top of it and lighting one of those cigars which Dr. Lunn had told him not to smoke. Other people came in, too, farmers and their wives and daughters, some of whom had never been in here before. They came in and bought a package of gum or a Coke and turned to say hello, just as if Bompasino had been there every day for twenty years.

He ordered some long-stemmed roses from a supply house, and brought them in, too, and when a woman came in and said hello, Bompasino offered one of the flowers with a sedentary although still chivalrous air, the gesture at once out of place and old-fashioned, like a horse-and-buggy on a freeway.

Mary Parker had never been in here, not even when Pearl Harbor was bombed, and I had had the only radio downtown. She'd stood in the street and shouted through the door, wanting to know if the Japanese were in Santa Barbara. But now she came inside and took one of those flowers from Bompasino, the two of them doing nothing more than an ancient kind of flirting, which probably took more grace than the easy kind of youth. Anyway, Bompasino went on smoking those forbidden cigars, breathing like a bellows with a hole in it, and drinking beer. He talked to the Indians and asked them for recipes for guinea hen and rabbit.

The place had the atmosphere of the training camp of a champion who has come out of retirement for one last fight and who is, beyond a shadow of a doubt, going to get himself knocked into the next county. At the same time there was an air of civility in the room, as though the men here weren't gambling and playing pool but on some European green, where people dressed in white and bowled balls the size of cantaloupes. Anyway, Bompasino sat there, smoking those black cigars, drinking beer, and breathing like some broken thing.

So it wasn't even a surprise when one day Bompasino turned to Ben and said, "Ben, I don't feel good."

Bompasino had the magazines on the table in front of him.

"Ben, do you hear me?"

"What's wrong?" said Ben.

"I can't breathe. My arm hurts too."

"Let's go see my father," said Ben.

"Maybe it will go away," said Bompasino.

Harold Wolf's Oldsmobile was parked in front of the pool hall. Harold took the keys for it and started the engine while the other men in the place picked Bompasino up and started toward the door. He was pale and some strands of hair waved softly around his head, and as he was carried out, belly up, he nevertheless put one hand out, and as he dragged the fingers of it across the table he picked up the two copies of what appeared to be *Time.* Then they went out, the men carrying him battering-ram style. Bompasino squinted in the sunlight, one hand grasping the magazines with an ownership that wasn't so much hysterical as ferocious. The men put him into the car, still carrying him battering-ram style, and from the sidewalk all you saw was his round belly, dark as an inner tube, and the soles of his shoes sticking up in front of it. Bompasino sat in the back, his eyes open, smoothing back the strands of his hair and straightening the lapels of his coat while he stared at the peeling paint and torn awning of his seed store.

In the waiting room of Dr. Lunn's office there were some Indians, one of whom was shaking with fever and staring at the wall opposite him, on which there was a photograph of some ducks landing on a cold pond. The ducks had their feet out and their black wings were spread. There were some women in the waiting room, and a failed dairy-farmer, a man by the name of Gerito. He wore his overalls and rubber boots and sat with his back straight and his hands on his thighs, and as he sat there, he looked out the window and saw the Oldsmobile. It came up the street, turned into the drive, and hit the bump there, and for that moment when all four tires were off the ground and the Oldsmobile seemed to hang in the air, the car looked like an old bird, spreading its wings for the last time. It came down with a crash and rolled up to the steps of the porch. Gerito blinked as the car stopped. He stood up, his knees making that lonely arthritic pop, and went to the window, where he pushed the curtains aside and said, his voice bland with fatalism, "It's that fat wop. Looks like he's about dead."

Ben, Harold, and Charley carried Bompasino up the porch steps and into the waiting room, where Bompasino sat down in a chair, still holding his magazines and trying to appear as though he had just stopped in, like any other citizen who had come to wait for Dr. Lunn, although Bompasino's color was waxy and his breathing sounded worse, as though the hole in the bellows had gotten bigger and was losing more air.

The door of Dr. Lunn's examination room was white, and Ben stood in front of it and knocked.

"Why, Ben, what's the trouble?" said Dr. Lunn.

"Bompasino. . . ." said Ben.

Dr. Lunn came out quickly, the front panels of his white

coat opening and showing that clean white shirt and bow tie. Bompasino still sat in the waiting room, opposite the other patients, all of whom kept their eyes averted, each one obviously hoping all this would go away, or at least that Bompasino wouldn't die in front of them. He blinked, and seemed to be concentrating, and there was about him, too, the air of a man who has not prayed in a long time, but who is seriously thinking of doing so again.

"Goddamn it," said Dr. Lunn, "you started smoking those goddamn cigars again, didn't you? And those heavy meals in the afternoon. . . ."

"I don't feel very good," said Bompasino.

"Where?" said Dr. Lunn. "In your chest? Your arm? Upper back? Do you want to throw up? Have you taken anything like Bromo-Seltzer?"

"Maybe I had too much for lunch," said Bompasino.

"Do you want to throw up?"

"I don't know. It's here," he said. He touched his chest.

"What?" said Dr. Lunn. "A pressure? Like a weight?"

"Like some bad thing," said Bompasino. "I don't know." All the patients looked at him now.

"Ben," said Dr. Lunn, "call the ambulance."

"No," said Bompasino, "I don't want to go in a rented car."

"All right," said Dr. Lunn, "call the hospital. Tell them I'm coming in." Then he took Bompasino by the arm and lifted him. Bompasino put down the magazines on the pile of others and said, "I can walk. No one has to carry me."

So Dr. Lunn and Bompasino went onto the porch, both of them wearing white coats, although Bompasino's was tight across the shoulders and Dr. Lunn's came down to his knees. The two of them went pretty fast, their legs looking like those from a donkey made by putting a sheet over two men. Dr. Lunn helped Bompasino into the Willys, and then he got in on the driver's side. He backed over the lawn and jumped the curb, landing in the street with a bang and a rattle. Bompasino sat on the passenger's side, squinting at the sky, obviously looking for vultures.

The Willys went down the street fast and turned onto
Main and then went straight over the flats, the car gliding into
the heat, slowly being submerged in it and then sinking or
disappearing altogether, leaving us with the memory of
Bompasino sitting in the car, his thin hair blowing in the
breeze, his eyes set on the empty sky. Then we went about our
business, waiting for the phone to ring or for Dr. Lunn to show
up, his face set in the expression that meant only one thing.

In the evening the Willys came out of the flats, not going
as fast as before, the front of it and that prudish windshield
materializing out of the pink air of sunset. Dr. Lunn parked
the car head-in on the street and got out, his bow tie and
starched shirt looking a little wilted. The door of the Willys
groaned and then Dr. Lunn climbed the curb and came into
the pool hall and said, "They don't know what's wrong with
him. Probably isn't a coronary. They're going to keep him for
a while." Then he went back to the Willys and drove home,
leaving the rest of us in that pink and golden air.

So, for a few hours anyway, it looked like we were going to
get back to normal. The thing that first made Dr. Lunn uneasy
was a piece of advice he had received in medical school: if a
working farmer comes into your office during daylight hours,
or worse, if a dairy farmer comes into your office before his
milking has been done, you have a certifiable medical emergency on your hands. Dr. Lunn's waiting room has eight or so
chairs in it, a couple of tables with lamps on them, a line of
wooden pegs in a board to hang your coat, and on the wall
there are some pictures, ducks and geese and bears, a raccoon,
and an ugly-looking condor. Mostly the waiting room is filled
with women, who, when they were alone with one another,
had expressions of a hardened intimacy, especially when they
were describing their symptoms, the pains that came as a
variety of honorable wounds and which were evidence of the
manner in which they fought life, the women having learned
a thing or two about resistance in this town or on the farms
around it, so that, at any particular time, the outcome of the
struggle between them and life was in doubt, or at least it is

fair to say that when it came to them, life was in for more than
it had expected.

So Bompasino went to the hospital. The day after he left,
Dr. Lunn went back to seeing his usual patients, one of whom
was Carrie Hartlund. Carrie is married to Bob Hartlund. It
was a little busy that morning because of the canceled ap-
pointments from the day before, and Carrie had to wait for a
while, flipping through the magazines that Dr. Lunn always
left out there on the tables by the chairs. When Carrie saw Dr.
Lunn, she wouldn't look him in the eyes, but Dr. Lunn was
busy and didn't have time to visit. He wrote a prescription for
her and she went home.

Soon, though, Bob Hartlund drove his red, flatbed truck
into town and parked it in Dr. Lunn's driveway. He came into
the office and stood there, blinking, a cap from Patz on his
head and his heavy frame covered by a plaid shirt, overalls,
and black rubber boots. Dr. Lunn had been in the examination room, stitching a cut, and he had just finished the dressing, laying on thick pieces of adhesive, when he heard the bell
on the door. He came out and saw Hartlund and said, "What's
wrong, Bob? Are you sick? Are you having chest pains?"

"I come to sit in the waiting room," said Hartlund.

"Well, sure, Bob," said Dr. Lunn, "you're always welcome
here."

Hartlund blinked at Dr. Lunn.

"Sit down, Bob," said Dr. Lunn. "If you need me, I'll be
right inside."

"I thought I'd just visit," said Hartlund.

"Well, sure," said Dr. Lunn. He stared at Hartlund. "Make
yourself at home."

"Much obliged," said Hartlund.

Hartlund sat down and put his hands on his knees. Dr.
Lunn went back to the examination room, glancing once
again over his shoulder, his gait suggesting a kind of medical
caution, if not excitement. Hartlund didn't move for a while,
and soon the waiting room went back to that state of mild,
bored expectation which was accompanied by the steady flick
and hush of the pages of magazines being turned. Hartlund

looked at the pile next to him, and after a while he picked up the first one and opened the cover, but after looking at the first page he put it down and picked up another, his air one of patient searching. When Dr. Lunn came out and said, "Next" (more like a barber than a doctor), he saw only that Hartlund's color was good.

In the morning Hartlund stood on Dr. Lunn's front porch. He didn't lean against the wall, or even sit on the wooden bench that was out there. He waited in front of the door, and when Dr. Lunn opened it, Hartlund said, "Can I come in now? I thought I'd visit. Much obliged." Then he went into the waiting room, his eyes set on the piles of *Time, Newsweek, Better Homes and Gardens, Popular Health,* and *Sunset,* and after the patients came in, he began to go through the magazines with a steady, farmerlike industry, his motions short and crisp but still having about them the quality of a man digging postholes. He went through one pile of magazines and then the next, moving around the room when a seat became vacant.

The women weren't reading magazines. Their attention was commanded by a spot in the middle of the room which seemed to hang there, about six feet off the floor, like some transparent balloon. Their faces were sour and no one said a thing to anyone else, and they sat with their pocketbooks in their laps, but their hands weren't draped over them. The women took a hard grip on the cheap metal of the top of the handbags.

So Dr. Lunn came out and said, "Next," and Mrs. Thomas came in and sat down on the table, not showing the purple welt or mole on her neck with her usual fear of cancer so much as with a kind of defiance which suggested, by the way she showed the mole, that this was another thing Dr. Lunn wasn't equal to. Dr. Lunn looked at what seemed to be a mole, the purple color of which suggested some malicious energy, like the darkness of the tornado.

Then Mrs. Thomas asked Dr. Lunn just who the hell he thought he was to have magazines like that in the waiting room. Dr. Lunn looked from that purple thing on her neck to her eyes. He straightened up. He went through the door and into the waiting room where Hartlund sat, and even though Dr. Lunn's hands were shaking with exasperation he said quietly, "Excuse me, Bob," and took from him a copy of what appeared to be *Time*. He flipped the pages back and forth and picked up the next copy of *Time*, too.

"I don't know what's gotten into *Time* these days, Bob. They used to be right wing. Why don't you take these home?" said Dr. Lunn, who then picked up the rest of the magazines and threw them into a corner in his office, where he turned to Mrs. Thomas and said, "You aren't dying. That's not cancer. It's just a tick," and then removed the thing.

In the evening, when Ben and Harold came into the dining room, Dr. Lunn was waiting at the sideboard, a glass of gin in his hand. Ben and Harold walked toward the table which the housekeeper had set, the two of them smelling the odor of corned beef and cabbage from the kitchen. The cabbage had been sliced and cooked quickly, just until the color of it darkened. The dining room was lighted by the Tiffany lamp, which Gloria had left behind as a monument to her belief in a world where people didn't just turn pale and blow away, and which the doctor kept as a thing to struggle against, almost as some of his patients stood up to their symptoms with a quiet, combative pride.

"I want some explaining," said Dr. Lunn. "There were some magazines in my waiting room today and I know goddamned good and well you had something to do with them. Two copies of *Time* filled with some pornographic . . ." He stopped for a moment. "I mean *pornographic* . . ." He stopped again, rattling the ice in his glass of gin and staring at the boys. "Well?"

The young men stopped when they heard his voice, and now they stood straight up, their shoulders square, their eyes, which were lighted by the Tiffany lamp, turned toward him.

"Do you think sick people are to be teased while they wait to see me?" said Dr. Lunn. "Are you that smug?"

"It's not that simple," said Ben.

"Yes, it is," said Dr. Lunn. "It is precisely that simple.

Either you had something to do with it or you didn't. Which is it?"

"I didn't intend—" said Ben.

"*Intend?*" said Dr. Lunn. "So you did have something to do with it, didn't you? How dare you? Life here is difficult enough without a bunch of smart shit like this. Those magazines are a violation of my oath, which clearly says the first thing is to do no harm. And I've spent a lot of time trying to live up to that, staying here in this place where people need me. Do you hear?"

"Yes," said Ben.

"Well?"

Ben just trembled a little as he looked at his father.

Harold stood beside Ben, his face reddish brown, his cowboy hat on his head and his T-shirt and bleached jeans lighted by the Tiffany lamp. The T-shirt was very white and clean and it made his face seem dark.

Dr. Lunn turned to him and said, "And what about you? Did you have anything to do with it? What did you intend?"

"I didn't intend anything," said Harold.

"But you knew about those magazines, didn't you?" said Dr. Lunn.

Harold shrugged.

"So what?" he said.

"*So what?*" said Dr. Lunn. "They ended up in my waiting room, that's what."

Harold stood there.

"If you knew about it, why didn't you tell me?" said Dr. Lunn. "And now you think you can come in here and eat food paid for by those people in the waiting room. What the hell's wrong with you? Why, you little . . ."

"You little what?" said Harold.

Dr. Lunn rattled the ice in his glass and stood under the lamp, the shadows of the soldered joints in it falling across the room like an enormous web.

"You little what?" said Harold. "Can't you say it? You *buck*, you redskin . . . ?"

"How dare you accuse me?" said Dr. Lunn.

He turned to Ben again.

"Why the hell are you waiting around in this town, why aren't you down in Berkeley where you belong?"

"I'm waiting," said Ben. "I came here to wait."

"Waiting?" said Dr. Lunn. "You must never wait. Never. Not for dark or dawn or any damn thing."

"Is that right?" said Ben, still trembling in his neck.

"Yes," said Dr. Lunn, "that's absolutely right."

Ben looked into his father's face, and the spiderweb pattern from the overhead lamp fell around them. The housekeeper made a noise in the kitchen.

"Well?" said Dr. Lunn. "Do you have anything to say? Do you dare?"

Ben swallowed.

"Well?" said Dr. Lunn. "Do you have something to say?"

"Is it all right to wait around for your young wife after she's left you?" Ben said. "Is it all right then?"

Dr. Lunn closed his eyes. Ben was still trembling.

"Ben, Ben," he said. "Oh . . ."

The housekeeper came into the room with a cutting board on which there was a piece of corned beef. She put it down and brought in two bowls, one filled with potatoes with parsley and the other filled with that crsip, shiny cabbage. She brought in a gravy boat of horseradish sauce.

"It's time to eat," she said.

Dr. Lunn took the sharpening steel from the sideboard and ran a knife along it, keeping his eyes lowered as he did so. He carved carefully and put the neat slices on a plate and added potatoes and cabbage and sauce. When there was a plate at each place, the three of them stood around the table, not one of them sure whether he would sit down, and each of them afraid not to.

Dr. Lunn went into the kitchen and came back with some beer, each bottle having a small white bulge of foam at the mouth, and when Dr. Lunn poured it into glasses there was a damp, almost sweet odor.

They sat down. They ate slowly, no one saying a word, and not looking at each other, either. There was the clink and movement, the noise of the eating men. They chewed the meat, their eyes on the table. At the end of the meal each of them looked up at the Tiffany lamp, and then each settled back into his chair, the anger in the room softening and finally disappearing, leaving behind an ordinary after-dinner clutter, in which the three men sat, their heads now lowered, bent in a kind of prayer or just fatigue.

Tubby Mars, The Cue Ball

Marlowe, Northern California

BOMPASINO CHECKED OUT OF THE HOSPITAL, UNDER HIS own power, and took a walk, probably swinging his legs out a little, unerringly looking for that part of town where years before he had been able to find a marriage broker, but now the buildings which years ago had been genteelly shabby were just run down, and the larger houses were rented by the single room. Bompasino checked into one of them, knowing that sooner or later someone from Marlowe would show up and bring him home.

It was dark when Ben and I came to get him. We went through the streets where in the days of the marriage brokers, inexpensive tailors, greengrocers, butchers, hatmakers, and florists had lived in a comfortable anticipation of domesticity, but now the storefronts of the milliners and tailors, greengrocers and butchers had given way to bars with opaque windows and movie theaters that were playing *Young Peaches, Velvet Lust, The Secrets of Sarah's Sister,* and *Meatball,* not to mention the signs that were in front of the theaters, on which there were enormous photographs of women, who usually reclined, nude, hair in a splash around their heads, the scale of the women making their desires seem beyond the experience of ordinary human beings. In bar windows there were signs that said, GIRLS GIRLS GIRLS, and when you passed, you saw a few solitary drinkers and beyond them a purplish, large jukebox. Between the bars and the doors of rooming houses there were women on the street, each one of them dressed in a short skirt and short top, all of them waiting, shifting their weight from one leg to the other, the movement appearing as a matter of frank commercial enterprise.

It was late when we brought Bompasino back across the flats. A moon was out and the scrubby brush, the road itself, and the telephone poles had a glow to them. The town was black and white, and the buildings looked clean and whitewashed, half bright, half black, and as I stopped I saw, at the side of Bompasino's loading platform, that Model T truck, which had been left there when Constantina died and hadn't been moved since.

"It's better to arrive at night," said Bompasino. "The town looks better then."

"Well, to be honest," I said, "I guess it does."

Bompasino looked at the seed store for a moment. Then he turned and said, "Ben, has your girl come home yet?"

"No," said Ben. "Not yet."

"I think she will come," said Bompasino.

"Do you?" said Ben.

"Yes," said Bompasino. "And when she does, you must ask her to dinner. You must cook for her. Pasta with seafood. Scallops and shrimp and maybe some clams. Parsley and a little wine, lemon, garlic, maybe a little crushed pepper. This is the way to her heart." Bompasino nodded in the moonlight. "These things must be done with care. Listen to me."

It was late spring now. Squeaky Hoskins drove into town in that Corvette with the patched front end. He parked in front of the pool hall and got out, his shadow running from his feet to the curb in a dark zag. He brought his aluminum cue case inside and flicked on the light over a table and said, "Sally Cooke is back. Doesn't ride a bike no more. Dresses like a snot.

She wears plaid skirts. Stockings and shoes with a little heel. White blouses. I saw her reading a copy of *Vogue* and carrying a book by Camiss," and then all we heard was the *kerschew, kerschew, kerschew* as he took the top off that aluminum case, his eyes combative, challenging us to tell him something other than what he already knew.

So we started waiting in earnest. We had the first dust storm, which appeared as a low brown cloud: it moved along the ground, for all the world looking as if there was some moisture in it, but it was dry. The wind blew the reddish-brown dust, which was the color of stinging ants and got into everything: you tasted it in your food and you saw it on any surface, a polished table, a mirror, a white wall, on pillowcases and sheets.

After the dust storm I saw Ben in town. He turned toward those mountains, above which the sailplanes climbed, their wings showing up as bright cuts in the sky. People asked him what the weather was going to be. Mostly he said it was going to be hot and dry.

The dry season began in earnest when, out of the heat, there appeared that truck with a trailer on which there was a patched cooker, the mismatched and obviously scavenged (if not stolen) tanks, tubes, and smokestack suggesting, in some nightmarish way, the plumbing and venting of a steam loco-motive. The truck came into town with the rainmaker at the wheel, his bald head out the window, his lips pulled back to show his large and very white false teeth. He didn't park head-in, but across six or seven places, the truck and trailer right next to the curb. Then he sat in the cab, giving the town one furious inventory, the pleasure of which he took as a snarling, unsatisfied ache. Then he climbed out of the cab and slammed the door. He walked into the shade of the awning, licking his lips and staring at the cooler.

Ben came down the street. He wore a bleached shirt and jeans, and as he came along the sidewalk, he glanced once at the machine on the trailer, where the patch on the cooker had the raised quality of a scar. Then Ben came along, into the shade of the awning, where he reached up and tapped the barometer. The rainmaker went on staring at the cooler, and without looking at Ben, he said, "Hey, you. Gimme a dime for a Coke."

Ben gave him one. The rainmaker reached into the cooler, pushing the sodas out of the way and taking one from the bottom with the same unnecessary violence as when he had slammed the door of the truck. He put the bottle into the opener and jerked the top off and then put the bottle to his face, not tilting his head back. He drank with his eyes open, and then put the bottle down.

"Nothing but sugar water," he said, turning his yellowish eyes on Ben. "Your name's Lunn, ain't it?"

"Yes," said Ben.

"Ben? They call you Ben?" said the rainmaker.

"Yes," said Ben. "That's right."

"They say you can tell when a storm's coming. Is that right? Can you do it?"

"Sometimes," said Ben.

"And I'll bet you don't charge nothing," said the rainmaker. "I'll bet you give it away. Ain't that right? And what about that tornado?" The rainmaker stepped closer, one eye now wide open, bulbous, glaring, the entire aspect of the rainmaker's face one of trembling curiosity. "Did you know it was coming, or was it lies? I heard you read a book about it. What book?"

"I got some out of the library in Sacramento," said Ben.

"*Library,*" said the rainmaker. He stepped back, his head jerking upward and his lips set as though he tasted something bad. The rainmaker spit onto the street, the gesture coming as a gift of bad luck. Then the two of them stood there in an unsociable silence, or, in the case of the rainmaker, a kind of professional rivalry, as though Ben didn't just predict the weather, but actually made it. The rainmaker held the soda bottle in his scaled fingers and squeezed it, and then threw it into the box with the other empties. He rubbed his head with an air that suggested concentration, as though he needed some bodily movement to go along with his thinking.

"*Library,*" said the rainmaker. "I should have known

there was a damn library in it someplace." Then he got back
into his truck, the green, iridescent color of his shirt, which
was like peacock herl, showing through the holes in his coat.
He started the engine, his eyes going over the town in a
languid and obviously pleasant curse. Then he drove into the
flats, the smokestack and copper tubing and cooker riding
unsteadily on the trailer.

The sun rose. The sun set. Bats rose from those attics
where they slept during the day, their wings flickering in the
sky as they looked for water. Ben went on buying cars from
Beauclerk, although now he went over each successive car a
little more carefully than the last, leaving Beauclerk and the
boys to stand out there beneath that sign or in front of their
trailer while Ben found, under their noses, the sawdust or
brake fluid or whatever else they had used to keep a car going
for a few hours more. Then, while Ben showed the stuff,
Beauclerk and his sons stood in the sunlight, blinking incredu-
lously, not that it was there, but that it had been found. On
these occasions Ben straightened up and wiped his hands and
said, "Well, I guess we're going to have to talk about a new
price for this one, don't you think? I know you boys want to be
fair."

In the worst of the heat Beauclerk and his sons stopped
showing Ben cars altogether as a kind of admission that they
had taught him all they knew and that it was time to stop
before it cost them real money. And through it all Ben had
gone about his lessons with a constant, steady patience, since
this learning was all he had, and in that endless search for what
was wrong and in the attempt to fix it (or at least not to be hurt
by it), there was a belief that somehow, if he learned or traded
well enough, he could somehow make the right woman appear.

Dr. Lunn watched Ben laying a new gasket over an open
engine block and said, "You think there's some magic in this,
don't you? That just doing this is going to get that girl down
here, is that it?"

"Yes," said Ben. "Can you hand me that wrench over there?"

Now Ben and his father barely spoke about his waiting, or about anything else, although they still kept each other's company. In the evenings, or in the mornings, they took walks together, both of them moving pretty fast, each of them having his hands in his pockets, both dressed in white pants and a white shirt, Dr. Lunn wearing a bow tie, both of them taking the air, their heads down, the atmosphere between them one of differing about a lot of things, theoretical and otherwise, but at the center of the disagreement was what it meant that Sally Cooke had come home but not to Marlowe.

So it was on one of these afternoon walks, the two of them going fast, all elbows and knees and forward motion, that the red car came toward town, the speed of it not any less than before, no matter what that eastern school had done to the driver of it. Ben and his father were by the seed store when they first saw the movement. And by the time Ben had stopped and turned toward Dr. Lunn and raised an eyebrow, they could already hear the faint but still definite sound of *Madame Butterfly*. Then the red car came into town, bringing behind it a trail of dust and the music, too. Sally Cooke was at the wheel, her hair blowing in the wind, her shoulders against the seat as she drove in a functional, straight-armed style.

She glided up to the curb and then reached over and turned off the tape recorder, the cessation of sound coming as a kind of greeting. She got out, her hair blowing around her face and her gray eyes now set on Ben. She was dressed in a silk blouse and shortish blue skirt, and she came away from the car in long, even strides. Sally held the car keys in one hand and twirled them around, the blur of them making a little circle. Behind her, as she walked toward us, there was the wolf-colored wood of Bompasino's, the slight creaking of the sign that still hung over what had been the grocery, and the dust in the street, out of which she emerged.

None of this took much time: the car came to a stop and she got out and walked across the street, where Ben and his father stood, watching, and when she stood next to them, Ben said, "Hello, Sally. You remember my father, don't you?"

"Why, sure. Hello, Dr. Lunn," she said. "How nice to see you again."

She put out her hand and smiled, and Dr. Lunn took it, holding it for a moment and looking at her.

"How nice to see you," he said. "Why don't you come up to the house for a cold drink? I think I can find something."

"I'd love to," she said.

She turned to Ben and Dr. Lunn said, "Well, I'll run up to the house. Come over when you want." Then he turned away, saying nothing more, and not looking at Ben either. He walked a little more slowly than before, his arms and legs not angular, his figure lonely against the golden streets of the afternoon.

"Hi, Ben," she said. "How have you been since I saw you last?"

"All right," he said.

"What have you been doing?" she said.

"I went down to Berkeley for a while."

She looked at him closely now.

"I'll bet you had a good time down there, didn't you?" she said.

"It was all right," he said.

"Was it, Ben?" she said. "I thought you'd call me up and invite me to some dumb movie or something. . . ."

"I thought you'd come down here," said Ben.

"Did you, Ben? Did you think I would?" she said. She swallowed. "I've been lazy, I guess, just sitting around the house. What a waste of time it's been, too. So I came down here. You wouldn't think an Oldsmobile could go that fast, would you?"

She laughed, keeping her eyes on him.

"I heard you were back," said Ben.

"Oh, yeah," she said, "I've come back for a while. You should have seen us, Ben, at that school I went to in Connecticut, all of us sitting at a table at dinner, with our napkins in our laps and with a straight back, holding our forks turned over, like you see in movies about England. It was a scream." She looked him full in the face when she said this, although she didn't smile at all. "You should have seen us."

"Do you still say *sucker*?" he said.

She smiled and shrugged and said, "Oh, I don't know. Why don't you come over to the car?"

Sally went a little ahead of Ben, her shoulders square and her head up, and every now and then she turned to see if he was still there, her hair swinging around her shoulders when she did so, her gait still a kind of fluid strolling, the sun falling over her and appearing as that same golden smear.

They stood in front of the car, talking, once putting their heads together, and when they touched they looked at the ground between them. Sally said, while looking at the ground, "I don't want anything pushing me around, not even this." Then she laughed, since both of them saw, even then, how little good defiance did. Sally opened the car door and leaned with one arm on the roof and one arm on the top of the door and watched as Ben walked around the hood and got in on the other side. Then she slid across the seat and picked up a blanket she had there and tossed it into the back of the car, the blanket opening before it fell. Sally pulled away from the curb, steering with the heel of her palm: the tires burned and the car went down the street, gaining speed and stretching into a blur of red metal and chrome, the car going toward the flats now, just as before.

So now that red car came back to town again, its arrival having about it that speed and music, which, as before, came as a well-known *ou-ah ou-ah*. Ben waited for her on a chair in the shade, reading a magazine.

We had some more summer dust storms. The high brown banks came toward town and before them the buildings seemed diminutive and frail, modellike, and when the wind blew, we heard the dry sifting of the dust against the outside walls. But even so, Sally came across the flats, where the dust drifted over the road like snow in the arctic. She came in here after one of these trips and stood at the door, using both hands to shake the dust out of her hair, and said, "It'll take the paint right off your car." I offered her a beer and she put her head back and drank. She looked at me and blinked, her eyes watering and her nose filled with the tang of hops. She said, "Oh, that's good, Tubby. Thanks." Then she went to Dr. Lunn's house, upstairs and into Ben's room, where Ben was waiting for her, surrounded by the things he had made or collected, the recording and aneroid barometers, hydrometers, books on extreme low pressure storms, and a photograph, taken from a satellite, on the day we had that tornado. Sally probably walked into the room, turned back the counterpane, and sat down, her entire air one of uncertainty, even in what she wore, since on these afternoons she was still dressing for the east, and as she sat down on the bed, her stockings made a small zipping sound against the sheets.

In the evening Dr. Lunn came into the kitchen and found Ben at the stove. There was a large pan on one burner, and in it Ben sauteed some garlic and added shrimp and scallops, some white wine, parsley, and a little crushed pepper. On another burner there was a large pot of boiling water. Sally sat at the table, barefoot, reading a murder mystery and giving Ben a one-line summary of each page ("He went up the stairs." "There was blood on the floor." "False alarm.").

"What are you cooking?" said Dr. Lunn.

"I thought I'd make some pasta. There's enough for all of us. Would you like some, too?"

"Yes," said Dr. Lunn. "Do I have time for a drink?"

Then they sat in the dining room, under the Tiffany lamp. Sally and Ben waited while Dr. Lunn served. Sally laughed and talked, but she sat with her napkin in her lap, her back straight, and her head up. She told stories about the girls' school, and she admitted, too, that the east terrified her, but not in a way that repelled her. It was the opposite of that, and she felt the terrifying pull just as a sky diver stands at the door of an airplane and feels the tug of the wind and space below. When she had been in the east, she had gone to New York with some of her classmates. She had gotten separated from them, and for a while she wandered by herself on Madison Avenue. There were shops and galleries, restaurants, and Sally walked along, seeing the lights and the cool space behind the heavy windows of the stores. It was early evening, and there were women on the street, wearing silk and having their hair done, their faces perfect and cool as they walked out to a car or taxi, and as Sally went, she looked carefully at the women, who seemed so self-assured and even haughty, but as she watched, Sally was convinced the women were terrified, too. Sally stood in front of a gallery and watched them, wondering what secret made them so scared and so excited. Then she went back down the avenue, seeing the half-lighted towers, the city rising ominously above her. As she spoke of the cold glitter of the east, of the terror of it, they heard the sound of the dust blowing against the house.

Sally sat under the Tiffany lamp, which had an almost unnoticeable sway because of the wind, and as she sat there, the bright, yellowish light fell over her face.

It was probably on that night things began to go sour. At the end of the evening Ben walked her into the front hall, where the brown wood of the walls and the staircase was covered with triangles of light from the overhead fixture. The dust blew outside. Ben said, "Just listen to that . . . sucker," and she turned to him, her eyes focusing now, and said, "I'm not supposed to say *sucker* anymore."

Soon, after the storms had blown away and the heat had come for good, Ben waited in the pool hall, reading one magazine and then another and then not even bothering to read so much as just sitting there, staring at the open pages. When the phone rang and I answered it and heard her voice, I handed the receiver to Ben, and he said, "Oh, sure, that's okay. I understand. Sure. Tomorrow, then."

Tomorrow came and that red car arrived again, Sally at the wheel. But it was clear, too, that as Sally had come across the flats, she had been thinking of fear or danger: she probably saw herself floating on a smooth, pleasant sea, beneath which, not far from her legs, there were schools of sharks, gray and moving, their malice obvious in every twitch of a fin, and as she floated over them, she was frightened and attracted to the thing that made them grand, and as she imagined getting a little closer to them, she arrived here and found Ben, just coming up to the car, to whom she said, "Hi, sugar. How ya been?"

In the evening they returned to Marlowe, where it was hot, and they stood in front of the pool hall. Ben reached into the cooler and handed her one of those dripping bottles. As she drank, he said, "Maybe it would help if I scared you more. Maybe you wouldn't want to get away so much to someplace that does."

She blinked at him and said, "Why, Ben, you don't scare me at all. Not a bit."

"But would it help if I did?" he said, his hands aching as he reached again into that cold water.

"I guess so," she said, looking down. "Maybe. But you don't, so let's not talk this way."

Now the dates were broken more often than not, sometimes without a phone call. Ben waited for an hour or so and then stood in front of me, his eyes having a fierce insistence in them as he said, "I'll see her tomorrow, I guess."

That red car did continue to show up here, though, and when it arrived, Sally sat at the wheel, the windows rolled down and the breeze still blowing her hair around. She didn't play the tape recorder so often and when she arrived she was announced by the impatient idling of the Oldsmobile out front rather than by an operatic *ou-ah ou-ah*. Now, when Ben went around the front of the car and got into the passenger's side, she stared straight through the windshield, her head no longer turning with that ease and no longer saying, either, "Well, sugar, what's cooking?" Ben slammed the door and stared straight ahead, too. Then both of them waited with a nervous impatience to get to the flats, where they could spread the blanket and deny, for a while anyway, the attractive terrors of the world.

I remember Ben waiting for her in the hottest part of the summer. The sky beyond the buildings had the same hot insistence we'd seen the day before and which we'd see the next day, too. Ben slid back the door of the cooler out front and the ice bobbed and clicked on the surface of the water. He took a

few cubes and threw them, skipping them across the hardtop
the way a child bounces a stone across a pond. Then the red
car came out of the flats, only this time it was going slow and it
hesitated there on the other side of the hollow where the road
dips, but then it came on, into town.

Sally parked the car head-in, under the shade, and then
got out. She was dressed in those white shorts and a T-shirt,
and when she stood in front of Ben, she put one long hand on
each side of his face and pulled him toward her. Their figures
were clear against that empty street, and as they stood there,
she gave him a wet, warm kiss good-bye. She looked at him
and said, "I'm going back east. It's just too scary to leave alone.
Do you understand?"

He nodded.

"No," she said, "I want you to say it."

"I understand," he said.

"Good," she said.

He put a hand to his forehead.

"What the hell do you want me to say?" she said.

"That you're not going to leave."

She put back her head and closed her eyes.

"Oh, shit," she said, "and I said I wasn't going to cry."

She looked around the town, the signs with the peeling
paint, at the shadows in the street.

"Let's talk things over," he said. "Why don't we go up to
the house . . . ?"

"No. There's nothing more to say. Not a goddamned
thing."

Ben stood there, looking at her.

"Is there?" she said. "Tell me if there is. I'd be glad to
listen."

"No," said Ben, "I guess there's not."

"Let me kiss you," she said. "Come on."

Ben shook his head, but even as he moved it from side to
side he bent forward, one of her hands then slipping around
his neck.

"Goddamn it," she said, letting him go. "Please, understand. I never planned on this, or anything like it. I never planned at all."

Ben nodded.

"I understand," he said. "I said I understood."

She turned toward him for a moment.

"Good-bye, Ben," she said. "Take care."

Then she got back into that red car and sat behind the wheel, her arms held in that straight, functional style. She backed up, turned around, and went north, going as fast as she could, her departure announced not by music, but by the horn, which came as a *honk!* and when she was at the edge of town and facing the flats, the car now having the speed of hysterical fleeing, there came a loud, long *HOONNNNKK, HOONNNNKK, HOONNNNKK,* which was repeated, the *HOONNNNKK, HOONNNNKK, HOONNNNKK* having the aspect of infuriated exasperation, but then, with the speed of the car, the horn didn't seem so loud, although it continued until the diminishing sound was so slight as to be almost imaginary.

Ben watched until the car and the sound were gone, and then he turned and saw the line of men who had the unerring instinct to be standing just behind the window of the pool hall. The cooler sat in front of him, and he put his hands on it, elbows straight, his head down. He slid back the door and picked up a handful of cubes and began to rub them over his face, but before they touched his cheeks, he threw them, each one of them skipping there on the hardtop, the handful of ice exploding into rays and leaving in the street the ugly rattle of anxiety itself.

In the evening he came into the pool hall, although he didn't take a table. For a moment he stood in the middle of the room, his head up, his eyes open and having in them the glitter of an overhead light. The Indians moved around. Someone put a coin into that red, yellow, and chrome machine and punched the buttons for "Ain't That a Shame." Fats Domino's voice came into the room. The Indians waited. Ben stood under the cone of light and looked at Bompasino, who sat alone at a table against the wall.

Ben picked up a cue ball from one of the pool tables and held the heavy thing in his hand. Bompasino's face was jowled, his chins piling up around his throat, and as Bompasino sat there, surrounded by others who had been here for years, he looked directly at Ben, Bompasino's eyes dark and aware, shining with the memory of things gone wrong, whether outraged menfolk showing up with guns, or his wife dying in the heat, and as he kept his eyes on Ben, he made a small shrug and turned up his hands as an admission that there never had been and never would be anything to do about a sense of loss.

So Bompasino lighted his forbidden cigar and took a sip of a beer, although he kept his eyes on Ben. For a moment Ben looked back, into the dark shine of Bompasino's eyes, and then he nodded, turned toward the front window, and sighed, and before I could say a word, he threw the ball.

It went like a white bird let out of a cage, and the men watched it, their faces half in shadow and their eyes glittering in the light, each one of them caught in an attitude of wonder as the ball went straight through the room and struck the window, just like in the old days, and there, for all to see, was the haunting spiderweb of cracks. Then the glass fell into the street, settling into a mess that looked like a load of ice had been dumped there by mistake.

The Indians barked with joy. There were three more windows along the front of the building, not to mention a lot of others up and down the street. Ben walked back to the pool table and picked up another ball, and as the Indians chanted and shouted, blue lights flashed in the street as Bertrand Gage, who works for the state police, pulled up in his car. Now he came in, wearing the Sam Browne belt and pistol, the jodhpurs, and khaki shirt the state police wear, not to mention that drill sergeant's hat with a flat brim: Gage came through the broken glass and took that short-barreled pistol from its holster and put the barrel into the middle of Ben's forehead and said, as he pulled back the hammer, the ratcheting sound of it loud enough for all of us to hear, "Ben, if you don't put down that cue ball I swear to God I'll kill you."

Ben dropped it on a pool table, and from around the room

there was an echo of that first ball hitting the table, a *thunk, thunk, thunk* as the Indians and farmers dropped the balls they'd picked up. Then Gage said, "Get the hell out of here. Go on home."

So they went out and Gage waited, holding the pistol against Ben's head, and finally, when the last Indian and ex-farmer had gone through the door or stepped through the broken window, Gage got out those chrome-plated handcuffs and put them on Ben, tightening them down. Then they went out, Ben's shoulders seeming especially broad with his hands behind his back.

When they were gone, Bompasino still sat in the corner, and he said, gesturing with his cigar, "Tubby, you come over to my place. We'll sit outside and have a glass of wine." So I went with him and sat on a chair on that loading platform, the two of us enormous at the small white table and both of us looking up at the stars.

We don't have a jail here. The closest one is in Knight River Junction, fifteen miles down the valley. Knight River Junction is a little bigger than Marlowe, and it has a train station, a plaza, a department store, and some supermarkets. There are telephone wires and power-lines running up and down the main street.

Dr. Lunn drove down there the next day. The air was already hot, and Dr. Lunn was dressed in his white shirt, flannel pants, and bow tie. The jail had the flavor of Mexican architecture: there was a tile roof, white walls, and doorways with arches at the top. There was a sign on the wall that said, MISDEMEANORS DROP YOUR PANTS, FELONS STRIP COMPLETELY.

Dr. Lunn found Ben in a cell. The bars had been painted many times and had a rough texture, although the last coat of paint was shiny. Ben was standing up, his hands on the bars, his head between his arms, and when he looked at his father, who stood directly in front of the cell, Ben said, "You're wrong. It's not lust that's a hard enemy. It's love."

"Come on," said Dr. Lunn, "let's go. I've paid your bail."

The Knight River is a slow, yellow stream, and it has so

little current as to look like a canal. It has steep banks. Dr.
Lunn and Ben came out of the jail and walked for a while, the
two of them saying little as they went along the wide sidewalks and through the plaza. At the end of town they came to
a bridge over the river, and there they went down to the
water and sat on the bank, both of them squatting, forearms
on knees, hands limp. The yellowish current was dimpled
here and there by small, thimble-sized eddies, and while Dr.
Lunn and Ben rested, the swallows flew overhead. Then the
birds nicked the surface of the river, splashed a little as they
did so, and flew away. The sky was enormous, filled with gray
and white clouds, and the two men sat next to the yellow
water, both of them silent now and looking fatigued, their
heads down, their figures small under the sky.

Ben didn't stay in Marlowe long. He cleaned up the mess
in front of my building and fixed the window, the Indians
watching him with the approval they reserved for people who
can't be trusted. Then he went back to that school in Berkeley
and studied physics and chemistry, paying his way by trading
those Chevrolets, Fords, Mercuries, and Pontiacs. He gradu-
ated and worked for the weather service, broadcasting the
forecasts. We have a little radio here that gets the weather
service. Once he said there was danger of a tornado on the
flats, and we listened to his voice as he said we should look out
for that black funnel.

So what could I say, when, after all those years, after Ben
had grown up and moved away, those reporters showed up,
asking about him? Did I think he could fall in love? Could he
be devoted to a woman? That's what they wanted to know.
Was he a friendly boy? Did he do his schoolwork? Was he
popular? What about girlfriends? Did I have an angle for
them? The reporters drove a rented car, and how the hell can
you trust someone like that: you can't tell where they're going
or where they've been. They just come down here from no-
where and ask about murder.

"Why, it just takes your breath away, doesn't it?" said
Mary Parker. "And to think that boy was so good with the
weather. Do you think the Russians are behind it?" Well, the

reporters got the usual from people here. Everyone said, "My, I just can't imagine Ben being involved with anything like that . . . he was on the track team and in the Science Club and I can still remember the time he ran the two twenty against Twin Falls . . . he went like the wind. . . ." That's the kind of blah-blah the reporters got. As for me, I looked at those rented cars and kept my mouth shut.

Book III

Faith Wheeler,
The Green Cadillac
Edwinville, Northern California

WE TURNED OFF THE MAIN ROAD, INTO THE FIELD, WHERE there was a building made of cinder blocks, the roof of it having only a slight pitch, the entire thing looking like a place where the town kept the trucks for the road crew. The last thing you'd think is that it was a church, although when you got close enough you saw a sign that said, THE CONGREGATION OF NEW SOULS. Behind it there was a cornfield, and a road, which was not more than two ruts in the earth with a strip of grass between them. The road went down to the river, or the irrigation canal, where the church held its baptisms.

The canal was about forty feet wide and the water in it came from the Sierras, which were in the distance, the peaks of them covered with snow and looking like triangles folded out of white paper. The banks and the bottom of the canal were concrete and the water was deep, blue, and it went fast. Next to it there was a telephone pole on which there hung a life preserver, a round one with a rope attached, and on it, in black letters, there were words which said, TO TAKE THIS IS TO TAKE A LIFE.

We went down to the river, passing the cornfield, in

which the plants were about five feet tall, shiny as the ocean. Beyond the corn there were twenty-five or thirty people who stood at the water's edge. They were surrounded by the clutter of cars and pickup trucks and station wagons, some of which had the names of businesses, dry cleaners and plumbers, painted onto their sides. There were tables there, too, covered with paper cloths and having on them platters of fried chicken and cold brisket and potato salad, the food under gauze nets to keep the flies away.

The reverend stood in the water, the current piling up around his hips. His white shirt was a little wet and his pink skin showed through. Then I got out of the car and walked through the dust, wearing a light, white dress. In the middle of the canal there was one long tongue of current, smooth and repetitive, as shiny as a piece of melting ice. I was nineteen, and I had dark hair, and my eyes were of different colors, one brown, the other brown and gray, the colors mixed like someone pouring one can of paint into another.

"Faith. The time has come," said the reverend. He smiled now, even in that cold water.

The current tugged at my skirt, the dry cloth floating away and then sinking as it went downstream, some of it going between my ankles, too. The concrete was rough on my feet, and I watched with a kind of fascination as the air billowed under my skirt.

The reverend put his hand over my nose and his other hand swept behind my knees, and then I went under, seeing the surface of the water over my head in a long, soft mirror, like the silver film they make balloons out of. My dress pulled at my waist, the hem moving in slow, peaceful undulations.

Above me, in the water, the ropes of current slid away, trailing bubbles which looked like pearls. Through the surface the man wavered, his face remote and unclear in the film, and as I kicked, my feet made splashes shaped like crowns. His fingers pushed against me with a calm, sad disapproval, and even then I thought, *I won't let you get away with this. I promise. I promise.*

The crowns drifted away, collapsed, disappeared. The

current came in a rush and gurgle, and there was the pressure of the man's fingers, just like a doctor's looking for the place where it hurt or where there was some swelling, the fingers themselves seeming to decide or to judge. So then I went limp, absolutely limp, not sure how much it was a lie and how much I gave right then, but only wanting to get out now, where I could breathe again. And as I waited, not moving, I thought, *You wait until I get my chance.*

It seemed there was some small black thing, like an ant, that climbed up my chest or along my neck and across my chin, maybe even into my mouth and onto the tip of my tongue, the maddening, slow, rising tickle of it finally making me shake my head from side to side and scream, the air from my mouth rising in one long bubble, exactly like one blown by a child out of a plastic ring dipped in soapy water, the shape undulant and smeared with rainbowlike colors.

He brought me up, and I stood, dripping water, breathing. My dress clung to me, my skin visible through it, pink now from the cold, and as I stood on the wet concrete, the congregation sang, "The Beautiful, Beautiful Riv-ver, . . ."

"You're washed clean now, Faith," said the reverend. He gave me a small push toward the bank, where I stood, breathing hard, now automatically looking for something on the ground, a stone, a club, but even then I thought, *Wait. The right time will come.*

I stepped a little farther up, my dress clinging to my legs and the wind hitting me now, too, the quick gust of it like a splash of kerosene, and as I turned away from the wind, or just turned to get it on my back, I saw a man, a stranger, walking in the ruts of the road.

He emerged from the green cornfield, his progress marked by the neat, dusty puffs thrown up by his feet. He was bareheaded, his blondish hair bright in the sunlight, most of it brushed to one side. He was youngish, about twenty-four, his face tanned, his eyes darkish. He wore a pair of jeans and a dark blue shirt, which looked like a gas flame against the green of the cornfield. He carried a small black bag, a little bigger than a doctor's, and when he came up to the cars he spent a minute looking from one of them to another and then came on again, his gait still marked by those definite puffs of dust.

By now the congregation had stopped singing, and the men and women slowly moved away from the river and walked toward the tables where the food was waiting. The stranger came toward them, carrying that bag. The men and women picked up plates, but they kept looking over their shoulders, not talking, not eating, just turning their heads every minute or so.

I still stood by the river, shivering there, the wet hair curled against the side of my face. The stranger came up to the table, his eyes going over me as though I didn't exist at all, and I thought, *He's being polite.*

For a moment he looked at the life saver on that black pole which had written on it, TO TAKE THIS IS TO TAKE A LIFE. He put down his black bag, carefully leaving it next to his foot, and then he said to a boy who hung back, keeping a collapsible lawn chair between himself and the stranger, "Hey, you know what, I'll bet you like cars, don't you? I'll bet you like Corvettes."

"Yes, sir," said the boy.

The stranger smiled then, his face moving over the people again, but still not appearing to know I existed. He just looked around, his tanned face and dark eyes passing over the silent congregation. Then he picked up that black bag and moved a little closer to the table, his eyes set for a moment on the enormous jar of pickle limes, the things pale and a little dented, or pocked, like fingers that have been in water too long. Mrs. Jackson stood there, next to the table, and said, "I made them myself. Would you like one?"

"Well, don't mind if I do," he said, reaching out for the round, greenish fruit Mrs. Jackson offered. No one else ate. The stranger held the thing between two fingers and took neat, largish bites, obviously tasting the bitter juice, eating all of it, the soft skin, too. Then he took a clean bandana handkerchief out of his pocket and wiped his lips.

"Delicious," he said.

"Care for another?" said Mrs. Jackson.

"Maybe some other time," said the stranger. Then he looked around again and said, "It sure was lucky for me to find you people here together. Going to save us all some time. I don't get up this way often. I'm looking for used cars. I pay good prices, so long as value's involved. Good transportation is what I want, no more than that, Dodges, Fords, Chevys. Nothing foreign or European. Too hard to get parts. And buying them isn't even patriotic, is it?"

The wind blew harder now, and I stood for a moment, looking at him, at the black bag, and then I started walking in his direction. He stood up straight, his head turned toward the people, his eyes moving once in my direction. When I got there I reached into the jar and took one of those limes. My dress clung to me, showing pink skin. One of the women brought me a blanket, which I put over my shoulders.

He stood at the other side of the table from me with the food and plates and paper napkins between us, so I started moving around the table, too, his eyes now moving more and more toward me. The men and women stood around, not saying much as I went between them. Then I came around to the other side, my fingers shaking now.

When I stood in front of him I looked into his eyes, my head back now, the hair plastered to it.

"That man right over there," I said, "—you see, the reverend. He's the one with the wet pants. I'll tell you something. He's always wanted a Cadillac. But he's never had the money." Then I stood a little closer and whispered so only he could hear. "I'd love to get a look at his face when someone sells him a lemon."

My teeth chattered a little as I looked at him.

"Lemon?" he said, smiling now. "I only deal in quality. Ask anyone." But he kept right on looking at me.

"What? What?" said the men on the other side. "What she say?"

"I don't know," said another. "Something about a car."

Now the stranger looked around, lingering for a moment on each face, giving the impression he spoke directly to each one.

"I'll be at the hotel. Bring some value around and everything will be just fine."

The reverend came up from the end of the table, wet
from the waist down, the water dripping from his black pants
onto the dust, the light-brown dirt immediately turning dark,
the color of gingerbread.

Now the stranger brushed his hair back, the motion of it
quick and impatient, the bright lock of it falling back into
place anyway, as though it was there not to be brushed back so
much as to give the stranger something to do when he was
thinking.

"That girl, that Faith," said the reverend. "What did she
say?"

"She said the water was damned cold," said the stranger.

"There's nothing wrong with a little cold water," said the
reverend.

The stranger looked at him for a moment, saying nothing.

"Well," he said, "my business is cars. I'll be over in the
hotel for a day or two for anyone who wants to talk. Can't say
how long I'll be there for sure. Something might come up. If
you want to talk, all details are in confidence. Here."

His eyes came back to the reverend now.

"My card."

He held it out, offering it, and then said, now still looking
directly at the reverend, "Maybe you'd like something from
the city?"

The reverend took the card.

"You Ben Lunn?"

"That's right," said the stranger. "I'll be over at the hotel.
Drop by."

He looked at the congregation again, his glance going
over those men and women who stood at the table, some of
them holding empty plates or paper cups of lemonade with a
kind of hesitation, as though a bomb might go off. Then he said
to Mrs. Jackson, "May I have another of those things? Pickle
limes? The trouble is, once you start you can't stop. I guess I'm
just a weakling about things like that. No willpower." And
then, when Mrs. Jackson had given him another of those

green, puckered limes, he took it, again between two fingers, but this time he turned and started walking, the bitter juice sometimes dripping from his hand, his progression against that green corn marked by the steady puffs of dust turned up by his boots. He carried his black bag in his left hand, the thing obviously heavy, not even being swung back and forth, the dark valise or tool kit going right along next to his knee, like a full pail of water.

The men and women at the table watched him go, and then they filled their paper plates with cold meat and chicken and potato salad, first one man and then another going up to the pickle-lime jar, peering in with a kind of barely subdued curiosity, which had always been resisted before. But now they reached in and took one, some of them spearing a lime with two widely forked fingers. The reverend held the card, his thumb going over one of its sharp corners and making a small flicking sound. A member of the congregation said to him, "Well, the man looks like a Christian, don't he? That's something, isn't it?"

"Maybe," said the reverend, "but you got to remember where cars are concerned, there's no such thing as being *completely* Christian."

He flicked that card again.

"How much money do you think he's carrying?" said the reverend.

I had come west to this town to live with my aunt and uncle. But even before I came here, I had begun to think there was something that didn't like me or didn't want me. If I was made pretty, why, then, some of it was taken back, too, like my eyes: one of them is brown and the other is brown and gray.

My mother and I lived in Cleveland, without my father, who had disappeared into British Columbia. He had wanted to have a homestead there, even in the twentieth century, in 1967, but my mother didn't want to live in a pine hut or to eat moose all winter. My father went alone. And if my eyes were the first thing that made me think I was being dealt a hand others didn't have to play, why, then, this was the second. My mother got along, typing letters in the office of a place that sold magic tricks through the mail, and then she added to this by working in a self-service gas station, making change, on Friday and Saturday nights. On the weekday evenings she brought home magic tricks, and after we had washed the dishes, she made a handkerchief disappear, or a coin, or a little rabbit, the disappearing tricks being her favorite.

When I was eleven, I had a high fever. A few days after it was gone, I was watching my mother do a magic trick, one with a rope tied into a lot of knots, and when she used the wand and the rope straightened out, the room seemed to be filled with purple light. It pulsed for a moment and then I fell back, feeling ill. It was a while before I woke up, and when I did, I felt stiff, as though I had been trying to pick up something that was too heavy for me, and I didn't remember things very well. But in a few hours I was okay. My mother was holding my hand when I woke, telling me she loved me, and that this was a secret no one would have to know about.

The seizures got better, though, and soon I'd just have them at night, and then only after I'd been upset during the day. My mother and I went on as before, the two of us eating at the kitchen table and my mother taking from her handbag a new trick, or one of the jokes her employer sold through the mail, too, a bag of "Certified Belly-Button Lint" or a rubber bag that made a noise when you sat down on it.

One night, when I was fourteen, my mother brought home a trick, but instead of showing it to me, she put it aside and said it was time to "have a talk." For a while my mother went through our finances, telling me how much we paid for rent, lights, food, and then she put out on the table what money she had for the week, the lead-colored coins and frayed paper showing how hard she had worked to get them. She told me it would be better for both of us if I went to live with my aunt and uncle in California, where there was "fresh air" just like in British Columbia.

Both of us believed that things had somehow conspired against us, or had singled us out for a special difficulty, but we believed, too, that it wasn't permanent and that our chance was coming, if we just knew how to recognize it. So, when my mother said she thought I should go, she raised an eyebrow, as though to say this might be a chance and that I would be a fool not to take it.

When we were packing my bag, she took me into her bedroom and opened the closet where she kept the magic tricks, all of them lined up on the shelves inside, and when she took down the first one, she said, "I don't want you to think there is such a thing as magic, either." And as she brought down one and then another, she explained each gimmick, showing me false bottoms or hollow tubes, or elastic cords attached to cups (these to make a handkerchief disappear), and when she had explained them all, she spread them out on the bed and said, "All right. Pick. Take the ones you want. Go on."

My aunt and uncle's house sat against a hillside on which there grew grass, eucalyptus trees, and wildflowers. The house was two stories and had flower boxes along the front. There were three derricklike towers on the hillside, too, each made of wood blackened with creosote, the cross supports looking like X's, one piled on top of another. There was a windmill at the top of each tower, and when there was a breeze, the windmills turned so fast as to become just a blur. The house needed paint, and the boards of the porch were so dry you could pull the nails out of them with your fingers.

My aunt and uncle had met in the thirties at a technical school for the blind, and then they moved to the farm which my uncle had inherited, and which in the forties and fifties had been run by a hired man, but which was now run by my cousin, Paul. It was a beef lot, a calving operation. There were pens in front of the house, all of them made of tubular aluminum panels, that were moved according to how much corral space we needed.

My aunt and uncle's church had been founded recently. Each woman dressed in white and wore handkerchiefs over her hair, and the men, on Sundays anyway, wore black pants and white shirts. In addition to the days when the church had baptisms, there were Sundays, and when the weather was good, the long tables were set up behind the church then, too, and on them, over the paper tablecloths, there were platters of fried chicken, cold brisket, and potato salad, all under small, umbrellalike things that were covered with gauze. There were pickles in cut-glass dishes and pitchers of Kool-Aid, fruit punch, and lemonade. After the service the men and women ate separately, sitting down at the long tables in the shade, the men in their black pants and white shirts suggesting a handful of mixed-up checkers.

On the first Sunday I went to church, the reverend took my hands in his and said, "Faith. Welcome." He was tall and heavy in the shoulders, with fuzzy, short-cropped brown hair, and he held my hands for a long time. He looked into my eyes and I glanced away, blushing, but still he didn't let go of my hands.

When I first came to stay with my aunt and uncle, I got sick in the night. I woke, knowing I had made that repetitive *huh, huh, huh,* and I lay there, thinking that the light of the room still seemed odd, a little purple, while I tried to figure out what that sound was (the *we, we, we)* of the windmills. Against my cheeks and forehead there was the blind touch of my aunt's and uncle's fingers. After a while I said, "Please. This gets better. I'm just not used to being here. That's all. My getting sick is a secret. Please. Don't tell anyone. It's not that bad."

"Hush, Faith," said my uncle. "Hush. Don't worry. It's between us."

"Who would we tell?" said my aunt.

"The reverend," I said.

When I felt better, I got up and looked out the window, beyond which there were the pens for the cattle and the drive that went between them, running into the distance. It was quiet in the house even though the artificial-insemination salesman was downstairs, talking to Paul about new genetic strains. Less fat, more muscle. I opened the closet and took down the magic tricks my mother had given me. I practiced them, getting them right, and finally it seemed as though things really did disappear under the touch of my fingers. There was a mirror on the inside of my closet door, and when I was lonely, or hoping for my chance, I stood in front of it and did the tricks I knew, one after another, the handkerchief vanishing, the coins disappearing, my eyes a little wide with the effort, not only to do the tricks perfectly, but with the regret that I lived without someone I trusted enough to show the tricks to. The closest I had come to being loved was when my mother had walked in the door and said, "Faith, what do you think? I've got a new one. Money magic, you know, coins and bills. We'll get to it right after dinner."

During the week the reverend kept a hardware and welding shop, and sometimes when I went to town, he'd be sitting on a box in front of the shop, watching me. When I was sixteen or seventeen, he stopped me and said, "Faith, I know what you're thinking. You're tempting me with it. Just look at the way you walk. You're in danger, Faith."

One afternoon, when Paul had taken my aunt and uncle to town, the reverend came to the house. It was hot and I gave him a drink on the front porch. The cattle moved in their pens, lowing in the heat. The reverend looked at me, and after a while I said, "I better go inside," and he went right on looking at me, as though he were angry. Then he got up and left, saying as he went, "I'm watching you. I understand you like no one else."

The church believed not only in gospel but in "technology," too, and it had helped Paul build the towers. Now the windmills produced electricity which the power company bought, sending each month a check for $9.50, or $13.20, or $6.20, and once, after a storm in the springtime, they even sent one for $21.50. Paul brought the checks from the mailbox, and when he came into the house he pinned them to the wallboard, along with the coupons for the supermarket, and turned away, saying nothing, quietly facing the thirty years it would take to pay off the cost of building the windmills in the first place: so he stuck them to the wall and turned away, the small shove of the pins coming no longer as a matter of commerce anymore but as one of faith, just as when he knelt to pray or sang in his booming voice, which made every piece of wood in the church hum.

There is no more lonely sound in the world than a slowly working windmill, and while I washed the dishes I listened to it. The reverend insisted that my skirts be made longer and that I braid my hair and keep it under cover. Paul watched me at home to make sure I did as I was told, but even so I kept lipstick hidden in a tree trunk and sometimes I used it, looking at myself in a small mirror I had bought with money saved from the housekeeping money. The directions on the lemonade can say to add four cans of water, but I put in five. Lemonade was sixty-nine cents, and if you stretched it one can more, that was thirteen cents.

I lost a year of school when my father left for British Columbia and I lost another when I came to California, so when I was nineteen, I was in my last year. The school was a large consolidated one, made of yellowish brick, attended by young men and women who lived on farms or in the towns spread up and down the valley. The girls' athletic building was two stories high, made of that same yellow brick, and when I walked into the first floor there was the odor of soap and steam and the sound of the girls' voices echoing off the tiled showers. There was a long row of gray lockers and a narrow bench in front of them. Girls came out of the shower room, their breasts moving as they walked, their bare feet leaving a long line of wet prints. They toweled their hair with a rough, nervous movement, showing their shaved underarms and emerging from the warm, whitish steam, their backs and their shaved legs pink from the heat of the water.

In the evenings, while I washed the dishes and heard that steady, pulsing squeak from the windmills, Paul and my aunt and uncle watched the news in the living room with Paul saying, "Chancellor's got on a new suit tonight, bluish with a red tie . . . looks like a million dollars. . . . Now there's a picture of a ship, smoke coming out of the side, helicopters around it. Chancellor again, holding his papers. Listen." After the news Paul went to look over the latest *Scientific American*, or something else that had come in the mail, and my aunt and uncle sat in the dark living room, reading their Braille Bibles or sometimes writing a letter, the *tip, tip, tip* of the typewriter going there in the dark, too.

On Sundays I helped my aunt into her clothes, brushed her hair, hearing the electric snap of it in the dry air, and then I braided it and pinned the braids on top of her head so they looked like a crown, although one that was the color of a galvanized tub. The car, that blue, square Pontiac, just a few years old, was parked in front of the porch, and my uncle was on the right-hand side and Paul was behind the wheel. The wood of the porch railing and the banister was so weathered the grain of it was raised and looked like strands of gray cord. I helped my aunt across the porch and down the wooden steps, her brown fingers touching the banister as they did every Sunday, her fingers first sensing that it was there and then reaching out, doing this exactly as though the world, or at least this piece of wood, had been invented again for her each Sunday morning.

The reverend watched me as he preached in that church with the poured concrete floor and the fluorescent lights overhead, the glow of them coming with a slight purple quality, which made me think that I might be getting sick. Outside, when we ate, he watched me, and when he had a chance, when no one was looking, he brushed against me. When I went to town, I stayed away from his shop, but sometimes I had to pass it.

Once, on a weekday evening, when the town was quiet and hot, with only the buzzing of insects around the outside lamps, he asked me to come into the shop, to the back, but I said, "No. Please."

"Come on, Faith. You step back here."

"No," I said. "I've got to get home."

"No one will know, Faith. I've got something for you."

"I'm late," I said.

"Faith, come to the back of the shop. Come on, now. It wouldn't hurt. I can promise you that. Just step inside."

I shook my head.

"What's wrong, Faith? You don't have to be afraid. I understand you like no one else."

"I'm late," I said.

"Your aunt and uncle can wait," said the reverend. "I'll call them. Everything will be just fine."

"No," I said. "No. Please."

I left him there, the clapboards of the building behind him, the window of the hardware store having a few tools and copper fittings in it, the street before him quiet. I turned to look over my shoulder and he was still staring, trembling a little, his eyes wide now.

At night I sat in my room, thinking about it. I shook my head, trying to forget it, or to think about something else, but I kept coming back to it. I was scared as I sat there, looking at the ceiling. Soon, I started getting sick again, first just once, but then more often, once every two weeks and then once a week. I woke with my aunt and uncle sitting in my room, their fingers going over me, their voices soft as they said, "Faith, Faith. We're here now. Faith."

But I went on worrying about it, afraid now that it would happen during the day. I woke in the morning, watching for that purple light, or the change in the way things appeared before it was about to happen. And I was superstitious about it, too, thinking if I just tied my shoes with small, tight bows, or walked down the street without touching the cracks, or if I always let the door close in a certain way, why, then, I'd have a chance. But I got sick during the day, too. I was walking in front of the reverend's shop, where he sat on that box, watching me, not hissing exactly, but calling to me with his eyes. Then I got sick.

In the evening the reverend and the elders of the church came to the house and sat at the kitchen table with my aunt and uncle and Paul, all of them talking in hushed voices. They asked how often I had been sick, and my aunt and uncle told them.

I hadn't been baptized before, and they thought it would help if I were baptized now. When I was alone with my aunt and uncle, I said, "It was a secret between us. You didn't have to say it had happened before. It was a *secret.*"

"Hush, Faith," my uncle said.

"You didn't have to tell," I said.

"Hush," said my uncle.

"The reverend knows best," my aunt said.

"No, no," I said. "That's where you're wrong."

"We'll have no insolence," said my uncle. "It's been decided."

I went into my room and sat down, listening to the sound of those windmills. Then I took down the magic tricks, doing one and then another, staring at the mirror, thinking, *Maybe he is only trying to scare me. Maybe he won't do anything.*

But then the day came when we turned off the road and went through the field, along those two ruts with the grass in the middle, toward the river where the reverend was waiting, saying, "Faith, the time has come."

So, on the first night the stranger was in town, the reverend sat on that box in front of his hardware and welding-repair, the door to his shop open behind him, the long, varnished plywood drawers of the store gleaming in the overhead fixtures, the contents of them, the carriage bolts and sheet metal and wood screws, washers, hinges and locks, plumbing fittings and solder all giving invisible substance to the place. The reverend drank a lemonade and sat in the heat of the evening, the moths fluttering around the overhead light, his eyes turning every now and then from the cracked sidewalk in front of him to the veranda of the hotel.

Paul and I went to town after dark and parked head-in, between the white lines painted out from the curb. Paul walked over to the reverend's shop, which was a hundred yards from the hotel. The hotel's veranda was dim, illuminated through the hotel's windows and having about it the air of an otherwise dark kitchen lighted by an open icebox door. The stranger was there, his presence revealed by the slow movement of the chair he rocked in and the thumbnail-shaped sweep of orange, which came from the cigarette he held in his hand. From time to time the stranger stopped rocking and reached to the floor, from which he picked up a half-pint bottle and drank from it, not with haste, or concealment, but with a short, practical movement.

It wasn't just being held underwater that made me go to see the stranger that first night, but other things, too, like my father's leaving for British Columbia, my mother's not making enough money to keep me, the sound of that windmill, the Sundays by the river, and the flies crawling on the white gauze over the fried chicken, not to mention those bitter pickled limes.

Usually in the evening it is quiet in the center of town, where those two roads come together at that Y-shaped intersection, in the triangle of which there is a small park and on the sides of which there are the hotel, the luncheonette, the court, jail, the two banks and shops and stores which are the town's lifeblood. To all appearances it was quiet, although there were a lot more cars than usual parked at the curb, Fords, Chevrolets, Dodges, Plymouths, most of them a little older than the ones the people here usually drove, which cars, until recently, had been sitting in a back lot or in an out-of-the-way garage.

The windows of the shops and stores were dim, filled with a bluish light, and in the grocery the neat pyramid of grapefruit looked like a pile of cannonballs. The moths around the lights made it seem as though there were a fruitless snow, one that kept falling but never piled up. I passed the veranda of the hotel, and out of the clutter of empty chairs there the stranger said, "Hello, Faith. It's a hot night, isn't it? Why don't you rest awhile?"

I climbed up, feeling the heat. There was a chair next to him and I sat in it, swinging back and forth now, too, and when I spoke, I kept my voice down.

"I meant what I said about sticking him with a lemon," I said.

"Did you?" he said.

"That's right," I said. I stopped for a moment. "They didn't have to dunk me."

He rocked back and forth now.

"They *didn't*," I said, turning toward him. "Can you tell me otherwise?"

He shrugged now.

"They didn't have to do that to me," I said.

"Here," he said, "would you like a drink?"

"I don't know," I said, "I never had one."

"Go on," he said. "It's dark here. No one can see you."

"I don't care if they can," I said.

He passed the smallish bottle over and I tasted liquor. It felt warm and good, like when my mother did a magic trick.

"I'd be pretty mad, too, if they stuck me in the river," he said.

"It's not just that," I said.

"What is it, then?" he asked.

"Lots of things. My father went to British Columbia and my mother couldn't keep me and . . ." I turned toward the lighted window so he could see my face. "I don't know . . . lots of things. Everyone says the reverend knows best."

The stranger reached over for that small bottle.

"Not so fast," I said.

We sat in the dark, hearing the squeak of the runners on the rocking chair.

"They didn't have to dunk me," I said.

"No, I guess, not," said the stranger. "The reverend sure looks like a man who wants to be buried facedown."

"Why's that?" I said.

"Oh, you know," said the stranger, "so his enemies will have to kiss his ass on their way to hell."

I laughed a little in the dark and held out the bottle.

"Well?" I said.

"Well, what?"

"Can you sell him a lemon?" I said.

He exhaled and reached over for the bottle and said, "I don't know."

"All right," I said, "you're afraid. I should have guessed it."

"I didn't say I was afraid—although, to be honest, trading

cars in these towns . . . well, you'd have to be crazy not to be careful."

He sat quietly in the dark, looking at the sky beyond the moths.

"Oh, God," I said, "I'm wasting my time. Good night."

There was that unconcealed, frank upward movement of that half-pint bottle. He went back to that easy rocking, saying nothing for a moment, his dark figure swinging back and forth, contemplative, shrewd, the motion there not calm so much as suggesting something being wound up, like a watch.

"Well, it sure is a pretty night. Look, you can see Orion, the bear star, Andromeda. . . ."

Now I walked to the steps of the veranda.

"All right," he said, "wait. Just wait a minute, will you? Listen. Can you drive a car?"

I turned back to him now, the bugs blowing behind me like snow.

"I need someone to show me the back roads around here," he said.

"Well, well," I said. "Well, well. You're all business, aren't you?"

"Not all," he said, and smiled.

"Are you offering me a job?" I said.

"Yes," he said. "I don't know the roads."

Now I smiled and said, "I'll think it over."

His chair stopped rocking as he leaned forward, looking into the steady, purplish light from the streetlamp. He sat quietly on the veranda, not rocking now or doing anything at all, but looking at me. I didn't like that purplish light, but I went on smiling.

Then I turned and went back through the park and past the reverend's shop, where the men stood outside, one saying to another, "I got a Chevy, you know, been sitting out by the garage a few years. I guess it's got to be worth something, don't it . . . ?"

There were some other men, too, who leaned against the wall of the shop, the yellowish clapboards there covered with a new cheap and shiny paint. The men were in their middle twenties, and during the spring, summer, and fall they worked on farms here, and in the winters they went to Oregon, where they worked in the potato cellars, lifting hundred-pound sacks. Now they looked across the park at the hotel, one of them saying, "Wasn't there an Armenian or something came through here a few years back, selling cars? Bob Marcher bought one. Block was cracked and he didn't get more than a week's use out of it."

"Yeah, it was Marcher," said a second.

"Well, I tell you this," said the first, "if this guy cheats anybody, he's going to have the chance to wish he'd never done it. That's not a threat. That's a promise."

The reverend sat on his box, listening and glancing to the hotel, saying once, "I wonder where he keeps the cars he wants to trade. Wonder if he's got a Cadillac. Anybody know?"

I waited in the car until Paul came away from the men. He walked across the street, and when he got into the car and sat behind the wheel, he said, his voice excited now, "You don't think that stranger is going to try to trade with the reverend, do you?"

"He's thinking it over," I said.

The next day Ben Lunn got up early and walked the fifteen steps from the hotel to the luncheonette next door, where he sat at the back, facing the counter and the entire place, waiting calmly while the platter of scrambled eggs and cinnamon-colored ham was put down before him. He ate slowly, chewing, looking out into the street. Then he took a stroll around the park, stopping in front of the jail where there is supposed to be an apparition in the window. A man who killed a woman spent six months in a cell at the top, and when he was finally taken out and hanged, his face began to appear in the glass of the cell's window. You can't spend any time here without someone pointing it out to you, and when the light is just right, a man's face *can* be seen in the window. When people go to the Methodist Church in town, they park at the jail, each one of them stepping from their car and looking up at that window, trying to see the face there, as though acknowledging the troubles of this world before going on to hear about the beauties of the next.

So Ben Lunn looked at the window, too, having had it pointed out to him by a boy in the park, and then he turned and went back to the veranda of the hotel, where he took a chair and started reading the paper. And as he sat there, people came to town and looked at him, however discreetly (from behind a shop window or over a bag of groceries), the people who were interested in making a few dollars doing so with the fear that he might vanish, like a genie back into a bottle.

Mrs. Anson was the first one to do more than just look at him. She lived outside of town in a big house, the clapboards of which had weathered to the color of ashes. Mrs. Anson's husband died and now she kept the house with a kind of greed, knocking her tin cans flat and tying them into bales, storing them in the barn next to the stacked and neatly tied bundles of aluminum trays TV dinners come in.

Mrs. Anson wore a black skirt and a black blouse and a man's black hat (which she must have seen in a fashion magazine twenty-five or thirty or even thirty-five years ago, when women in Paris were wearing them). She owned a Dodge, a newish one, which she drove herself, and at dusk on the third evening, Mrs. Anson drove up and parked directly in front of it and got out, making her way onto that dimly lighted porch, where she stood opposite that dark figure and those empty rocking chairs and said, "Hey, you. I hear you're offering money for cars. I got one at my place. Ford. Good rubber."

"Ma'am?" said the stranger.

"You want it or don't you?" she said. "My name's Anson. You ask anybody where I live."

The others came after that, one man at a time walking up to the veranda and just standing, not taking one of those chairs, and then the stranger and the man in a work shirt or overalls went up to the stranger's room in the hotel, where they talked for a while. Later, the man emerged, coming downstairs and slinking away from the hotel, not wanting to be seen, if only because nothing had been definitely resolved and there was still the possibility of falling into some unseen and embarrassing trap. But they kept right on coming, climbing those steps to the veranda and then to the room at the top of the hotel.

Ben Lunn called in the morning and asked if I'd come to the hotel, and when I pulled up in front of the veranda, he was sitting in that same rocking chair, looking at me over the paper. I opened the passenger's door for him, swinging it outward like an invitation. There were people in the street who stopped and stared, but soon they went on with their business, since they obviously believed a man who was buying used cars didn't have much time for anything else, and that even if he did, the people here, under the circumstances, were willing to bend propriety a little for the sake of commerce.

"All right," Ben said, "Mrs. Anson's. Do you know where she lives?"

That black bag of his sat on the floor, by his boots, and he put his hand on the back of the seat, about three or four inches from my shoulder. His hand was tanned, strong, and had greenish-blue veins on the back.

Mrs. Anson sat on the porch, waiting for us.

"Car's in the barn," said Mrs. Anson.

He went into it, carrying that black bag. I walked in after him, the dust moving around the hem of my skirt.

"Can I help?" I said.

He shook his head.

The light came in between the boards and fell in slats across the ground. The car was black, slumped down on flat tires, which had the quality of an old man without his teeth. He worked quickly now, taking things from his bag and then leaning over the fender, sometimes with both of his legs in the air. It was quiet and private in the barn. I looked down at my white dress, the light falling across the cloth in stripes like gold foil.

"Well," I said, "have you thought about it?"

He went on working, a tool clattering now.

"I haven't decided anything," he said.

"Look," I said, "I liked you when I first saw you, even when I was shivering there by the river. I wouldn't ask if I didn't like you."

He dropped a tool.

"I wasn't planning on cheating anybody," he said. "Not the reverend or anyone else."

"It's not cheating," I said, "It's giving someone what he deserves. If someone acts like a son of a bitch long enough, he's just inviting someone to come along and give him what he's got coming. Isn't that right?"

He looked at me and then down at his black case, where he began to search for something.

"Of course it's right," I said. "You know it. Anyway, one time isn't going to hurt, is it? You must know something about cars that look good but aren't, otherwise you'd already have gone broke."

He was silent for a while, but then he sighed and said, "Does the reverend trade cars?"

"Him? He wouldn't know the difference between a Chevrolet and a Ford."

He brought his head out from under the hood and looked at me.

"Well," I said, "all right. Maybe he's sold a car or two. What difference does that make?"

Then he went on working, his movements quick now, taking tools and an instrument with a dial from his bag and finally a can of something he sprayed into the carburetor. When the engine started he got out and listened for a while, putting a stethoscope against the water hoses. He had a compressor in that bag, a small one, and he plugged it into the cigarette lighter and then filled the tires with air. Mrs. Anson came into the barn, slipping through those slats of light and saying, "I'll be damned."

"Are those original miles?" said Ben.

"Yes," said Mrs. Anson.

"All right," said Ben. "Sixty dollars."

"Well, I . . ."

"Seventy-five," said Ben.

Mrs. Anson looked from him to the black car, the dust and hay still on the roof and trunk.

"Well, mister, you just bought yourself a car," said Mrs. Anson.

On the front porch Ben passed over the money, neat twenties and a ten and a five. Mrs. Anson showed us a photograph, in which she and her husband stood in front of the car.

"We used to drive out at night, you know, in the moonlight. . . ." said Mrs. Anson as she signed the papers and handed them over. "Well, it's yours now."

Ben put the papers in his pocket and carried that black bag out to the Pontiac. Then, when we sat there together, he said, "All right. All right. What's next? Skrips? Parker? Where are they?" But as we went along those back roads, passing those houses here and there on that brown, grassy land, he stared ahead, pushing that hair out of his face and saying, "How do you know the reverend wants a Cadillac?"

"Everybody knows," I said.

We went to Skrips's, Parker's, Baily's, Marshall's, and Brown's, at each place Ben getting out of the car with that bag and approaching the cars he had agreed to look at, throwing open the hoods, sampling the oil with a stick, looking at the black, ancient crud there and maybe even rubbing a little between his fingers, standing waist deep in weeds or in those sheds or barns, where the dust rose like billows of smoke when he sat on one of the car seats. Then he slammed the doors or hoods and walked into the yard, where he stood next to a porch or in the shade of a tree and said to the man or woman who had been watching him work, "I'm sorry. I had something else in mind. Much obliged for your time." But even so, by the end of the day, he owned not only Mrs. Anson's black Ford, but a yellow Chevrolet which had belonged to Mike Wallis, and a red Buick, a Roadmaster, which had been owned by Robert Van, in each case Ben taking money from his wallet and counting out the green twenties and tens and fives, eighty-five dollars to Wallis and a hundred to Robert Van, their brown hands outstretched to catch the bills.

In the late afternoon we drove back toward town, but when we came to the reservoir road, I turned into it and stopped. The road was lined with trees, poplars, all planted in two long windbreaks, one on each side of the road. It reminded me of the roads I'd read about in France, the ones along which Napoleon had planted trees so his troops could march in the shade. The road was cool and the ground was dappled with light. At the end of the road, about a mile away, there was the lake, which was filled with blue water and the reflections of clouds.

We got out and started to walk. It was cooling off now and I wore a jacket over my dress. Both of us were glad to be away from those barns and dusty garages and back lots where we had looked at the cars, and as we went, in the cool, trembling shadows, I looked at him from time to time, just enjoying walking along now, a little tense, but otherwise all right. Up ahead the water flashed in the afternoon sunlight. When we got to the beach, we sat down next to the slight wash of the waves.

"How are you going to make money off those cars?" I said.

He turned and looked at me for a long time.

"I fix them up and sell them to students in Berkeley," he said.

"Oh?" I said. "They pay well?"

"I do all right," he said.

"Soon you're going to leave, aren't you?" I said.

"Yes," he said.

"I can't believe anyone can just get in a car and drive out of here."

"Why not?" he said.

I shrugged.

"I don't know. I guess I'd need someone to go with," I said, blushing hard. "Look, do you see the clouds there? What do you see in them?"

"Oh, horses and bears," he said. "A dragon."

"Where?" I said.

"Over there," he said, "see? Right there."

As we sat there, I said, "I've started trusting you, you know that?"

"Listen," he said, "I—"

"Don't argue with me," I said.

He turned and looked at me.

"I can see it in your eyes," I said. "It's all right to trust you."

I lay back now on the ground, feeling the weight of the sun. Then I said, "You wait here. I'm going to go over there behind that tree for a moment." And then I got up and walked away, reaching into my pocket for a gimmick I had with me. It was a small cup with a piece of elastic attached to it, one used to make a handkerchief disappear. I pinned it to my clothes and came back and said, "Here. Watch. I take this handkerchief like this and stuff it into my hand . . . see? . . ."

I watched his face as I made the handkerchief vanish, his eyes widening as it did so, his expression not so much shaken by the magic, but looking precisely as though he had been searching for something, or more accurately, someone, and had just found her. He looked uneasy, too, that she might disappear on him, just like the handkerchief.

He laughed now, but the laughter was a little nervous.

"How did you do that?" he said.

"Oh, I've had some time to practice," I said. "Would you like to see another?"

I reached into his thick, sandy hair and brought out a quarter, the thing bright in the afternoon sun. He laughed again, looking into my eyes, and I let him see that one was a different color from the other. Then I sat down again and we looked at the water and the shapes in the clouds, wispy, bearded horses and ragged ships.

We started walking back between those trees, the afternoon wind making the leaves shimmer.

"Are you going to buy any more cars here?" I said.

"I guess not," he said. "I guess I'm fresh out of money. Money goes through my fingers like I don't know what."

"You can save," I said. "This spring I saved three dollars by putting an extra can of water in the lemonade. It adds up."

"Three dollars," he said, looking at me.

"You'd be surprised how it adds up. Because lemonade is sixty-nine cents, and if you stretch it one can further, that's thirteen cents."

"That's right, isn't it?" he said and reached down and took my hand in his.

The afternoon breeze was cool and smelled of the trees.

"Are you going to do what I asked?" I said.

"Well," he said, "I can tell you this. It isn't going to do me much good when word gets around I've been selling . . . less than quality."

I smiled then.

"No promises," he said. "I've been beat before."

"Maybe you'll get lucky," I said.

"When it comes to cars," he said, "luck is the last thing you want to depend upon."

It didn't take long for word to get around that cars had changed hands, although the precise amounts of the sales were a little vague. Now, in the evening, when Ben sat on the veranda of the hotel, the men who approached him did so with as much stealth as before, or maybe even more so, since this group had actually seen money, or anyway had heard about it, and so they didn't come with curiosity so much as the desire to make a quick, clean killing. They parked in the side streets and walked up to the hotel, all of them coming out of the shadows and approaching that dark figure in the chair, the cigarette in his hand making the curved sweep as he rocked. The talk of makes of cars, mileage, rubber, and transmissions drifted into the street, not to mention the jokes about rear ends filled with sawdust, banana peels, eggplants, STP, and janitor's compound, these last suggested to see if the mentioning of such things came as a surprise or not. At the end, though, there was Ben's voice saying, "What do you take me for? I've been buying cars here all day. You've heard what I've paid, haven't you? Maybe I'm interested in selling a car now. What about that man across the square there, sitting on a box? The reverend there?"

"I heard he wants a Cadillac," said a man in the dark.

"Is that right? Well, I got a Cadillac. I don't know if I want to part with it, though."

But that was all. Then the men who had come up to the veranda went back into the night, now slinking away with the air of men who have waited too long. They went into the shadows and across the park chastising themselves for letting easy money slip through their fingers. Not one of them failed to stop by the hardware, where the reverend sat on his box, drinking a lemonade and being surrounded by the flutter of moths attracted to the light.

I had come to town like everyone else, and after I had spent time in the park, or walking up and down the main street looking into the shop windows, I went past the reverend, too.

"Faith," he said, "that boy's up to no good. Do you hear me? I'm not going to let you slip through my fingers, Faith. Do you understand? He's got a tendril around you now, Faith, can't you feel it pull?"

Then I went home and got into my bed, where I looked out the window, seeing the black night sky and thinking about that shape rocking back and forth, the dark veranda marked by a streamer of orange.

He left in the morning, first driving Mrs. Anson's black Ford to the city, the hood and roof of it covered with droppings from the bats that lived in Mrs. Anson's barn. He returned in the morning, on the bus, to ferry back the next car, that Chevrolet he had bought from Mike Wallis, and then finally he drove off for good in that faded, Rustoleum-colored Roadmaster, which had belonged to Robert Van. I watched that Buick disappear toward that mountain range between us and the coast, the galvanized tin color of the exhaust mixing with the sky. Then I went home and stood at the kitchen window, seeing the windmills and hearing that *we, we, we, we, we* as they turned in the light breeze.

After he'd been gone a week, I told myself that he'd be back soon, but after he'd been gone two weeks I wasn't so sure anymore, and then it occurred to me that even if he did come back, how could things go farther than they already had? What would happen when I told him that I got sick at night? What then?

After the heat of each day I went to town, seeing the swallows come out of their nests, which sat like small, primitive jugs under the eaves of the jail. Then I watched the road. And, as each day passed, as I began to get more desperate, it became apparent that there were a large number of strands of my life, like being abandoned and my sickness, and that these were being braided together with other strands, like having a chance to get away, and that for better or worse they were all tied together in one knot, which was the reverend buying the wrong car.

Ben came back about six weeks later, in the middle of summer. It was evening when he arrived, that hour when the houses and buildings around the center of town were beginning to look black against the pale horizon and when trees were shaggy against the sky. Then you think of some soft, warm kiss on a porch or barely hidden place. The houses seem cozy, the kitchens sizzling with dinner, and in the yards there are sheets of buttery light from the windows.

He was driving a black car, and it came into town with an even, constant purring of the engine, the sound itself subdued and appropriate to those dark shapes of the houses against the sky, not to mention the voices that floated away from the porches and verandas, the words husky and intimate. The black car was shiny, so much so as to make the paint seem still wet.

In town the shops were closed, and in that hour before the moths came out the street was filled with warm August air. The car coasted up to the hotel, the engine running in that smooth putter, and as it stopped, there was a definite odor of new paint hanging around it like a cloud. The engine died and the lights went out, the glow of them turning a smoky color on the wall of the hotel before disappearing. Ben sat at the wheel, the fingers of one hand draped over it, his eyes dark in the half light of the evening, and even as I stood there, looking through the windshield, I had to think twice before realizing where the car had come from.

"Hi, Faith," he said. "Beautiful night, isn't it?"

"Yes," I said. "Yes, it is. I'm glad to see you. What's this?"

"Oh," he said, "I thought Mrs. Anson might like to have her car back. It's fixed up some. What do you think?"

For a moment I waited, looking at him, neither one of us saying a thing.

"I can't see how selling this car back to Mrs. Anson is going to do any good at all."

He turned and blinked at me.

"Well?" I said. "How is it going to do a thing?"

But he just blinked at me again and said, "Do you suppose you could follow me out to Mrs. Anson's?"

It was almost dark when we pulled into the yard, and the house was dark, although the kitchen was lighted, the bales of tin cans and aluminum TV trays stacked along the front porch. When Mrs. Anson saw the car in the yard she came out to the porch, where she stood with a white apron around her skirt, her hair thick and pulled into a braid. The bugs flicked around the porch light, the shadows of them busy on the floor. Mrs. Anson's dog came out of the kitchen, too, and looked at the car, which puttered into the yard and stopped, the dust swirling around it in delicate curves, like the front of a sleigh runner.

Then Mrs. Anson came down from the porch, not saying a word, at least not then, her fingers touching the paint and the chrome, her legs moving through the dust, the bugs around her head like confetti. She looked at the tires, too, which were new and shiny, and inside there were seat covers, plaid ones like the original cloth.

Ben got out of the car and brought with him the papers and the keys and handed them over, or at least offered them, and Mrs. Anson said, "I've still got the seventy-five you gave me to begin with. I've got another hundred and twenty-five. That makes two hundred. Is that enough?"

"Yes," said Ben, "that'll do."

Mrs. Anson returned to the house and rummaged around

while Ben and I stood in the yard, looking at the stars. Then she came back, now standing in the last slow tendrils of dust, counting out the money, the bills and even some silver dollars, which were the color of her hair.

"Listen," I said, when we were back in my uncle's Pontiac, "I don't see you making any money on this. You paid seventy-five for the car and sold it for two hundred. But that doesn't count expenses, doesn't count the hotel, the bus, and meals, not to mention what it took to get the car to look like that. That takes money, doesn't it?"

"Yes," he said, "it takes money."

Then he sat in the car, looking out the window at the dark fields and the sky beyond them, although after a while he reached out and put his hand on the seat, and I put mine on top of it.

Word got around fast, too, since Mrs. Anson didn't wait more than a few hours before she drove the Ford to town, going around the three sides of the park, the car gliding along like some smooth phantom. Now when I went to town, Mike Wallis and Robert Van said to me, "Faith, did that boy say when he was coming back?"

The reverend sat on that box in front of his store, saying to the men who now stood around him, "Boys, you know how you kill a bear, don't you? One of these rogues that are always getting into people's garbage and making a mess? You take one of these five-gallon cans and cut a hole in the top, just a little smaller than the bear's head. You put a piece of pipe in the ground and attach the can to the pipe. You put some honey in the can and wait. That bear will shove his head in there no matter what, and then he can't get it out. That's when you shoot it. Yeah, the bear just can't stay away from that can. Do you think that boy's got any money left at all?" His voice was flat, uninflected, but still having that energetic combination of wrath and commerce.

The men who worked on farms and in potato cellars leaned against the wall next to the reverend, their faces inscrutable, their arms crossed now, each one waiting, suspicious.

A week later the people in the park and in front of the courthouse and jail, or those hanging around the luncheonette and hotel, heard the faintly antiquated but nevertheless constant purr of an engine. This time it was the green Chevrolet that had belonged to Mike Wallis, and just like that black Ford, it had been resurrected, the paint dark green now, the sides and hood covered with long, shiny streaks of chrome, the tires new and as shiny as licorice. The car pulled up to the hotel and stopped.

A man on the veranda of the hotel said, "Someone better call Faith Wheeler. I guess she'll have to follow him out to Mike Wallis's."

When we got there, Wallis was already standing in the yard, his hand outstretched and already holding money, his eyes set on the Chevrolet as it turned into his yard, and when Ben got out of it, Wallis said, "I've been thinking it over. Can't imagine why I ever sold that car in the first place. Here's your eighty-five dollars. How about a hundred more? What do you say? Have you got the papers? You know, I started feeling bad about selling that car the moment I did it." And two days later, when Robert Van saw that Red Buick, now bright as a fire engine, pull into his yard, he said, "Here. Take the damn money. Give me the keys."

After that last car was sold back to Robert Van, Ben returned to town, still carrying that black bag, and then he went into the hotel and rented a room. In the evening he sat on the veranda, rocking in one of those chairs while a lemonade from the luncheonette stood on the floor beside him. He sat in the shadows, not talking much, aside from saying to the people who stopped by to see him, "Well, hot as a furnace, isn't it? You've got a car for sale, you say? Well, good luck. A De Soto? Isn't that something?" Then he went back to that steady, patient rocking, the stroke of it neither fast nor slow.

In the early evening the colors of the houses and storefronts seemed to reappear after the harsh light of day, the blues, reds, oranges, and whites now having a soothing, dusty quality. Soon, against the gray and yellow sky, there were the black shapes of houses, and the air was filled with husky, conversational voices.

It was about eight-thirty when the reverend walked across the park to see Ben. Before that the reverend had been standing in the doorway of his shop, his arms across his chest. The traffic around that three-sided park had diminished, and the lights in the shops had gone out, one by one. Then there was only that dusty light and the peaceful air of evening. The reverend came away from his shop door, his legs, in those black pants, moving like enormous scissors, and as he came there was above him the face of the clock on the courthouse, which looked like a yellow moon. In the shadows there were men who stood quietly, each one of whom had told his wife not to put a plate on the table. The reverend came across the park now, his hands swinging at his sides. Then he stopped in front of the hotel.

"Pssst, hey," he said. "You."

Now Ben rocked a little more slowly than before.

"Pssst, pssst. You," said the reverend. "All right, then. You, Ben. Isn't that what they call you?"

"I guess so," said Ben.

"All right," said the reverend. "I got a car for you. You're interested in cars, aren't you? You're still buying them, aren't you? You can just tell me if you aren't up to it anymore."

"I don't know," said Ben, "I'm about done trading cars. Anyway, I already got a car."

"What car is that?" said the reverend.

"Oh, you wouldn't be interested in it," said Ben. "It's a Cadillac."

The reverend watched sharply now. Ben looked away, toward the mountains, as though the car were visible there.

"Seven years old, but it runs like a top. Paint is clear and clean. Clean interior. Got those fuzzy seats, you know. Fifty thousand original miles. I'm happy with it," said Ben.

"Where is it?" said the reverend.

"You wouldn't be interested."

"I said, where is it?"

Ben started rocking harder now, the chair sweeping back and forth. The light from the hotel was bluish and cold.

"I already got a car," said Ben.

"That Cadillac?" said the reverend. "Well, I'll tell you something. Maybe I'd be interested in it."

"I'd like to help you," said Ben, "but I don't think this one is for you. Maybe some other time."

"Listen," said the reverend, "I've got a position here, can't you see? A good respectable car is what I need. Not something new and flashy. That's all there is to it. I'm telling you what everyone knows. Well?"

Ben stopped for a moment and lighted a cigarette and then went back to rocking, the streak of the cigarette, the sound the runners made on the wooden veranda suggesting a patient considering of things, the air of it not necessarily friendly, not necessarily warm or considerate, just steady, blank. Finally he said, "Well, all right. If you're going to twist my arm. I'll have it here tomorrow. Let's say about one o'clock in the afternoon?"

"Good," said the reverend.

Then the black chair started moving again. The reverend turned and walked across the park, passing the benches, which were blue-black in the dark, his passage steady, wrathful, unrelenting, and as he went there was that squeak, squeak of the runners of the rocking chair on the floor of the veranda, not mocking, but having about it that same blank air of considering.

The luncheonette was dark, too, and when I stepped away from it, I saw that steady movement and heard Ben say, "Good night, Faith."

The reverend went into the door of his welding shop. There was a long bench there, above which there were fan belts, new black ones shaped like a rubber band and hung in order, each one a little larger than the last. On the bench there were wrenches, screwdrivers, a mallet, calipers, and pliers, a vise, and a grinder. The reverend took a Coleman lantern from a hook and lighted it, the sound of it constant, like the hiss of escaping steam. He carried it to the back of the repair shop and put it down next to the back door. It was like a barn door, made of wood, and it had twenty-five or thirty license plates nailed to it. When it was pushed open the bottom of it hissed over the unmowed grass behind the shop. Then the reverend picked up the lantern and went into the dark, the circle of light swinging around his legs as he passed some cardboard barrels, a harrow, a rake, a baler with its drive shaft unconnected and hanging at a forlorn angle. Beyond these things, half obscured by the weeds and appearing as though it was partially sunk into them, there was a car, a white 1957 Ford.

The reverend put the lantern down in front of it, the hood ornament falling in a blade-shaped shadow over the hood. For a moment the car looked not so much abandoned in the weeds as having somehow just crashed into them. The lantern gave the lot the air of something being done irregularly and with haste, like robbing a grave. The reverend opened the hood and lifted the light so he could look at the engine, the round shape of the air filter emerging from the darkness there. Then he came into his shop to get his tools and a block and pulley that had a chain rather than a rope, the clink of it muffled as he dragged it through the dry grass.

I came back about noon the next day. By then the car wasn't in the back lot anymore but on the other side of the park, in front of the hotel, and it didn't look like it had been slowly sinking into the weeds with a lot of broken-down farm machinery, either. It had been washed and there were new tires on it (real ones, not recaps) and the seats had been vacuumed, not to mention that the chrome had been shined up and wiped dry. It was parked head-in and seemed ordinary there against the curb, distinguished only by the fact that it was a little cleaner than the other cars on the street. The reverend watched it from the front of his shop, where he sat on that box, his eyes red from lack of sleep, his hand holding one of those large white styrofoam cups of coffee that came from the luncheonette.

It was a warm, hazy day, the sky not so much gray as

having a high, thin fog. Nothing cast a shadow. The town appeared in muted colors, and the people went about their business without being careful to walk in the shade. It was quiet and the birds pecked along the sidewalks, or at the popcorn kids had thrown in the gutter. But even though it was quiet, we didn't hear the hushed, purring engine of the Cadillac until the car was almost here. It rolled into town without a squeak. We just looked up and saw the thing pull into a parking space in front of the hotel, appearing there with a kind of surprise one associates with magic. It was about six years old, green like a pond at dusk.

The reverend put down his styrofoam cup. The paint on the car was new, just as it had been on the other cars Ben had brought back, but not only did the car have the appearance of one that had been well kept, it looked pampered, too. The chrome wasn't pitted, and the aerial was new and tall. When the car came to a stop, the brake lights were as bright as coals. The reverend stood now, his eyes bloodshot, the bland sunlight washing over him as he stared.

He came across the park, walking with the slow but irritated air of a man who has gone without sleep for a night. Ben stepped out of the Cadillac, pushing the door away from him and then shutting it, the tight, ice-box like sound of it rushing out to meet the reverend. The two men went through the business of opening the hoods of the cars, first the Cadillac and then the Ford, all of this done in a slow two-step, first one way and then the next, the oil caps being removed and the engines started, the thin ribbons of smoke rising from the crankcases, the dipsticks being removed and examined and then shoved back in again, just as a bullfighter puts a sword into the soft spot between a bull's shoulders. As Ben tapped and listened to the engine, as he removed a spark plug, the reverend kept looking at the Cadillac, even when he spoke of the Ford. The Cadillac sat against the curb, the color of it green and bright.

Now the two of them sat down on the veranda, Ben rocking back and forth and the reverend in a chair that he didn't move at all. They each had a glass of lemonade from the luncheonette, which each sipped slowly, tasting the sticky, cold, and sweetish drink, both of them staring into the street, the reverend's eyes fiercely set on the Cadillac. They spoke to one another like two men at a baseball game, not steadily but with a certain regularity, as though discussing each play.

When I walked out of the luncheonette and strolled past the hotel, Ben said to the reverend, "Well, that's all right. I don't hold it against you. But if you don't come up with more cash than that, why, I'll just take my car back to the city. That's fine." Then I was out of hearing, but the reverend leaned a little closer to Ben, talking quickly now into the ear which slowly and steadily swung back and forth in front of his lips. Soon I turned and went back up the street, appearing to be wandering aimlessly around, but in fact getting closer again. The windows of the grocery, the lawyer's and the accountant's office, the dry cleaner's with the stale dummy beyond it, and the shaded windows of the luncheonette passed with a slow, steady regularity. Above, the hands of the clock on the courthouse looked like enormous black spears.

Then I passed the veranda again, where Ben said, "Well, you go out there and ask Mrs. Anson, or Mike Wallis, or Bob Van. Maybe they'll tell you what they think of the cars I fixed up. It's up to you. I'm just as happy either way."

At four in the afternoon the reverend stood up and walked over to the bank, his gait steady and fierce, his head bent forward, his hands not exactly clinched, but held in front of his thighs. He emerged from the heavy doors almost instantly, coming out of the place as though expelled, and then he walked back across the street to the hotel, carrying the small white envelope he had been given in the bank and which was thick with money. Then he went up to the veranda again and started counting bills into Ben's outstretched and faintly curved hand, the twenties adding up, twenty forty sixty eighty, one hundred, two hundred, three hundred, the counting continuing, the reverend's voice quiet, but still fierce, as he dropped each bill.

They exchanged keys and titles, and the reverend left, the two men separating as though they didn't know the other existed. The reverend got into the Cadillac and sat for a moment, running his fingers over the fuzzy material. Then he started the engine and drove the car around the square, where he parked in front of his shop.

The square was quiet, still warm from the day. I walked back to the hotel, and then went up and sat in a chair. After a while Ben said, "Well, Faith, I guess I better drive the thing sometime, don't you think?"

The reverend sat down on the box in front of his store and drank a cup of coffee. Ben stood and walked down the steps of the veranda and over to the Ford, letting the keys swing back and forth in his hand. Then he got in and started the engine, backed up and turned and went down one side of the park, the car just rumbling along in first gear.

The town was quiet, but watchful, and here and there someone came to the front of a store window and looked out, the faces streaked in the old glass. The car made its steady passage, first emerging from the end of the park and going out of town, disappearing there with that same cautious or suspicious speed. But as it turned at the last street in town, we heard the pace pick up, although even from a distance there was that air of Ben looking for what he knew was wrong, the entire passage suggesting one long, tentative exercise in fatalism. Then the white car emerged again, on the other side of the park, but this time coming back toward the hotel. The engine was powerful, a little ragged, the occasional pop it made having about it an irregular quality that suggested nothing.

Now Ben turned and passed the hotel again, making another circuit, although this time he went faster, especially down the back street beyond the park, and when he was out of sight, we heard a high-pitched roar, like the sound of an old prop-driven plane which is about to take off.

The car came around the park again. This time, as it went by the hotel, it looked as though it had hit a mine. There was a flash of light, a platinum-colored pulse that spread under the car, the color and intensity of it something like steel being poured in a foundry: it splashed against the pavement and dispersed, running to both sides of the street as the *BANG* of the explosion came and went, leaving behind the slight, nervous rattling of store windows.

For a moment the car was airborne, or seemed to be, the hood snapping open and being flung against the windshield, a door springing outward, too, but even in its flapping disarray it still moved forward. There was a second bang, not so loud as the first and having about it a hard metallic crash and rattle as the car hit the ground. There it skidded and left two curved black marks from the rear tires, since, even in the air, Ben had put on the brakes and kept them on.

The car sat there, in the street, about twenty feet from the curb. The hood was half open, and from under it there came some smoke, which curled around the edges of the hood and converged on itself again, forming a thick column which rose straight into the air. There was no wind and the smoke rose with a calm, deliberate quality, as though someone were burning a pile of damp leaves. The day was still warm, but the heat was giving way to the coolness of the late-afternoon shadows.

Ben got out of the car, stepping back and slamming the door as he did so, putting his arm and shoulder into it, as though he were throwing a heavy rock. He looked around the street, his arms crossed over his chest, everything about him, even the obvious trembling of his legs, suggesting not fear or even surprise so much as defiance. Then he went to the hood and threw it all the way open, the smoke now coming together in a large puff which roiled there, turning into itself as it rose. Ben reached into the engine compartment, into the smoke, touching the engine gingerly because of the heat, but nevertheless still looking until he found, on the underside of the intake manifold, five new, neatly drilled holes, through which gas, or worse yet, gas vapor, had leaked into the engine compartment, where it had been ignited by two stripped wires, between which there had been a small, almost invisible spark.

The smoke and some steam rose over his arms, shoulders, and face, the only sound now coming from the front of the hardware. There the reverend sat on that wooden box, a large Styrofoam cup of coffee in his hand, the brown stuff spilling as he laughed, his head going up and down, the bright lines of tears running from his eyes as he did so. After a while he stopped, but then began again, his face collapsing into horizontal lines and his head going up and down again, as though he were praying in a mosque.

"Well, well," said Ben, looking up from the engine, his eyes going over the people who were in the street, "I guess that just goes to show you better be damn careful who you buy a car from, doesn't it?"

He stood there, the smoke still rising from the car. Then he opened the door and pushed against the frame, straining there, trembling. The car didn't move much and he looked around again, saying, "I need help pushing my car. Who will help?"

The men and women in the street heard that laughing and hesitated. Next to the reverend, there were those men who worked on farms, and they stood with their arms crossed, but now, at the corners of their lips, there was a slight smile. Ben turned back to the car again, the clock high above him.

"Faith! Faith!" said Ben. "Where's Faith Wheeler?"

The reverend sat on his box, the coffee dripping from his hand as he went right on laughing. But when I started walking toward Ben the reverend said, his voice loud, "Faith, we've all had enough fun now. No one likes a good time better than me, but enough's enough. This young man is going back where he came from. You go on home with your cousin. Paul? Where's Paul Wheeler?"

Ben looked around the town, nodding, saying nothing.

"Listen," Ben said, speaking to the people in the square, "listen. There's got to be an auto parts store around someplace, isn't there?"

"Next town over," said Robert Van.

"If I can just get over there . . ." said Ben, still breathing hard now.

"Get in my car," said Robert Van. "I'll give you a lift."

In the morning Ben came out of the hotel and went to work, putting that black bag of tools on the curb and then lying in the sunlight, where he took off the old manifold and put on a new one, gaskets and all. The old one he stuck in a trash can in the alley by the hotel, and then he went upstairs and took a bath and came back to the veranda, where he drank a lemonade and said to the people who came by, "Did I think I was going to the moon? Well, you could say that. But let me tell you something. Years ago the Indians were scared to come up to this part of California, and you know why? They were afraid of getting skinned. Well, some people will do about anything to get their hands on a Cadillac."

He sipped his drink.

"But you look at that Ford now. Just needed a new manifold, that's all. I wouldn't sell it for anything. Not now."

In the evening, when I passed the reverend's shop, he sat there on that box, looking at me, saying, "Faith. Come to the back of the shop. I want to talk to you about something."

I went on, down the street, my eyes turned toward the veranda of the hotel.

The next day Ben was still at the hotel, getting up early and going into the luncheonette and eating his breakfast, and then he went back to the veranda with the newspaper, which he read slowly, his entire aspect one of patient waiting. Every now and then there was the sad, slow sound of the runners of his rocking chair.

Ben didn't look up when the reverend came out of his shop and got into the Cadillac. The reverend sat behind the wheel, taking it in his hands while he pushed against the comforting fuzz of the seat. He fingered the knobs for the radio, the controls for the air-conditioner and heater, all of which were large and substantial. He looked at the interior light, too, and at the seats, all of which were sedate, if not downright formal and suggestive of some bleak thing, like a funeral. The reverend lingered for a minute, hearing that steady creak of the rockers, or seeing Ben slowly turning the pages of the paper. The reverend twisted the knobs again, giving them a good jerk, as though to prove there was nothing wrong with them, and when he started the engine, he pulled away from the curb with a seallike bark of tires, these actions all taken with the air of a man who is kicking a dog that has bitten other people but which the man is certain will not bite him.

In the evening the reverend came out of his shop and saw me strolling along the street, a large brown bag in my arms, parsley and celery tops sticking out, my passage seemingly aimless but surely going to the hotel. At his glance I stopped and even started backing up, now just a few feet from the veranda, from which there came that *creak, creak, creak.* The reverend said nothing, but he walked up to the Cadillac and got behind the wheel, slamming the door behind him.

He started the engine and drove into the square. The car was running smoothly, and as he made the turns, now passing the hotel, he went fast, the automobile going in one long algae-colored smear. He came to the courthouse and jail, and as he made the turn there, he jerked the wheel, just as he always did now. The car made the turn, the tires not even squealing that much, but a sound, a new one I had never heard before, rose from the car and spread into the shadows of the evening. It was loud and like ice breaking up on a lake at the end of winter or like someone taking a bite of a large carrot. So, from the street in front of the courthouse, there was a loud *CRACK.*

Ben stopped rocking now, and let the paper down, too, the sheets folding in the middle and collapsing into his lap. The Cadillac went through the turn, but after the sound it didn't seem to be made from steel, aluminum, and tin anymore, but something more soft and pliable, like Jell-O. There was a barely audible hiss, too, like someone opening an enormous canned ham, the kind with a little key that winds up a strip of metal. So as the frame snapped, as there was that crack and hiss, the reverend sat behind the wheel, now feeling the car sag into a swaybacked shape, the roof creasing as the pieces of the frame dragged, the front end of the Cadillac looking for all the world as though it were going up a mountain, while the back half seemed to be going downhill. For a moment, the green car seemed to quiver (just like a plate of mint Jell-O), and then the frame hit the pavement, the sparks from it now spewing behind the car, the long spray of them looking like the white cinder-marked chaos of a welder's torch. As the Cadillac came out of the turn, the frame scraping on the pavement, the rear part of the car no longer tracked behind the front. Then the car came to a stop and the quiet air of the evening was filled with the firecracker stink of burned metal.

Ben's chair had been motionless for a moment, but now it started again, his figure dark there as he looked into the square, which was lighted only by the face of that dough-colored clock. After a moment he turned to me and said, "Well, Faith, I guess I can go home now, can't I?"

"Yes," I said, "I guess you can."

"Why don't you come and sit for a minute?" he said.

I climbed the steps and put down my bag. He reached over and took my hand, pulling me just close enough to kiss me, to touch my lips for just a moment, while out there in the square that car still smoked.

"Yeah," he said, "I guess I got rid of that Cadillac at just the right time. Who would have known?"—his voice not angry, or vindictive, but his eyes looking into mine.

"You're going to leave soon, aren't you?" I said.

His eyes moved away from my face once, toward those men who stood along the street, their eyes turned toward us.

"Yes," he said, "I'm done here. I didn't do so badly, take it all around."

"What'll I do when you're gone?" I said.

"I don't know," he said. "Maybe you should leave, too."

"Yes," I said, "that's what I was thinking."

"Were you?" he said.

"Yes. I was thinking how it would be just to . . . wake up someplace else."

He nodded, looking out to the park.

"Do you understand?" I said.

"What do you mean?" he said.

"I want to come with you," I said. "Don't you see? There's

nothing to think about. You can't imagine me staying here, can you? Oh, God, can't you see?"

He sighed now.

"You're sure?" he said.

"Yes," I said.

He nodded, looking down now.

"That's good," he said. "I didn't plan on leaving here without you."

"You won't back out on me, will you? You won't leave me with my bag packed and—"

He started laughing now.

"What?" he said. "After all these cars, after nearly getting killed in that Ford? No, you don't have to worry. . ."

I went home and made dinner, hearing the windmill, although the sound of it seemed a little easier to take. There was a peach pie for dessert, and I sat with my aunt and uncle, all of us eating, tasting that crust and the sweetness of the peaches. Then I went upstairs and got into bed, where I pulled the sheet over me and slept.

In the morning I went up beyond the house, passing the towers on the ridge, the X's of them piled up one on top of another. There was a swale beyond the ridge, and then another ridge, and beyond that a long, gently sloping hill. It was some ways off and took a while to get there. There were still some flowers left from the springtime, lupine, poppies, but they were dry now, although still fragrant, and as I went, the dry grass and flowers brushed against my legs. At the top of the hill, when the house and farm and those towers were so far away as to seem as though they hardly existed at all, I sat down and stretched out, feeling the heat of the sun on my blouse and over the front of my skirt. Up above there were mare's tails, which were the color of cotton string. After a while the sun felt very hot. Around me there were the swish and cracklings of the dry grass, of the lupine and poppies, and the constant hush of the wind. My skin got burned, even through that white dress, but as I sat there, my eyes closed now, I thought of the hillside in the spring, the colors of it a little muted, like a tweed coat. There were some swallows and I felt the shadows of them through my clothes. Then I stood and went back down the hill and into the house.

I had told my aunt the night before, and we had argued. But now she stood there, waiting to say good-bye.

"Are you in love, Faith?" she said.

"Yes," I said, "I think so. We'll be all right. He can always make money trading cars, I guess. He says he's studying in that school down there. He's going to be a weatherman. They must make something."

"Maybe your uncle should talk to the reverend," said my aunt.

"No," I said.

"We could stop you," said my aunt.

"No," I said, "you're wrong."

"Are you in love, Faith? Are you really?"

"Yes. He can always make something. You can stretch a dollar if you have to. It adds up. We'll get along. I don't know about the weather business, but he says he's good at it."

My aunt kissed me, her blind expression exaggerated now.

I picked up the bag and went out, putting my hand on the wooden banister of the steps. The dust blew away from my feet in small, definite puffs as I went down the drive. Below there was that white car, but it didn't turn into the drive, if only because Ben knew I wanted to walk out of there alive, carrying that bag with the magic tricks inside.

We drove over the mountains and into the coastal plain, where there were some low rolling hills and some trees that were dry and isolated on the grasslands. Soon, though, the hills were covered with houses, a smooth, complete conglomeration of them that made it impossible to see the land at all. We drove into the hills in Berkeley and stopped in front of a small red house. It was below the road, surrounded by eucalyptus, and from the bedroom you could see the bay and the bridge, too, and as I sat on the bed, my bag at my feet, I saw the cables of the Golden Gate, all of them looking like the strings of a harp. There was a bathroom off the bedroom, and as I took off my shoes and put them neatly under the foot of the bed, heels and toes together, I heard a steady *drip, drip, drip,* from the shower head. I imagined the drops forming and swelling. I took off my dress and lay down, under the sheet, having around me the scent of dried grass, poppies, and lupine, the dust of them still on my skin, which still seemed to have a little warmth from the sun. In the heat of the room I heard that constant dripping and imagined the drops making crown-shaped splashes on the floor of the shower.

In the middle of the night I was sick, the sense of it coming over me in a rush. I made that noise, that steady *huh, huh, huh,* and when I woke he was sitting next to me.

"Who are you?" I said.

"Me?" he said. "You don't know me?"

"No," I said. "I want to go home."

"Home?" he said. "Oh, Faith. What should I do?"

"Wait a little," I said. "I've been sick. Please, don't tell on me."

"I won't tell," he said.

Later, after we slept, I went into the kitchen and stood in the brown gloom of morning. There were pans on the shelf, which had a curtain for a door, and one of the pans was the right size for making coffee. I picked it up and then turned toward the sink, which was squarish and deep, covered with porcelain so old it wasn't shiny anymore. Water dripped from the tap. I put my finger and then the palm of my hand into the cold pulse of it. The water wasn't cold enough, though, not even when it had run for a while. I made a cup of my hand and splashed some onto my face and breasts and stomach, but even then I thought of putting ice into a pitcher and then adding water, which would get as cold as the rivers that run out of the Sierras, and then I could stand in the shower and pour it over me while I said, "Ah, ah, ah." Instead I stood in the kitchen, bent at the waist, my hand under the faucet, my head on the cold, hard porcelain, my shoulders dripping.

Ben came into the doorway of the kitchen and looked at me.

"There," I said, "isn't that enough? I've been punished for

it. All right? Isn't that what you want to do? Hold me in cold water? Well, it's already done."

He shook his head now, his hand reaching out to my back and shoulders, which were slippery with the water.

"Faith, listen. . . ."

"I have broad shoulders," I said. "I can take the blame. For this or anything else. You don't have to worry about me," I said.

The water beaded on my skin and ran downward, the paths of it coming as long, cool tickles along my sides and down my legs. Ben brought a towel and I rubbed my skin hard. Then I went into the bedroom and climbed into bed, pulling the sheet up to my shoulder.

In the afternoon he brought me tea and toast on a tray, the triangles of toast brown and crisp and still warm and without crusts either. The muscles in my legs and arms were stiff, just as though I had been lifting sacks of concrete onto a truck.

He stretched out on the bed next to me, curled up along my side and back. I felt his steady, warm breath through the sheet.

"I love you, Faith," he said. "I love you, Faith Wheeler."

"Do you, Ben?" I said.

He nodded.

"Why? Tell me why."

He shrugged and said, "Maybe I started thinking about things, like about a woman who has to put an extra can of water into the lemonade."

Faith Wheeler,
Tying the Knot

Northern California

SOON IT WAS FALL, AND WITH IT CAME THOSE CLEAR SEPTEM-
ber days in California: from the bedroom window the Golden
Gate Bridge seemed sharp and clear, the cables separate, the
construction of the thing so obvious as to make me believe I
saw the round head of each bolt and the seams between pieces
of steel. The bay was visible, and each facet of the windy chop
on the surface was shiny and shaped like the bowl of a spoon.

Ben went back to school now, and when he did so, he
asked if I wanted to go, too. I took a few classes, but during the
first year I read Descartes and said to myself, *Do I know I exist
because I think? Have I lost my mind to the extent that I sit
here worrying about this?* Right then I got up and looked in
the mirror and said, *It's time to get a job. Right now. At least I
can make some money.*

I began to check groceries at the A & P, and there the
women who worked with me didn't talk about Spinoza or
Locke or Hobbes or any of the rest. I was glad to be away from
those dustyheads and their complications, and the young men
and women who sat through those classes, the women with
their long braids and blue jeans and the men with their san-

dals and wire-rimmed glasses. At the store we laughed and told jokes, some of which I brought home, and when Ben sat there over his books, his face bent forward, one hand in that sandy, golden hair, I said, "Hey, listen . . . have you heard about the scientist who . . ."

There was a magic shop near the A & P and I stopped there after work, or on payday, and I bought some new gimmick, and after I told Ben a joke I made a flower appear or did a rope trick with a wand. Then he laughed and said, "Faith, I love you, you know that?"

"Do you, Ben?" I said, but even then I kept an eye on those books, not quite hating them yet, but already being suspicious of them, not for what was in them so much as what they would do to the two of us once he was finished with them. "Maybe you do now, but what about when you aren't just a student anymore? What are you going to do when you've got a real job?"

"What?" he said.

"You're going to live with me now and when the time comes to start a real life, you're going to find someone else. A little blondie from the east, I'll bet. From Mount Holyoke or Smith or even some place like Radcliffe . . . a brainy little—"

"Faith," he said, looking up from that golden light, the pages of those books shiny with it, "Faith, what's wrong?"

"I don't know," I said. "But I'll tell you this. No one is going to look down his nose at me. No one."

He ran his hand through his hair.

"I'm not doing that, Faith," he said.

He closed his books now and said, "What do you say we get out of here for a while? Let's go down and get a cold glass of beer. Would you like that?"

"Yes," I said, "I would. I can't think of anything I'd like better. I don't know what's gotten into me." But even as we put on our coats against the fog, I looked at those books on his desk as though they were a kind of indictment.

I have always dreamed of being in Afghanistan, or India, or the foothills of the Himalayas. I'd have a duty in these places, and I'd unflinchingly perform it in the midst of a plague or a war or some upheaval and misery: perhaps I'd be a nurse or the head of some hospital, and in the middle of a battle I'd work day and night. I'd even be wounded. There would be a time when, with the blood showing on my white clothes, I'd turn and look at an officer in the army (someone like Richard Burton), and in that moment, in the stink of the battle, in the smoke of it, in the funeral pyres of people who gave their lives, he would understand what I'd been through. Now, after I'd had a seizure, I turned to Ben and said, "Don't worry. I'll get by," the tone of my voice not a whine exactly, but one that showed how difficult things had been for me. His sorrow washed over me like a sweet, comforting thing, one better even than love.

I brought home my paychecks and pinned them to the bulletin board, each one of them cementing what was between us, the money making it seem I was useful and that these days had no other reality than the domestic life of that small rented house.

While Ben studied, he had a job, too, driving a tow truck. He had an office, or at least a place where he waited for calls, in a gas station near the bay. The place no longer sold gas and was surrounded by a cyclone fence, topped by barbed wire, and around the place there was a sparkling crust of broken glass. He sat there at night, in his blue, starched uniform, a copy of *Banke's Mathematical Models* propped up there by the two-way radio. I brought him his lunch, a piece of cold fried chicken, a small container of potato salad, a few black olives, carrot sticks and celery in a plastic bag, a napkin and a fork, all of it packed into a shoe box I had saved. There was a thermos of black coffee, too, which had a top you could drink out of. He sat in that service station building, the radio and his book illuminated by one bare overhead bulb. I arrived, stepping over the broken glass, and when I came in, I said, "Here. I brought you your lunch."

When a call came, he got into a tow truck and drove onto the freeway, where he hitched up to what was left of cars, the engine compartments and wheel wells all showing as a kind of black accordion, just like those old portrait cameras, not to mention the clutter of broken glass and twisted fenders and hoods or the things that were plainly no longer identifiable. Before he hauled the things away, he walked around them, sometimes picking up a woman's shoe or some other piece of clothing and throwing it into what was left of the car, the shoe or handbag or belt making a short, straight path into gray-brown gloom.

I was waiting when he came into the gas station lot, the crushed piece of metal he towed squeaking in the chains that held it. I walked out, over that broken glass, which so filled the lot as to appear like an enormous swimming pool with the green surface rocking back and forth after someone had gone for a swim. I stood there and looked at the car, or what was left of it, and said, "Look at the cracks in the windshield. God. And look at that steering wheel. Did anybody live?"

Then I went home and stood in front of the mirror and thought, *I'm pretty, really. Especially if I turn like that. Maybe a little eye shadow would help, like Marge at the store.* Then I put my head down, remembering what I had learned in that small bed at home, hearing the windmills turn at night, the things squeaking at the top of those black piles of X's: infinite patience and loneliness, too.

We spent time in the kitchen together, cooking from a book he'd bought, the *Larousse Gastronomique*. We made stock and sauces, poached chicken under paper, made raspberry soufflés for dessert. When we sat down, I said, "This is pretty good. What's it called?" my eyes flashing at him a little when I heard the name in French.

We had some friends, Paul and Sharon, and one night we invited them over for dinner. Paul was tall and fat and had blond hair and thick glasses. He spoke slowly about his experiments with U-235. Sharon wore blue jeans and had long hair and didn't wear a brassiere. In the middle of dinner, when they were talking about someone, Sharon said, "You know, she has a kind of stupid expression on her face. Like a checker in a supermarket who's made a mistake."

"There's nothing wrong with working in a supermarket," I said.

"Oh, God, Faith," said Sharon, "I didn't mean—"

"I know what you meant," I said. "I have ears. I work in a supermarket and I'll tell you something else. The food you're eating was paid for by my working there."

"I'm sorry," said Sharon. "Please."

I stopped eating now and drank the wine, listening to the conversation. Ben changed the subject and told a joke: I hated him then for making it go away so easily, so gracefully. Everyone laughed too hard and I drank some more wine. Ben told a story about how he had helped a friend put together a mass spectrometer: the parts of it that held liquid nitrogen had to be bolted together and each bolt had to be under a certain number of foot-pounds of torque. Ben was able to do it, not because of his knowledge of physics, but because he had spent so much time buying and selling cars, opening up the engine heads and then putting them back together, using a torque wrench for each bolt. His friend was so clumsy that when it was time to pour in the liquid nitrogen, he spilled some of it on the floor: a drop fell into Ben's shoes. He showed the scar. When they finally went home, I said, "I'm going to bed. I don't want to talk about it."

"Listen," he said, "I'm sorry."

"No, you aren't," I said.

"Faith, *I* didn't say anything."

"That's right," I said. "That's absolutely right. You didn't say a thing when you should have thrown her ass right outside."

"I didn't think that was the best thing to do," he said.

"Think. Think. I'm so tired of *thinking*. Oh, shit, I'm going to be sick tonight. Goddamn you."

I went in and got into my nightgown and pulled back the sheets, and when I lay there I heard him washing the dishes and cleaning up, the sounds steady, rattling, clinging. The water ran in the sink, splashing there, and when the plug was pulled, the water pulsed in the walls. He came in and sat on the bed and then undressed and got under the covers, saying, "Good night, Faith."

In the night I was sick, the power of it coming with that purple light and that sense of being nauseated, or dizzy, as though I had had too much to drink and that the bed was rocking up and down, just like seawater. Then I was in the dark, floating there, but it was worse than sleep, a long stifling, strangling time which left me feeling that stiffness in my neck and arms and stomach, not to mention that continual sense of the bed softly moving.

Ben sat next to me, a damp cloth in his hand where he had mopped my face and around my mouth. There was a stink in the room, too, like an outhouse. There were no sheets on the bed and I was lying on the striped mattress ticking.

"Who are you?" I said.

"Ben," he said, "I'm a friend."

"Oh, Ben," I said.

I turned to the side now and felt ill, as though wounded. I put a hand to my head.

"I'm sorry," he said.

I blinked now and looked around and into the living room, where there was a light on and where I could still see those books.

"You don't have to worry about it," I said. "I can take care of myself."

He nodded.

"Yes, I'm sure of that," he said.

I looked at those books, the things enormous, dark there on the desk, the collection of them looking like registers in the county courthouse.

"I love you," he said, the sorrow in his voice bringing me that same cool relief.

A few days later, at breakfast, he said, "I went to see my father. He wants you to come down for a visit. I think it would be a good idea."

"You talked to him about me?" I said.

"I . . ." he said. "Yes. I did."

"So you've been going around my back. Listen, my

mother took me to a doctor and there's nothing that can be done."

"Things have changed," he said. "That was years ago. There are new drugs—"

"No," I said. "It's no use. It's just humiliating."

"Don't you think this is humiliating?"

"How dare you? I stand up to it."

But it didn't end there, either. Because a few weeks later he came back with a bottle of pills, which he put on the kitchen table.

"I got them from my father. He's says if you're in good health otherwise, you might try one of these a day."

"You've been going behind my back again, haven't you?" I said, "I thought it was a secret, just between us."

"These may help," he said.

"No. No," I said.

He closed his eyes now.

"I'm not damaged goods," I said. "I'm not. No matter what you think."

He went into the living room and opened his books. I took the pills into the bathroom and flushed them away, as though to fight against the sense of being a freak, or against what I believed, that the disease was a symptom of our being different and that pills or not, cured or not, he would leave me. I felt better, just as soon as the pills swirled around in that cold water. I went out and sat next to him and said, "I'm sorry. I'm just a little jumpy, I guess."

I was proud of him, too, and when he finished his studies, I went into that football stadium in Berkeley and saw him get his degree. There were thousands of men and women, in black and white gowns, the entire ceremony having about it the air of the end of expectation. It was a clear, warm summer day, and I took Ben's picture and he took mine, while I said to him, already beginning to laugh, "We're like brides, you know that? We know we're going to get it, but we don't know how much."

By the time he was finished I was in my middle twenties. Then he began to look for what we called a "real job," one that required a Ph.D. in meteorology, and the two of us passed through our days like any other seemingly normal couple, splitting our time between looking at where we'd been and thinking about where we were going.

Now, though, he had gotten into the habit of being careful not to upset me. This came as a kind of insult: his tiptoeing around was proof, as far as I was concerned, that he was getting ready to find that blondie from Radcliffe or Smith.

"Listen," I said, "you don't have to do that."

He looked at me now.

"I'm fine. Just fine," I said. "There's nothing wrong with me."

"All right," he said, "I've been offered a job. In the Sierras. It will be frightening sometimes. If you don't want to come along, I'll come down to visit you on the weekends."

"What?" I said. "And leave me here? No. I'll come."

The job was for the Steigmetz Institute. During the summer we lived in a cabin at the top of a mountain, the small, one-room place being filled with instruments and having, as part of its appeal, the fact that there were not groceries to check. So we sat there, Ben carefully adjusting his instruments and taking notes, waiting for lightning, which came both day and night, the closeness of it making my hair rise like metal shavings on a magnet. The bolts were too close to sound like *pffffft*, or even like the tearing of a sheet. They came as sudden bangs, and at night, in a storm, there weren't flashes so much as sudden appearances of enormous tubes, as big around as a barrel, their shapes running one way and another into the sky, the color of them suggesting an enormous purple and irregular neon tube. Ben wrote in his neat script, his eyes going up to his instruments as he said, "Good, good, good. A little closer now."

The *BANG* made the dishes rattle on the shelf, and the fear washed over my skin, infinitely pointed, as definite as flakes of snow. For a moment the room had a slight purple tinge to it, but I shook it off. Ben watched his instruments, but every now and then he turned toward me, his eyes filled not with fear of the lightning but of what would happen if I had a spell. Yet there was a certain relief for both of us there, in that fear which was so overwhelming as to make things disappear. Then, when it was all right for him to stop writing, we got into bed, with me a little brazen in a way I usually was not, that cold sparkle washing over my skin again while I said, "Ah. Ah. Ah."

I started fighting back, or just showing that being this frightened wasn't going to make me sick and that I wasn't a freak or someone to be frowned upon. Passion was close to the surface then. So, when we were surrounded by those tall, wavering columns of light and when the dishes started rattling with the explosions, I got up and went to the small butane stove, even though I was having trouble with my legs and hands, and there I began to cook, making scrambled eggs (not trusting myself to any other kind). In the worst of it I brought the plate over and put it down in front of him, saying, "Here. I made you something to eat."

So now Ben was trapped, too, since he knew I would see any attempt to shield me from things as condescension. And this he wouldn't do: so now I egged him on, insisting that we stay in the cabin, if only to prove to him that I was all right. So, he felt that terror, too, not only from the lightning around us, but from the possibility of my having so bad a time as to hold him to account for it, as though bringing me up here were his fault, no matter whose idea it had been in the first place.

Near the end of the summer, when he sat down at his instruments, the black dials of them moving with quick, nervous twitches, I didn't light the butane stove, but went over to my bag and took out a gimmick and in the worst of it I swallowed hard, barely able to speak, my voice coming with an endless quaver, as I said, "Look. You see this handkerchief. Presto. . . ."

In the fall we went back to our ordinary life in that small rented house in Berkeley, neither one of us saying a thing, Ben now supposedly looking for an ordinary job, but in fact still finding short-term work, a six-months' contract with the Navy, a consultantship for a trader in grain futures. I took a job in the post office. Now I looked over his shoulder at the job announcements he brought home, and I eavesdropped when a friend of his called to say there was an opening here or there. When he pulled away from a job because there was some danger, I said, "No. You don't have to do that. I'm fine."

One afternoon, when I came home, he was throwing away a letter offering him a job with the National Atmospheric Project. I stood in front of him, wearing my blue post-office blouse with the patch on the sleeve, and said, "What's that?"

"You know, Faith," he said, "those people in Tulsa. We'd have to go down to Oklahoma for the summer, but I was thinking maybe I'd tell them we wouldn't come."

"Why?" I said, looking right at him, challenging him to insult me.

"Oklahoma is what they call tornado alley," he said.

"Well," I said, "fine. Let's go."

We packed and went out there, too, neither one of us talking about it, the two of us going like any unmarried couple, although now we were a little older yet, the two of us sitting in the front seat of Ben's plain new '74 Chevrolet. We listened to the radio and went through southern California, Arizona, and New Mexico, stopping at diners and staying in motels, the atmosphere between us brittle sometimes.

Before we started to work, he explained what we were going to do, his voice a little cautious, as though still giving me a way out, his eyes plainly suggesting that we could stop anytime I wanted. If nothing else, I began to understand how I had raised the stakes, because now we weren't going to sit in a cabin at the top of a hill (that was protected by a lightning rod) but instead we were going to load a pickup truck with a portable box of instruments, a kind of washing-machine-sized thing with handles on it. Then we were going to pursue tornadoes, or try to, and when we got as close as we wanted or dared to, we were supposed to stop the truck and leave the instruments, hoping the storm would go right over them. The instruments had a radio transmitter.

On the day we started there was cold air moving quickly out of the north, pushing into the plains, and there was a long line of thunderstorms. Ben and I went out to the yellow pickup truck that had been assigned to us, Ben carrying the map that had been marked up for him. Then we got into the cab of the truck, both of us looking through the windshield with a restrained fear, not necessarily of the funnel (until we saw one: that, at least, was enough to make us begin to worry about the right thing), but of the two of us, so neatly trapped by the tacit agreement we had made: I'd prove to him what I wanted to prove and he'd take the blame if I couldn't.

"You know, Faith," said Ben, "the truth is, a tornado packs the same energy as an A-bomb. Not a big one, but an A-bomb. Well? Any last-minute ideas?"

"No," I said.

It rained hard the next week, the streaks of water hitting the ground and splashing up, making a white mist as high as my chin. We drove through it, neither of us saying anything while the truck went back and forth over the section we were supposed to patrol. Over the radio, when someone spoke, there was only static, but the voice could still be heard, insistent, excited, demanding something. The rain stopped and a tornado appeared, the point of it coming down in a field and its funnel stained black by the fertilized earth, the shape of it, the movement, the color of it, all suggesting we'd made a mistake. There was that turbulent noise, too, just like at the airport when you want to turn your head away from a jet engine, but it was larger, harsher than that. As it moved toward us, at about thirty miles an hour, the engine of the truck died. Ben turned the key and ground the engine.

"I'll take a look," he said, taking some tools from the glove box and stepping outside. It was raining again now and he stood in that rain and raised the hood while I looked through the side window that was streaked with water but through which the thing could still be seen. From time to time I put my head down, praying now, not just mouthing the words, but saying them with conviction while I felt around me, in the cab, the moist, quick heat of terror.

Ben stood in front of the open hood, his head under it, the tools clinking against the engine while the funnel came toward us, the thing now moving into fields that had been planted and which were already green and knee high with corn. Ben slammed the hood, the yellow piece of metal falling away and showing the flat horizon and that black thing against it. He looked at me through the glass, the funnel now over his shoulder, his expression having about it the frank, greasy look of terror, and not just because of the tornado, either. He got into the truck and threw the tools onto the floor, the pliers, screwdriver, and socket wrenches twisting end over end. He turned to me, and I looked out the window again, seeing the funnel, the black shape suggestive of every human error.

"All right," I said, "why don't you try to get a little closer?"

Ben gripped the wheel, his forehead bright now, but not with rainwater. Outside, the funnel looked like smoke coming from a steam locomotive, the shape of it bent across the fields in front of us, the thing getting larger or just higher above us as it approached. Ben still gripped the wheel as he said, "Faith, you know what? You really slay me." He got out of the cab and grabbed that two-hundred-and-fifty-pound package of instruments, swinging it onto the ground and depositing it there somewhat like a man smoothly rolling a ball down a bowling alley. Then he got back inside and slammed the door, reaching over and pulling the truck into gear as he did so, and saying to me, too, "You really slay me, Faith. But let's get the hell out of here."

The truck bumped in the ditch as he turned around, and then we went quickly, about as fast as the truck could go, the hood and cab shuddering in the wind, the rain hitting the windshield in grape-size drops. As we went, Ben picked up the microphone of the radio and started describing the funnel, its shape and direction. I put my hand to my face and the light, constant shaking of my fingers was like having a moth fluttering against my cheek. Then we stopped at the side of the road, smelling ozone, and as the windows misted over I said, "Look. Everything's fine. You can do anything you want. Okay? Isn't there a project that flies into thunderclouds?"

"Yes," he said.

"I'll go," I said, "don't think I won't."

The long black road in front of us was wet and as shiny as a piano top. After a while we came to our motel, and there, in the parking lot, we turned on the radio and listened for word about the next one. At night, when we had dinner, Ben looked across the table and said, "Please, Faith, listen. I never want to condescend to you. Do you understand that? But sooner or later this is going to cause trouble. You know that. Let's stop this. Please."

We went home, back to that small rented house in Berkeley, and when we got there, it seemed that we did so on my terms: he had begged off, perhaps not because he was convinced I was fine, but certainly in respect of how far I'd go. When I was alone I closed my eyes with the secret pleasure only power gives.

Ben went out and got a job with the National Weather Service, where he made forecasts and read them over the radio, and now he wore a jacket and tie and showed up at the door in the evening with a bag full of groceries, his appearance having about it all the frank comfort of domestic life. I continued in the post office. We began to save a little money.

In the springtime, when Ben had a day off, we went out to take walks: now we climbed the hills there together, seeing the bay and smelling the eucalyptus trees. We drove to the northern peninsula, where we climbed small mountains, from the top of which you could see the wind-streaked ocean. We went into the redwoods, where there was enormous green moss at the base of the trees.

I told him I wanted to go into the Sierras, up toward Disaster Peak, which is on the other side of the valley. We both took some time off. Ben packed a lunch and put it in the car.

We drove east and north, seeing the purplish mountains ahead of us rising out of the valley, their peaks regular and looking like saw teeth against the horizon. There was a map on the seat between us, but Ben didn't look at it very often, just once or twice, even though we went on Forestry Service roads, dirt ones, and when we came to the end of the last one, we parked and started to climb, Ben taking the small blue pack from the car. I was behind him as we went uphill and around the pines, and he walked with a slightly wooden gait. When he stopped and turned to look below, his back was straight and unmoving, like a cigar-store Indian's. Around us there was the smell of rosin where the pines oozed bubbly sap, and the needles between the trees were cinnamon colored and so deep that when you walked through them it was like wading at the beach with the water curling around your ankles.

We went on walking now, going over the flowers, small yellow and white ones, like bread and butter. There were stones on the slope, and some of them were as large as bathtubs and covered with flaky white and greenish lichen. After a while the tree line was far beneath us and we saw for miles, the valley below filled with a mixture of thin clouds and air that suggested a misty lake. It made the mountain seem like an island. The sun was hot and we were warm, especially after the climb, and Ben took off the pack, removing from it a bottle of champagne, wrapped in a white tea towel, and two long-stemmed glasses, too. He opened the bottle and poured the champagne, and we stood there, hot and tired, but feeling cool where the wind hit the damp places.

Below there was the rocky, treeless mountain, the grasses and stones and small flowers, the collection of them stark and vulnerable.

"Have you got me up here to make love to me?" I said.

"Oh, I don't know," said Ben. "I was thinking of something riskier than that."

"What?" I said, "Do you think I can be frightened? After what we've been through? Can you still think there's something wrong, or something I can't handle?"

"No. No. It's not like that," said Ben. "No. Maybe we should get married and have some kids."

I went right on looking at him, seeing his figure on the slope immediately below me, his head turned upward, his hair sandy in that light, the trees, that barren landscape, the misty air beyond him, and as I stared, there came over me the same terror as when we had sat through those storms or chased a tornado, the cold points of it like flakes of snow. I finished the champagne, and then I unzipped my blue jeans and pulled them down, removing my underwear and folding both, making a small monument to the domestic. The champagne glass sat next to the neatly folded things, the grass and sky and my legs elongated in the stem.

"All right," I said, "do you think I'd stop there? Do you?"

There was the tickle of the grass around my ankles, the warm sun on my legs, the odor of the grasses and hot stones, not to mention the blue, distant mist below. On the slope, in the breeze, there was the pulsing sheen of the grass, the effect of it like seeing infinitely small fish swimming in a current. I sat down now, feeling more of that grass, the sensation of it dry and somehow certain, not at all like that thrill of terror, but still a thrill, although one that now was warm and infinitely pleasurable.

After a while we stood up and dressed awkwardly, each of us first standing on one leg and then the other. The effect of the champagne had gone and our clothes seemed to drag against the skin when we put them on. It had gotten colder. We sat back to back when we tied our shoes, the bump and brush of each other coming as reassurance while the mountain became gray-blue with shadows.

Ben put the glasses and the bottle back into the pack and we started downhill, toward the tree line. I went behind him, his head and shoulders and the pack all having a steady up-and-down movement, not cheerful or swaggering, but businesslike now. It was getting late. We walked quickly in the heavy shadows, and as we went there came over me that tingling shock or realization, just like, I imagine, the reverend felt when that Cadillac turned into a large piece of Jell-O. I put my head up and walked, wondering if Ben knew that after enough terrifying times, each one taken as defiance, I'd face this moment just like any other bolt of lightning or gust of wind. At the top of the mountain, where the sun still shined, the cone of the peak was butter-colored in the last, warm light of the day. We went into the trees, the stones with the scaly patches of lichen and the grass disappearing behind us in the clutter of trunks. I still watched that up-and-down movement of his head and shoulders, and in that slight fatigue from the champagne, I thought that maybe the earlier fear had been just a warm-up to this one, and in the terror of what we were doing (no longer scaring ourselves with getting killed, but the reverse, with actually bringing life into the world), I had an odd, bitter moment, just like biting on a loose, itchy tooth and tasting the blood, since I realized I hadn't understood what was happening at all.

The realization of it came as a soft, maddening caress. It was clear that while we had been struggling with one another (with Ben trying to prove he wouldn't condescend to me and me trying to prove I was all right, not damaged, not a freak), we had in fact been trapped by something else. I was so frightened and amazed that we had been watched (and were now being made use of) that everything around me had a kind of glassy brightness, and even now I can close my eyes and see the trees, the rill-like creases in the bark, the milky bubbles of sap, and the rust-colored needles we walked through. And, as though to acknowledge the difficulties we faced and maybe even the treachery we'd begun, or maybe just in humility before the fact that we had been trapped by life simply loving life, Ben went before me, making a list, out loud, of every lemon he'd ever bought, starting with a Hudson Hornet with a cracked block, the water from the radiator of which slowly leaked into the crankcase so that, in the beginning, Ben had the impression he could drive the thing forever and not add any oil, since the crankcase seemed to fill all by itself.

We got back into that serviceable station wagon and drove across the valley, and after dark, when we went along the straight roads, we heard the flatland preachers on the radio, their voices rising and falling, the sound coming as a sweet, genuine rapture. Later we heard those stations you only get at night in the San Joaquin Valley, the small, one-horse transmitters where the disc jockeys are probably also engineers between songs, and from them we heard Howlin' Wolf. Ben sang along with him, staring straight ahead, the car going fast now, the lights of the city in the distance not beckoning us so much as attracting us, like moths to a flame.

So we went along, Ben laughing every now and then about a car he'd gotten screwed on, like a big Pontiac with a smashed-in front end and a leaky fuel pump and bad carburetor, and me still feeling that terror, as though it were some slimy thing like egg white slipping over my skin, but even so, as we went, I smelled around us the odor of grass, flowers, those enormous dry stones, not to mention our own salty, sweaty scent, and while I remembered the afternoon, I heard him say, "And you know what happened after that Chevrolet? Well, I'll tell you. I got stuck with a Dodge, I mean a real dog, and let me tell you . . ." and I said, "Hush, just hush now. Let me hold your hand for a minute, will you?"

But it didn't happen quite so fast, and for a while there we lived in a kind of heightened, alert stasis. Ben got up for work every morning, knotting his tie in the mirror, appearing there for all the world like responsibility itself. When he was gone, I got up and took a shower and dressed, too, combing out my hair before the mirror and looking into my eyes, one of them brown, the other brown and gray, and while I felt the tug of the comb or brush I thought of my aunt and uncle. I prayed that my child, when or if I ever got pregnant, wouldn't be blind.

So we lived in that continual state of excitement: we didn't think this would go on forever, but yet we couldn't imagine things being different. But even then I was still suspicious of him, or not quite certain that this wasn't all some joke, or another thing I would look back on with regret. I needed some hard, three-dimensional thing to remind me that we were going ahead after all. On Saturdays I opened the newspaper to the real-estate section where there were pictures of houses, each one of them suggesting certainty and regularity. Now I said, my voice having about it something of Ben's when he had wanted to buy or sell a car (which proved, if nothing else, that I had learned something while living with him), "You know, Ben, there are some ads in the newspaper for houses. I wonder if you think any of them are worth looking at. It's all the same to me."

So we got into Ben's plain Chevrolet and looked at houses, going through the empty rooms, or rooms with people in them, their eyes turned toward us with a kind of wariness, as though we weren't thinking about buying so much as just moving in, for free.

In the end we found a two-story house at the end of a road, back against the hillside. The backyard was big and overgrown, the orange and avocado trees there surrounded by weeds and having in front of them some lawn chairs, which stuck up through the grass like things left afloat after an ocean liner has sunk. On one side of the house there was an overgrown orchard, too, the trees unpruned, the recent growth of them spikelike and forming a cloud of brush. Deer came into the orchard to eat the apples. Big mule deer.

Now, as we stood in the quiet, overgrown yard, Ben turned and asked me if I wanted the house, and I said yes, without even batting an eye.

After we had wandered around some more in those waist-high weeds, kicking unseen toys and garden tools that had been left behind, Ben got behind the wheel of that plain Chevrolet and drove to the bank, where he went in, his gait one of fierce directness, as though things had been decided and between him and the realization of what he had promised there were only some nagging, bureaucratic details. And in the evening he sat at the kitchen table, a calculator on one side and those green forms from the bank on the other, carefully filling in the blanks and probably realizing right then that we didn't have anywhere near enough money.

Then, without hesitating, even though he had never asked his father for a thing before, he picked up the phone, and called Dr. Lunn and asked to borrow thirty-five thousand dollars to buy a house and to get married, too. He'd pay it back, of course. With interest. Would his father come to dinner and talk it over?

I made some food, pork chops and applesauce, mashed potatoes and string beans. Apple pie and cheese for dessert. When I cooked, when I rolled out the dough or peeled and cut the apples and sprinkled them with sugar and cinnamon, I did it with a vengeance, taking things out of the icebox or off the shelf and putting them down with a bang and a clatter, not seemingly rude or overly noisy, just a little fast and sharp, as though I'd seen a tentacle of the thing that had trapped us and that I was driving it back where it came from with a hot platter.

Ben's father was a tall man in his late sixties with short, silver hair, a silver mustache, dark-brown eyes, and reddish cheeks. When he came to dinner he wore a brown suit and a green tie, both looking beautiful and expensive. He was a little drunk.

We had met before, but then it had seemed more as though Ben and I had been on a date. Now he came into our rented house and looked around. The pie was on the counter, cooling. You could see he wanted to ask, *Have you gone to college? Oh, you haven't? You work in the post office sometime? And you've had a seizure or two?* Instead, he avoided my eyes, one brown and the other brown and gray, and asked Ben for something to drink.

We sat in the living room, and in the distance there was the bridge and the fog piled up behind it. Ben's father looked out the window and around the room and finally at me. I smiled. He stared back, now a little drunker than before, rattling the ice in his glass. When he asked Ben for another drink, he said, "This time hit me with a little meat." Then we sat down to dinner, the three of us around the kitchen table on which I'd put a tablecloth and our ordinary, studentlike plates and silverware. Ben's father went on drinking at the table, eating only the mashed potatoes, now looking directly at me and then at Ben and saying to his son, "You remember the time you threw a cue ball through that window and I had to get you out of jail?"

"I remember," said Ben.

I sat between them, watching the food get cold. It was a good dinner and looked nice on the plates.

"You didn't know anything about love, Ben. Not the first thing," said Dr. Lunn.

"Let's talk about something else," said Ben.

"I didn't mean to upset you," said Dr. Lunn.

"I'm not upset," said Ben.

"Good, good," said Dr. Lunn.

He had another sip of his drink and turned toward me. "I don't want to upset anybody," he said. "Especially not you, Faith. But I think it's time we talked about the difficulties you've been having."

"What difficulties?" I said.

"Seizures," he said. "Epilepsy."

He looked at my face, eyes, my hands.

"Ben shouldn't have told you," I said. "It was a secret."

"A *secret,*" he said. "Listen, young lady, you are thinking about having children and—"

"This has gone far enough," said Ben.

"When did you first have them?" said his father.

"After a high fever," I said.

"No brothers, sisters, no parents with the same problem?" I shook my head. He sighed.

"That's something," he said. "At least your children aren't likely—"

"Stop it!" said Ben.

My fingers began to shake a little now. Dr. Lunn looked at them and said, "Do you know you're having an occurrence now? Jacksonian tremors."

"No," I said. "I'm just self-conscious. That's all."

"Well, it looks like—" he said.

"How dare you?" said Ben. "How dare you come in here shit-faced and start this?"

Dr. Lunn turned toward his son now, both obviously trembling. Ben swallowed and looked down a little.

"I'm sorry," said Ben. "I didn't mean to talk like that to you . . ."

"Oh, Christ," said Dr. Lunn, "I'm ruining your dinner. Now, that's just what I didn't want to do."

Dr. Lunn slapped the table, the silverware jumping and the water in the glasses swaying from side to side, as though we were on a ship.

"Will you accept my apology?" said Dr. Lunn.

Ben closed his eyes and nodded.

"Faith?" said Dr. Lunn. "Will you accept it, too?"

"Yes. Of course," I said, holding my hands under the table, pressing the fingertips together.

Dr. Lunn turned back to Ben and said, "What I wanted to say is you're doing fine, just fine now. You know that, don't you? Everything's turned around. Just fine." Now he reached across the table and put his arm on Ben's shoulder. "I can still put my arm around my own son, can't I?"

Ben nodded and said, "Sure you can. Why don't you have something to eat?"

"More potatoes, Dr. Lunn?" I said, holding the bowl out. I held it steady, watching him.

"Yes, Faith, please," said Dr. Lunn, and then he got up and went into the bathroom, where he knelt and started throwing up, the repetitive sound of it seeming loud as it echoed from the porcelain bowl where he had put his head. Ben and I sat there, looking at one another.

"The dinner looked real nice, didn't you think?" I said.

In the morning, though, Ben's father was up early, dressed and gone, leaving on the kitchen table a check for thirty-five thousand dollars, made out to both of us and left there with all the quietness of grief and shame. Ben came into the kitchen and picked it up, the long rectangular slip of paper held between his thumb and forefinger. Then he put it on the bulletin board, the shove of the pin having about it the knowledge of just what a marriage was made out of after all.

Our wedding was in San Francisco. Anthony Bompasino was best man. It was a small wedding with just some friends from Berkeley and Ben's father. My aunt and uncle came, and I wore white. My mother came from Cleveland, too, and when we were alone, she said, "You see? There is something better. Just imagine. My daughter marrying a weatherman. Isn't that something?"

Ben wore a new, dark suit from Brooks Brothers and he had a carnation in his lapel, although at the height of the ceremony, when I stepped up to kiss him, he felt the frank, dutiful pressure of my lips, not cold, not even uncaring really, but just matter of fact: the knowledge of it passed between us. After the reception we drove up to the house, which was now ours, but that was about all: it was still surrounded by weeds, and the old lawn furniture still stuck out of them. We got out of the car, and then Ben picked me up and carried me through the front door, putting me down quickly, my heels hitting the floor with an empty sound. Then he took my hand and led me to the backyard, where he stood for a moment, touching his lips. There was a shovel by the back door, and he picked it up and began digging, still in his dark suit and those Brooks Brothers shoes, saying, as he did so, "You see, Faith, along here I'm going to plant some bulbs, tulips and daffodils, or maybe narcissus. Do you have to force bulbs in California? Maybe some poppies, too. Can you see? Right in here."

After we moved in Dr. Lunn called to say Ben's mother had died. Ben stood in the kitchen, holding the phone to his ear, nodding, his eyes closed, saying, "All right. We'll be ready tomorrow morning. We'll be waiting in front of the house."

That was on Monday evening. The funeral was on Tuesday afternoon, in Los Angeles. On Tuesday morning Ben woke at first light, both of us curled together, my knees with a pillow between them and his knees curled behind me, holding that same pillow: we slept like people riding a bicycle built for two. Outside the sky was yellow and it had a sheen to it like a piece of satin. Here and there the stars were still out, bright as an airplane's landing lights, and this made the sky look like a pale yellow slip on which someone had spilled a few rhinestones.

Ben sat at the side of the bed, looking out the window, his hands on his knees. Then I got up, too, and sat next to him, both of us looking at that yellow-gray sky. We sat there, neither one of us wanting to get dressed and to start waiting outside, but even so, there was a cold, heavy weight in the room.

"Do you think I should wear black shoes, too?" he said.

"Yes," I said, "I think that's right."

"Okay," he said.

We sat there for a moment more, the room getting a little brighter, but not much warmer. The sky was smooth, and there was about it the suggestion of the softest skin imaginable. Ben sat next to me, looking out the window.

"I'm sorry, Ben," I said.

He nodded now, taking my hand for a moment.

"I know you are," he said, and then he got up and took a shower, leaving plenty of hot water for me. When he came out, he said, "I feel lonely sometimes. Just as lonely as . . ." He closed his eyes and swallowed. "Just too goddamned lonely for words."

"I understand," I said.

"Oh, Faith," he said, looking at me, "you know what? I bet you really do."

I put on a black dress and black shoes, and when I came into the kitchen Ben was wearing a dark blue suit, the same one he had worn to be married. There was a can of Kiwi shoe polish on the kitchen table next to him, the cake inside greasy and coal-colored. He had a shoe in one hand and a rag with wax on it in the other. Soon the shoes were shined, but his fingers were stained. Then he stood at the sink, scrubbing them, saying, "How can I get that off? Why the hell do those marks have to be there?"

"Here," I said, bringing out the bleach and putting a little on the spot. There was still a little mark there, but you'd have to look hard to see it.

He went on rubbing it for a while. Then we went outside and stood in the driveway. The sky got lighter, the yellow of it now becoming brighter, more buff-colored, like a peach. There was no breeze. Dr. Lunn pulled into the drive in his new Chevrolet station wagon, the car floating over the bump at the street with a smooth, soundless action. The tires were new and shiny, too.

"Good morning, Faith," he said.

"Hello," I said.

"You better drive, Ben," said Dr. Lunn, shoving over and sitting on the right-hand side, wearing his dark blue suit and a dark tie, the two of them looking almost exactly alike. On Dr.

Lunn's thumb and forefinger there were black stains from shoe polish, and when he saw me looking at it, he said, "I tried to get it off. That's the best I could do."

The car smelled of the adhesive tape he had in the back, along with gauze bandages in waxed, crinkly paper, syringes, cases of bottles with rubber stoppers, pints of glucose, and his black bag, which sat there like an enormous lunch box. The odor of the paper wrappers, the rubber stoppers, the small, clean bottles was reassuring.

For a while, as we drove, we said nothing. The hills, covered with houses, gave way to the flat land of the valley, where the houses lay along straight streets. Then we came to some of the large farms.

"I wonder," said Dr. Lunn to Ben, "do you think they'll ask me to say anything?"

"I don't know," he said.

"Maybe I could tell a story," he said, "you know? Just some small, pleasant thing. What do you remember?"

The white lines on the road were new, bright and white, clean.

"When she came back she had a trunk with her," Ben said. "It was covered with crocodile skin. Her clothes hung in it like in a closet, and it had some drawers, too. I thought it was the most beautiful thing I'd ever seen."

"Well," Dr. Lunn said after a minute, "I probably won't have to say anything."

Then we were quiet until we arrived. The service was held in a small commercial chapel in West Hollywood. It was newish, but already well used, and the carpets were gray where people had walked up and down the aisle. In the foyer there were some artificial flowers, but they were new and weren't dusty. The place smelled of furniture polish. An Episcopal minister stood in his black robes, waiting as Ben's mother's friends came in, not many of whom were crying, although the few who did so cried hard. There were women who looked as though they were trying to hide the fact that they had gotten old, and women who looked like waitresses, secretaries, barmaids, and maybe even a few who worked in department stores, selling clothes and running the cash register. There were a few, too, who had a flowing, theatrical carriage, their shoulders moving from side to side, their locomotion coming as one long fluid sweep down to the altar where Ben's mother lay. I recognized a man from a TV series, his stature as the only working actor there having about it the air of a blessing. The coffin was open and the people filed by, Dr. Lunn and Ben included, both of them glancing down for a moment. I found a seat in the back and waited there.

Ben and Dr. Lunn sat down next to me, all of us with our heads down now, listening. The minister said, reading from the Psalm, "Lord, let me know mine end, and the number of my days . . . Hear my prayer, O Lord, and with thine eyes consider my calling; hold not thy peace at my tears; for I am a stranger with thee, and a sojourner, as all my fathers were . . ."

Then the minister said, "Let us pray," and on the bench next to me Ben and Dr. Lunn did so, both trembling with the effort. Their hands were together, Dr. Lunn's arm against mine, and the wood of the bench had a slight, constant tremor in it. I put my hands together, too. Then the both of them sat there, in the back row, identical in their suits and ties, their stained fingers, each with his head down, one silver haired, the other sandy and just touched by gray.

The organ played and we walked out and got into the car and started driving through the streets of Los Angeles. As we drove, Dr. Lunn put his hands together again, watching those shiny, glittering streets, the trash in them bright with sunlight and blowing dust.

"I'm sorry," I said.

"Yeah, well . . . it had been a while since I'd seen her," said Dr. Lunn. "Maybe we should stop for something. Faith, would you like a drink?"

"Yes," I said. "I'd like something."

"I'll stop at the next place," said Ben.

"It doesn't have to be fancy," said Dr. Lunn. "Anything will be fine."

We stopped at a brick, one-story restaurant that was

called the Night Cap. It was daytime still, but at night the sign
would have blue and green lights shining on it from the lamps
in plants along the sidewalk. It was dark and cool inside, and
almost empty, aside from two men who sat silently at the bar,
smoking cigarettes and drinking from small glasses of flat
beer.

"Until she died I thought she might pack a bag and . . .
you know, maybe that small town I live in wouldn't look so bad
to her when she got older," said Dr. Lunn. "I thought she'd
come home. How could I have been so full of shit?"

"Father," said Ben.

"Here's what waiting gets you," said Dr. Lunn.

One of his hands moved toward the cool, empty room
where an island of cigarette smoke hung about five feet off the
floor.

"Yeah," said Dr. Lunn, "that suitcase was beautiful. She
had shoes to match, too. Did you know that? Real crocodile.
They were something. They really were."

He closed his eyes and cried.

"Dad," said Ben, "Dad."

"Ah, Ben, give me your hand for a minute, will you? That
would be a big help now."

They put their hands out, gripping the other's, so there
was a large knot of flesh on the table, their fingers, stained
with that black polish, now intertwined. It looked as if they
were closing some long, difficult, and probably futile deal.
Then they each had a drink in a shot glass, pouring it down
quickly.

We spent the night in a motel, one that smelled of some
familiar thing, like the inside of a new refrigerator. I slept
alone and Ben and Dr. Lunn sat up in the other room. In the
morning we started the long drive north, not having to say
much, and after a while the car was filled with the sound of Dr.
Lunn's gentle snoring as he slept against the window.

At home we all got out of the car, each of us looking as
though we'd slept in our clothes. Dr. Lunn's hands shook a
little. The light breeze blew his dark tie and the front panels of
his jacket, which swung open and showed the wrinkled shirt

underneath. After a while Ben and Dr. Lunn walked around
to the rear of the house and sat on the back steps, each of them
with his forearms across his knees.

Beyond them there was the yard, the grass now cut, but
you could still see the burrows the gophers were making. For a
while the two of them stared at those long green welts in the
grass. Ben got up and walked over them, seeming indifferent
to them, but in fact going into the half-rotting shed from
which he took a gopher trap. It was a square, wooden thing,
about the size of a shoe box and having a spring-loaded bar
that went through it, bottom to top. The trap was supposed to
be put into a burrow and then the gopher would run along it
and try to go through the trap, too. Ben took a shovel out of
the shed and dug into one of the burrows, doing so in his
Brooks Brothers suit and good shoes. He knelt in the dirt to
put the trap into the hole he had dug, raking the dirt over it
with his hands and patting it down so no light would get in.

Ben went into the kitchen and took two bottles of beer
out of the icebox. His father sat in the afternoon sunlight,
putting up his hand to take the cool, sweating, brown bottle of
beer. They didn't say much then, and they sat there, side by
side, drinking the beer in that pale yellow light. An hour
passed before the trap was sprung, the thing making a sound
like someone hitting a mink coat with the flat of a knife. Then
Ben got up and lifted the trap out of the ground, the gopher
neatly caught in it, its teeth long and yellow, its body hanging
there. He turned the trap over and gave it one angry shake
and looked up at his father and said, "Look at the little bastard.
Just look. How are we going to get rid of them? How the hell
am I going to stop them?" His father just shrugged, though,
and then got up and hugged his son, and turned out toward
the driveway, where he got into that new car and began the
long drive home.

"Come into the house," I said. "It doesn't do any good to
sit out here. Come inside. There's something I want to tell
you."

"What's that?" I said .

"Well, come inside," I said. "I'll show you a magic trick."

"What's that?"

"Come in," I said, "Here. Reach inside my blouse. Let me help you. Do you feel how swollen I am? And how hot the skin is?"

"Yes," he said.

"And tender. I can't tell you. I'm way overdue."

He nodded, still touching me.

"That's wonderful," he said.

The pregnancy came as one long progression, and when we lay in a bedroom of that large empty house (with the weeds now cut down and the lawn furniture now painted), there was the sense not only of my own child, but of others, too, not yet born, not yet inside me, but desperately wanting to be. I felt them around me, the faceless shapes of them stretching into the dark, the color of them hard to see in the soft gloom where they were unable to do anything aside from that quiet, insistent, even desperate waiting to get into the world through me. The room glistened with the terror of it. And along with this there was the certainty, too, that while life delighted in life in general, it didn't give a damn about much else, certainly not about one bear, or one seal, or one lion, and certainly not one woman, lying in an old house in California. Once, during the day, I found a children's book about caribou and discovered how a wolf hunts them: he chases the entire herd until one can't keep up. I sat there, holding the book, nodding, agreeing with it, realizing, for the first time, what we'd got ourselves into.

Genny, our first child, was a cranky baby, and most of the time I didn't feel well enough to get up with her. Ben got out of bed, his legs visibly trembling near dawn on those nights when the baby screamed if he stopped carrying her. After the sun rose he shaved, dressed, and then brought Genny into her bed, where I rolled over and said, "Please. Don't bring her in here."

"I've got to go to work," he said.

"Oh, God," I said, "I hardly slept."

So, after the first child came, we weren't so cheerful or

maybe just not so spunky anymore, since we didn't have the time or the energy to climb mountains and make love or to sit through a thunderstorm or chase tornadoes, either. And now I didn't have the energy or the desire to prove anything to him, aside from making it clear that something terrible had happened to me, the proof of it being that I was sick a lot more now than before.

When I was sick at night the sound of it woke Genny, and when I came out of that long blackness I found Ben bending over me, mopping my face where I had spit up. He held the damp washcloth in one hand and had Genny tucked under his arm, where she screamed, her eyes closed, her fists clinched, her feet kicking at him. The sheets were dirty where I'd lost control, and there hadn't been time to change them, not with the baby screaming. The room had a harsh, acidic odor, too. When I looked at him, my eyes still a little confused, I said, "Please. Can you get the baby quiet?" He took Genny down the hall and got her quiet and into bed, and then came back and changed the sheets, rolling the dirty ones into large balls around the stains. He washed me, too, and changed the sheets and helped me into bed, his expression never really satisfying me.

Now I was glad to be sick, since it wasn't only that I wanted to get Ben's attention, I was angry at what having a child had done: it was another thing for which I'd been dealt a dirty hand. When I was sick now, it was a way of saying, *How did you get me into this?*

At night after we got Genny to sleep, we went to bed. Sometimes he reached across those cold sheets and I said, "Please. Please don't touch me. I don't want to get sick later."

Now we didn't even talk about going to a doctor anymore: Ben knew I wouldn't, and around us, in the house, there was the presence of something momentous about to happen. I was left with the sickness to show him how I felt.

I liked to go out on Saturday, and there were times when he had a day off in the middle of the week and then we went to lunch, at the Mark Hopkins, and looked at the Pacific or just at people. There were friends of his from school or work and sometimes we went to a party. Once, when we came home, I said, "We're beginning to look a little shabby, do you know that? I saw someone looking at your jacket."

"Who was looking at it?" said Ben.

"Oh, someone from the weather service. I don't know his name. All the names sound alike to me. Rolston and Peterson and Larson. Who can keep them straight?"

"There's nothing wrong with my jacket," he said.

"*I* didn't say there was," I said, "I just said people were looking at it. And at my clothes, too."

"Look," he said, "we've got the mortgage, the house to paint, the payments for the new furnace . . . Weathermen just don't make that much money."

"What was all that studying about, then?" I said.

"I *like* what I do," said Ben.

"Well, what about me?" I said. "All I see is the paycheck."

"You can go back to work when the kids are older," he said.

"That's *years* away," I said.

He sighed now.

"I'm sorry," I said. "I just got tired of people looking at you that way."

Ben took a part-time job. Now one evening a week he went into town and changed the signs on a theater marquee, carrying those enormous red plastic *A*'s, *B*'s, *C*'s up a ladder and spelling out, against the lighted panels of the marquee, *The Spy Who Came in from the Cold, The Pawnbroker, Around the World in Eighty Days.* Each letter was two feet high and had, close up, the scale of a kite. Ben went every Wednesday night, driving that serviceable Chevrolet (which was now six years old) and stopping in front of those enormous, lighted marquees where he looked up and read the words he had put up the previous week. Mostly he went late at night, when there weren't many people around.

Sometimes after I'd been sick and was resting, he'd get up and dress and ask a neighbor to look in on the baby, and then he'd drive into the city and climb that ladder with those enormous letters, clipping the words on with a steady, patient attempt to put things right.

He bought his own letters and began branching out, dressing the marquee not only for the theater where he had begun, but others, too. He built a shed in the backyard, a small wooden one, and that's where he kept the letters, the enormous *A*'s, *B*'s, *C*'s all hung on twenty-penny nails. Now, at night, when he couldn't sleep, he got up and dressed and went out there, where he stood before the regular arrangements of letters, the conglomeration of them making no sense at all, but the size of them being almost noisy. He took down a list of the titles he'd need for the next week and started putting them together, a letter at a time, slapping each one down and tying each word into a bundle. There were times when I rolled over and found him gone, and then I went outside, too, dressed in a bathrobe and slippers, and stood in the door of that small shed, hearing the letters come down *slap, slap, slap,* the cool breeze blowing the front panels of the robe open and showing, in the light that came from the shed, the few small blue veins that were on my legs now: the first child had done that. He had the list of titles on a clipboard in front of him, and I stood there, watching him, seeing those big letters pile up into a word, which was tied together with a navy knot.

By now our second child, Sarah, was three years old, and Genny was eight. Ben went on with putting the letters up, making a little more extra money, although the movie theaters were changing, one after another, and they didn't need signs saying *The Spy Who Came in from the Cold* or *Around the World in Eighty Days,* but ones saying *Blanche's Secret, Slippery When Wet, Swedish Twins, Hot Summer, White Slaves, Girls in Love, In Heat,* and just as the theaters had changed so had the people who went to them. Now Ben went out to the shed in the middle of the night and slapped the letters into *Young Lust,* or *French Maids,* and then took the bundles of words into the city, where he climbed the ladder and stood in the breeze, finishing one theater and going to the next, occasionally hearing a voice from below saying, "Hey, buster, where can you get laid around here?"

On weekends Ben worked around the house. Genny helped him. She wore blue overalls and had her hair in a ponytail, and when Ben fixed a leaking faucet, she carried a bucketful of washers, which she dumped on the floor, picking from among the clutter the one Ben needed. In the evening they sat by the radio in the kitchen, listening to a show that played old rock and roll songs, Ben having a glass of beer and Genny a glass of soda, and both talking about whether a song was "hard-driving rock and roll." Fats Domino, Buddy Holly, Elvis Presley were hard driving. Jerry Lee Lewis was, too. They listened to Fats Domino singing "I'm Ready" and "Ain't That a Shame." To Rosie and the Elegants singing "Angel Baby," the Diamonds "Little Darlin'," Richie Valens "Donna," and other songs, too, "Stand by Me," "In the Still of the Night." On Ben's fortieth birthday we had a small party for him, and then he and Genny listened to the radio, the two of them comfortably settled on a sofa in the corner of the kitchen, and when Jerry Lee Lewis sang "Whole Lot of Shakin' Goin' On," Ben listened as though watching the approach of a tornado or of those bright, purple columns of lightning, the memory of the power of them clearly on his face.

"Dad," said Genny, "where were you when you listened to 'Ain't That a Shame'? I don't mean as an oldie. I mean for real."

"Oh, I don't know," he said.

"Tell me," she said. "You remember."

He put his arm around her and said, "It must have been where I grew up. I guess that's where I heard it last."

In the fall I looked out the window at the orchard. Ben and the children were there, picking the apples, wanting to save as many as they could from rotting on the ground. They'd planned to go to Sears to buy a small cider press, one you cranked by hand. Even from the kitchen I felt excluded. I knew, too, that this was another thing that was somehow unexpected: how lonely I felt when I saw Ben with the children, all of them having a kind of unencumbered joy. Ben had a burlap sack filled with apples, and as he carried it away from the trees, the children followed him, jumping up on him, so filled with love for him that they couldn't just walk, they had to bound and shriek with it. They swung from his arms, pulled on his clothes, and even from a distance I saw his face as they gave him those small, sweet tugs. The kids' hands were sticky from the windfalls, and at the side of the house Ben turned on the hose so they could wash, but soon the kids were jumping through the water, or grabbing the hose, squirting each other and Ben. The backyard was filled with sudden bright plumes of water, the mist of them breaking into a rainbow. All of them laughed, and then they came into the kitchen, dripping water, all of them still smiling and dragging the now wet bag of apples.

"You're making a mess of the floor," I said.

"Oh, Mom, look at the apples . . ." said Genny.

"No," I said, "I want you to look at the floor. Ben, can't you be a little more considerate?"

He stopped there in the kitchen, his hand just touching Genny's head, gently pressing against her wet hair.

"We were just having a good time," he said. "I'm sorry it got out of hand."

"*A good time,*" I said. "What about this floor?"

"Come on, girls," he said, "let's go outside and get dried off there."

They turned and went out, a little quieter now, but as soon as they were outside, they were happy again. Ben brought some towels, and the girls sat before him, their blond heads reddish-gold in the fall sunlight after he had dried their hair. The children sat still for a moment, Ben's arms around both of them, hugging them a little, if only to remind himself he wasn't dreaming and that the children really existed after all.

At night, after their bath, I saw him cleaning Genny's ears. She held her hair away from her head, her neck bare and white in the overhead fixture, Ben's fingers just touching her, gently doing the job.

"That didn't hurt, did it?" said Ben.

"No," she said, dropping her hair and yawning now.

I went downstairs and had another cup of coffee, putting more sugar in it, somehow or other never able to get it sweet enough.

When I was alone on a dim December afternoon, I stood in the bedroom and took off my clothes and looked at the small blue veins on my legs, at the shape of my breasts, the marks on my hips, all of which were proof that I had been trapped, that I hadn't gotten away at all, or that life had used me and wasn't even half done. I sat down on the bed and stared, and then I looked away.

At night I said to Ben, "I didn't think you'd let things get this way. I thought we'd be better off. And to think there was a time when I thought you were smart."

Ben got out of bed and stood there, turned toward me, not saying a thing. Then he took a blanket from the closet and went downstairs, where he made himself a bed on the couch. When he came back for a pillow, his hands trembling as he tried to pick it up, I said, "What if I'm sick?"

"I'll hear you," he said, "I'll come up. Don't worry."

I woke early, in the quiet brown shadows of the morning. No one was in the bed next to me and I slipped my hand between the cool, empty sheets. Then I went downstairs and sat on the sofa, putting my hand on his head.

"I'm sorry," I said. "I just wish you could understand how things are for me."

He turned and looked at me.

"I understand," he said.

"Do you?" I said. "I don't think so."

He shrugged.

"I never said I was smart," he said. "The only thing I ever promised you is that I'd do my best."

He looked down now.

"That's what I'm doing. I can't do better. So if I were you, I'd tread a little lighter."

One December evening, Genny and Sarah came into the kitchen where Ben sat with the checkbook and a pile of bills. It was warm there and the room was filled with the aroma of a pie in the oven. The girls told Ben what they wanted for Christmas, and he said, "We'll see. We'll see."

On Saturday, Ben and I went shopping, and when we saw things that would make good presents, I reached over and picked up the price tag and showed it to Ben. Then he turned away, saying, "I don't know. Let's look a little more. Everything can't be that steep, can it?" Genny wanted a bike, a racer, and we went to three stores, the bikes lined up in long lines, one next to another, like a parking lot in China. Then we came home without buying anything.

Ben sat at the table, looking through the checkbook. Then he went upstairs and stood in front of a closet in our bedroom. It was locked and he fumbled in his pocket for the keys, and then he took from inside a shotgun his father had given him. It was an L. C. Smith, field grade, in good condition, and as he wiped the oil off it, he said, "You know, my father and I don't get out to hunt pheasants the way we thought we would. He's a little too old for it and I'm not so sure I want to hunt with him anymore. And these days the birds are all canned. You know, they're stocked. And I'm tired of having it around anyway, worrying about the kids getting into it."

On Christmas there were packages under the tree, a large one which was obviously the racing bike. The kids opened the packages, shrieking, ripping the paper. Ben watched and turned to me, smiling now. The sound of the ripping paper came like an echo, infinitely repeated, and then the light in the room got a little purple.

When I sat up, feeling stiff, there was around me the scent of balsam fir and that outhouse smell, too. Genny and Sarah were crying, Sarah saying, "Is she going to be all right, Dad? Is she?"

"Why don't you go in the other room?" said Ben.

"Is she going to be all right?" said Genny.

"Yes. You know how your mother is. It usually happens at night," he said. "You understand that, don't you?"

"Why did it happen now?" said Genny.

"I don't know," said Ben.

The children started crying again. He knelt over me with

a damp napkin in his hand. There were shiny bits on it, sparkles that came from a broken Christmas ball.

"I'm scared," said Sarah.

I moved then, hearing the ripped paper rustle around
me.

"I'll be all right," I said. "Don't worry."

Genny and Sarah sat side by side, holding hands.

Ben moved the paper away now, his hands coming out of
the fir branches above me. Then he brought a blanket and
said, "Can you walk to the bathroom? Maybe that would be
best." He helped me up and wrapped the blanket around me.
"Genny. Sarah," he said. "Everything's all right now. Everything's going to be fine. Everything's okay now."

Ben met the girl a week later. It was winter and he was
driving back from seeing his father. The road from Marlowe
goes into the mountains that separate the valley from the
coast. It is a pretty road and from it you can see the brownish
hillsides and some eucalyptus trees, the leaves of which are
the color of dirty money. The girl was in an MG, a blue one,
and she had short auburn hair. She passed Ben. It was a cool
day, and it was warm inside her car and the windows were
misted over. Ben couldn't really see what she looked like, or
that she was upset. All he knew is that she passed him and
then, after a while, she slowed down, her face turned toward
the land. So Ben went by the car, but soon she was coming up
behind him and gaining ground fast. They went on that way,
going between those brown, grassy, and rolling hills. After a
while, when she was passing him, she reached over and wrote
Lunch? in the misted-up window on the passenger's side, the
word spelled backward so he could read it.

She followed him to the next exit, and when he pulled
into a parking lot, in front of a restaurant, she got out, swinging her legs from under the wheel, and walked straight toward him, the pale sunlight falling over her hair. Her stockings had long runs in them and there was a bruise, the color of

a ripe plum, around her eye and on the side of her face. She came toward him with a kind of desperation, almost as though someone was after her, and said, "Hi, I'm Christine Taylor. What's your name?"

Book IV

Christine Taylor / Marie Boule
Wham, Wham, Wham

ON THE BUS OUT OF BAXTER I HAD TROUBLE SITTING STILL, since right from the first moment I left the hills, the birch, and the popple behind, I didn't get the relief I wanted, not from the speed of the bus or from the disappearance of familiar landscape. I wanted to get up and walk in the aisle, where at least my own locomotion would make me feel better, no matter that the bus itself was going sixty miles an hour. Just fleeing wasn't enough. I put my hands to my cheeks, just as though I had been surprised or shocked, and then I smelled the burned gunpowder on my skin from having shot at those machines in the store. And when I turned, with my hand to my face, and looked at the dull hills and leafless trees go by, what came to me first was that smell of gunpowder, a cloying, sometimes almost sweet, odor like the stink of a firecracker.

After the border of Ohio the land was flatter, and every now and then there was a farmhouse, a silo next to it and a windbreak along the fields. The houses were isolated and had a chill about them, not from the moisture of the air, although this seemed to be part of it, but because of a grubby sense of futility and lack of tenderness. I looked at the farms and pulled my coat closer to my neck, feeling the cheap rabbit fur under my chin. And with each passing mile the coolness of the farmhouses seemed to increase, and the rush of the bus, the sense of moving toward nothing more than a name on a map came as a quiet, nagging dread. What I knew about San Francisco were the things I had seen in an advertisement on TV for a rice with artificial flavoring.

More and more I just stared at the land with a kind of fascination, the passing of it giving me comfort, since so long as I passed over it I avoided the cold moment that would surely come at the end of the line. The Mississippi slipped behind me, too, when the bus went over a bridge, beneath which the water flashed and shimmered in the frigid light of spring. In Nebraska the land was flat and black, the large silos standing on it like rockets about to go to the moon. Now I put my hands to my face, smelling that burned gunpowder and almost believing it didn't come from my fingers so much as from the land I was headed into. I pulled my collar up again while I thought about my arrival in the dirty light of the Oakland terminal. It would probably be worse than Pittsburgh.

So, in the first part of Nebraska I still wanted to get up and walk back and forth, but instead I put my hand into my pocket as I had done every hour from the moment I left Baxter, and inside the worn lining I put my hand over the bills there, which were folded in half like a matchbook, the total amount of them, when I crossed the Mississippi, amounting to one hundred and ninety-seven dollars. A little change, too, quarters to put into the locks on the doors where you were charged even to use the bathroom: the slam of those metal doors had about them the arrogance of things designed to deal with unknown people who were just betwixt and between. I kept my hand on those bills, judging the thickness of the small pile, the ones and fives disappearing every time I went into a bus stop and bought a cheese sandwich or a cup of coffee at prices even my father would have shied away from as being not only unfair or greedy but maybe even immoral. When I bought something the money just evaporated, leaving my hand outstretched and then closing on the air where I expected my change to be.

In Chicago two Asian girls got on the bus. They wore dresses cut from the same pattern and which were made at home, the only difference between them being in the colors of the cotton material out of which the dresses were made, one with red flowers, the other with green. The girls came into the bus, one behind the other, their dark eyes going over the people in the seats with a darting, constant suspicion. They sat down opposite me, each of them folding her hands into her lap, the fingers laced together in the same prayerful way. They sat and looked out the window, the one closest to it speaking every now and then, saying the same words over and over and the other one nodding: they were counting Toyotas they saw on the road. *Bug ini. Bug ini.* There's another one. There's another one.

In Lincoln, Nebraska, the bus pulled into the parking lot of a barbecue restaurant. On the roof there was a neon sign with a figure of a cowboy dressed in a hat and vest and chaps. He had a lasso, and the loop of it went around his head, the path of it defined by circles of light that flicked on and off. It was cool and damp, the wind blowing along those fields that were ready for planting. Inside the restaurant I bought a barbecued beef sandwich, which was wrapped in tin foil, and then I brought it back to the bus, where I sat down and folded back the foil. The anonymous crinkle and the sudden, shameful odor, as though I were cooking in a rented room, spread from my seat. I looked down at it for a moment, and then wrapped it up again, feeling the warmth of the sandwich against my thighs. I sat for a while, thinking about what it had cost.

The Asian girls hadn't eaten since Chicago, and I leaned across the aisle and said, "Here. Would you like some? I lost my appetite."

The one on the aisle turned and looked at me, her dark eyes on mine: they were steady, incurious.

"I haven't touched it," I said. "I haven't put my cooties on it. There's no germs."

"No money. No English," said the girl. "No need talk."

"No. No," I said. "I'm not selling it."

"No money," said the girl.

"It's yours," I said. "You can share it with your sister. Here."

I held it out.

"No need talk," she said and then turned to her sister and said, her hand moving slightly, once, in my direction, *"Bug ini."* There's another one.

"Here," I said to the Asian girl, "I'll leave it on the seat. If you get hungry you can have it."

Outside, beyond the restaurant, there was a motel, a one-story building in which there was a line of rooms, each having a sliding glass door. The parking lot was empty and it was late afternoon, the spring sunlight bright but not warm. Beyond the building and the parking lot there was that flat land and the sky above it. The shadows from the few trees, the restaurant, and the building were all long and gray. At the side of the parking lot, in front of the office, there was a woman. She was tall and thin and she was wearing a long green dress, a "cocktail dress." Her hair had been nicely fixed up so it was shiny and curled, and she was obviously drunk. She stood with her arms across her chest, wobbling a little on her high heels, everything about her suggesting that she was asking some mystifying question ("Why the hell did he have to do *that*?") Above her there was a sign from last fall on the marquee of the motel, which said, NEBRASKA FOOTBALL WEEKEND. GO CORN-HUSKERS. ALL THE WAY.

After a while I slept, doing so with my hand on that shrinking pile of bills in my pocket, and while I did so, there still came from time to time that jerk and sway of the bus, the abrupt jar of it waking me up, leaving me a little sick, since that half-sleep made me feel as though I were in one long, unstoppable fall. So, in the dim light of the bus, I thought of the things I knew, or just the objects I possessed, my bag and the things in it, the lotions, the clothes, the belts, the black leather skirt and silk blouse, the canister with the light ashes inside. With a kind of sigh, or as a blessing, I slept, and when I woke at the next bus stop the Asian girls were gone and the sandwich, now cold, still sat on the seat next to me. It was early, six o'clock or so, and I took the sandwich back on my lap, but when I tried to eat it, I closed my eyes and put it away again. At the next stop I got off, carrying the cold foil, and outside I put it into the trash, feeling nothing but shame as the thing fell into the barrel. Then I went back to my seat, where I started to cry, even then knowing it would do no good in the face of where I was headed, the bus station where I would be greeted with the *wham, wham, wham* of the pinball machines, the sound of which caused a kind of anonymous ache.

I was still crying when more passengers got on, the first one a woman who wore a pink dress and who had a beehive hairdo, the thing sprayed until it had a sheen. She was a little heavy, about fifty, and she carried a shopping bag filled with used clothes for children. When she sat down, I was looking in my jacket pockets for a Kleenex.

"My allergies drive me crazy this time of the year, too," she said. "Here. You want a Dristan? It dries me up. And you know what, sugar, it will take down the puffiness."

"Thanks," I said, taking the pill and swallowing it with the last cold coffee in a Styrofoam cup.

"Oak flowers. Popple flowers. Maple. Any flowering tree. You just show me one of those little red flowers and it's curtains for me. Does mullen or goldenrod get you in the fall?"

"Not so much," I said.

"You know what I'd like? In the springtime? I'd like to have a house that's sealed. You know? Plastic over the doors and windows and around the foundation. It's the only way to win. In another life I must have been a pirate or a murderer to deserve these sinuses. Do you believe in reincarnation?"

"No," I said, finding a Kleenex and putting it to my nose, "One time is enough for me."

"Sugar, you don't know what you're missing. You got to work up from the lower bardos. Like crocodiles. Or snapping turtles. Then you get to come back as Princess Di."

"Do you think Princess Di was a snapping turtle?" I said.

"Of course she was. We all were. There's nothing to be

ashamed of, sugar. Here, let me give you some literature. Have you seen the new *Out of Body* and *Whole Earth Health*?"

She took a magazine from her bag and passed it over to me.

"There's a great section on griefwork," she said. "Right here, where the page is turned down."

For a while I looked out the window, the magazine in my lap, one hand to my cheek, and on it I smelled that lingering scent of gunpowder.

The road to Cheyenne was straight, although not so flat, since the plains started rising, the slope of them gradual but constant. The bus stopped at a store and gas station, which was just to the side of the road, and beyond it there were the grasslands, the clumps of green blades spread evenly all the way to the horizon. The store and gas station sat in a hollow, where there was some protection from the harshness of the wind, but even so the dust blew around the pumps and made the screen door creak. Inside, around the cash register, there were racks for chips, and on the shelves there were the small cans, too. On the wall there was a Pepsi thermometer, stained and rusted like the one in front of my father's store. In the distance the dull-brown hills rose from the land. The air was heavy, damp and suggested the arrival of snow. I looked into the store, where the racks of chips and piles of Day-Glo sweatshirts sat on the counter, and while the cash register rang, the sound of it echoed over the miles I had come. The wind blew across the dirt around the gasoline pumps. A dust devil formed there and swept up to the wall of the store, where I stood, holding that money in my pocket. Then, in the brief chaos of the dust and wind, which tugged at my coat and blew my hair and left grit in my eyes and mouth, I heard that constant ringing of the cash register, the grind and bells making me put my hand to my face. There, in the transcontinental echo of the cash register, I thought of the names that had meant so much to my father, Edison, Bell, Ford, the words now disappearing into the last shreds of the dust devil.

Inside the gas station the sandwiches were four dollars

apiece. I said to the woman behind the counter, "I guess I'll just have some chips. How much?"

They were seventy-five cents. I turned and went back to the bus with the bag in my pocket, glad to have something with me I was worried about breaking, or just sitting on. Now, as the bus climbed, there were antelope at the side of the road, some of them lying down. I forked the chips out of the bag, one at a time, tasting the salt and watching the antelope, the appearance of them having the startling quality of something that has only been dreamed about. They seemed aloof and quietly stubborn, as though the size of the grasslands and sky meant nothing to them, and as I ate the chips and watched the antelope, I felt that moist air of spring and the harshness of the land, its frank brutality and the cost of the pleasures it offered. I was cold and thirsty and there was still some grit in my eyes. But even so, I put my head back and made a sound that was half grief and half laughter as I wondered if someone came out here, too, and shot an antelope so a man could get laid in peace and quiet.

"Have you been reading the *Out of Body*?" said the woman next to me. "It all makes sense, doesn't it? The bardos, I mean. You see, you start as bacteria and work up. I started laughing, too, when I got the message straight. It takes your breath away thinking about the possibilities. Just think where we've been. When I think about earlier lives, I always get a kind of Egypt feeling. What about you?"

"Me?" I said.

"You've got Eskimo written all over you. Plain as the nose on your face. Here, read the next article."

It was snowing in Cheyenne. There were brick buildings along the street, all of them two stories, the bricks stained black from the tar on the roof. The snow blew through the streets in long, corded lines. Opposite the bus stop there were stockyards, the chutes and runs and loading platforms all standing out of the snow. Now two cowboys walked out of the bus station, both carrying saddles, which they threw into the bay for luggage. Then they climbed on board, both wearing jeans, wool coats, and hats, and their clothes had the sour smell of horses. One of them had a copy of *Penthouse,* which he opened and looked at as though he were reading but there was only a picture on the page.

The snow piled up. The clumps of grass disappeared and only the thin blades stood up, looking dark now, green as spinach. I pulled my jacket together and tried to get warm, watching the snow, and while I felt the thirst from the chips, I took the money out of my pocket and counted it again, making sure it hadn't somehow disappeared altogether, and as I looked at the fives and tens and the twenties (which had the other bills folded around them), I thought, *In San Francisco the cheapest room can't be less than twenty dollars a day. Then there will be food, too. So that's five days.*

The snow blew across the grass, just like dust or sand, streaming around the blades, and I held the fur to my throat, already knowing what the room would be like: a single bed with a thin, stained mattress on some creaking springs. One pillow. A Bible in the drawer. Green shades. A bureau with a mirror, the dust on it making you look the way you will in ten years. There will be the smell of leaking gas and of people cooking onions and meat in a pan on a hot plate.

The cowboys didn't even look at the snow. But for me there was a fascination in it, since the last thing in the world I wanted was to feel it on my skin, the points of it, the claustrophobic lightness of it suggesting everything that was wrong and that I wanted to get away from: I watched it the way you would a shark in an aquarium.

It was still snowing hard in Salt Lake City. The bus station there was large, and the buses were lined up side by side, the bays for them all on an angle. When the driver opened the door there was the clean smell of the storm.

Graham Hardy got on the bus in Salt Lake City. He was drunk. You could see it even as his head first rose from the steps at the front of the bus, his movements not sloppy or even clumsy so much as distracted. He was about twenty-five years old, a little heavy, and he had blond hair and blue eyes and a little blond mustache. Even as he came up the aisle his eyes looked pale, like a piece of blue glass that has been polished smooth on the beach: whitish, a little misty. He looked for a seat, and he carried an airline bag and a suitcase, which was made of leather and had a sheen like caramel. His face was flushed, but it didn't look like it was from the cold or from being outdoors. He was wearing the most beautiful sweater I have ever seen. It was handmade from blue and white yarn, and on it, in circular patterns from the neck down over the shoulders and across the back and front, there was a regular pattern of animals, caribou, wolves, ducks, geese, foxes. The sweater looked as if it weighed ten pounds. His jeans were new and they fit him perfectly and he wore a pair of brown leather boots that had a sheen, too, and looked like they'd been made in some other country. Even the smell of bourbon on his breath seemed expensive.

Outside, the bus drivers stood together, all in blue-gray uniforms and wearing hats like those of airplane pilots. They talked about the snow, their voices sawing against the throb of the engine. I put a hand to my hair, fluffing it up a little, smelling the odor of the storm outside and thinking, *There's got to be a way to get ahold of things. I can't go on falling like this, can't just be pushed across the country until I'm dumped in the ocean.* I remembered the time, just months before, when I had had dreams of love, or romance, the ease of them like silk or satin or some texture that was beguiling to the skin. Now all I wanted was to stand up to that current, or whatever it was that was pushing me toward the ocean: lack of money, lack of someone, the lack of everything but the cold, greasy atmosphere of the stations where the bus stopped.

I got up and crossed the aisle, carrying that magazine, and sat down next to the man in the sweater. He was looking at his hands and it was a second or two before he turned toward me, the movement of his head having about it the suggestion of weight or fatigue.

"Hi," I said. "What are you drinking?"

"Bourbon," he said. "You want a sip? I've got a bottle in my bag."

"Sure," I said. "It's cold. I'm about crazy with being on the bus. I've been on it ever since Pennsylvania."

He took a pint bottle from his airline bag and passed it over, without the cap. When I was done he had a sip and put the bottle away, the top making a small *kerscrew*.

"My name's Graham Hardy," he said.

"Christine Taylor," I said.

"What's that you're reading?" he said, looking at the magazine.

"It's a health magazine," I said. "It has vegetarian recipes and articles about reincarnation, you know? Like Calvin Coolidge coming back as Michael Jackson."

"That's what I need, all right," he said. "What I need is to be fucking reincarnated. Maybe as a lizard."

"How about another drink," I said. "Do you think we're going to get through the snow?"

"Who the hell knows?" he said. "Anything can happen up here this time of the year." He shook his head. "The Donner party got caught up here in the spring, didn't they?"

"The Donner party?" I said.

"A hundred years ago a bunch of pioneers got caught up in a pass up here. Snowed in. They ended up as cannibals."

"Oh," I said.

"Jesus, what a weekend this has been," he said.

I opened the magazine now.

"I cracked up my car," he said. "My skis were on it, too. Total loss. I got to get back to San Francisco to see my shrink. Is he going to be pissed."

"What kind of car was it?" I said.

"Well, this time it was a Camaro. Red. Got to keep those poor bastards in Detroit at work somehow, I guess."

He took another sip now, putting his head back quickly, like a boy who is showing off. He offered the bottle, but I shook my head.

"Yeah, some of that stuff you were reading about is pretty interesting. I took a macrobiotic cure once. The thing about it is they don't let you have enough vitamins, so when you're done, you go out and buy them back in LSD. Bad medicine, that stuff, take my word for it. Say, look at the snow now."

It came in large, soapy clumps. The grass had almost disappeared and on the road the tracks of the cars that went ahead of us were disappearing.

"Come on, snow!" he said. "If it snows enough I won't have to see my shrink."

"Hush," I said, "people are looking."

"Let them look," he said, "they don't have to deal with Gerald T. Mishkin, M.D. Or my uncle, either. He's going to be pissed, too."

"Your uncle?" I said.

"Yeah. He's a real prince," said Graham.

Now, as we went uphill, the bus slithered from side to side and the tires made a tearing sound. Outside, through the blowing snow, the white land disappeared beyond the air speckled with snow. I put my hands in my pockets, but they were still cold, even though the heater was on, the warmish air coming out the vents in a dry rush. Now the cowboys turned to the window, their frostbitten faces a little rough over the nose and cheeks. They sat there, both heads turned the same way, watching the snow, their eyes not wide exactly, but intent, alarmed.

"Tell me about your uncle," I said.

"My uncle's a prince," Graham said, "didn't I tell you? Jesus, look at it snow." He looked out the window now, away from me. "My uncle's always careful about things, you know. When he has some cherries, he arranges the pits on his plate in a little pattern, like a little half moon. That's the secret of him. It's right there. *Attention to detail.* The buttons on the sleeve of his suits *unbutton.* If he could get away with it, he'd have his shoelaces ironed. You can't argue with him."

"He must have money," I said.

"Yeah, you could say that," said Graham. "Everything he touches turns to gold. When you shake his hand you can feel it happening to your palm and fingers."

"I could use a little of that," I said. "He can shake my hand anytime."

"That's what you say now. Wait. Just wait until it happens," Graham said. He reached down for the bottle and had another sip, puckering up to the mouth of it, his expression one of pondering some faraway secret.

"Here," he said, "want another?"

"Thanks," I said, taking another small sip. "What about your aunt?"

He shrugged.

"Hell, she's lived with him for thirty years," he said. "That's got to take it out of you, right? You know what her motto is? Keep a Valium in case of capture. Not bad advice, if you want to know the truth."

The windshield wipers became misshapen with snow, and they swept back and forth, no longer cleaning the glass, their movement having a dumb, useless quality. The driver pulled to the side of the road and got out to clean them, letting in the air from outside, which smelled like the inside of a freezer. The cowboys looked up when they smelled it. Now, when the driver started again, the bus slipped farther to the side of the road, deeper into the drift. The snow came down now in a white shimmer.

"I'm sorry," said the driver, "but we're going to have to wait for the plow."

The woman across the aisle looked at me and said, "I just knew there was Eskimo in you. Snow karma. You watch, sugar, you got plenty to learn about where you been."

The heater didn't seem to do much good. Every now and then there was a sound, or what appeared to be a sound, coming from the road behind us, but it wasn't the plow. The cowboys and Graham started a card game and they were joined by another man. He was tall and white-haired, although his hair was cut short. He was a retired submarine captain, and when he told a story about being on the bottom of the Pacific with dead batteries, he did so with the air of a man untroubled by claustrophobia. His skin seemed white, too, and tight fitting. He looked back at me once and raised a brow, not smiling, just curious as to how I was taking the claustrophobia of the storm. In his glance there was the indifference of those cold bus stations, the large, half-empty rooms where people waited. I looked right back, knowing I had no place to go aside from that dusty room with the mirror and the creaking bed.

They cleaned Graham out in a couple of hours, and he came back up the aisle and sat down next to me.

"I'll have to ask Gerald T. Mishkin, M.D., if it's self-destructive to try to draw to an inside straight," he said.

Now he took large sips, finishing one pint and moving on to another he had in his bag. He was asleep when the plow arrived in the dirty light before dawn.

It came with a grating rumble, and when it passed sparks spread onto the road from the bottom of the blade, the truck disappearing in a rush of snow and gold colored streaks. Then the driver got the bus onto the road again and we started the long drop into California. We came to the valley, where not only was there no snow, the fields were planted and green. The sun emerged from the clouds, the edges of them lacy and bright, the same color as the gold streaks from the blade of the plow.

Graham slept, his snoring gentle and quiet, although every now and then his head swung toward the window where it made a thump. There wasn't anything to make a pillow out of, so I sat there, hearing the sound whenever the bus changed lanes. He woke in the Oakland station.

"Where are we?" he said.

"Oakland," I said.

People got their things together and walked down the aisle, the cowboys going first, their scaled, red faces turned toward the greenish light of the garage. Graham watched them go, and then he started sweating, the drops appearing on his upper lip and forehead. Now he held his head in his hands and closed his eyes, trembling there against the window.

"What's wrong?" I said.

"Oh, shit," he said, "I got the *willies.*" Now he put his hands together and squeezed them between his knees. "Something's going to happen. Oh, shit."

His face was damp when he turned toward me.

"What's wrong?"

"I don't know. I'm just scared. I got the willies."

He rocked back and forth a little, sweating, his hands squeezed together. The rest of the people got up and walked off the bus, a few looking at him, but most just going outside. The driver stood outside, his face dark with his unshaved beard.

"Look," Graham said. "Look in my bag, will you? There's some pills. Two bottles. One has Ativan in it. Can you give me two? Can you just do that?"

I put the airline bag on my lap and went through it, touching the things inside carefully so as to be polite about it. There were some dirty clothes, a book, a kit, and a checkbook. There was a bathrobe, some slippers, and some forms, like an accident report. I didn't see any pills.

"Right in there," he said. "In the *kit.*"

He took the pills without water, just throwing his head back and swallowing, his larynx going up and down until the pills were gone. He closed his eyes now and said, "I can't take it in here anymore. I can't stay here."

"Sure," I said. "I know how you feel."

"No, you don't. Oh, no you don't," he said. "Oh, shit. I got the willies."

Graham closed his eyes while I got his suitcase down from the rack. The bus was empty and it had about it the air of a deserted movie theater. The sweat on Graham's upper lip and forehead was unnaturally clear, like gin.

In the terminal there was the *wham, wham, wham* and jingle of a pinball machine. There was a jukebox playing, too, and people sat in the waiting room, their faces blank, as though they heard nothing. I could smell a little sea air, the scent of it coming as the reminder that I was finally here after all. I breathed deeply, trying to think, but all that came to mind was the jingle from the advertisement for spiced rice, "The San Francisco Treat . . ." I looked out the window, but there weren't any cable cars.

"I got to sit down," said Graham. "That's all I can take. Let's rest."

The benches were long, shiny, and made of wood. My suitcase sat on the floor next to Graham's, which made mine look just like where it had come from, which was the K mart. Before, I had been able to kid myself about it. There was nothing in the room that seemed familiar, aside from the anonymous things I had seen in stations in every city we had stopped in since Pennsylvania, the accumulation of the times I had seen them making me want to do anything to get away, into the air outside. I pushed the bags one way and another, unable to sit still.

"Please," said Graham, "stop that."

I sat with my back against the wooden seat, my hands in my lap, my legs crossed at the ankle, waiting now, not moving, thinking, *I wish they'd stop playing that pinball machine. Then I could think about what to do.*

"Where's your uncle's house?" I said. "Maybe we could go there."

"It's in the city," he said, "on the other side of the bridge. I don't know about getting there. I couldn't stand the city bus. I couldn't take that right now. Oh, shit. Goddamn Ativan has such a slow rate of absorption."

"We don't have to take the bus," I said. "We can get a taxi."

"I haven't got the money," he said. "I got wiped out playing cards. Those bastards wanted to play for my Visa card. Can you believe that?"

"How much is a taxi?" I said.

"Thirty dollars," he said.

Thirty dollars. That's one and a half nights. The pinball machines kept making that noise, like someone slamming a drawerful of silverware. Graham was sweating in the fluorescent light of the waiting room.

"Look," I said, "I've got thirty dollars. All right?"

"Will you come with me?" he said. "I don't want to be alone. Oh, shit."

"I'll come," I said, "but I need a place to stay."

"Sure, sure," he said. "Let's get a taxi."

"Do you understand?" I said. "I need a place to stay. Will you keep your word?"

"Let's get the taxi," he said.

He didn't want to carry his suitcase because he couldn't stand the weight of it tugging on him. People looked at us now, Graham next to me, his head down, watching the floor while I carried both bags, thinking, *How can you trust him? He's about crazy. What if he doesn't have an uncle at all or anyplace to stay?*

Outside the sunshine was the pale yellow of popple leaves in the fall. Our shadows were blobs at our feet and I thought, *Well, that's something. No seasons.* I stood in the street, seeing the dirty storefronts, the cars with blue-and-yellow license plates, the telephone and power-line poles, the endless black crosses of them. Even then I remembered my father as he had sat in the kitchen in January, saying, "Sunbelt real estate, Sherry. That's where the smart money is."

Up the street there was a bar with a Budweiser sign in the window, the red, white, and blue colors of it having a patriotic air. The front of the place was dark glass.

"A drink would help," Graham said. "A drink would get that Ativan working."

"All right," I said.

Inside there was a long wooden bar, at the end of which there was a metal cage with gold bars, thin ones like in a pawn shop, and inside a woman danced on a small platform. She was wearing only a G-string. I brought the bags in and put them by the door, and Graham sat down and asked for a bourbon. He never looked at the dancer. The linoleum on the floor was torn and you could see the concrete underneath. It was smoky in the room and a little damp, too.

Graham took his drink quickly and waited, his head bent forward, still sweating but now obviously trying to keep the bourbon down. Then he sighed and said to me, "Thanks. You're so goddamned wonderful." He closed his eyes. "Wonderful. Just wonderful."

We got a cab, which went across the Bay Bridge, the water on both sides of it blue and roughened by the wind. I saw some gulls hovering along the bridge, but I didn't look at them for long. I kept my eyes on the meter, watching the numbers flash up, $7.50, $8.00, $8.50, $9.00, while I thought, *What if I can't stay? What if they won't let me stay?*

The house was at the top of a hill in San Francisco. The land was flat there. The taxi stopped in front of a three-story house that was made of pink stone and which had wrought iron balconies in front of the upstairs windows. The street was clean. There was even a small yard where some grass and flowers grew, the beds and the lawn perfectly weeded and trimmed. The dirt in the flower bed was black. The steps to the house were a pinkish stone, just like the walls, and the front door was a heavy piece of glass in a wood frame. It smelled of Windex.

It was cool inside. Behind the door there was an Oriental rug, a palm in the corner, and a wooden bench next to an umbrella rack. There was the sound of someone walking in the upstairs hall.

"Graham? Graham?" said a man's voice. "Is that you?"

"Just my luck," said Graham. "He's home."

Graham's uncle wore a blue, pinstriped suit, a red silk tie, and brown shoes. There was a handkerchief in his breast pocket. His hands were short and thick-fingered and his nose was covered with skin that had a texture like an orange. His hair was thin, combed back from his high, shiny forehead. And as he stood at the top of the stairs he looked down at his nephew, not with disgust or even amazement but as he would at a difficult crossword puzzle.

"Who's this?" he said, looking at me now.

"She helped me home," said Graham. "I wasn't feeling well. Her name's Christine."

"Christine Taylor," I said.

I stood, still holding my bag, looking upward. I smiled now.

"I have a hangover," said Graham. "I want to lie down."

He picked up his bag and started climbing the stairs. I watched him go, standing there in the hall.

"Christine's going to spend the night," said Graham.

"Is she?" said Graham's uncle.

"He said you wouldn't mind," I said. "He said it would be all right."

Graham's uncle walked down the stairs.

"Do you mind, because if you do . . ."

"It's all right," he said. "There's a room upstairs, next to Graham's."

"Thanks," I said.

"I'm Robert Hardy," he said, offering his hand. "How nice to meet you."

He looked right at me now, not missing a thing. He took a quick look at my bag.

"Make yourself at home," he said. "I'm going out now. But I'll be back tonight. You'll have dinner with us, won't you? Good. My wife's away, and both Graham and I could use some company."

Then he turned and went out the door, into the pale sunshine, the gleam of it on his hair and on the skin of his bald spot. I waited behind the door, wanting to have the sense of the house quiet around me, and when Robert disappeared I looked at the green palm in the corner, at the Oriental rug I stood on, and thought, *All right, so at least I didn't get pushed all the way into the ocean, right into the Pacific.*

Graham was asleep in his room, curled up on his bed. It was a nice room with a desk, a bookshelf, a model airplane hanging from the ceiling, and a row of empty champagne bottles, with names written on the labels, on the bureau. There were silver brushes and a closetful of clothes. There was some scuba gear in the closet, too. On the wall there was a framed letter which told Graham Hardy III that he had been expelled from Stanford University.

There was a bathroom next to my room, and after I got out of the tub, I toweled hard, as though the texture of the new, expensive terry-cloth could take care of the memory of those bus stations. Then I sat down on the bed, toweling my hair, and when I stopped and looked out the window, I didn't want to sit still here, either, even in the cool, comfortable room with a view of the city. I felt the house wanted me outside, as though my presence were somehow humiliating to it and to the people who had lived here for years.

I put on my robe and fastened it with the large safety pin I always used, and then I went out into the hall and started along it, looking at the things on the walls, the pictures and photographs. Downstairs there was a dining room, a living room, and a library, and I went through all of them, touching the sofas, end tables, Chinese jars, curtains, books, crystal figures, and vases with cut flowers, white orchids mostly. There was a bowl with some gardenias in it and I touched them, too, but then remembered this would turn the petals brown. They had a wonderful aroma, and as I bent there, over the bowl, smelling them, the scent came as another reminder, just as everything else in the room did, that I didn't belong here. I sat down on the sofa, feeling the wet hair around my face and on my neck, and when I closed my eyes, there was the endless sensation of the bus swaying from side to side. By the door, next to the hall, there was a grandfather clock, which made a steady *tick, tick, tick.*

In the evening we had dinner. Graham wore a clean white shirt and a pair of slacks, and he had his hair brushed back. Before dinner he took a couple of pills and sat there quietly, eating his lamb and string beans. Robert said, "Graham, would you like some wine?"

"No," said Graham, "I'm fine."

"Restraint is built up one moment at a time," said Robert. "I'm glad you're learning that."

Graham nodded.

"It's just a matter of paying attention . . ." said Robert.

". . . to the details of the moment," said Graham.

After dinner Graham and I watched television, the programs the same here as in Pennsylvania. It was time to go to bed before the movies came on, and when Graham and I walked upstairs, both of us not so much tired as bored, we stopped in front of the door to his room.

"You don't want to come in here, do you?" he said. "You know . . . in here with me, do you? That would be treating you like an object, wouldn't it?"

"Yes, I guess that's right," I said.

"Well," he said, "I just don't want to treat you as an object. It would be insulting if I wanted to sleep with you. I'm above that now."

I looked at him.

"So, it's for the best," he said.

"Yes," I said. "That's right, isn't it? Good night."

I closed the door to my room. He went into the door next to mine. I heard him sit down on his bed, the sigh of it coming through the wall, and then I sat down, too, looking in his direction. I turned back the sheets and got under them, feeling their cool caress, but I couldn't sleep, since I had taken a nap during the day. It was dark in the room, a steady, deep purple. I sat there, my arms behind my head, thinking, *No one said a thing about tomorrow. Not a word.*

I got up and turned on the light and took the money from my jacket pocket and counted it again, laying the bills across the bed as though I were playing a game of solitaire, the money coming as a reminder of how little there was between me and the outside. Downstairs, in the hall, I heard that steady ticking. Then I opened my suitcase and looked at the things inside, the lotions, clothes, and that canister with the ashes inside. Then I thought, Thomas Edison. Bell. Einstein. Sunbelt real estate. Knowing the market. Taking the plunge. Isn't that what's needed, Al? I sat on the side of the bed now, my eyes closed.

I tried to sleep, but I only lay there. At one o'clock I turned on the light again and put on my bathrobe, fastening it as always with that oversized safety pin. I just wanted to walk now, to move for a while, to have that sense of locomotion. In the hall there was only one dim light, and when I came to the top of the stairs, my shadow went before me, zigzagging down to the bottom. The banister made a polished squeak under my fingers and my feet made a subdued thump on the carpeted stairs. In the dim light of the living room I went by the furniture, feeling that each piece of it was building a case against me.

There was a light in the hall, and by it the palm cast

striped shadows on the library floor. The books were in shelves that went from floor to ceiling, and some of the titles were printed in gold, the letters appearing soft in the light, like foil through fog or mist. There was a desk, on which there was a bottle of brandy, a glass, and some papers, too, where Robert had been working. I stood there, my hand just at the edge of the desk, one finger touching the edge of it. Now everything about my fleeing, about being unconnected to anything at all, came down to the touch of that piece of furniture against my finger. The light showed through the brandy, the color of it like old wood. I stood there, thinking, my brow wrinkled, trying to face the danger in the infinitely vague, but nevertheless vicious things that lay in wait for me.

Robert now stood in the doorway, appearing there as a silhouette against the smoky light. Then his shadow moved along the bookshelves as he came quietly into the room, the gold titles winking out as he passed. His feet, in slippers, made a steady *pfit, pfit,* on the carpet, and there was a liquid hush in the movement of his silk robe. Now the light from the hall fell across part of my face, from my lips downward, the safety pin bright as an ornament on the front of my robe. Robert stood opposite me. I walked a little closer, saying to him in a whisper, "I'm having trouble sleeping. Aren't you?" while I took the safety pin in my fingers and undid it, the small, almost inaudible *flick* of it piercing the silence of the room, the undoing of it and the slight opening of the panels of the robe coming as an attempt to resolve two things, the desire to rip this place apart and not wanting to be pushed (that's what I hated, that pushing) into the outside world where there seemed to be shadows behind every door, just phantoms of people, none able to do more than just grub for himself. And upstairs, when we were in that oversized bed, where there lingered the perfume of Robert's wife, there were times when he began to cry out, the sound beginning as a muffled, amazed *ah, ah,* and I said, my mouth close to his ear, "Hush now. Hush."

After he had gone downstairs and brought himself a glass of brandy and stretched out again, one arm behind his head, I sat in a chair opposite him and said, "Don't you think this was an accident or a mistake. I knew what I was doing."

"No. I don't think it was a mistake. I've been waiting for you for years," he said. "I can't believe you just walked into my house, all by yourself. I couldn't live without you."

I got up and walked away, not saying a thing, not putting on the robe, either, but just dragging it behind me like a sheet. The hall was quiet and cool, which came as a relief after the cloying odor of that enormous bed, and when I went down it, glad to have the cool air flowing over me, I passed Graham's door, which was open just a crack. He stood just inside, watching as I obviously walked away from his uncle's room, dragging my robe behind me. Graham looked carefully, his eyes bright, and then he closed the door.

In the morning Robert made scrambled eggs and sausage and freshly squeezed grapefruit juice. I sat down at my place, putting the heavy napkin in my lap. I hadn't showered, and my cheeks were pink from Robert's beard. Robert was wearing a robe, too, and there was about both of us an intimate dishevelment that comes from only one thing. The housekeeper had the day off and we ate in the kitchen.

I asked Robert if he believed in reincarnation. He said he did. I asked him if he had been a snapping turtle or a crocodile. He asked what I had been and I just smiled, saying "Wouldn't you like to know?"

"Oh, I can tell," he said.

Graham came in and stood for a moment at the place that had been set for him.

"I hope I'm not interrupting," he said.

"Oh, no," said his uncle, "we've been waiting for you."

"Have you?" he said.

Graham went to the icebox, where he took out a bottle of beer. He opened it and had a drink, his lips in an ugly pucker as he put the bottle up with a quick toss.

"We were just talking about reincarnation," said Robert.

"That's fucking perfect," said Graham.

"Why don't you have something to eat?" said Robert.

"I'll make something for myself," he said. "I'm not hungry."

"I made eggs for you," he said. "Soft. Just the way you like them."

"I don't want them," said Graham.

"They'll never be better than they are now," said Robert.

Graham turned that bottle up, the gesture of it that same upward toss of rage. He stood behind the chair at the place that had been set for him, looking at his uncle. Then he put the bottle down with a bang and went to the icebox, where he took another, opening it with a jerk and turning it up, too.

"Why did you have to sleep with him?" he said to me.

"Is that your business?" I said.

"Oh, shit," he said. "I don't know. Why didn't you come to see me? What's wrong with *me*?" He closed his eyes now and sat down on the floor, crying. "Please, please, just tell me."

Graham sat there, shaking his head, holding the bottle. I sat at the table, looking down, pulling at the napkin, watching the food get cold on my plate. Then Graham got up and went out, taking the bottle with him. Robert went out, too, and I heard them talking upstairs, Robert's voice quiet, comforting, soothing.

In fifteen minutes Robert came downstairs, dressed now, shaved, smelling of cologne.

"I want to talk to you," he said.

"Let's talk tonight. I'll see you then," I said.

"Sure. That's best," he said. "I'm late. But you'll be here, won't you?"

I smiled.

"Good," he said, "I'll see you then."

He went into the hall and through that heavy glass door, his dark suit, as he emerged into the sunshine, looking like a million dollars. Then I went upstairs and dressed and packed my bag, folding my robe and fingering, for a moment, the oversized pin, but then shoving it in, too, with the rest.

In the room next door Graham paced back and forth. I spread the newspaper on the bed and opened it to the classifieds, running my finger down the long columns of type, finding what I was looking for and then calling a taxi. It arrived quickly, gliding up to the door.

I went without a word, just vanishing: the empty room where I had stayed suggested that Robert's luck and pleasure had turned to nothing. I sent this surprise as greetings from my world to his. As I sat in the cab, seeing the cable cars and hearing that spiced-rice jingle, I thought, *Well, what do you think of my greetings? Has some unexpected thing come into your life? What can be done about it now? Wouldn't it be nice to pretty things up again or to think chaos can be managed after all?*

The cable cars seemed from another time, each one having a roof like a small gazebo. The poles on them were brass and the conductors wore blue uniforms, the levers they managed looking like machinery from the nineteenth century. The cars seemed to have escaped time or progress and now they went up and down the hill with an ageless innocence. My father would have loved a ride on them, watching the city roll by, saying, "Marie, oh, Marie, these cars were a good idea. A good idea never goes out of fashion."

My room was in a building that had a door with a broken lock downstairs and a sign that said, NO JUNKIES. The room was not quite as I had imagined it, dustier for one thing and having a floor that wasn't quite flat. The venetian blinds were gray with dust, and slats of light fell across the room, breaking over the bureau like a child's drawing of lightning. The mattress was thin and sat on some creaking springs. There was a bureau, with a few clothes still inside, men's things that had been left behind. No pictures on the wall. A torn shower curtain. Cracks in the ceiling. Dark stains on the floor near the window. An odor in the hall of people cooking meat and onions on a hot plate. I paid for a week, passing the money over and getting my sheets and blankets, and then I made the bed and sat for a while in the bars of sunlight.

Now, just as I had accepted the room as the stamp of who I was and where I had come from, I opened the paper again and turned to the want ads, running my fingers over the long columns of jobs, the list of them familiar and almost comforting, since these were the things my father and his father and my mother, too, had always done, laboring, working in factories, waiting tables, driving trucks or taxis, our entire economic life having about it a quality that was at once low paying and anonymous. These were the things that were always done in new places (until, of course, my father got his hands on enough money by making loans at usurious rates of interest to be able to buy the grocery, Al Boule's Hilltop Store). Now I did as I knew I always would, turning the sheets of newsprint with a quiet, businesslike air, not to mention a certain comforting fatalism.

The Tree Park Cafeteria was in the middle of a block of dry cleaners and laundries, Chinese restaurants and lunch stands, beauty parlors and shoe repairs, one-horse groceries and pharmacies with bleached window dressings, all of them having a pale, dusty vitality: they neither went out of business nor expanded, until each of them was sold, dusty windows and worn doorknobs and peeling linoleum and all, to the next soul who put up a little more money than the place was worth and hung on for the next forty years.

The Tree Park Cafeteria had an aluminum front, large panels of it below the window, and strips of it along the top. The overall effect of it was that the place looked as if it had been decorated with stainless-steel sinks. Inside there were long, brown tables with stools and there was sawdust on the floor. On the tables there were pots of hot mustard, and sticking out of them there were wooden tongue depressors, which were used as knives. John Kiri, who owned the Tree Park, believed that almost anything would be eaten without complaint if the mustard on it was hot enough. He used the tongue depressors because he thought it was a good idea to keep the knives in the place down to a minimum, even though most of the clientele consisted of old men who bought a meal ticket, a little coupon like a bus transfer, and used it to eat the rest of the week. Even so, fights broke out between two old men, who grunted alongside overturned stools, kicking sawdust and slashing at each other with a spoon or a fork or a mustard-smeared tongue depressor until someone broke it up.

John Kiri came from Iceland, and there most food was cooked by boiling it. He was a short man with gray hair and dark eyes and a face wrinkled like an Eskimo's. He sat in the back of the Tree Park in his white shirt, white pants, ice-cream man's hat, and white apron, watching the people who sat at the tables. He cashed Social Security checks, money orders, and he lent money, too, at rates just like my father's. He said the secret to making the mustard was to put a little beer into it and to let it sit in the icebox for a while. He liked salmon, too, in the Icelandic style, marinated with oil and herbs. Once a month he bought a salmon, prepared the oil and herbs for it, wrapped it in a plastic bag, and then dug a hole in the small backyard of the Tree Park. He put the salmon in with some stones on top of it and then covered it with dirt, tamping it down with the end of his shovel. It took about a month to ripen properly. At the end of the month he dug it up and ate it, putting the pink slices on thin pumpernickel bread.

When I came in the door of the Tree Park, carrying the newspaper, he kept his eyes on me while I walked to the back of the room, unerringly picking out the man who acted like he owned the place. He said, "You want the job? Why do you want it? You could get a job in a cocktail lounge. What are you doing in a crummy cafeteria filled with old men?"

"I want an honest job," I said.

He looked at me for a moment.

"All right. You got it. When you eat something, it comes out of your pay. No discount. See Blanche. She'll break you in."

I stood behind the counter and when a man or woman wanted something from the steam tables, I served them, passing over the stewed tomatoes or meat loaf or brown beef and gray beans. I kept the trays stacked, the tables clear, and I cut the Jell-O into neat, quivery squares.

At the end of the first day, when I sat at the back of the room, eating a plate of turkey stuffing and a scoop of cottage cheese (to save money), John Kiri sat down next to me, keeping his eyes on the room but obviously wanting to talk things over. He had ideas, like about what the first astronauts on Mars would eat (boiled food with hot mustard), but more than anything else he was interested in a kind of philosophy: he believed that there was a time to die, and if you missed it, you were condemned to years of misery. He believed there was a force that brought the right moment about, and when someone was killed, and the circumstances of it were correct (a bank robber who was fleeing with the money, say), he said to me with a wink of philosophical savvy and with the air, too, of sharing a secret with a sympathetic soul, "Car crash in a high-speed chase last night, Christine."

He began the day by putting a large green cigar into his mouth, but he never lighted it, since "people don't like smoke when they're eating, especially the geezers here with asthma," but the cigar disappeared anyway by a slow, constant lipping and chewing. When I sat at the back of the room with my turkey stuffing and cottage cheese, Kiri said, looking at the old men in the room. "Don't tell me, Christine, that these guys didn't miss the *moment*. Jesus, look what happened to them. Something went wrong someplace."

A man came to repay a loan. He counted out the money he had borrowed and the enormous interest, which was calculated by the week, and, as the money slid across the wooden cafeteria table, I smiled at Mr. Kiri, my face having about it the expression of someone who's seen an old friend. Then he said, "Christine, you know what? My salmon's almost done. You come out to the backyard." There we pushed aside the dirt and dragged the fish out, and in the kitchen Kiri scraped off the skin and sliced the pink flesh, putting a little on a piece of pumpernickel and passing it over. It was the most delicious thing I have ever eaten. "Yeah, that's good, ain't it?" he said, "You listen, Christine, you got to remember where you came from. That's what will make you happy."

Now, in the evenings when I took my break, Kiri fleshed out the rest of the things he believed. He made amends in his will for the things his sons, wife, daughters, brothers, and sisters had done wrong, enumerating to me in a slow, patient voice the list of people to whom he was going to leave "one lousy buck." All this was said with a less philosophical air (". . . and to that little prick Harold . . ."), as though to show that where satisfaction was concerned, disinheritance beat philosophy all hollow.

In the evenings I walked along the streets of the city, looking into the department-store windows, feeling around me the people who seemed businesslike, aloof, and with some-place to go. I found the Music Box, which was a record store where you could sit in a glass booth and listen to records. I found some of the songs my mother and father liked (Teresa Brewer singing "Music! Music! Music!"), but soon I was listening to things I knew nothing about, Beethoven, Brahms, Schubert, or any of the records from the Deutsche Grammophon Gesellschaft, the music loud there in the glass booth, where I sat with my eyes closed, feeling the music around me and in my arms and chest and head, and with the booming of it I was able to recall those hours when my father was dying ("It's the money that counts, Marie"), or to feel the weight of the miles that had piled up behind me. Then I changed the record, going through composers and musicians whose names I couldn't pronounce (Chopin, Tchaikovsky), but nevertheless sitting there in that glass booth, pressing my fingers against it, leaving my fingerprints on it while I trembled, feeling the music and, worse, the things it stirred up. I went home and opened the pint bottle of bourbon I kept in the drawer by the bed, and then I sat there, carefully measuring how much I poured into the glass, wanting just enough to make me sleep, but not so much I'd wake at three or four in the morning, nervous and tired. I swirled the dark liquor around in a water glass while from the building there came the sound of televisions and radios and the smell of the onions and cheap meat being fried on hot plates, the room where I sat having in it only the creaking of the bed when I stretched out and the steady *tick, tick, tick* of the wind-up clock I had bought. In the room above me a man coughed, over and over again, spitting into a glass jar, which he showed to the people who visited, the man saying, "Jesus, look at it. I got it here in this jar. Look."

In the morning I got up and dressed and went to the Tree Park, where I stood behind the counter, punching those small red tickets. The cafeteria had a familiarity about it, since it was a reminder of construction gangs and taxi companies and high-interest loans. Mr. Kiri sat in the back, the unlighted cigar in his mouth, contemplating the growing list of people who were going to get a dollar while puzzling out the problem of how he was going to be there when the will was read.

On my third payday I went to the bank and cashed my check and withdrew the two hundred and fifty dollars I had saved from the previous weeks, folding the money neatly in half and carrying it in my pocket with my hand on it. At Lord and Taylor I bought a silk dress, a pair of shoes, and a pair of stockings, all of which I took home and spread out on the bed, where they looked fresh and full of promise. Now I took the jar of Nivea I had bought and spread the cream over my hands and then I put surgical gloves over it so my hands would absorb the moisture and heal quickly. I sat at the side of the bed, my hands in the gloves, drinking that bourbon. I did this each night, my hands getting a little softer each time, and when they were about right, I went up to the corner and put a dime in the phone, the *ding* coming as the announcement of how long it had been since I'd called anyone.

Robert answered and I said, "Hi. Guess who?"

"Christine, Christine," he said. "My God, where have you been?"

"Here and there," I said. "Why don't we have lunch?"

I dressed in those new clothes and looked at myself in the mirror, the dust on it and the slats of light coming in the window making it look as though I were a fashionable woman who was having a fling in some dingy hotel room. In the restaurant Robert sat opposite me, not so much relieved as excited and romantic. He couldn't believe his luck, or that things weren't so chaotic as he had imagined. Just seeing me across the table gave him reassurance about that. And when we went to a hotel, a good one, I took off my dress and carefully hung it up and said, turning toward him, "Come on. Tell me. What did you think when I left?"

In the afternoon, in the street, I laughed off his requests for a phone number or an address or just a PO box where he could leave a message for me. I smiled and said, "I'll call you."

I went back to sitting in my room, drinking bourbon after going to the Music Box. I had gone through most of the records now and knew which would give me the most . . . access to those things I usually didn't or couldn't think about. In the morning I woke to the hammering of that cheap alarm clock and went to work, cutting those large trays of Jell-O into squares and seeing the old men smear mustard on the boiled meat and potatoes and gray vegetables.

"High-speed chase last night, Christine," said Mr. Kiri. "*Very* high speed."

Two weeks went by.

I called Robert, and he said, "Oh, sweet Jesus, where have you been? I've been desperate. I've been worried."

"How about lunch? I'll meet you in an hour," I said.

"I've got a meeting," he said. "People from all over are coming in here to—"

"Maybe some other time," I said.

"No, no," he said. "Wait. Where? Where do you want to meet?"

"You pick a place," I said.

It was a restaurant with white tablecloths and friendly waiters in black jackets and bow ties. We drank a little champagne and ate stuffed endives and pâté (which I learned to pronounce right then), and when we sat opposite one another, he said, "Christine, please. I've made a lot of money. So I'm able to help. Maybe with an apartment. Or some money. Please, don't be insulted. Money is not dirty bills, you know, it's like magic."

"Magic," I said.

"Yes," he said. "That's right. Well?"

I kept looking at him.

"Sure," I said. "All right. I need help."

The apartment I picked out was in a building with an elevator, and it had a doorman who stood out front in his brown uniform and brown cap. There was an awning, too, and the front of the building was glass and metal and the floor of the lobby was covered with a shiny, hard stone on which the heels of my shoes made a clicking sound. The apartment had a view of the city, and I bought some chrome-and-leather furniture, an Oriental rug, some glass bookshelves and books at a secondhand store, a palm in a terra-cotta pot, some things for the kitchen, a toaster oven and a frying pan, a coffee maker, and I didn't let him give me a credit card or a charge account for it: I got cash.

Now I saw Robert on Tuesdays and Thursdays when his wife was in town, and on the weekends, too, when she was gone, and that was fine, because on weekends, when she was away, we went to parties in Sonoma where friends of Robert's owned a vineyard. We drove up there, the rows of vines sweeping by like spokes on some enormous, flat wheel. The repetition of the vines was reassuring, one row always behind another: there were no surprises in those vineyards, each one regularly planted and carefully cultivated. And when a man looked at me across the room or hesitated when he shook my hand or made an excuse to come back and talk to me again, I got his telephone number (out of the book, or from a friend, or the host . . . always giving some excuse, some bland, perfectly acceptable reason), and during the week, on Monday, Wednesday, or Friday, I'd call him up and say, "Hi. Do you remember me? My name's Christine Taylor. Why don't we have lunch?"

I never brought them to my apartment. Never. Not if they weren't paying the rent themselves. We'd meet for lunch and go to a hotel, and then I'd disappear. For a while. And this gave them time to think it over, especially during those silent hours with their wives, or when they were at some dull, deadly dinner party, or at work. When I called back, a week or two or three later, they said, "My God, where have you been?"

I always got cash, too, even though there were men who wanted to give me a charge account or a credit card, each of which could evaporate at any time. Credit is a good friend but a hard enemy. Cash is constant, like the speed of light. There were some struggles about this, because it is easy for a man to write a check to Lord and Taylor or Jax or some other place, especially if his wife has a well-used account there. It is an unusual check that causes trouble. Like to a woman. Cash was always the solution, and when a man was squeamish about it, I said, "Money is like magic. Think of it that way."

It didn't take much to get by at these parties and among these people. A couple of French words, the knowledge of a few snotty things, the lyrics, say, of the "Eton Boating Song," the knowledge that if Harvard loses the Yale–Harvard game a nude picture in a bar in Boston is covered with a black sheet, the names of a few designers, Lord Ripon's advice on wing shooting ("Aim high, keep the barrel moving, and never check"), a line or two of Latin, an occasional reference to a father ("Daddy always said the time to buy is in a falling market"), the names of legendary bird-dogs, or the slang concerning them ("blinkers," "potterers," etc.), the name of a Greek island, or an Indonesian one, the menu of the *Concorde*, the drill at Foxcroft . . . I let these bits and pieces fall without any obvious guile. There wasn't much you needed to know, aside from some basics. Never be impressed by anything or anyone. Dismiss people by their clothes. And, if a bad moment came up, a bit of cross-examination that was dangerous, the weapon was always the same: a look of cold boredom, as though you'd just seen something about a man that made it impossible ever to sleep with him, or even to think about it.

Every six or nine months I moved, going from one man who would pay the rent on an apartment to the next, usually getting rid of the last by vanishing, by just packing up and disappearing after new arrangements had been made. The men I saw on the side were easier to handle, since they didn't know where I lived. Every now and then, if a man got unpleasant, or possessive in a nasty way, I didn't only disappear, I sent his wife a postcard, too, giving times and dates I'd spent with her husband, and that settled his hash.

When I called the movers and had the chrome-and-leather furniture, the Japanese bed, the chrome lamps, the glass bookshelves, the Oriental rug, the potted palm taken from one apartment to the next (which was indistinguishable from the last, being different only in its address), I took with me the list of names, George, Peter, Paul, Mick, Mickie, Mike, Michael, Mark, Don, Page, Bill, William, Willie, Charles, Chuck, Dick, Douglas, Doug, Bob, Robert, Sam, Sammy. In the new apartment, as in the old one, I had two phone lines, each with a jack. When I needed money or wanted to . . . work, I called three or four of the men, leaving messages with a secretary, and the first man who called back was the one I saw. Sometimes, for the others, I left an answering machine, and then, when I came home and sat in the quiet apartment, I had a glass of cold champagne and listened to their recorded voices.

Once a week I went to the Tree Park, where I sat in the back, wearing designer jeans, a T-shirt, and maybe a sweater too. Mr. Kiri sat opposite me, looking at my hands or eyes, seeing a bruise sometimes, but never asking about it or anything else. He just nodded when I walked in and said, "High-speed chase last night, Christine. Did you see it in the paper? How about some salmon. Yes?"

Then I sat in the back, eating the thin slices of pumpernickel and feeling a kind of relief, as though here at least there were no lies, and, if nothing else, I was a little closer, sitting in this room with the sawdust on the floor and the men with the meal tickets, to my father's failed enthusiasm and to my mother and her flimflam man, all of which, at one time, I had wanted to get away from. Mr. Kiri sat with his unlighted cigar and told me about Iceland, the coast there, the rocks webbed with cracks, the grass, the rolling hills, the lack of trees, the constant wind, the rivers, the sheep. . . . What did I miss? he asked.

When he asked this I had just moved again, and my apartment was a chaos of furniture and boxes. On the way home I went to the Music Box, where I played those Deutsche Grammophon Gesellschaft recordings of Beethoven, Schubert, Brahms, Chopin, the sound coming over me while I stood and looked out the glass booth. Then I went to Chinatown, seeing the ideograms in neon and on plastic signs, and when I finally stood in a tattoo parlor, I crossed my arms in front of myself, grabbed the bottom of the T-shirt, and pulled it over my head. The Chinese man who stood in front of me kept his eyes on mine as I said, "I want a small deer. About an inch long. With antlers. Right here. How much do you charge?"

Then I went into the street, feeling the heat of the tattoo and walking under those yellow and red neon signs. When I came into the apartment, it was dark, the light slashing out of the bathroom door and falling across the brown boxes and the unmade bed. No one could see me on the balcony of the new apartment. It was foggy there. When I moved an arm, white ribbons of fog trailed away from it, the shape of them like strands of smoke from a cigarette. I raised the T-shirt and the fog touched my skin, the infinitely small sparkles cooling the new tattoo while I thought, *All right. That's an identifying mark, one I can depend on.* The fog felt good, and I took off my clothes and stood there, the moisture collecting on my skin and eyelashes, in the hair between my legs, the drops small, like dew.

I started shivering and went inside, but I was still cold, and as I pushed the boxes around, trying to find one with the blankets in it, I saw the suitcase I had brought when I had come from Pennsylvania, and inside there were the same things I had put in it four years ago (those plastic bottles of cheap lotion and hair conditioner, my underwear from K mart, a leather skirt), all of it being carried from apartment to apartment as a reminder not only of where I had been, but of where I wanted to go, too. Now I just stared at it, shaking my head, having come up against the limits of how far I could run. I found a towel and rubbed my skin until it burned. When I looked down, I saw in the suitcase the chrome pistol I had taken off the shelf in my father's store, not to mention the ammunition for it, the cartridges held in a piece of Styrofoam that looked like a child's peg game. I picked the pistol up and held the familiar, cool weight in my hand, the pressure coming like a handshake from a judge, and then I put it on the shelf in the closet as insurance against the time when I'd make a mistake.

I met Charles DeLucia at a party on a boat in Sausalito. At

first I liked him because he carried around a roll of money. It was vulgar and shocking, but then most things about DeLucia were like that. I should have left him alone, but without giving it more than a thought I got his number and called and said, "Hi, remember me? I'm Christine Taylor." He was a tall, heavy man in his fifties and he wore silver suits and blue shirts and metallic-looking ties. French-toe shoes, perfectly shined. A handkerchief in his breast pocket. An expensive hairpiece. When he walked, his head rocked back and forth on his shoulders, like one of those figures, on springs, people put in the rear window of their cars. He liked to grab me when we were in bed and shake me like a doll, leaving bruises, but then he left enough money so it was all right, or almost all right. He had made a fortune in real estate. Sunbelt real estate. He paid the rent and was one of those who knew where I lived.

He had me followed, and when he discovered I was seeing other men, he came into the apartment and knocked the books off the shelf and grabbed me, shaking me hard. Then he sat down and breathed for a while, his hand to his forehead. He called me names, and stood up again, catching me by the arm. He told me what belonged to him and put his hand under my skirt and hurt me. Then he pushed the furniture around and went out. I sat on the floor, feeling a stiff numbness in my arm, and those other places where it hurt. He said he'd better not find me seeing anyone else again.

I began to look for another apartment, and when I found one I called the movers. There was the expense involved, the deposit, the cleaning fee. I got the money for it and started packing the boxes and bags. DeLucia came back while I was folding towels, letting himself in with a key and slapping me full in the face. Then he went through the apartment, kicking the boxes I had packed, turning them over, spilling my clothes onto the floor. He shook me again and spit on me and he hit me hard, harder than before. Then I sat down on the floor, both hands over my face, but he went right ahead now, using those French-toe shoes, his entire aspect one of anger mixed with pleasure. He turned back to the boxes I had packed, ripping them open, finally coming to the bag I had brought

from Pennsylvania, and there he found those bottles of lotions
and the canister, too, which he knocked against the wall. It
spilled there, just like a cosmetic box, the ashy powder and grit
making a conical pile on the floor, the tip of it smoking like a
miniature volcano. Then I stood up, one hand to my face,
trying not to give in to being dizzy or throwing up, but instead
walking directly to that closet where the pistol was, not only
wanting to get my hands on it but knowing that I would use it,
too. I walked out of the room and opened the closet door, but
when I reached up for it, he was right behind me. He shook
me again and brought me back into the living room, where he
left me on the floor, next to the suitcase. He stood in the
doorway and called names into the hall, where everyone
could hear, and then he slammed the door, the sound of it
coming like thunder.

I found a piece of paper and I scooped that gray powder
and grit back into the galvanized can, my fingers shaking so
much I couldn't hold the paper steady, that ashy powder spilling over the sides of the dented canister and into my hand,
which was wet with blood and sweat, and as I cried now, as I
looked at my hands, I said, "Where's Thomas Edison now?
Where the fuck is he? Or Bell. Or Einstein. Father, Father,
what good can they do me now?"

In the morning I sat on the unmade bed, sitting up and
touching my hair, the side of my face. There was the hum of
the icebox, a slow, steady drone. I put on my shoes and walked
into the living room, where I sat down, seeing the runs in my
stocking. I found a razor blade and chopped out two lines of
blow, taking it through a one-dollar bill. I took two Valium and
a shot of aquavit.

Outside it was a pale, sunny day. The pigeons flew overhead, their wings popping as they took off. There were gulls,
too, gliding on their wings, and on the bay there was a sailboat,
heeled over in the wind, the people in it wearing all-weather
gear which was the color of daffodils. In the square at the end
of the avenue there was a statue of a man on a horse, and I sat
on the steps beneath it, watching the traffic go by. From time

to time I touched the side of my face or my hair, feeling where it was matted.

There was a bench opposite the steps and a young man sat there, reading a book. After a while he came over and said, "Do you need help?"

"Me?" I said. "The only thing that's going to help is reincarnation. Do you believe in reincarnation?"

"No," said the man. "How about a drink? Maybe that would help."

"Yeah," I said. "Maybe it would."

We spent the afternoon in a bar, where he did most of the talking. The bar was quiet and cool and when it got dark outside the lights were kept low. The man sat opposite me, looking at my face, but not asking about it. Sometimes I put a napkin in a glass of water and put it to my cheek. After a while we were both in bad shape, and when it was late, he took me outside and got a cab, giving me the money for it through the window, and when I took it, I looked at him and said, "I didn't say I didn't have money. I just wanted a little company, that's all." The cab pulled into traffic and I threw the ten-dollar bill into the street, the bit of paper leaving the tips of my fingers and disappearing into the night.

"Where to?" said the driver.

"Do you know a place called the Music Box?" I said.

I went into one of those glass booths and played Schubert and Beethoven, the sound rolling over me while I sat with my hands in my lap, remembering that push from Baxter, the salmon in the Tree Park Cafeteria, the power of the music making me put my head down as I said, "I need him now. The right man. Where the hell is he?"

Christine Taylor/ Marie Boule
The City at Night
San Francisco, California

IN MY APARTMENT THE BOXES I HAD PACKED WERE NO longer neatly stacked one on top of another, but thrown around the room and ripped open, the clothes hanging out of them like long tongues. I turned on the light and began pushing the things back inside and then sealing the cardboard flaps, the tape coming off the roll with a sound like someone skinning a deer. And while I put the things back in the boxes, I thought of the new apartment I'd rented, one which was almost exactly like this one, a living room, with a bedroom alongside it and a bathroom in the hall between them. A kitchen off the living room. In the new place I'd know where the light switches were without having to look for them. This was like the man who came into the Tree Park: he was blind and asked me to cut up his meat for him, and when I did so, he told me that he liked to travel, but that he always stayed in a Holiday Inn. That way he never got lost in the hall or had trouble finding the ice machine or anything else: the places were all the same.

I stretched out on the unmade bed, taking off just my shoes, knowing I had had too much to drink and not wanting

to take more Valium. So I stared at the ceiling, hearing the hiss
of the cars on the wet street outside, feeling the bed rock from
side to side, the endless shifting of it coming as a slow, wheeling confusion. Then I got up and stood on the balcony. The
night sky was dark and had a sheen like the bluing on a pistol. I
took some Valium anyway, just wanting to sleep, to get away
from things for a while.

The movers came in the morning and woke me by banging on the door, the sound of it loud in the apartment with no
pictures on the walls and with the rug rolled up. I sat up, one
hand to the side of my face, where it hurt when I squinted.
The room had a slight nauseating roll. I went into the bathroom and drank from my hand, keeping my eyes closed, swallowing hard. In the daylight the walls were the color of nico-
tine stains, broken only by the fish-belly-white rectangles
where the pictures had hung. Then I let the movers in, checking first through the peephole to make sure it was only them.
The three men came through the door, two of them tall and
heavy, one short and heavy, each one of them looking at my
face and then picking up the first box and going out. I sat in my
bedroom, one hand to my face, staring at the runs in my
stockings until they came to get the bed, too.

The walls of the new apartment were cleaner, and now
the boxes and rug and furniture sat in the same chaotic pile as
in the apartment I had just left. I opened the box with the
coffee maker in it and boiled some water and poured it onto
the coffee grounds, but the steady dripping, the loneliness of
it, made me pour everything into the sink. Then I started
walking back and forth, stopping in front of the bag I had
brought from Baxter, which I now opened, if only to make
sure that the canister, now taped shut, was where I had left it.

Against those piles of brown boxes there was a framed
poster. It was two feet by three feet and it was an enlargement
of the picture of George Washington on a dollar bill: I had
bought it as a joke, or as a talisman, thinking the father of the
country was a good thing to face from time to time if only to be
reminded that money had a picture of a man on it, an appropriate decoration considering how I was making it. Now I

stood before that slight half-smile on Washington's face, as though the picture was there to remind me that not only was money like magic, but that it came at a price, too. I sat down before it, my head in both hands, seeing the runs in my stockings.

Outside, the sunshine filled the street like thin smoke. There was an alley where I had parked my car, a small blue MG. I got behind the wheel and drove across the Golden Gate Bridge, seeing the water below, the texture of it like a suit of mail. I kept on driving, up into the hills, squeezing the wheel hard, not able to think about how things had turned out and not wanting to, either. I just liked seeing those white lines on the macadam. Every now and then some doves rose from the side of the road, pairs that fluttered into the distance, their tails, with a flame-shaped mark down the middle, straight out behind them. I began to turn around and go home, but I thought about those boxes, the chaos of the apartment and the knowing smirk on George Washington's face. I want farther, keeping my eyes on the lines.

Once, when I was going slow, staring at some quail in the grass at the side of the road, the covey of them moving with a fast skitter, a car, an ordinary Chevrolet, went by me. It was driven by a man who had sandy-colored hair. His face was tanned, not deeply lined, his features definite and even. And when I speeded up again and passed him, he kept his eyes straight forward, not looking at all.

There were no other cars on the road. We went through brownish grassland which had a eucalyptus or two in the distance. There were only a few white houses against the ridge. The sky was blue and hazy. We just drove along together, and as we went I had the sense of an intimate warmth, which seemed to be not only in the car around me, but in the sky and in the sunlight on the brownish land. When a car passed from the opposite direction, I squeezed the wheel and looked away, not wanting even that small interruption. I relaxed now, forgetting about that empty apartment, the unmade bed there, or the panic of facing those unpacked boxes (again), and for as long as that car stayed in sight, the smirk on George Washington's face and the silence of the apartment didn't effect me so much. When I went through a turn and the sight of that car was lost, the sense of warmth disappeared, too, just as surely as if the shadow of a cloud had passed over the landscape.

He passed again and looked over, his expression suggesting that he understood, too, and that he was enjoying the sunlight, the smell of the ocean, and the speed, the getting away from something. What could have been more innocent? Now I blushed, the heat of it in my cheeks and ears coming as a pleasure, if only because it reminded me of the way I used to be. I squeezed the wheel hard, wanting to make sure that things wouldn't disappear. I concentrated on the passing of the white lines and on the man in the Chevrolet.

There was a softness to the way he handled a car, a lack of abruptness that seemed as though he was not in any hurry at all, and when the car approached there was a tactile sense of its closeness, like the fuzz of static electricity. When he passed, I raised a brow, already wanting to ask a question, the particulars of it having no importance at all, the impulse behind it being an attempt to prolong things: I wanted to make idle conversation, just waiting-room talk, the words themselves being of no consequence at all or only an excuse to hear a comforting voice. We drove next to each other, just enjoying things. I looked over to see if there were any obvious marks on him, a black eye or a scar or something that explained how he could possibly understand. Then I kept my eyes on the lines, not knowing what to do, or how to talk to him: for a moment I thought of going ahead and pulling over, but what if he stopped or turned off before then? So I reached over and wrote in the fogged window on the passenger's side, *Lunch?*, the tip of my finger feeling the long, cool slickness of each letter.

We stopped at a gas station, where I got out of the car, the runs in my stockings showing as I walked through the pale sunlight. In his glance there was that same quality as when we had been in the cars: the awareness of the two of us being somehow separate from the rest of the world. It was friendly, too. I walked up to his window and said, "Hi. My name's Christine . . . Taylor. What's your name?"

"Hi," he said. "Beautiful day, isn't it? My name's Ben Lunn."

"Well, hello, Ben Lunn," I said. "Where are we going for lunch?"

Beyond us there was the gas station and the brownish land. A breeze had come up now, and I felt my hair moving a little, and when I smiled the side of my face hurt, but even the sea breeze didn't seem very cold. Both of us ignored the black eye, the wrinkled clothes, the runs in my stockings.

"Why don't you follow me back to the city?" I said.

He went on looking at me.

"All right," he said.

I got into my car, swinging my legs under the steering wheel. I had a small handbag, a red leather one with a snap that didn't close, and when I threw it onto the passenger's seat, the things inside flew out, the lipstick and compact tumbling over, the pillbox and Kleenex disappearing into the darkness below the steering wheel, the change, the dimes, nickels, and quarters winking as they fell, some of them dropping onto my thighs and between my legs, their presence on my skin coming as a cool lick. I picked them up, having to reach onto the seat for them, picking up one and another, bringing my hand into the patch of sunlight where the coins looked like drops of quicksilver, and even then, feeling the coins in my hand, I thought, *Look at you. Just look. What's this?*

Soon, though, I forgot about it, and the certainty of sharing some innocent thing came back. It was dark and foggy when we got into the city, and the lights of the cars looked enormous and fuzzy. We parked in the alley around the corner from my new building, and when he got out of his car the sound of his steps echoed on the damp, shiny walls. He opened the door for me and I got out, exposing on the seat some of the coins that I had spilled, all of them looking like drops of silver paint. We both glanced down, the dimes and quarters and nickels glowing in the alley's dim light and looking like stains.

We went down the street and turned onto the avenue where there were restaurants and stores. Ben took my arm as we crossed the street. His fingers rested on a bruise there, but his touch was so gentle it didn't hurt. Instead there was some warm ebb and flow, some sense of fuzziness between us, as though where we began and ended wasn't so definite. Now, on the other side of the street, he let me go, and then I hugged myself in the cold, mystified now.

As someone came out of a restaurant, the white tendrils of mist curled outward, the shape of them like the coils of a streamer, and through the open door there was dark wood and soft yellow lights, tables with white linen tablecloths, and men and women at them, their heads close together, their voices hushed. We passed in front of the windows, from which the light slanted into the street. We went into the dark again, where I stopped and said, "Wait a minute. Please, maybe I should just go on home. . . . I need some rest. . . ." But I kept looking at him, seeing his features, which seemed familiar. We stood there, just touching in the fog, my knees trembling against him, my fingers awkward on his shoulders, as I said, "You're shaking, too, aren't you?"

"Yes. That's right. Can you feel it?" he said. "Let's get out of the cold. There's a place."

We went in, passing the long dark bar, where men and women sat, smoke rising from cigarettes, the women dressed in silk, the men in jackets, their hair gleaming in the light. We sat at a table in the back against a dark wooden wall and drank brandy.

I put my head down for a moment, one hand over the black eye and the bruise at the side of my face, and as I sat there, I began to relax again.

"Look," he said, "if I haven't ever seen a black eye, it's time I did, and if I already have, one more time isn't going to hurt me, is it?"

"No," I said, smiling now and dropping my hand, hearing the hushed voices of the restaurant, the clink of silverware on plates, the striking of a match. I went on looking at him.

We had another brandy, and the warmth of it and the

sound of the people around us, the steady conversation and the occasional laugh had about them a reassuring quality, as though we could sit here as long as we wanted. I didn't listen very closely and he didn't, either, since both of us were doing the same thing, just relaxing, forgetting about things, each moment having about it the sense that we weren't expecting anything at all. That's what I liked about it, one moment leading to absolutely nothing at all. I watched him now, over my glass, still just hearing his voice, but after an hour had gone by, I found myself squeezing my glass, trying to find a way to get another hour. And when I got up and went into the bathroom, the same thing happened as when we had been driving those turns up in the mountain and had gotten separated: that comfort just disappeared and the thought of my apartment, the chaos of boxes there, came back with a cold, greasy rush.

We paid the check and the waiter brought the change, which was left in a tray, the coins, like drops of solder, spread on top of the bills. I put my finger on a quarter, on the profile of George Washington, feeling the shape of his nose and forehead. And when we were outside again, the moisture from the fog collecting in our hair, eyelashes, and on our jackets, and the mist streaming away from our mouths, I didn't even hesitate to say, "Listen. Why don't you come with me to a place I go to sometimes? It's a store where you can listen to records. Everyone gets a glass booth. Sometimes I spend a couple hours there. Please"—the last word hanging there, the suddenness of it coming as a surprise.

At the Music Box he sat in a booth, his hands folded neatly in his lap, his blondish hair shining in the light, his eyes looking through the glass. I played my favorites for him, bringing in one record after another, the music and his presence getting me the same thing we had had in the afternoon and in the restaurant, and now when I went out of the booth for another record, I did so with a direct, quick searching, flipping the albums back and forth as though they would give me what I wanted, not only music but more time (more of that calm escape). So I found the ones I knew and liked, slipping them out of the jackets, expertly holding each one by the edge with my fingers and having my thumb just on the hole. I put them on the player, feeling, in the moment the needle slipped into the groove, that I was safe for a while longer. He listened, glancing up at me and nodding from time to time, not in an attempt to say he understood the music, but that we understood the same thing, just as we had understood speed, that warm landscape, and the smell of the ocean. Then I went out again, flipping the album covers back and forth, searching with a kind of frenzy now, but finding nothing, and while my fingers flicked through the records, he said, emerging from a section of the store I knew nothing about, "Here. Have you heard this?"

We sat down again, one of us on each side of the booth, opposite one another, although now we weren't smiling so much as just admitting we were up to the same thing here, too, each of us trying for more time, not to mention playing for the other these albums as though they contained all we needed to know about one another, at least if we were going to limit things to just an afternoon. He put the needle into the groove of the record, and we listened to a duet from *The Pearl Fishers* (something I knew nothing about), the sound of it taking me by surprise, so much so I started crying right there, putting a hand to my face and saying, "I'm sorry. I didn't think I was so upset. It's funny how that can happen. You think you're fine and then"—I snapped my fingers—"just like that you end up . . ." I stopped now and looked through my pockets for a Kleenex, and when I couldn't find one, I said, "If you give me a handkerchief I'll wring your neck. I'd rather just sit here with a wet face. . . ." And when he handed a clean handkerchief over, I took it, squeezing his hand, and then I wiped my eyes while he looked out the window.

But that was too close, too soon: we weren't up to that, at least not then. We didn't need to know about each other being panicky. What we knew and all we needed to know was in the general understanding that began when we were driving those cars. If we got around to admitting specifics, why, then, neither one of us was sure, or at least I wasn't sure, that we'd still have those hours of innocent reassurance: that's what I craved, the sense that I wasn't doomed, that I had a chance, and a calmness that let me remember my first longings and innocent desires.

We took a taxi back to where our cars were parked, and when we got out, we stood there in the darkish street, but now I had nothing to use, nothing to keep those hours going, and as I heard a foghorn from the bay, I looked at him and said, "Why don't you come up for a drink. I've got some brandy. Okay? Please."

We stood at the front of the alley where the cars were, and next to it, on one side, there was a brownstone building with a black metal rail along the steps that lead up from the street. The rail was wet and the moisture fell to the concrete beneath it with an endless *drip, drip, drip,* the sound of it coming as a reminder that now he could just turn and go, leaving me to face the emptiness of that apartment. As I heard that sound and saw the splash of the drops on the stone, I turned and looked at him again. He waited, the fog behind him, those drops falling in lines straight as banjo strings.

"All right," he said, his eyes set on mine.

"I warn you," I said, "everything's in boxes. It's a mess, the plants are on the floor . . . even the toaster's wrapped up. . . ."

I walked along, feeling the pounding of the concrete in my legs, in my head, and as we went I sighed a little, not thinking of tomorrow or the day after or even when I would have to try to sleep, since now the only important thing was keeping away that moment when I had to face the silent rooms where I had come to live. It meant everything now to have him smiling, nodding sometimes, listening to my voice as though I sounded like someone who was really fine, just fine.

The lobby of the building was deserted, aside from the doorman, who stood in a blue uniform with gold piping on it, his movements when he opened the door quick and exaggerated, since he was drunk and trying not to show it. The stone floor had been polished and was bright now, like the top of a piano. Upstairs we got out of the elevator and stopped in front of the buff-colored door with the peephole in it, the small, wet-looking lens there the same as in the other places I had lived. The key was new, bright as tinsel, and my fingers were trembling a little so I had trouble getting it into the lock.

The apartment smelled of new paint, and for that I was glad, since the atmosphere was one of starting fresh. We moved the boxes out of the way and pulled a sofa and a chair together. He sat down, folding his hands in his lap. I went into the kitchen and rinsed out two glasses and took a bottle of brandy out of a box. Then I came out again, and even in the midst of the things I disliked we sat together as before, and around us there was a calm, delicious ease, which came to the skin like mink. We had both been frightened, since it had seemed, before we had arrived, that this pleasure was bound to the places we had been, on the road or in that restaurant, and that somehow the feeling of being together couldn't take being moved, although this turned out not to be true. We sat there, not curious exactly that the transit had been made and that no damage had been done, since we were too much in the middle of it to admit to anything aside from the warm sense of being alone. It was late now and the building was quiet, and the silence added to the privacy of the room. I had put a sheet over the window, and the light of the streetlamp, with its peachlike color, came inside.

But then I began to brood again, realizing that now there was nothing to stop him from finishing his drink and going, leaving behind that darkening sense (as in the shadow of a cloud): when he left, the apartment would seem ugly and oppressive. Now we sat with our knees almost touching, our faces close together, but even there, in the scent of our breath, in the aroma of brandy, there was no expectation of any kind. Our fingers touched once as we both reached for our glasses, and there was a shock or charge or surprise, but we both . . . went on, ignoring it. He looked up and smiled and then sat back, and I did, too, watching him, pleased now that he had denied that accidental touch. We both insisted that everything was as innocent as though a chaperone were sitting in the shadows beyond the lamp. Now we were silent, feeling that clutter around us, and the sense of being comfortably alone was even more pronounced than before, since he understood I didn't want to change anything at all, or to take a chance on damaging things by getting into bed, and that the youthful, simple afternoon was everything.

We spoke quietly, both of us feeling our way through this, neither one of us knowing how to proceed. All I wanted was time, and it was after midnight. He put down his glass and said, "I've got to go."

I nodded, closing my eyes, already feeling the room as it would become when the door closed.

"I know," I said.

"Thanks for the afternoon," he said. "I had a . . . good time."

"Did you?" I said. "Did you really?"

"Yes," he said. "It was nice to get away from things. Just for a few hours."

"Look," I said. "Let me give you my telephone number. Will you call me?"

I went through my handbag, looking for the letter from the telephone company which gave the numbers of the two lines that ran into the apartment. I wrote down the private one, the one that was never unplugged, and held it out, saying with that same explosive suddenness, "Please. There are other afternoons. . . . I'm not always like this. People won't stare at us when my face is better. Look." I reached into my bag and took out some photographs of me.

"You look very nice," he said.

I blushed, the heat coming so hard and with such pleasure that my eyes watered.

"Here's the number," I said. "Can I have yours?"

"I don't think so," he said. "I'm married. I have two children. I'm forty years old. Do you think I have business here?"

"Yes," I said. "There's nothing wrong with today. Absolutely nothing."

He took a deep breath and began to speak, but before he did I said, "Please. Take the number. You can think it over. We can spend some innocent afternoon . . . like today. That's all.

You can't tell me there was anything wrong with today, can you?"

He looked at me and shook his head.

"No," he said.

"Here," I said. "Take it."

I put the number into his hand, my fingers pushing against his palm through the paper. I smiled and said, "I had a nice afternoon. Call soon, okay?"

"Okay," he said.

"Maybe you'd like to stay a little longer," I said. "I could make some coffee."

He shook his head.

"I'm late. My wife is probably worried. My oldest daughter is probably awake, waiting . . . she gets worried when I'm late."

I nodded, not even really listening so much as concentrating on the piece of paper I had put into his hand, and even then I was imagining the sound of the phone ringing. Perhaps we'd have lunch someplace. . . . It was just a matter of waiting, of getting through the hours, of unpacking the boxes, all of which could be done so long as I knew there'd be a little . . . break. And even his wife and daughter helped, since they acted as a kind of ballast, or an invisible chaperone that would keep things proper. We'd be polite, as we had been today, about our mutual desperation to make things stop just for an afternoon.

We stood at the door, each of us remembering the fog or the brownish landscape, the damp streets, all of which were somehow different than before, and as we stood there we were as skittish as kids, or as the kid I had been a few years before, the jumpiness or awkwardness having a pleasure to it as well, so much so that I reached up and kissed him sweetly on the lips and said, "Thanks," and then closed the door and turned to face the chaos of the room.

So I started to wait right then. I began to move the boxes around, looking into them, telling myself that each one was a unit of time, and if I just got them right, if the things were put on the shelves or hung in the closet or arranged in the drawers, why, then, I'd have a chance for a little more relief.

After a while I filled the bathtub. I took off the dirty clothes, the ruined stockings, and threw them into an empty box in the hall. In the tub I ran a washcloth over the money-colored bruises on my arms and legs, all the while feeling the warmth of the water. I put my head back and closed my eyes, concentrating on that delicate, crucial thing that had happened in the afternoon, those hours when I thought I wasn't doomed after all. I put my head back like some child of eighteen who thinks things are possible after all, and when I smiled now, still with my eyes closed, it was while savoring a delicious moment, the innocence of the memory only adding to the pleasure.

Then I toweled hard, feeling the heat on my skin. I let the water out of the tub and sprinkled scouring powder into it. The stuff got wet and dark, and I knelt down with a piece of steel wool and started working, making the chrome shine and scrubbing the porcelain until it looked like pearls.

In the morning the moon-colored light came through the sheets over the window, and around me there was the dry rustle of the bedclothes, not to mention their seductive warmth. There was the scent of cleanser on my hands, and I lay there, smelling it and staring at the telephone. I dressed and went down the street to the corner, where there is a coffee shop, and there, in a booth at the back, I ate grapefruit, scrambled eggs and ham, toast with jelly, the food steamy and yellow and brown, the butter melting into the toast. I hadn't slept so well in months and was already telling myself I was fine now. I started unpacking the boxes, arranging my clothes and shoes, stacking the sheets and towels in the closet, hanging the pictures, tapping the brads into the wall for them. While I piled up the sheets or folded a comforter I kept stopping, amazed that for now even the waiting was pleasurable, the entire episode having about it the quality of a decent woman who is waiting for a decent man. There was no shame in this, not even any embarrassment, or if there was, it came as a pleasure, too.

But I still kept watching the phone, and when the apartment was in order, when my few dishes and pots and pans were arranged in the kitchen, when there was nothing left to do, I sat on that chrome-and-leather furniture, no longer certain he would call at all, the panic or desperation of this allowing the things I wanted to keep in the shadows, like the memories of the nights I had spent, to come a little closer than I wanted. Then I got up and started straightening the already immaculate piles of towels, somehow thinking that each folded piece of terry cloth, when stacked perfectly against another, was a sign of good luck.

I gave the number to no one else, and by doing so I thought I would save myself a few seconds, since when the phone rang I wouldn't have to wait to answer it: I would know at the first sound. But it rang anyway: a wrong number, a woman selling magazines, a man telling me I'd won one of three unnamed prizes. I asked him if there were any fees involved in claiming one and the man said, "Have we contacted you before?"

So, when Ben called and we agreed to meet, I put down the phone with a kind of pleased relief. I dressed in a pair of jeans and a T-shirt and a sweater, and when I looked at myself in the mirror I saw what I wanted, a young woman who was on her way to some safe, reassuring place. I began to put some makeup over the bruise, but then I put down the jar, knowing I didn't have to hide anything at all. I waited with the last banana-colored marks under the skin.

Now, when he came into the apartment, it was the same as before: the room became pleasant. We sat by the balcony and talked for a while, each glancing at the other with a frank acknowledgment of what the time had been like since we had last met. That sense of escape was right there again. Right *there*. I could touch it with my finger, could feel it on any glass I picked up, on the jacket I took from the closet when we went out.

We took a cable car down to the bay, and while we sat there, side by side, looking at the water and at the white crests of the waves, there was a slight tension, too, like that for any couple who are going on a "date" for the first time, and in the steady movement of the car, in the ratcheting of the levers that made the thing go, I enjoyed that momentary awkwardness between us, the sense of it suggesting precisely what I wanted: our mutual knowledge that we had something to protect.

We had an Irish coffee in a restaurant by the bay. We talked now, the conversation having to it a frankness that was new, and for a moment troubling, since I wasn't sure we were ready, or that we would ever be ready, for more than pleasant chitchat. But it wasn't what was said, so much as how. Each of us let down just a little, relaxing, taking a deep breath of that sea air and then tasting the coffee and the sweetness of the whipped cream. So I didn't even think about it, or hesitate when I lifted the hair from the side of my face and said, "See? It's healing. It's almost gone," the words, and his steady nod, his acceptance of it indistinguishable from the ease of our surroundings, the white tablecloths, the scent of coffee, the large glass windows, the blue, white-topped water on the bay.

He didn't have much time. An hour, or perhaps two, and even as we sat there, I began thinking, *That's it? That's all? How long do I have to wait again?* I put my hands together, under the table, pushing the knuckles together.

Ben came up to the apartment, where I felt helpless in the face of the time. He had to go. What could I offer? So we stood at the doorway, talking there, my fingers brushing his as I reached up to my hair . . . but we still denied the shock of touching, the surprise of it: neither of us was able to do anything but . . . smile, nod, each of us protecting the other, or those unentangled hours we spent together. But I thought, *Please. Please. Just a quarter of an hour more. Can't we just sit by the window? Just think of how much time I've waited. . . .*

I was afraid to give him a sweet, innocent kiss. Instead I said, "There was nothing wrong with this, either. I'd like to know when I'll see you again. You can understand that, can't you?"

"Yes," he said. "Next Tuesday, then. Same time. All right?"

I nodded quickly, moving my head as though to say, *Yes, yes, yes. That's fine.*

He turned and went to the elevator and I closed the door and leaned against it, glad that at least I had a date, a particular time to use against the silence of the apartment and those memories that waited in the shadows.

Now, though, things began to change. Before, when we had driven those cars together or when we had gone to the Music Box, there had been about us that innocent sense of just being together, as though nothing had ever gone wrong for either one of us and that we still had infinite possibilities. But as I stood against the door, I blushed again, feeling in the heat of it more pleasure than before, since, if originally we had seemed innocently unentangled, I began to think about how I was attracted, or interested. I was like any eighteen-year-old girl who is examining, with a sense of wonder, just what she would do if she had the chance. So, now, not only was there that sense of innocence, there was that sense of wonder as well, between the two of which I would have been hard pressed to choose one as being more important or giving me a better weapon against the shadows around me.

Now I went to the Music Box and bought records and brought them home, being able, in anticipation of the time we would spend together, to play the music at home, unafraid that the apartment would do the music any harm at all. I listened to Brahms, or Schubert, or Beethoven.

Sometimes I went to new places, like the Planetarium, being reminded, as I stood in the marble hall of the place where there were pictures of stars and distant galaxies, of how I had wanted my father to take me to the Museum of Natural History, but we had never had the time or money when we had gone to New York to the trade shows. But he had always said, "Outer Space, Marie. That's the future. Manufacturing. They will make a perfect ball bearing there one day. Can you imagine? A perfect ball bearing!"

In the theater of the Planetarium there were rows of seats, and I sat in the dark, in the afternoon, surrounded by schoolchildren while that enormous, antlike thing made stars appear on the ceiling. I stared at them and memorized the names of the constellations, Sagittarius, Orion, Andromeda, the stars themselves looking cool, blue and clean. There, watching the heavens, it seemed as though the possibilities were endless. The voice of a man at a lectern filled the air with a steady drone, the dome overhead finally turning white as a star blew up, the brightness of it looking like white satin.

Ben came back on Tuesday. We took the streetcar to the Tree Park, and there Mr. Kiri shook Ben by the hand and made us sit down while he went into the backyard and dug up some salmon. While he was gone, Ben and I sat against the wall. There was the odor of hot mustard, of the sawdust on the floor, and the old men who sat in their damp overcoats and musty clothes. I said nothing then, and Ben didn't, either, both of us just sitting there, the entire visit done as a kind of surrogate for my bringing him home to parents who would have embarrassed me. In the steamy atmosphere of the counter, in the boiled beef and around the red meal tickets, there was the suggestion of the places where my family and I had come from, the construction gangs and shape-ups and cheap cafeterias where waitresses wore support hose and shoes with rubber soles. While Ben and I waited, I looked at him to make sure he understood. I wanted to say something, but I knew I would ruin it if I had to ask, "Do you really understand . . . I brought you here to show you where I came from?" Instead I looked for a sign that he knew what was going on. As we waited, there wasn't so much a sense of comfort as of panic. What if he thought we were slumming? That would have been it, right there. Then Mr. Kiri brought out the salmon on those thin slices of pumpernickel, and a bottle of aquavit from the freezer. The bottle was in a block of ice, and he poured out three small shot-glasses, the clear fluid in them coming right up to the rim. Ben came around the table and sat opposite me, and when he drank the cold, burning fluid he did so in one *BANG*, putting the shot glass down on the table with a knock, while he looked me in the eye and said, "My father is a small-town doctor. My mother ran off years ago . . . it was a scandal the town still talks about. We were hicks. You understand? Nothing special. Nothing fancy."

There were times when a week or so went by and Ben didn't call or even come over, either, and then he wrote a note, the words definite and clear as I read them in the silence of the morning in that apartment: he said that when we were apart he felt a kind of panic, as though he'd been under water too long.

We found out, too, how futile it was to resist. On the next Tuesday, when we sat together in the restaurant by the bay, there was a slight uneasiness from kidding ourselves, or from trying to say that a door hadn't been forever opened and that we weren't already halfway into the room beyond . . . both of us smiled and talked, just as before, but it was different, and both of us knew (and admitted it, just by looking at one another), that the pleasure of the hours we spent together depended on the two of us doing things we had never done before (like meeting on the road, or following a stranger into the city for lunch . . .).

In my apartment we tried again, each of us wanting to make sure that the mild comfort we had had together was gone forever. Or maybe it is better to say that the comfort we had had before now seemed mild . . . and somehow used up. We sat together in the living room, making idle conversation (the news, politics, earthquakes, small memories of one kind or another), and you could see him straining, or deciding what to do. I could almost hear him thinking, *All right. This and no more. I have no business in anything beyond this.*

But then . . . we drew a little closer, telling each other more than just small memories. Each small advancement, each small step toward unexplored things had about it an unavoidable quality. We were cautious, both of us enjoying the sense of being on a precipice and wanting to stay there for as long as possible. We sat together for a few hours and there was a little more . . . acknowledgment (a smile, a hint, and best of all a *blush* . . . from a man of forty). It seemed nothing tawdry, nothing that made me want to look the other way could ever happen here.

Now, before he arrived, I picked the things I wore, trying on one blouse or skirt and then another, standing in front of the mirror, wondering just how I should appear. I blushed while I unbuttoned one more button, not because of the image before me, but because I realized (by his constant decisions to keep coming back) I had been granted the right to a seduction. I woke up in the morning and stood by the terrace, laughing at the freedom of it. There was nothing wrong here, either.

I went to the florist's and bought orchids and put them in a vase near where we sat, the petals of them pinkish and delicate. I left the door to the bedroom half open, beyond which there was the bed, neatly made with the covers turned back, and in the corner there was a dressing screen, over which there hung a flowered dressing gown and a pair of stockings. I went to the stationery store and bought a notebook and a pen, and in the evenings I wrote there, in my clear, still girlish hand, some things . . . dreams or musings of one kind or another, all of them about him. I left it open for him to see, or at least to see his name, and then I walked into the other room, although I watched to see if he read the thing. He made that continuous struggle to be correct: he wanted to see what was written there, but he stood up and looked away. When he waited at the door (as he got ready to leave . . . now trembling with the effort), he said, "I shouldn't come back. We both know that, don't we?"

"No," I said, "no, I don't. Everything about this is right. How can you think of being separated, or of doing without those few hours. . . . Could you live without them?"

He stood there, shaking his head.

"No," he said, "I'll see you Tuesday."

So I waited for him, cleaning the apartment and then buying a sweet, a raspberry tart, which I brought home, carrying it by a handle hooked through the string the box was tied with, the parcel light and perfect and somehow suggesting order. When he came back, just as he said he would, I opened the door and let him in. I was dressed as I used to be in Pennsylvania, in blue jeans and a T-shirt, and when he came into the apartment I said, "You know I love you, don't you? I don't think I've ever loved anyone so much or at all." He closed his eyes, almost as though I'd slapped him. "Is there anything wrong?" I said. "No, no," he said. "Why don't we lie down. . . ."

In that room with the covers neatly folded back and with the orchids in a vase on the nightstand, I surrendered like any teenage girl who has finally realized some things were not only inevitable, but necessary, too. The day slowly disappeared outside, the light from the white curtains over the windows turning from pale blue (like the light of a freezer) to that peachlike glow when the streetlights came on, the time passing in one long series of moments when we looked into one another's eyes and with me finally asking him to call me *Marie, Marie, Marie.*

We lay there, hearing the shoes going by on the pavement below, the endless scuffle or click and tap of them. There were voices, too, blowing along like scraps of old newspaper. Then I got up and brought in the box I had brought home. I bit through the string and we ate the raspberry tart, getting the jam on our fingers and cheeks and drinking drafts of milk from the pitcher in the icebox.

When he left, I went out to dinner alone.

I went out to a Chinese restaurant, where I sat in a booth, seeing the men in black trousers and white shirts come and go, speaking a language I didn't understand. I sat there, not eating the food, not even taking the stainless steel covers off of it, just drinking tea and smoking cigarettes, saying nothing, only thinking, *There's nothing else I want but more time.* The waiter came and said, "Miss? Something wrong, miss?"

In my apartment I sat at the kitchen table, with the boxes the restaurant had packed sitting in front of me, the food uneaten here just as it had been in the restaurant, the beef and broccoli and shrimp in oyster sauce cold now after having been carried through the fog. I made a drink and stood in front of the TV and the VCR. I thought of those movies I had watched behind the store in my father's house, the ones where women wore silver dresses and had the light shimmering over their hair, backs, hips, and legs like an endless thrill of satisfaction, and now it seemed that I had not only found that world, but one better, a clean, reassuring place where nothing I did seemed to be wrong.

Now there were letters from the phone company and the electric company, wanting money. The rent was seven hundred dollars. There was twelve hundred in the bank. I started making dates. At first I wasn't aware I was speaking frankly to these men, and I didn't really notice the puzzled expressions or the raised brows.

The man from Chicago was a grain merchant, or futures broker, and he had money in his pockets. A date had been arranged with him through a man I saw from time to time. The man from Chicago was tall, over six two or three, and he wore a beautiful suit, the material soft to the touch and perfectly tailored. The man was young, not more than twenty-five, but still he had a triple chin, and he must have weighed three hundred pounds. He was almost bald, and wore a ring on his little finger. It was a gold ring, thick and broad, and in it there was the biggest diamond I have ever seen: it was circular and cut around the edge in triangular facets, hundreds of them, the clear sections coming together like the triangles of a geodesic dome. When he moved his hand, the diamond flashed, the light coming as a small, definite weight, but it came again and then again, the flick of it getting worse all the time. I watched the diamond. The man was heavy, but since he was young, his stomach was hard, like a ham. We sat in an apartment with a view of the bay and Treasure Island and Alcatraz, and we drank champagne, the color of the bubbles like the light from the diamond. I told the man that my father had read *The Wall Street Journal,* and that he had bought a futures contract once. The man had a little mirror and a razor blade and as I spoke, he chopped his white powder, the razor making a *chit, chit, chit* on the glass.

"What did your father do for a living?" he said.

"He had a store in a small town in Pennsylvania. He sold gas and guns and groceries. Mostly canned goods."

"And he bought a futures contract?" said the man, looking at me. "Why? Did he know what he was doing? Did someone give him a tip?"

"No," I said. "He thought it was a good idea. He put a certain amount of time aside each day to think about new ways of making money. He always wanted people to see him on the street and say, 'That's Al Boule. He's got a wad.' "

"Did he make any money?" said the man.

"No," I said. "He sold some vacuum cleaners door to door. I guess he did all right there."

"Is that where the money for the futures contract came from?"

"Yes," I said.

"And he lost money, didn't he?" said the man.

"Yes," I said. "He always lost money on things like that."

The man started laughing, his hard, hamlike stomach bouncing up and down, his chins moving, the tears coming out of his eyes. He laughed until his brow and almost bald head began to sweat a little. "Oh. God," he said, "isn't that the limit. Wait until I tell . . ." Then he started laughing again, the ring moving now, the light sweeping across my face, and as I sat there, looking at him, hearing that laughter, I wished I had brought that pistol from my father's store, and that I'd take the thing and put it next to the man's head. Maybe the shot would come like a flash of the diamond's light. The man went on laughing, his head still sweating. He did a little more chopping with the razor blade and then took the powder through a rolled-up bill, putting his head up quickly and sniffing as though he had a cold. When he was finished, he said, looking at me with a smirk, "I guess I'm as ready as I'll ever be. What about you?"

I took care of him and went into the bathroom to wash, seeing my face in the mirror when I looked up, my skin white, my eyes deep now, shiny as polished glass. Then I got dressed, pulling the things on with a jerk, my foot shaking as I tried to push it into a shoe, and when I got outside I realized I had forgotten the money. So I stood in the hall, slapping the door, hitting it hard, and then going back in, passing that hard, hamlike stomach and picking up what I'd left.

Ben had given me a crystal radio set, one that received the weather predictions he broadcast, and when I got home I turned it on, hearing Ben's voice: winds were out of the west, high pressure was building. There was some warm, moist air in the south Pacific, and there was some wind there, too, but it was a long way off. Rainy weather ahead. I listened to his voice, and then I threw open the wardrobe and looked at the clothes hanging there, the silk and wool and cotton having about them a maddeningly insubstantial quality: they hadn't helped me at all. I pulled open the drawers in the bureau and looked there, too, seeing the things that were of no more help than a costume. I slammed the drawers shut, my hands shaking. And as I stood there, as the forecast was repeated every few minutes, the sound of Ben's voice came into the room with a kind of seduction, as though if he were just here, I'd be all right. I'd be able to sleep. I wouldn't tell assholes about my family anymore. I went around the apartment, opening cabinets now and slamming them, enjoying the *whoosh* of air and the noise, but I couldn't slam them hard enough. Then I stood in front of the radio, hearing that voice. While he went on about those winds, about that moist air, I put both hands to the front of my blouse and ripped it off and then the skirt, too, in a fury at where I had been. I sat and looked at the material on the floor, which lay there in sleek folds, the edges of the tears unraveling.

Now, while I waited for Ben to visit, I went to the pharmacy and bought conditioners and lotions, shampoos, creams, aloe, and mousse. I had read that beer was good for hair, and I had a bottle of beer, too. When he came into the kitchen I said, "Take off your jacket, Ben, will you?" I brought a chair in and he put a telephone book on it, and then I sat down, bending my head back into the sink, baring my neck to him, saying, "I couldn't get to the hairdresser. Will you give me a hand? You can use that hose there, the one to rinse dishes." He rolled up his sleeves while looking at the plastic bottles and smelling the sweet, chemical odor of them. "Just wash my hair, will you? I want to feel your fingers against my scalp, okay? Do you see this picture in *Vogue*? How about that flip? What do you think of that? Do you like it? Just talk for a while, will you?"

"You have beautiful hair," he said.

"Do I?" I said. "That's nice, isn't it?"

For a while we were all right. He arrived on those days he could get away, and then the apartment seemed cool and clean and white, and there was about the time we spent together the authority of people who have a right to the things they did, not to mention the privacy that went along with it. When he left, the shadows around me seemed to press a little closer, and I crossed my arms, hugging my shoulders, trying to get away from the closeness of that anonymous world outside, the cruel streets, the flophouses and cheap restaurants, not to mention the memory of the man from Chicago, and the *chit, chit, chit* of his chopping, his laughter, the flash of the diamond on his finger, all of which came as a reminder of how I had run out of ideas about everything aside from making sure I had those safe, reassuring hours.

In the beginning Ben had asked what I did for a living, and I had said, "Ah, I'm a . . . photographer. Was a photographer in the east. I saved some money and came out here to start . . . again. I'm looking for a job."

Now, when he came into the apartment, or when we met in the restaurant down by the bay, he said, "How's the job hunting?"

"Okay," I said. "All right. Things are a little slow."

He nodded.

"Yeah," he said, "every time one of the aerospace plants loses a contract, the entire town seems to close up for a while. It'll turn around. Don't worry."

"I'm trying to be careful about money," I said.

"We can get by just by . . . you know, spending some time together and going for a walk and having an Irish coffee. That would leave a little something. Maybe you could use it. It wouldn't be much."

I put my head down.

"Listen," he said, "I understand. I know how things can be. I haven't got much. There's a mortgage and life insurance and the kids are always needing things. When they need something, they get it. My wife does, too. But I can help. . . ."

"I need help," I said.

"All right," he said, "I'll see what I can do."

"I wouldn't take it if I didn't need it," I said. "I've been having a little trouble. . . ."

I still had my head down.

"Let's not talk about it," he said. "Come on. Things get a little tough sometimes. So what?"

"I'll pay it back," I said, "every cent."

"Sure you will," he said. "I believe you."

He smiled. Beyond him there were the windows and the bay, the seagulls there, their wings braced against the breeze. To my left there were more tables, and beyond them there was dark woodwork and brass and the opening for the dumb-waiter beyond the bar. There were waiters wearing black jackets and bow ties, the entire air of the place one of relaxed enjoyment.

"Don't worry," he said. "We'll be okay."

In the morning I got up and dressed and went to an employment agency. I sat down and filled out a form and then talked to a woman who was about fifty, who wore a pink dress and whose makeup gave her face a wooden quality, as though her features had been carved and then sanded down, although the sawdust was still there. She told me to come back after I'd learned to type.

On the way home I went into a stationery store and bought a teach-yourself-to-type book and a keyboard. The keyboard had a little display and it flashed up letters and you were supposed to hit the right key. Now, in the mornings or evenings I sat with the keyboard, typing *asdfg asdfg ;lkjh ;lkjh,* the steady *click, click, click* having the sound of futility, but I kept at it, working up to some three-letter words ("The Bat Ate the Cat. . . ."). I typed those, too, thinking about those trips my father and I used to take to the inventors' shows, where the men sat, watching for someone to come along and buy what they had to sell. Then I got up and walked back and forth, looking down at the small red keyboard, shaking my head as I realized I could now type, after two weeks' work, "The Bat Ate the Cat. . . ."

Ben had gone to school and I hadn't, and as though to make up for it, or maybe just to do something about it, I went to bookstores and bought things I couldn't possibly read or understand, philosophy and logic, and at night I ripped the pages out, one at a time, enjoying the sound, which came as an endlessly repeated unzipping while I thought, *All right. So I'm not educated. I'm hurt.*

I saw him once or twice a week. When he came to see me I was waiting for him, and we didn't sit anymore by the window looking at the city. Now we went into the bedroom (after Ben gave me money, saying, "We've got to be careful for a while. . . ."), the two of us not so much looking forward to this time as just giving up, and when I grabbed his hair, when I asked him to call me Marie, it was all done with the air of letting chaos into our lives, the approach of it having, as its first announcement, the alien whiff of something we had never done before. I lay next to him, feeling the cool air in the room, or hearing voices in the street.

"Marie, why are you trembling?" said Ben.

"I don't know," I said. "Why are you?"

But we went right ahead now. One morning we went shopping. The store I had in mind was expensive, one where the manikins in the windows were wearing silk dresses, their hands not quite real and looking a little like flippers. Behind them there were clouds made from long puffs of cotton and hung by wire. Inside the store the clothes were in muted colors, browns and grays, in silks and wools, and the women who shopped there were tall and small hipped. They spoke with crisp voices and smoked long cigarettes and smelled of expensive perfume.

We went upstairs where there were blouses. Ben sat down while I tried some on, and when I came out of the dressing room, I stood in front of the mirrors, seeing three figures. The air was heavy with the odor of sizing, silk, and wool, the scent of it like money from the bank. While he watched me, it was with a comfortable, intimate air. I stood next to his chair and leaned over him, the silk blouse I wore not far from his face, and said, whispering against his ear, "I need two pairs of stockings. Red ones. Don't buy them."

He looked back at me now, the two of us having that sense of standing on the threshold. He didn't blink or even change his expression, although both of us now admitted how far we would go to keep alive that sense of leaving the world behind. I changed into my own clothes and then we went down the counter, Ben a little behind me, the room seeming bright now, the edges of the glass cabinets shining like a newly sharpened knife. The footsteps on the carpet, the sound of a cigarette lighter making a flame, the crush of tissue in a box, all seemed as light and as substantial as feathers. The curtain of a dressing room swung to the side, just like a skirt, and inside a woman stood, wearing just a pair of briefs, her back and legs bare, one of her hands holding a silk dress.

We stood at the counter where the stockings were displayed, the pairs spread in half circles just like a hand of cards, the color of them going from black through blue, brown, orange, and red, the toes and heels of them looking empty and flat, transparent. Ben kept his eyes on mine while he reached out and picked up two pairs of stockings, red as maple leaves in the fall, and without looking around, or even acknowledging the people in the room, he put them into his pocket.

We walked over that heavy carpet, hearing the women talk, their voices soft in the languid air. There was a trunk in front of elevator and on it there were some wool skirts and silk blouses, the color of them suggesting cinnamon, rust, and paprika.

When we got home and into the bedroom, I knelt over him and said, "Do you want to see what the stockings were for?" Then I took them and tied his ankles and his wrists . . . and began . . . went over him with my fingers and the tip . . . of my tongue. I watched his eyes, put my hands into his hair, pulled him against me. The room seemed dry and as light as that cotton hung in the department-store window to suggest clouds.

Outside there were voices and the sound of footsteps. Then I took his hair in my hands, pulled his face next to mine, the scent of my breath and even fear, too, falling over him as I said, "Let me see your eyes. Let me look at them. Why don't you call me Marie? Marie Boule. Do you hear that? Will you say it? *Marie.*" I bit my lip and put my head down, next to his, saying, "All right. Hush now. Just hush. Just don't say a thing. I want to breathe now. Hush."

More often now, when he gave me money, he said, "Things are a little tough this week. There's something wrong with the furnace and the kids need clothes and Faith wants to see a doctor. . . ."

Once he came into the apartment and asked for a pen. Then he sat down in the kitchen and spread out before him an application for a second mortgage, or two applications, one to work on and one to finish, and after he sat there, holding his hand in a peculiar way to sign his wife's name, I said, "Are you sure you want to do this?"

"No," he said, "I don't want to do this. I hate the idea of it. There's just nothing else to do. . . ."

The loan was approved and Ben brought money into the apartment, putting it down on the chrome table in the living room, not saying a thing. But now, when we were out together, when we stopped to get gas for the car, he looked at the gas station's cash-register drawer. One evening, when I was restless, when I knew I'd spend another night trying to sleep and hearing the almost itchy, uncomfortable darkness around me, I went for a walk, hoping that would do some good. I went a long way, passing the stores, restaurants, bars, markets, and theaters. Finally I turned onto Mission Street where there are pawnshops, and in the windows there were those sad drums and guitars, knives and pistols, trumpets and clarinets. The windows were dusty and streaked and they had silver tape on them for the burglar alarm. Overhead there was a fixture with three enormous bulbs.

Ben stood at the counter, in front of which there was a cage, the bars of it as regular as those in an old elevator's gate. He was wearing a tie and a jacket, and his hair was neatly combed. The pawnbroker was behind the bars, and Ben was offering him an enormous instrument, a brass barometer, the thing as big around as a dinner plate and as thick as a dictionary. It was the color of those trumpets hung in the window, although more shiny. The pawnbroker took it and held it, turned it over, shook it. He looked at the metal and then he put it down and said something. Ben spoke back now, pointing at the instrument, and then turned both hands up in amazement. He went on talking, looking directly at the pawnbroker, and finally, while still looking the man right in the eyes, he nodded and put out his hands for the bills that were pushed from under the bars.

Sometimes when he came to see me, we went to the Tree Park, where Mr. Kiri gave us aquavit out of that bottle which was frozen in a piece of ice. The old men in the cafeteria had a chess set, and they played by the hour. Now they asked Ben to play, and he sat opposite them, moving the pieces, picking up the small plastic knights, rooks, bishops. And, with each passing week, as there was more trouble about the money and as we surely made our own advancement, he played a little more seriously, at first just having a good time, but soon he was bearing down, concentrating, intent. He beat one old man and then another (some of whom were good), each one of whom got up and looked at Ben with a kind of dismay, since the old men weren't sure if they had just gotten older or if Ben was as good as he seemed. Ben sat at the table, taking a drink from Mr. Kiri and having it in that one *BANG* before saying to the next old man, "Okay. Are you ready?" Soon he spoke again, the timber of his voice one of carefully controlled desperation, as he said, "Check."

At night, when I was alone, I walked around the apartment, desperate for some small detail, some hint as to what Ben had at home, his entire life there having about it the air of mystery. It seemed if I just knew a few details, why, then, I could struggle with what I was really up against, the thing that kept him from simply giving up and coming to me. There were times when Faith and his children were so much a part of my life, even though I had never seen them, that we seemed to be one large family. I wanted to take the kids' temperature, to look at the bright line of mercury, to make dinner for them, anything to get an idea about what his hours were like when he wasn't here.

Now Faith insisted that Ben spend more time with her, not quite adding up the hours of those few mornings or afternoons Ben and I spent together, but somehow coming close. She wanted to know what was keeping him away from the house. . . . And why didn't he get another raise? The house needed to be painted. And when were they going to get a new car? Were they saving for the kids' college education? He was never around, now, when she wanted him. She hadn't been feeling well. She nervously said Ben was acting like he was having an affair, but she was sure she didn't even have to ask him about a thing like that, did she? It was going to make her sick. Did he want that? All she wanted was some reassurance. Why wasn't he paying more attention? She knew something was wrong.

Ben took his kids to the zoo. The day of the trip was one of those clear September days in California, when even the sea doesn't have haze over it and you can see the horizon, the line of it looking like an almost invisible wire. I woke, feeling stiff, and as I sat at the side of the bed, staring at my feet, the painted nails of them chipped and looking cheap, I told myself that I needed a little time, that a drive out toward the zoo was what I needed: I'd look at the leopards, the tigers, and polar bears in their cages. I was ready to hear the roar and screech of the place, the endless, inarticulate cries. I wanted to sit there and eat peanuts and listen. I put on a white blouse, a pair of blue jeans, and a pair of tennis shoes, looking, for all the world, like a young, fashionable woman who doesn't realize she's made out of money and who thinks most things are pretty simple, when you get right down to it.

The parking lot was large and freshly painted, the white lines marked on an angle, so that there seemed to be row after

row of pretty patterns like the bones of enormous fish. I
walked up to the gate, the turnstile there shiny and cranking
in the early-morning light. There were eucalyptus trees
around the entrance, and some bushes, too, that had been
planted to hide the fence. I bought a ticket and a bag of
peanuts, the paper of it striped and warm. I walked past the
pens of the ostriches and camels, ocelots, porcupines, zebras,
and kangaroos. The zebras looked like small white horses over
which someone had laid narrow pennants of black cloth. The
elephants had enormous gray ears, and when they moved
them, they made a sound like the door flap of a heavy canvas
tent moving in the wind. Their trunks, or at least the ends of
them, were pink and wet. I went into the center of the zoo,
where there were tigers, hyenas, lions, leopards, cheetahs,
wolves and coyotes, North American bobcats, cougars, and
jaguars. The leopards went back and forth in their cages, the
movement of them like a piece of water sliding over the top of
some falls. The tigers were there, too, striped like the zebras,
although their coloring was different, their eyes green and
bright, shiny as marbles. They hissed like someone ripping a
piece of silk. I sat there, my legs out before me, slowly cracking the peanuts and wondering what rejoicing there would be
if the lions, the tigers, and cougars were free. I thought of
them going into the high grassy places you see at the side of
the roads, or of them waiting, their claws beautiful and
curved, their teeth white and sharp, their whiskers pale and
glass colored as they waited in the fog along a street in the city
where there were restaurants, where people walked home,
the animals all breathing softly, alert, bringing with them not
so much knowledge as an unrelenting vengeance. I sat there,
cracking open the shells, looking around the cages and wondering what was confined there and what it would do if it had
the chance. There were some more cries, half articulate and
repeated, and that endless throaty hiss like the tearing of silk.
So I sat there, hearing the roars and cries, the distant splash of
the seals, or the almost silent padding of the feet of one of the
tigers, and when I looked up, I saw, about twenty feet away,
Ben sitting with his wife and children.

They were sitting at a picnic table, the two children blond, one in overalls, the other in a dress made out of blue-jean cloth, the two of them sitting side by side, one smaller than the other, but both looking very much alike. They both had blond hair, both wearing ponytails. The younger of them swung her feet back and forth. The older one had a small tape recorder with headphones. Ben sat with his back to me, and his wife was opposite him.

She wore a madras shirt and a pair of brown khaki pants. Her hair was in a bandana, and what stuck out was half brown, half blond, the color of the hills in the fall. It looked dry and in need of being cut. She wore no makeup, but her skin was tanned, although a little lined around her mouth and eyes. She had been pretty, but it was as though the beauty had gotten tired. She stared at the animals, not looking at Ben when he spoke to her or answering him, either.

Ben had a brown paper sack with him, and he took four homemade and carefully wrapped sandwiches from it. He opened three of them and put one, in its wax paper, in front of each child and one in front of Faith, too. She looked at it and then went back to staring at the cages, where the twenty or so cats went back and forth on the other side of the bars.

"I don't want a sandwich," said the youngest child. "I want a hot dog."

"We haven't got the money for hot dogs," said Ben. "That's a good tuna sandwich."

"I want a hot dog," said the young one. She started to cry.

"Take a bite of the sandwich," he said. "I made it with celery. It's crunchy. . . ."

"You don't like the sandwich," said the young one. "You aren't eating yours."

"Oh?" said Ben, "Is that the problem? Here." He reached into the bag, unwrapped the sandwich, and started eating. "It's good."

The little girl shook her head. The older one took a bite, and then put on the headphones and turned on the machine. The animals howled.

"Why haven't we got money for hot dogs?" said Faith.

"We've been through all that," said Ben.

"Have we?" said Faith.

"Listen," said Ben, "I'll get more money . . . don't worry. We'll talk about it later. Okay?"

Faith looked down now, at the unwrapped sandwich in front of her, but she didn't touch it. Then she looked up, not crying but close to it. "Ben, do you remember when we were first together? We were always doing some crazy thing, like going up to the top of a mountain? . . ." She put her head down now.

"Please," said Ben. "Please. Not in front of the kids."

"You're getting even with me because I was sick, aren't you?"

"No," said Ben. "No."

"I didn't mean any harm. I wanted to get your attention. You paid attention when I was sick."

"I'll do anything you want, Faith, I promise," he said, "so long as we don't talk this way now."

"I didn't think it would be like this," she said.

"Please," he said.

"Why do you have to get even?"

"I'm not getting even. . . ." he said. "It has nothing to do with getting even."

"So there is someone, isn't there?"

"Not in front of the children," he said.

She put her head up and blinked and then looked around again, her eyes moving from one cage to another, from the panther to the tiger. The cages were made of galvanized posts and cyclone fence.

"I want something to drink," said the youngest child.

"All right, I think we can manage that," said Ben. "What kind?"

"Wild cherry," said the girl.

"Me, too," said the other. "I want one, too. Goofy Grape."

Now Ben saw me sitting on the bench.

For a moment we heard the slight breeze moving around us, the hush of the eucalyptus leaves, the sound of the water splashing in the pool where the seals dived and barked, their skins shiny in the sunlight.

Then he got up and went to the other side of the plaza where there was a place to buy food and cold drinks. He walked quickly, and then came back, carrying the drinks for the children, the seals barking as he arrived. He sat down with his back to me and stared at his wife, taking her hand again.

"It will be all right," he said. "Come on, Genny, Sarah. Eat your sandwiches. Then we'll go home."

"But we haven't seen the snake house," said Genny.

"Fine," said Ben, "then we'll go look at the snakes. How about the aviary? How about seeing some birds?"

"They just poop on you," said Sarah.

"Some of them are beautiful,"

"Like what kinds?" said Genny.

"Flamingos. Swans. Wood ducks. Herons."

"What about pelicans?" said Sarah.

"They have pelicans there," said Ben.

"Pelicans smell like dead fish," said Sarah. "Yuck."

"It's not so bad if you're a pelican," said Ben.

"Oh, Daddy," said Genny, "Sarah's not a *pelican.*"

The kids laughed now. Faith wrapped up her uneaten sandwich.

"I don't want to see the birds," said Sarah.

"All right," said Ben. "we can look at the snakes then. Maybe they have a spitting cobra. Or a python. Eat your lunch now."

The children ate and then Ben picked up their wrappers and empty cans and all of them walked down the macadam path, the kids stopping and putting their hands up to the wire, Ben pointing something out, Faith just watching, walking along, looking at everything quickly. I sat in the sunlight, seeing my shadow at my feet. There were some pigeons moving around the macadam, all of them looking mechanical, their beaks picking things up as though they were windup toys. They smelled real enough, though.

I didn't move for a long time. The peanuts didn't taste good anymore, and I fed them to the pigeons, one at a time, the shells falling from my fingers and making a light *tick* when they hit the ground. I was down to the last two or three when Ben came back alone. He sat down next to me.

"I haven't got long," he said.

"No, I guess not," I said.

"I'll be over later. We'll forget this. You'll see. We'll go for a walk . . . it'll be like in the beginning."

"Yes. Sure," I said. "I'll be waiting for you. You won't just abandon me, will you? Not after all this time?"

He shook his head.

There was a splash of water and the barking of the seals. Some kids went by holding hands with their father. Then Ben stood up, too.

"I'll wait for you," I said. "Don't be long. Please. Don't make me sit in that apartment alone."

He stayed there for a moment but Genny came running up. She took his hand and said, "Dad, Dad, who's this?"

"This is a friend," said Ben. "Her name is Marie."

"Your father made a mistake, honey," I said, looking into the girl's face, smelling the young odor of her. "My name is Christine."

Then both of them turned and went along the macadam path, passing the cages farther down in which there were polar and brown bears, Kodiak and black bears, the animals quiet, sleepy in that September sunlight. Then I went up to the tiger cage in front of me, and while I stood next to the slick, polished rail, I looked up, leaning forward, keeping my eyes on the animal, its coat light brown and black, the stripes coming in dark stabs, and as it went back and forth, I thought, *Yes, wouldn't you like to get out of there? Wouldn't you just love it?*

Now I started to wait, thinking, *He can't last too much longer. He will break. He will leave her. He will come to me and we will start over together. I will give him children . . . they will take the sting out of the ones he will lose. Everything makes perfect sense now.*

There seemed to be less money than before, and we spent

more time in the apartment, in that blue-white light that came through the white curtains over the window. If we went out, it was to the Tree Park, where Ben played those old men, beating all of them now. When he walked into the place they still perked up, though, each one forever thinking he still had a chance.

Faith knew about us, but said nothing. They spent silent evenings at home. The bills piled up. I couldn't work. I sat for hours at the keyboard of the typewriter, picking out, "The quick red fox jumps over the lazy brown dog. . . ."

A psychiatrist lived in the apartment next to mine, and he had his office beyond the wall of my bedroom. His patients stretched out on a sofa next to the wall. The building had been built in the early sixties and the walls were as thin as cardboard. The voices of the patients came into the room, and you could hear the words if you concentrated or if it was very quiet.

Now, after we'd spent the morning together, Ben sat up and listened, his expression intent, and as the weeks passed, as he brought what money he could, as he and Faith got through each day, as the bill collectors began to call and the credit cards were canceled, he sat there, listening to what went on beyond the wall, and as he did so his expression was one of a man who has discovered a sign or an omen or a clue of some kind. He sat on the edge of the bed, bent forward, drinking the brandy we were more careful about now. Then we went down to the Tree Park, where Ben played chess with those old men, his moves sudden, precise, always winning, his air one of concentration at the task at hand.

In the evening, when he left, I said, "I need a little money."

He sighed, turning toward me.

"We have to go easy," he said. "This month there's . . ." He stopped now and shook his head, "I'll find some more money. Somehow. Maybe you could get some part-time work, just . . . you know, anything."

"I'll try," I said.

"Anything . . . you know, as a waitress . . . some easy, anonymous job."

"I'll try," I said.

He turned toward the door now, but I said, "Isn't this driving you crazy? You have to be with Faith when you know I love you. Why don't you just give up and leave her? Do you really think you have to stand up to everything, the lack of money, the endless pressure of trying to live this way, of being someplace aside from with me? You have some *idea* about this, some damned morality, don't you? You're worried about doing the wrong thing, aren't you?"

"Yes," he said.

"I want you to leave her," I said. "We'll start again. I'll give you children."

He stood there, watching me.

"No," he said.

"But why?" I said. "I love you. You've told me yourself that you've never been loved. Isn't that right? Never?"

He closed his eyes.

"You don't understand," he said. "Kids aren't interchangeable. I love the ones I have."

"And you can stand this, you can continue . . . ?"

He closed his eyes.

"If I have to."

"Well, you know what, you're just fucking me up."

He stood there, looking at me, concentrating, trying to find the right thing to say.

"I love you," he said.

"What fucking good is it?" I said.

"I don't know," he said. "That's what I've got. It's the best I can do."

I stood there, looking at him.

"The best you can do," I said. "Listen. Tell me something. Why won't you break? What's it going to take? Why aren't you moving in here? Oh, sugar, can't you see that's the only thing that makes sense."

"I'm doing my best," he said. "Good night. I'll call soon."

Then he left.

I went into the bedroom and stood in the open closet, where I had put that pistol from my father's store. It sat on the shelf, the trigger guard looking in the dark like a sliver of a new moon. I picked up the pistol and walked around the apartment, feeling the comforting, familiar weight of it and seeing the buttonlike ends of the cartridges when I snapped the cylinder open. I swung the barrel over the television set, the glasses on the shelves, the photographs on the walls, the icebox, pointed it at the tub in the bathroom, which I now kept white as a bride's gown. I went back into the living room, now carrying not only the pistol, but a glass of brandy, too, and there I pointed the pistol at the chrome-and-leather chairs, the books, the ferns hanging like green lace. In the bedroom I went into the long wardrobe, the clothes hanging in one long row, the dresses, jackets, suits, coats, nightgowns, and robes looking like a varicolored curtain. For a moment I thought of putting the pistol against the first dress and shooting, the bullet going through all of them, passing through every dream of escape and power I ever had. Then I sat down on the bed, still holding the pistol, shaking my head, the clothes in the closet, the VCR, the entire apartment coming as proof I had gotten no place and that I was condemned to being a small-town hick with a broken heart.

There was no hesitation when I picked up the phone and dialed, and when Faith answered, I said, "Hello. Don't you think it's time we met?"

She hesitated for a moment. In the background the kids were arguing, and Faith said, "Genny, I told you to put that down. I meant it. Now, I want both of you quiet. I mean quiet." She turned back to the phone, sighing there, or maybe she just blew air upward, making her hair move a little. Then she said, "Yes. I guess we better."

The kids started up again, and Faith reached out and spanked one hard enough to make a little noise. "Now, I meant *quiet. . . .*" she said. One of the kids started crying. "All right," said Faith, "I'll try to get a sitter."

"Do you want the number?" I said. "You can call me back."

"That's all right," said Faith, "I've already got it. I found it in Ben's pocket. All I need is the address."

The kids went on crying.

"What about tonight?" said Faith. "Is that all right? Ben's working, isn't he?"

I took the vacuum cleaner from the closet and ran it back and forth over the rug, seeing that pattern it made, one like enormous roses. I cleaned the bathroom, too, scrubbed the porcelain, and then shined the fixtures. I put out some new hand towels, paper ones, and some more tissue. Then I went down to the florist on the corner and got some flowers, small ones with a shape like a sheet of paper rolled tight, the corner sticking out of the curl. When I was done, I took a shower, scrubbing my face until it shone, and then I got into a pair of jeans and a blue shirt from Brooks Brothers. I wore nothing underneath and left the top buttons undone. My hair was dry and fluffy and I wore no makeup. I went into the bedroom and closed the wardrobe closet, and as the large, accordionlike door swung shut, I saw the pistol.

In the evening the fog was thick and the cars went by, their taillights appearing as reddish puffs. The sounds were muted, soft, the voices out there hesitant or maybe just inquisitive. I sat in the living room, turning the pages of a *Vogue*, the faces there looking out at me with a cool aloofness. I turned the pages, the magazine itself having the odor of a department-store section where you can try on makeup and perfume.

When I answered the door, Faith stood in the hall, her parka and her hair sparkling with drops from the fog. She came in and started looking around, her eyes already moving from one object to another. She was a little heavy in the hips, and she wore a pair of khaki slacks, a sweater, and a pair of running shoes. There was a rustle of her parka when she went into the living room. Her eyes went over the hanging plants in their terra-cotta pots, the chrome-and-leather furniture, the

brass lamps with the half-spherical shades. Then she took off
the parka, put it on the floor, and sat down on the edge of the
sofa.

"I'm glad you came," I said.

"Are you?" said Faith.

"Yes," I said. "I wanted to . . . talk to you."

"How old are you?" said Faith.

"Twenty-five," I said.

Faith looked around the apartment again, nodding now,
saying, "Twenty-five. What the hell do you know?"

I sat there, looking at her, watching her face. She spoke in
a flat, uninflected voice.

"I think we should have a drink," I said, "don't you?"

Faith sighed.

"I don't know," she said. "Yes. I guess so."

I brought out a bottle of brandy and two glasses. She took
a good sip out of her glass.

"Can I look around?" said Faith.

"Sure," I said, "if you want to."

Faith got up and looked into the kitchen, the bathroom,
the bedroom, where she stood for a moment, looking at that
large Japanese bed. The room was filled with peach-colored
light from the streetlamp. Faith went up to the closet and
opened it, throwing back the door of it with a jerk, as though
someone were hiding there.

"How much was this?" asked Faith, touching a skirt.

"I don't know," I said. "Couple of hundred dollars."

"A couple of hundred," said Faith. "Do you know what I'd
do for a couple of hundred dollars?"

She looked at me now.

"Look," said Faith, "I just want you to leave him
alone. . . ."

"I know," I said. "I understand."

"Do you?" said Faith.

Faith sighed and walked back to the living room. This
time she didn't sit on the edge of the chrome-and-leather sofa.

"Can you imagine what it would be like to be alone with
two kids and no money?" she said.

"I never had kids," I said.

Faith sighed and shook her head.

"It's not like what you think," she said. "Just not at all. Women don't tell you what it's really like. Everyone just says, Oh, you're going to have a baby, how wonderful. You'll be so happy. . . ." She took a good sip now. "Look, I want you to leave him alone. This can't mean anything to you. . . ."

I kept my eyes on her.

"Oh, maybe you're sentimental. . . ." she said.

"Maybe. . . ." I said.

"He hasn't got much money . . . we're in debt. There just isn't anything for you. . . ." she said.

I sat there, trying not to slap her. Then I poured a little more brandy into her glass. It was good brandy.

"Well, maybe you're right," I said. "But we haven't talked about you, have we?"

"You can just leave him alone," she said. "I'll be fine."

"But aren't you lonely," I said, "and tired? Who's looking after you?"

"That's not important," Faith said. "I have broad shoulders. I can hold the fort. I run the house. You know you can save five dollars a week if you—"

She stopped and had a sip of her brandy.

"Sure," she said, "I've been lonely. I don't think you can really understand. How can you? You're young and pretty. . . ."

I held my glass with both hands.

"Maybe I have an idea about it. . . ." I said.

"Please. . . ." she said. "I don't want to beg you to leave him alone."

"You don't have to do that," I said.

I took my brandy and sat next to her. She started crying a little, and I poured some more brandy into her glass.

"Drink some more brandy. It's cold outside. I think you've got a chill."

Faith looked around the apartment now, her eyes slowly moving from one object to another.

"Hush," I said. "You've got a chill. I know how tired you are."

"You must have a chill, too," Faith said. "You're trembling."

"Am I?" I said. "Well, it can't be much." I put my arm around her, gently holding her. She slowly moved over, sighing, just leaning against me, her head on my shoulder. She left her glass on the sofa and put her hand in her lap. She rested, and when she moved her head, when she was about to pull away, I put my fingers to the front of my shirt, lifting it, making the light on the skin seem as though it came through a pale blue tent.

"Look," I said. "I have a tattoo. It's all right to touch it. It's nice to touch."

As though she weren't thinking at all, she put her hand under the material, the texture of her palm a little rough against me.

Outside there was the steady, almost indifferent calling of the foghorns. The fog filled the streets, muffling the sounds, making the cars drive slowly past the building, the wet tear of their tires going endlessly by.

"Hush. Hush. Hush," I said to Faith, "I know how tired you are." The room was white and clean, and I saw the bright, hard reflections on the chrome and brass, on the doorknobs and glasses, on the bottle of brandy. Then we walked down the hall. She took off the sweater and those brown pants, and the large, cheap underwear from K mart. She had a round, full stomach from having children, and her hips and legs were a little pitted, the hair between her legs thick. We stood on opposite sides of the bed, and she said, "My God, you're so young." We lay there, and as we did so, I thought of the zoo, of those cages in which the lions and tigers went back and forth, and as I heard the foghorns, I thought about my fingers touching the locks and latches, of swinging the doors open, the animals stretching in one long jump into the night, the gleam of their sides smooth and looking like water going around a stone.

I finished with her. We lay under the sheet, warm. Then

Faith stood up, looking around the room, at the books, the handles on the wardrobe, the heavy carpet, the curtains. She reached down and began to pick up her clothes, putting on the big underwear from K mart, crying now, saying only, "Please . . . please. What can he mean to you? That's what I came to say."

I sat with the sheet at my waist.

"What was all this about?" she said, making a gesture toward the bed. "Did you want to prove how lonely I am? Who the hell isn't lonely? You had to look at me, didn't you? You had to see the veins in my legs, didn't you? Is that it? Did you think women stay young forever?"

"No," I said.

"Why did you have to humiliate me?" she said. "You can't think this is going to make any difference, can you?"

"It's crossed my mind," I said. "Who knows? Maybe it's the straw that breaks the camel's back."

She started crying again.

"You know, the wolves are going to pull you down," she said.

"The only wolves I know are safe in the zoo," I said.

"Wait a few years," she said.

Then she went down the hall, picked up her jacket, and went out. She pulled the door gently shut behind her. I got up and walked back and forth, putting on a silk gown, not stopping, thinking again of those tigers, of panthers, their coats damp with the fog, their claws the color of mothballs.

Now, when he came over, we went down the hall into the bedroom, and with the steady murmur of the patients beyond the wall, I . . . got him to the point where he felt he was about to dissolve into nothing, or into no one, or that he was only kept in this world through my lips or fingers or clinging pressure, through my odor, or sweat, or panting. . . . I watched from an enormous distance (with a sting of pleasure at how remote I was now). It was a way of being angry now, letting him think I was right there with him, when in fact I was trembling with rage. I wasn't going to be cheated out of mocking what we had been, not for a moment less than I needed it. Watching from a distance gave relief. The distance was greater each time I saw him, and each time I was angrier, too, since I'd made the mistake of thinking I was in love when I was a girl, and now I'd done the same thing again. And if I'd had the illusion of innocence, now I had the certainty of having been twice seduced. Mostly now we didn't talk. Sometimes we sat for a moment, having a brandy before we went down the hall to that room with the white walls and the large bed. I didn't want to talk anymore.

One Tuesday he knocked on the door, and when I let him in, he went into the living room. I stood in the hall, looking back at him over my shoulder.

"Come on. We haven't got much time," I said.

"Not right now," he said.

I sat down opposite him.

"What's wrong?" I said. "Why don't we step down the hall?"

"I'm tired," he said. "Why don't we just sit here? Let's just talk . . . you know, a little harmless talk."

"Why don't we lie down?"

"No," he said, "not for a while."

I was shaking now.

"There are things I'll do," I said, "things you haven't even dreamed. . . . Come on. Don't you want it?"

I started unbuttoning my blouse, looking at him.

He got up and went into the kitchen and brought back a bottle of brandy and two glasses.

"Let's talk," he said, "the way we used to. Remember? We'd just get away from things for a while."

"So," I said, "you're not interested. Fine."

I turned and went down the hall, leaving him there. I reached into the closet and took that pistol from the shelf, the glint of it in the dark looking like chaos itself. I walked down the hall, holding the thing in my hand, reassured by the cool weight. But when I came into the room, he just stood there, facing the pistol as though it didn't exist.

"You just won't break, will you?" I said. "You're just going to go on and on. . . . You won't leave Faith. You won't leave your kids. You're just fucking me up."

"Marie," he said. "Marie. I love you."

"Don't call me that," I said. "My name's Christine Taylor."

"Is that your professional name?" he said. "Does it have something to do with photography?"

Now I laughed.

"Yeah," I said, "that's right."

"What's that for?" he said, pointing at the gun.

"I just like having it," I said. "It makes me feel better."

I pulled the hammer back, hearing the reassuring clicks. He went on staring at me.

"You haven't got enough money," I said. "You know, it's the money that counts."

"Marie, Marie," he said.

"Don't call me that," I said.

"Do you want me to leave?" he said. "I'll go now. All right?"

"You're going to go?" I said. "That's just *perfect.*"

I looked around the room, already feeling the shadows flowing into the apartment.

"I saw Faith," I said.

"What?" he said.

"I called her up," I said. "She came for a visit."

Now we both waited, hearing the cars in the street, the steady click of someone walking down the sidewalk. It was evening, and the room was filled with the peach-colored light from the streetlamp.

"What happened when she was here?"

"I made her feel good," I said.

"What do you mean?" he said.

"In there. In bed," I said. "She was just about desperate."

He picked up the bottle and stepped forward, holding it by the neck like a club.

"That's supposed to frighten me?" I said. "You don't frighten me at all."

"Why won't you stop?" he said.

"*Me?* I'm not going to stop. Not now. Not ever. You know what you should do? I'll tell you. The first thing is to go out and buy your wife some new underwear. Not that cheap shit she wears from K mart. . . . Then you should spend more time with your kids."

"You're lecturing me?" he said. "*You.* Who the hell are you to lecture me?"

"Someone has to," I said.

"*You?*" he said. "You're going to act as though you're superior? As though we didn't do this together? How dare you?"

I stood there, still holding the pistol, already wanting to hear the noise of it. Through the curtains there came that peach-colored light. On the wall there was the framed poster of George Washington. His forehead was high, his hair around his ears like an old woman's, his nose bent to one side, his lips compressed in one straight line, and his expression was one of infinite understanding, just as though he had been a witness to every bad moment I'd ever had. The face on the wall looked down on me, the eyes acknowledging the barrier I kept hitting, over and over again, that infuriating sense of love and loss.

Ben stood in front of me, trembling, holding that bottle by the neck. I raised the pistol and pointed it at him and said, now abandoning all hope, "I'll tell you what you should do. I'll tell you exactly what to do. . . . I'll tell you how to live, how to fuck your wife . . ."

"How to do what?" he said.

"You heard me," I said.

I pulled the trigger. The hammer snapped forward, the thing looking like a mechanical woodpecker, and even as I flinched, I heard the sad, ineffectual *click.* We stood there, hearing that metallic *tick*, which confirmed every betrayal I'd had, right down to being stuck with a cheap gun and lousy ammunition from my father's failure of a store.

"That's just perfect," I said, trembling now, trying to get both thumbs over the hammer to pull it back again.

Ben stood opposite, watching my eyes.

"You care that little?" he said.

I put both thumbs on the hammer, one on top of another, and pulled it back, already beginning to raise the pistol again. He swung the bottle, the thing moving in one shiny arc toward me, the impact of it coming as a numbness, and as the bottle shattered, the pieces of it fell to the floor, where they looked sea-green and slick as the ocean. "Oh," I said. The numbness spread from the side of my head through my neck, into my eyes. My arm fell straight down now, the pistol at the end. I went along the wall, stumbling once, trying to slink toward the door. Beyond him there was the furniture in the living room, the chrome-and-leather sofa, the potted plants, the brass lamps. Ben followed now, saying nothing, looking at me. I felt I was falling backward onto some hard and cold surface, like ice, and then I broke through it, the green-brown water washing over me, and as the chill took me, I heard an echo of some words,

Coffee and Doughnuts
Coffee and Doughnuts
just about as ready as I'll ever be
What about you?

the sound disappearing, diminishing, gone.

Book V

Ben Lunn,
Figures in the Clouds

Marlowe, Northern California

AT FIRST I JUST DROVE AROUND, WANTING ONLY TO FEEL that continual motion, and in the stink of exhaust on Mission Street, or in the pseudo-calm of Golden Gate Park, it came back to me, leaving me shaking my head, and still in love. I had picked her up, surprised at how light she was as I said, "Oh, sugar, oh, honey, oh, no. No." Then I put her down, on the bed, and sat there, my head between my hands, hearing through the wall that *buzz mumble, buzz mumble* of the patient on the couch next door. My father had taught me how to be sure if someone was dead. There was no need to call for help.

I kept driving. There was a parking ticket on the windshield of the car and I stopped, got out and took it from under the wiper blade, glad to be that much more inconspicuous.

At the end of the next block there was a church, a large one with a romanesque façade, which was made from pinkish adobe. . . . I began to look for a place to park. Inside there were dark pews and long aisles and along one side there were candles burning, the red flicker of them diminutive in the gloom of the place. At the back of it, in the cool air, I sat down, leaning forward, my head against the seat in front of me, still thinking, *Oh, sugar. Oh, darling.* Old women came in, their skirts rustling in the aisles, their voices murmuring prayers for the dead. I put my hands together and thought, *Please, please, please. . . . I never loved anyone more. What do I do now?*

In the bright light of the street, in the traffic again, I kept driving, stopping once for gas and seeing the twelve dollars in my wallet. The credit cards had been canceled. The sun glinted off the chrome of the cars, off the windows, and off the water in the bay when I crossed the bridge: with each passing moment I became more certain about where I was going, the place having its own unstoppable tug.

On the way out of the city there were mare's tails in the sky, the color of them the same as the white lines on a blueprint, and I stared at them, looking for some sign, some indication as to what I could do: the color of them suggested unavoidable plans. High pressure. You could feel the air falling into the valley, heating up now, and making the barometer rise. The air had a clean, dry smell: there wasn't much moisture and the high pressure suppressed the scent of the earth. Low pressure released it, and just before the rain, you could smell what was on the ground, the aroma of it rising like mist from a hot cup of coffee. From the top of the ridge the town looked brown and smoke colored and there were some glints, too, from the windows that faced west, toward the setting sun.

The radio was on in the car and there was a station that played old rock and roll, Fats Domino ("Ain't That a Shame") and Jerry Lee Lewis ("A Whole Lot of Shakin' Goin' On"), but I kept going from one channel to another, doing this with the illusion of accomplishing something, searching for the news, hearing the announcers' voices, which were slicker, better than those of the weathermen at the National Service. Better than mine. Faith had always hoped I'd end up on TV, but I knew only about weather. I kept twisting the dial, but after a while I switched the thing off. It wouldn't be there quite so fast.

My father's house sat a little back from the street: it was a squarish building, had two stories plus a room in the attic under the pitch of the roof, and in front of the lawn there were the stumps of trees that had been killed by the Dutch elm disease. All the windows were dark, aside from those in the living room, and the light from them collected in golden rectangles on the porch.

From the driveway the house loomed above me. The deep purple of it against the evening sky, the shape of the roof and the dark windows and the presence of the things inside (those first barometers, the clippings on the wall in my room, the furniture in the house) all suggested the place held a half-forgotten secret which, if just remembered, would give me the one clear moment I was looking for. If nothing else, the place offered the illusion of comfort.

The street was quiet. I stood on the lawn, which wasn't so thick as it used to be. There were patches of dirt here and there and the grass was brown, or sunburned. My father watered it in the heat of the day now. When I was growing up, the lawn had been green and thick, which gave rise to rumors so constant they were believed as truth: that the lawn was green because my father treated it with tainted blood he got from the Red Cross.

As I stood there, looking at the house, I remembered taking a fall from the porch. I fell with the sense of the world tilted over and rushing up with a bang. My shoulder hurt. My father came out from his office, wearing his white coat, his stethoscope hanging from his pocket, his hair thick, his eyes brown. He said, "I don't even have to touch you, Ben. I can see from here you broke your shoulder. Come into the office, and I'll fix you up. I'll bet you have trouble trying to lift it above your head, don't you? Sure, sure, come on in. I'll have you patched up in a jiffy. It could be worse, couldn't it?"

The collarbone healed with a lump in the middle, halfway between my neck and shoulder. When the weather changed, when rain approached, the lump began to ache. Now, as I stood in front of the house, I slipped my hand inside my shirt, feeling that old, constant throb, even though the sky was clear and the first star came out, as bright as a penlight.

I knocked on the door and said, "Father. It's Ben. I'm in trouble," my voice soft, but insistent.

Farther down the porch there was the door of my father's waiting room, and on it there was the small plastic clock that said WILL RETURN AT set at five-thirty, even though my father hadn't seen a patient (aside from an emergency, like a car wreck) for three years. Beyond the door, which had panes of glass in it, top to bottom, there was the waiting room, but now in addition to the furniture and magazines, there were the things my father had stored there, a lawn mower, shovels, a canvas tent, a sawhorse and scraps of lumber, two old television sets, a beach umbrella, a croquet set, wicker chairs, and jars of nails, and screws, sorted by size and variety. There were bales of medical journals, still in their brown mailing wrappers, the piles of them held together with string tied with a surgeon's knot. In the examination room there were still the table, the small flashlight on an electric cord, the electrocardiogram machine, the instrument for taking blood pressure, the canisters filled with cotton balls, the sterilizer, the shelves with glass doors. All of it had a layer of dust now, which was the gray color of a rabbit.

The front door of the house had glass panes, too, but one of them was broken. It had been patched with plastic from a large Baggie, the thing gently swelling in the breeze and looking like an enormous blister. Inside, the tile in the bathrooms had been patched with toothpaste, and all the faucets dripped.

The house began to tremble. The earthquake came with a short prying sound of the nails in the wood of the porch and the liquid squeak of the roots of a tree which shook in the yard. The tremor grew stronger so that it felt like a train was approaching and getting quite close, the earth thumping under my feet. I put my head against the door frame, trying to decide if the tremor was going to get worse, and while it lasted, while the constant shaking of it made the door of the house tremble against my fingers, the steady quaking made it seem as though the world was getting ready to come apart at the seams. We'd been having these small quakes for months now, and while I concentrated on it, there was a clue in it, too, the power of it suggesting just how suddenly things can change. Down below, the fault moved, the stone turning to liquid under the pressure. The tremors got weaker and finally disappeared, leaving me sweating on the porch, thinking things over and waiting by the door.

My father came out of the living room, away from the gray-white blur of light from the television. He walked with a slight limp and his clothes didn't fit as well as they used to. The sleeves of his white shirt were too big for his wrists and his bow tie was twisted, badly tied, so that it went more up and down than it did from side to side. One arm hung straight by his side, and at the end of it, held firmly in his hand, there was a pistol, the sheen of it, in the darkness, looking like the skin of an eggplant.

"Who's there?" he said.

"It's Ben," I said. "I'm in trouble."

"Oh, hell," he said, "it can't be all that bad. Come on in."

He started working a new brass night-chain, which rattled on the other side of the door. He had to use both hands, still holding the pistol when he did so.

"What's the gun for?" I said.

"You get these junkies up from the city looking for small-town doctors' offices. Well, they come up here and they're going to get a surprise."

I stepped inside now and he closed the door behind me, fastening the night-chain again.

"I felt a little tremor just now. Did you? At my age sometimes it's hard to tell what's going on. Glasses made a little noise on the shelf."

For a moment, in the sense of being confined to the house, I looked out the window, wanting to be certain I hadn't been followed. The cars parked in the empty street had a blue sheen. Nothing moved. We stood behind the door in the half-light of the living-room light and the glow from the television, both of us now looking out the window. The lingering presence of the tremor made the shadows outside somehow alive and ill-meaning.

"I'll tell you," my father said, "this is one town the junkies better stay the hell away from."

"Look," I said, "I'm in trouble."

"Trouble?" said my father. "You're too young to know what trouble is. Wait until you're my age. Then you begin to see the light. We'll talk later. I was just watching Groucho Marx. Come on. I want to see the rest."

We stood opposite one another, my father still holding the pistol, the thing gleaming in the dark.

"Groucho Marx hasn't been on TV for twenty-five years," I said.

"I get tapes from the gas-station store," he said. "You can get Groucho and W. C. Fields and Laurel and Hardy. . . ."

In the living room he put the pistol down on a pile of medical journals next to his chair. It was a recliner, a green one covered with imitation leather, and the footrest was up. The journals were issues of *Geras, Studies in Geriatric Medicine,* and the *Quarterly of the Society of American Geriatrics.* There were medical books, too, piled on the table next to the recliner, where there was a half-eaten TV dinner, all of them open to sections dealing with hardening of the arteries and senility. The sound had been turned down on the television and Groucho Marx glided back and forth, his tailcoat too big for him, his eyebrows moving, a black cigar held between the fingers of his right hand.

My father pointed to the books and said, "You know, when I go to the supermarket, I spend an hour looking for my car. And sometimes I look for that Willys I used to have. Can't remember anything that's just happened. But I remember medical school just fine."

Now Groucho stopped and put his hands behind his back, his eyes wide with recognition of the way things really were. Then he started walking again, his knees moving up and down as though he were riding an enormous tricycle, and as he went, his presence, in that black-and-white flicker of the television, came into the room as a phantom or unexpected messenger, the cigar, the black eyebrows and mustache all suggesting the terrors which my father knew were waiting for him in the shadows of the house.

"In our anatomy section there was a woman by the name of Rachel Mackenzie," said my father. "She had red hair and freckles and blue eyes. In those days there were probably only three women in our class. I had a crush on her. You know why? In the anatomy section we each got a cadaver. Rachel's was a female. Well, somebody cut the pecker off his cadaver and stuck it in Rachel's cadaver. These were medical students. So they stuck the thing in some intimate place. You can imagine. You know what happened when Rachel came in the next morning? I'll tell you. She threw back the sheet and said, 'All right, which one of you guys left here in a hurry last night?' "

We sat together, looking at the screen. My father turned up the sound.

"Can you turn that off?" I said.

"It's almost over," he said. "We can talk while I rewind."

"Will you do me a favor?" I said.

"It's almost over, Ben," said my father. "Relax for a minute. Just look at this. Jesus Christ. How could anyone move like that?"

My father laughed, and I sat next to him while the screen flickered. In the dining room, which was dark, there hung the black outline of the Tiffany lamp. I sat in a straight-backed chair, my hands together, glancing at my father's face from time to time. There were some aftershocks now, little tremors that made the glasses in the kitchen clink, the sound of them coming into the living room as a slight *ting*. I looked at the features of my father's face, the lines, the faintly vacuous eyes, the bushy brows, all of them holding some secret I wasn't quite able to understand (some stubbornness or stupidity, some flaw that had brought me here, one that if I could just see clearly in my father would give me that clear, untroubled look into the heart of things). I put my hands together, feeling a tremor there and not knowing if it was me or an earthquake.

"I'm rewinding now," said my father. "I can do it from here. You see this little gizmo?"

He held up a thing about the size of a small calculator. It

had a cord running to the tape deck. The machine made a little click and started to rewind. My father turned toward me, his hand flopped open, the controller in it.

"I'm in trouble," I said.

"It can't be that bad," he said. "You need help with the mortgage? You know I haven't got much, Ben, God knows there are people who still owe me money. I'm the poorest doctor in the San Joaquin Valley, but—"

"It's not like that," I said.

"Are you sleeping all right?"

"No," I said. "I haven't slept right."

"I'll give you something to sleep. I got my pad right here. How about some Dalmane?"

"I never had it," I said.

"It's good," he said, "I take it."

My father wrote for a while and then tore the slip off and held it out. I took it and said, "Thanks."

"Sure," said my father.

"Look," I said, "I met a woman. . . ."

My father blinked now, nodding.

We sat there for a while, doing nothing. The faucet dripped in the kitchen and in the downstairs bathroom, too, both of them at a different rate.

"That's right," he said, "her name was Sally something. Cooke. You told her that tornado was going to come through here . . . you remember those books you got from the library in Sacramento?"

"No," I said, "that was a long time ago. No. I mean recently. Last winter."

"Winter?" he said.

"Yes," I said. "I met her by chance. I was driving back home from visiting you and she passed me in a little car and I—"

"But, Ben, the tornado was in the summer, when it was hot. You should know that."

"That was some other time," I said.

"Was it?" my father said.

"Yes," I said, "that was when I was a kid. This happened

just recently. In the beginning I was careful . . . you know, we just sat together and talked. I helped her, you know, just by being with her."

"Sure, sure," said my father. "I know who you're talking about. You met her in the valley. In some jerkwater town where you were trading cars. You were just kids, remember?"

"I just want you to listen to me! Just listen!" I said, "I'm in trouble."

"I don't know, Ben," he said. "Now I'm all upset."

"I fell in love. . . ." I said. "Do you understand?"

"Sure, sure," said my father.

"There's a lot of pressure these days. I thought I could do everything right. Everything. . . ."

"That's right," my father said, "I remember. Her name was Faith. . . ."

"No, no," I said, shaking my head. "that was years ago."

"I'm not getting it, Ben," he said.

The machine came to the end now with a click.

"I killed somebody," I said.

My father sat back, his face turned toward me, his skin gray now with age, his eyes set on my face.

"How do you know the person was dead?" he said.

"No pulse in the carotid artery. No breath. Not even on a mirror."

He went on looking at me, blinking, holding the controller.

"Any rigor mortis?"

"No," I said.

"You're sure about the carotid?"

"Yes," I said.

"Pupils wide open?"

"Yes."

He nodded.

"I think I'm going to have a drink," he said. "You want one, too?"

We went into the kitchen. On the counter there was a bottle opener without the piece of plastic that used to go on the handle. In the icebox there was an ice tray, but it had only three cubes in it. There were some glasses on the shelf, none of them exactly the same size. I put two ice cubes in his glass, and one in mine. We went back to the living room.

"Do you understand?" I said.

"Yeah," said my father. "You got to make a run for it."

"I don't know," I said.

"Sure you do," he said.

"I just don't know," I said, "I came up here to decide what to do."

He nodded.

"Do you really understand?" I said.

"Yes," he said. "You lost your temper. Then you threw the ball through that window in the pool hall. Now I have to keep the cops away from you."

I finished the drink and put the glass down.

"You got to make a run for it," he said.

"Do I?" I said.

"Yeah. The cops up here hate me. They called me a thousand times to take a look at some guy who had a coronary, and you know there was nothing I could do. Nothing. They hold it against me for every poor bastard who ever died up here. If they catch you, they'll take it out on you."

"You mind if I have another drink?" I said.

"No," he said, "go ahead. I'll help you though. It's nothing to get too upset about. It's just a broken window. It'll be all right, Ben."

"Yes," I said, "I guess it will. It'll work out."

"I'll help you," he said. "You'll see. We'll think of something in the morning."

It was quiet in the kitchen, aside from the steady throb of the icebox, the *unh-unh-unh* having about it the sound of some machine not quite able to do what it was supposed to. The ice cube in my glass hadn't melted yet and I poured more bourbon on top of it. In the drawers there were broken can openers and carving forks, dull knives, a rusted potato masher and broken vegetable peeler, a pastry bag without a nozzle, the accumulation of these things having about them all the certainty of passed time. I moved toward the phone, instinctively wanting to call Marie, but then I turned back to the counter where I picked up the drink and poured it into the sink, watching the dark, varnish-colored fluid swirl around the drain.

"Hey, Ben," said my father, "you want to watch Laurel and Hardy? I got the one where they move a piano. You remember? They get the thing up all those stairs? It's a riot."

"No," I said. "I thought I'd turn in. I'll be here just for one night."

"Sure," he said, "go ahead. This tape has another Laurel and Hardy on it, too. You know the one where they cook for a convict and they have no food? They make meatballs out of a sponge and—"

"I remember," I said. "Good night."

"Good night, Ben," he said. "You want me to check on you? I used to give you good dreams. Remember? You want some good dreams?"

"Sure," I said.

"Here," he said. He made as though to throw me something, a palmful of flower petals, or some dust.

"Oh," he said, "I forgot. You know what?"

"What?"

"That Sally Cooke girl came back to visit her father. Except her name is Scott now. I guess she's still up there. I thought you might want to know."

He put the tape onto the machine and sat back in the recliner.

"The Laurel and Hardy I want to get is the one where Ollie is allergic to horns . . . you remember?"

"Sure," I said, "I remember. Good night."

My room was filled with stale air, and on the shelf the barometers and hydrometer were covered with dust. The window opened with a bump and the air came into the room with a cool pressure, the dusty curtains brushing against me. There were some pictures of a tornado on the wall, a clipping of a photograph from a newspaper of a boy straining toward the end of a race, and the caption said, BEN LUNN, LOCAL BOY,

SETS COUNTY RECORD IN THE TWO TWENTY. I sat down on the
bed and stared at the face of the boy on the yellowing newsprint. His eyes were closed, jaws clenched, fingers outstretched, arms thrown wildly backward as he stumbled into
the tape, one shoe in the air behind him: everything about
him, the grimace, the awkward lunge, the pained gasping
were all part of his devotion to the one simple thing he had
begun. There was a diploma from Berkeley. The weather
instruments were on a shelf, the collection of these objects
suggesting, as everything else about the house did, that there
was something to be understood here, just for the picking up,
for the proper arranging of what I had left behind.

I found a windbreaker that still fit, and I put it on and sat
in the breeze from the window.

Sally Cooke's telephone number was in the book in the
hall, and I dialed it, thinking of this as a kind of test of my
father's mind, since there was no way of telling now when she
had come back . . . last year, two years ago, or never.

"Hello," said a man, his voice a little gravelly with age.

"Hello," I said, "Mr. Cooke? This is Ben Lunn. I'm calling
from down in Marlowe."

"Hello, Ben," said Mr. Cooke. "It's been a long time,
hasn't it? I guess you want to talk to Sally, don't you?"

Downstairs there was the sound of my father's laughter,
and in the bathroom I heard the steady dripping of the faucet
and the shower head.

"Yes," I said. "Please."

He put the phone down on some hard surface.

"Hello," said Sally. "Ben? Is that really you? Well. How
the hell are you? Where you been? You been getting into
trouble?"

I swallowed now, holding the phone.

"Oh, I'm all right. Are you still living in the east?"

"Oh, yes. I brought the kids for a visit. They wanted to see
California, you know? They think everyone out here wears a
hat and rides a horse. They were disappointed to find that the
Indians drive pickup trucks and cars."

I nodded, my eyes closed.

"Well, I guess that's right. My kids think New York is just a place with the Statue of Liberty in it. And a street with walls. You make money there," I said.

Sally laughed, but not with pleasure.

"My husband is an investment banker," she said. "He'll love that about the street with walls."

"Well," I said, "how you been?"

"All right," she said.

From the television in the living room there came the sound of men pushing a piano upstairs.

"Look," she said, "my kids are in bed and I can get out for a while. Why don't we meet? You know that little turnoff halfway on the road from here to Marlowe? It's a dirt road on the left, coming from your direction. We can meet there. That way it's only about ten miles for both of us. All right?"

"I don't know . . ." I said. "I . . ."

"Oh, come on," she said. "Have you still got your hair? Are you bald?"

"No, I've still got my hair."

"Prove it," she said.

"Well, maybe some other time."

"I want to see your hair. Are you lying about it?"

"No," I said, "I'm not."

"Well?"

I sighed.

"Okay. I'll meet you there. I know the spot."

"Whoever said men weren't vain? You wait a minute or two before walking out the door. I want to brush my hair. See you."

In the bathroom I splashed water on my face and then sat down on the edge of the tub, holding a towel. The breeze from the window in the bedroom made my skin feel cold. For a moment I stood in the middle of my bedroom, looking at the squiggly line on the paper wrapped around the drum of the recording barometer. While I stared at the faded ink and felt that steady throb in my shoulder, I was finally convinced of how little I was able to escape, the constant ache at the change in the weather, or a flaw in myself which I could never quite see, never fully grasp (stubbornness or endless hope), and which I knew only by its effect.

I sat down on the bed again and looked out the window. Marie always made me feel when we were together, as though I had no flaws. Isn't that how she seduced me the most, by making me believe I wasn't entire without her? That unless we were together I was like some jigsaw puzzle in a box, but when we were in the same room the puzzle was done by magic, all the pieces together, the corners square, the edges straight? *No flaws.* I closed my eyes now, remembering the moment when such a horrible illusion came unglued.

Downstairs my father slept in front of the television. Laurel and Hardy had the piano in a small fishpond. Stan looked confused. Ollie was angry. I left a note for my father, sticking it onto the screen with some adhesive tape that had a reassuring, curative scent.

The road out of town was straight. The tumbleweeds at the side of the road were silver colored in the moonlight and the asphalt had a sheen to it. The air was dry and warm and there was only a slight odor of sage and dirt. The telephone poles at the side of the road were burnished with moonlight, too. I drove down to the turnoff.

She wasn't there yet. But it didn't take long. A new rented car came along the road, not with quite the same speed as when Sally used to come down to town. The car pulled into the dirt road and stopped alongside mine. Overhead there were the stars and the blue-black sky. Sally got out and said, "Well, well. Let me look at you."

The cars seemed blue in the moonlight, and we stood between them. Sally had short hair, and around her mouth and eyes there were small lines. She'd gained a little weight, and her skin was not so smooth. Her smile hadn't changed, though, and she raised a brow with that same hint of sultry understanding.

"It's good to see you," she said.

"Yes," I said. "It's good to see you."

"Here," she said, and reached into the front seat of her

car, where there were two bottles of beer. She handed one to me and gave me a bottle opener.

"You know what?" she said. "When I went out the door from the house into the garage, I picked up a blanket, which my father still keeps on a shelf."

The blanket sat in the backseat, folded neatly, the thing a little forlorn in the moonlight.

"Don't get any ideas," she said. "I just thought it was funny. That's all."

I nodded. From under the hood of each car there came a steady ticking as the engines cooled.

"Your husband works on Wall Street?" I said.

"Mmmm-huh," she said, putting the bottle to her lips, swallowing there in the half-light. "Yeah. He makes a lot of money. I spend it as fast as I can."

We laughed now.

"Did they make you a lady?" I said.

"Oh, sure," she said. "You know what a lady is? Somebody who never tells the truth. I was made for it."

"That's all there is to it?" I said.

"Oh, you've got to know which fork to use. . . ."

She put her head back and took another drink of beer, looking at the stars now.

"Just look at those suckers," she said, and then turned back to me. "Oh, Ben, we were just kids back then. Just kids. What the hell did we know?"

"Not much," I said.

"No," she said, "we didn't know anything at all. We used to think that time helped out, that if something happened . . . you got over it. Like someone dying. But you know what? That's all wrong. The sense of loss gets worse, doesn't it?"

"Yes," I said, closing my eyes for a moment. "I guess that's true, isn't it?"

Her face was turned toward me with the dark hills beyond her.

"What's wrong?" she said.

I shook my head.

"Nothing," I said.

"Did I break your heart? Do you forgive me for running out years ago?" she said. "That would mean a lot to me."

"I forgive you," I said.

She put the back of her wrist to the side of one of her eyes and said, "Oh, shit, I shouldn't have come out here. I just wanted to say hello. Now I'm crying."

"Tell me about your kids," I said.

"No," she said, "no. I came out here to tell you something. You know what it is? A few years back I was going through my things and I found a letter you'd written me years ago. When I first went east. It was the nicest love letter and the only love letter I ever got. I cried until I thought I couldn't stop. What the hell did we know back then?"

I shrugged.

"Nothing," I said.

"Listen," she said, "I'm going now. I just came to tell you about the letter. It was good to see you, Ben. Now I'm going to get in the car before I say something stupid or make a fool of myself. Okay?"

"All right," I said. "It was nice to see you."

"Was it?" she said. "Well, I'm glad of that. Good-bye, Ben."

She got into the car and started the engine and turned on the lights, and when she backed up she turned the wheel with the heel of her palm. The lights of the car swept over the flat land, the brush there bright against the black sky. She kept her eyes on the road now as she put the car into gear and started down the long strip of macadam, the surface of it like a lake at night. Now she went fast, just as fast as when she was young, the taillights quickly diminishing and the horn making a *hoooonnnnk, hoooonnnnkkk, HOOOONNNNKKK,* the sound of it coming not only over the flats, but through the years, too, although it wasn't so much a matter of farewell as an admission of how we were bound together by only half-remembered things. I stood under the stars, smelling the exhaust, and then I reached over and leaned on the horn, the *hooooonnnnk, hooooonk* seeming loud, enormous there on the flat land. Then I got into the car and drove back to town.

The sign in front of what had been Bompasino's seed store was gone now and all that was left of the original store was the brass fixture on the door, which still looked like the trigger guard of an enormous shotgun. The place was boarded up. I sat for a moment on the steps. On the other side of the street there were two Indians, sharing a bottle in a paper sack, both of them squatting on their heels and leaning against the boarded up front of what had been Tubby Mars's pool hall.

At home my father had gone to bed, and I went upstairs and stretched out, trying to sleep, but unable to do so. Every now and then I sat up and said, out of the dark, "Marie." Then I stretched out again and tried to sleep, thinking of things like the steady *scritch, scritch, scritch* of Bompasino's record player, the sound of it like the end of romance itself. He used to sit in his backyard, sleeping in the afternoon, with just the sound of the needle going around at the end of the record.

But that took a while.

After Constantina died, Bompasino cleaned out the bedroom he had shared with her, leaving, when he was done, few signs that anyone else had ever lived there. He had taken away her clothes, her wraps, and shawls, but he left the hooks and nails she'd hung them on, and from each of them there trailed away a smoky shape, like the wake of a snag in a river. Bompasino had put into the closet her photographs of a small town in Italy and of her mother and father. On the wall, where the photographs had been, there were some rectangles, the centers of which were a pale white.

Bompasino still went into the room to take his nap on Sunday afternoons, although he didn't sleep as well as before. He continued selling flowers, although now he bought them from the wholesaler, and finally he abandoned the real ones in favor of those made out of plastic. When there were only a few artificial poinsettias on the chicken-wire display he had put up in the flower shop, he put an ad in the San Francisco paper that said, *Seed Store and Apartment. Good Business Opportunity in No Fail Location. Growth Possibilities Unlimited. Inquire, Anthony Bompasino, Marlowe, CA.*

The store was sold to a short, bald man and his wife, who started the seed business and the nursery again, replacing the windows in the greenhouse and building tables for the flats of seedlings. My father said, "Well, hell, the people who bought this store are going to pay for Tony to be buried in style. That's the thing you got to remember. It's going to be just the way he wants it. A big black horse-drawn hearse, and someone from the San Francisco opera to sing from *Martha. . . .*"

Bompasino moved his furniture from his apartment into a new house trailer just outside of town, where he planted a small garden and put up some four-by-four posts, topped with some two-by-fours, over which he got some grapevines to grow. He sat there in the early evenings of summer, the green dappled light falling over him and the first breeze of twilight bringing through the grape leaves the scent of sage from the desert. Then he wound up his Victrola and listened to his 78 rpm recordings of Caruso, the noise drifting along the seldom-used blacktop in front of the house trailer.

I brought Parmesan cheese from San Francisco, the crumbly texture and the color of it like a brick from an old house in Italy. And provolone cheese, too, wrapped in rope and dipped in wax, and when I got to Bompasino's, he sliced it and served it with tomato vinaigrette, and parsley. We drank wine and listened to the noise of the record player. Bompasino read from Caesar's account of the war in Gaul, remarked on the earthworks, the engineering of bridges and fortifications.

There were some dogs in the road in front of the house, walking along, one behind the other, black ones and brown ones, panting in the heat, waiting, each with a long red tongue. A boy in town had taught the dogs to howl at the sound of opera, and they made long, quavering wails. Mostly, now, when Bompasino wanted to play records, he chased the dogs away first.

He asked me if I'd stay for dinner. I said I would. He took his TV dinner out of the freezer and cut it in half with tin-snips and put both halves in the oven. We ate them under the grapevines, looking into the flats. He watched for vultures, seeing them in the distance.

My father found him a week later. Bompasino was in the bathroom. This was just after my father had given up his practice. He came into the trailer and saw those enormous legs sticking into the house trailer's hall, the black patent leather shoes odd there against the indoor-outdoor carpet. My father sat on the floor for a while, putting his head into his arms, and then he tried to move the body. He could barely lift one of the legs. Outside the *scritch, scritch, scritch* of the record player was endlessly repeated under the arbor.

My father went to town and asked for help, admitting even to himself that he had come to the point where he couldn't turn over the body of one of his closest friends.

Some of the townspeople who came to help were the same men who, years before, had been the ones to carry Constantina from the seed store into the truck bed filled with ice. Now the Indians, farmers, and shopkeepers walked in a long, fragile line from the center of town to the trailer, going through the afternoon sunlight. Dogs joined the procession, each of them hanging its head, too, especially the dogs the boy had taught to howl in the street in front of Bompasino's house.

"Shall we call an ambulance?" said a man.

"He wouldn't want that," said another.

"What the hell, call an ambulance. The fat wop can't object much now, can he?" said the first.

"Put him in my car," said my father, "I'll take him."

The men went into the trailer, lifted the enormous body from the doorway, and carried him out, his now bald head shining in the light of the afternoon, the last strands of his hair hanging down like a limp, leftover thing. They put him onto the backseat of the car and covered him up, and my father got behind the wheel. The front yard wasn't much bigger than a plot in a cemetery, and men and women stood in it and looked at the sky, keeping an eye out for those large black birds, but instead seeing only the light, chilling movement of the bats, which had come awake and were looking for water. My father backed out of the dirt drive and left town, passing the seed store, which had been boarded up, and while he drove, his expression was seemingly blank, or just businesslike in dealing with one more dead man, but as he drove across that flat land toward Knight's River Junction, where there was a funeral home, he said, or hissed, "Goddamn it, Tony. Goddamn it. How dare you do this? How dare you?"

In the first light of morning I sat on my old bed in my father's house. The window was still open and beyond it there were the mountains in the distance, the peaks reddish in the light of the rising sun. The bases of the mountains were dark blue in the shadows and the line separating the light and darkness was so straight it looked like a high-water mark. I made the bed, doing the corners in regulation hospital style (as my father had always insisted), and as I smoothed the sheets I heard him in his room down the hall, where he took long, dry breaths. From the doorway of his room his legs looked like pieces of two-inch pipe laid side by side under the blanket.

On the walls in the hall there were framed prints of flowers and herbs that had medicinal qualities (Camomile, Foxglove), and I stood before them, still desperately trying to find something that made sense. The prints were antiquated, and the leaves, stems, and flowers were labeled with a black script. The order and correctness of the prints was tantalizing now, the scientific labeling not impossible to understand so much as having no importance any longer: science, order, regularity, predictability . . . these things had become as useless now as the broken utensils in the drawer downstairs. I sat on the top step of the stairs and said, "Marie," the sound of the word lingering in the dim light of morning.

In the kitchen I drank a cup of coffee, standing by the counter. In front of me there was the open drawer of worn-out utensils, and from time to time I turned one over, like a bear looking for something in a dump. I picked up a spatula, a steel rod for sharpening knives, a carving fork with a handle made out of horn, all of them a reminder of how my father and I had tried to hold things together years ago: we had set the table, or cooked, or eaten the food the housekeeper had made just as though there had been nothing freakish about us at all. Recently, when I had come to visit, my father had taken a print from the wall, or a book off a shelf, or showed me a well-made old table, and said, "I'm leaving this to you," his voice clear and his meaning unmistakable: it was one of the things he had gotten out of the world, however difficult it may have been, and although by other men's standards it might not have been much, it was what he had.

"The smell of coffee woke me up," my father said as he stood in the doorway. "Is there some for me?"

He wore a striped cotton bathrobe and a pair of slippers, and after I had given him a cup, he went into the living room, where he sat on the recliner, now with the footrest down so he could sit on the edge of the chair and look through the medical books, journals, and the *Physicians' Desk Reference,* in which he read up on the drugs mentioned in the articles, the benefits of each now being weighed against the side effects.

From time to time he looked around at me, and with each moment he brightened a little, not becoming cheerful exactly, but with a certain animated decision making. I sat in a chair next to him, holding my lukewarm cup. My father stopped flipping the pages of the *Desk Reference* altogether and stared, blinking, still considering. He said nothing for a while and sat there exactly like a man who is going over all that he has in order to pick the most prized possession to give to his son.

I went up to the corner and bought the paper, but there was nothing in it, and when I came back into the house, with the paper folded under my arm, my father said, "I remember about last night."

"Do you?" I said.

He nodded. He was dressed now, his pants pulled tight by a belt he had put an extra hole in with a hammer and a nail.

"That's right. Here."

He held out an envelope, one of those he used to use for billing. It had DR. K. D. LUNN, M.D., MARLOWE, CALIFORNIA, printed on the corner.

"There's a thousand dollars in it," he said.

"What for?" I said.

"You got to make a run for it," he said.

He held out the envelope.

"Well?" he said.

"I don't know," I said.

"Listen," he said, "my sticking with you is what we got."

Now the room was bright with light from the rising sun. Next to the television there was the pile of the Laurel and Hardy and Marx Brothers tapes, and from the kitchen and bathroom there was that steady dripping.

"I just don't know," I said.

"I am offering this to you," he said. "It's not just money. It's letting me help."

The envelope trembled in his hand.

"Don't you see?"

"I've been trying to think things over. . . ." I said.

"You haven't got time now," he said.

I closed my eyes and turned away.

"This is what I want to give you," he said. "Are you going to take it? Between you and me, sticking together is the only important thing. You won't deny me now, will you?"

Now he came a little closer, shuffling like a man who is wearing bedroom slippers and is having trouble keeping them on. He licked his lips as the envelope trembled in his hand.

"I'm scared you won't take it," he said.

His eyes watered.

"Don't you dare make me beg you," he said.

"All right," I said.

"Here," he said. "Take it, then."

I put out my hand and he dropped the envelope into it.

"All right," he said. "Get a warm jacket from upstairs. I've already called the airfield. The plane has an open cockpit. You'll need a pair of gloves, too."

It was still cool at the airfield, and the small hangars, the macadam, and the terminal were in the blue shadow of the mountain. Beyond the last hangar there was a small shack, made of pine planks and having a flattish, corrugated tin roof. There were battens over the cracks between the planks, and over the door there was a sign that said, GERALD LIPSILL. CROP DUSTING. EXCURSIONS. SMALL PACKAGE COURIER. AERIAL PHOTOGRAPHER. PRICES NEGOTIABLE.

My father and I got out of his station wagon and walked through the shadows and the damp smell of the macadam. Beyond the shack there was a two-seat, tandem-cockpit airplane, which sat on the apron of the runway. It was painted white and red, like a stunt plane for an airshow, but there the similarity ended. The red paint was of two different colors, and the plane had about it a shabby quality, like an automobile with a flat tire at the back of a used-car lot. The engine cowling was marked with greasy fingerprints and the propeller was multicolored, like a skin graft, since the varnish on it had come off in distinct patches.

We opened the door and entered the shack. Inside there was a workbench with tools on it, socket wrenches, calipers, screwdrivers, and above it there was a calendar with an Oriental woman on it. There were spark plugs and a can of starting fluid on a shelf above the bench. Against a wall there was a small sofa with only three legs, and next to the bench there was a hot plate on a card table, above which there were three cans of Dinty Moore beef stew on a plank shelf. On the wall there was a list of insecticide prices.

Lipsill sat on the sofa, drinking black coffee from a white enamel cup. He was in his forties, thin, and his face had one thin scar that ran from his hair down his forehead. On a shelf above the sofa, there was a series of objects, each one looking like the vanes of a small windmill. These were prototypes for an invention which Lipsill had come up with and which my father had put money into: the vanes, when attached to the tire of an airplane wheel, were supposed to make it turn. This was supposed to make airplane tires last longer, since if they were turning, they wouldn't skid or mark the runway when an airplane came in to land. Lipsill had destroyed two planes in crashes while trying the things out and my father had signed one check after another for a patent lawyer (doing so after stitching Lipsill's cuts and gashes and setting his broken bones). In the end my father and Lipsill received a pile of drawings done by other inventors trying to solve the same problem, all of which ideas had failed, too. Now the prototypes were displayed like things honorably obtained, like deer antlers.

My father and I stood in the doorway.

"All right," said my father, "here we are. Do you think you can get to Canada without being seen or noticed?"

"Does a bear do it in the woods?" said Lipsill. "Listen, I'll go along the coast and then we'll go inland and come in at tree level. I'll put green streaks on the wings from brushing the treetops. There isn't radar in the world that can keep track of me. . . ."

My father nodded and offered an envelope here, too, but Lipsill just shook his head and said, "You can't spend your money here, Doc. Especially not doing something I might get thrown in jail for."

"Who said anything about jail?" said my father.

Lipsill looked away from my father and handed me a helmet, saying only, "Wear this. The wind makes your hair hurt after a while if you don't. Are you ready?"

I nodded, turning outside into the blue light of morning.

We walked to the airplane and I got into the rear cockpit. Lipsill opened the cowling and checked the oil, and my father stood by the wing, his head bare, his wrists too small for his white shirt. Then he turned and walked back toward the shack, going with the same definite gait as when we had come from the house, both of us walking like men who had finally come to a decision. Now I sat at my set of controls, the stick moving as Lipsill checked the plane over and worked the control surfaces by hand.

Even here, in the disappearance of the shadows and with my father sitting on a bench at the side of the shack, his elbows on his knees, and with the controls moving in that ghostlike fashion, I still looked at the mountains with that same desperate attempt to make sense of what surrounded me, not to mention wanting to get away from the chaos that seemed to lurk just beneath the surface of things.

Now I thought of Marie as she walked toward the bed in her apartment, her carriage straight, her nakedness smooth in the moonlike light that came through the white curtain. She sat down next to me and began, as she usually did, carefully touching, licking, biting . . . not saying a word until she suddenly put her face opposite mine and said, "You've never felt this way before, have you? I dare you to say you have. And you know why? I fit you like a glove. Not only here—" she put her hand into the flat between her legs—"I fit you everywhere, in your fears, in your secrets, in your anger, in your desires, everywhere"—her face above mine, the words and then the almost barklike sounds coming in scented puffs, her hands holding my hair and jerking it, her eyes set on mine with an infinite curiosity. Then she got up and turned away, walking toward the bathroom, shaking her head, mystified. "Please," she said, "be careful. Don't do anything stupid. I couldn't live without you now."

The propeller spun into a transparent blur, perfectly round, through which there were those distant mountains, still red-gold in the sunlight. We went down to the end of the runway and turned and faced the long, flat macadam ahead of us. The pitch of the engine increased. For a moment there was just the noise, but then Lipsill slipped the brakes and we began. The runway sped toward us, the tire marks on it flicking by in a speckled rush.

We flew over the mountains and along the coast, the wings slowly tilting from side to side in the updrafts. The steady drone of the engine, the constant pressure of the wind, and the morning glitter on the water below made for a sleepy lull. Below, about a mile from shore, there were a few whales, their wakes looking like small V's, their tails breaking the surface before they sounded, the broad and scarred shapes waving in the air before sliding into the depths.

The plane crossed back into the valley. The mountains were blue-green, and in the valley the farms were cut into squares and rectangles, either green or brown, neat, precisely drawn. From the altitude of the plane the earth stretched into the distance, the horizon hazy, or smoky up toward Oregon, which wasn't far away now. There were clouds in the west, misty and fog colored. Beneath them there was the contour of the brown hills, at the bottom of which there were some gullies, which, from the air, looked prehistoric. Some birds circled in a flock. In the green-and-brown arrangement of the fields below, or in the irregular stands of trees, there was the tug of the earth, the steady pull of it so strong as to have the effect of making you feel that here, at last, there was something to trust. It had the effect of the power of a place, or a moment, which overwhelms, like dawn in the wilderness. It suggested not just the physical, but the depth of human attachment. I looked over the side now, feeling that tug, and watching those neat rectangles below, the colors, the distant mist, the glint of the sun off the aluminum silos and the windows of automobiles all contributing to that reassuring pull.

When we landed, Lipsill said, "What?"

"I'm going back," I said.

"Look," he said, "I'll get you there. Don't worry. There's a little airfield I know outside of Vancouver . . . no one there but an old drunk and his Indian wife. They'd help you . . ."

I shook my head.

"I'm going back," I said. "Do you need more money?"

"No," he said. "Look, I promised your father. He never asked for a favor before. . . ."

"I understand," I said.

"He said it meant a lot," he said. "I wouldn't have agreed otherwise. He's getting old . . . who the hell knows what he means."

"It's hard sometimes," I said. "I'm going back now."

Lipsill stood there, his back against the plane.

"I was thinking I wanted to get up to Oregon anyway," he said, "to arrange for some work for next springtime. There are apple orchards up there that need spraying. . . . I usually go for a couple of weeks when the trees are blooming. It's always good to go up in advance. . . . you know, to get it all set up."

"Go ahead," I said. "I'll take the bus back. Is there a town near here?"

"Yeah," he said, "I'll go and see about getting you a ride."

I took the bus to Marlowe. It groaned into town and

stopped in front of the stationer's, just as it had years ago, the winter after the tornado when I had come home to wait. It was evening and I walked up to my father's house, where he was sitting on the front porch, reading the paper.

"So," he said, "you're going back?"

I nodded.

"Yes," I said. "I just needed a couple of days to think things over. Thanks."

"Well, well," he said. "You poor son of a bitch. What the hell are you going back for?"

"I want to see my kids," I said.

"Don't you think the cops know that?" he said. "Oh, Ben, why the hell did you break that window? Just look at the trouble it's caused."

I reached out and took his hand.

"Thanks," I said, "for sticking by me."

"That's what we had. That's all we really ever had," he said.

"I'm going to go now," I said. "You take care of yourself."

My father leaned forward and took that pistol out of his lap.

"Here," he said. "You poor son of a bitch. You better take this. It's about all I can give you now."

I picked up the thing and put it in my jacket pocket and then turned toward my car.

My father stood up, the open sheets of the paper trembling in his fingers, some of the pages falling to the porch like small grayish tents before collapsing altogether. Behind him there was the waiting room filled with garden tools and dusty piles of old journals, the old television sets and the jars of sorted screws.

"I did what I could," he said.

I turned toward him now, looking right at him.

"Good-bye, Ben," he said.

He sat down, staring into the blue gloom of evening, the paper around his feet where it had fallen. It was a warm evening, and the bats had come out, their shapes black against the almost purple sky. I backed my car out of the drive and turned south, toward the city. For a moment, in the rearview mirror, there was the porch of my father's house, where he sat and waited.

Ben Lunn,
The Poachers at Night

Los Reyes, California

AT WORK I DID THE LATE-EVENING AND EARLY-MORNING broadcast: there was no one else around, and I sat in the meteorologist's room. There was a computer terminal against the wall, a radar screen, a telex for reports from the Pacific, and the facsimile machine for the satellite photographs. There were some enlargements of photographs on the wall: a hurricane off the coast of Florida, a typhoon near Japan, the storms appearing like pictures of spiral galaxies. I came home at dawn, buying the early paper, listening to the radio when I drove the car. There hadn't been any news. I slept during the day.

At dawn, when I drove up to the house, I stood in front of it, seeing the peeling paint, the weeds in the beds where I had planted bulbs, the children's toys on the lawn, bikes and bubble sticks, kitchen utensils left in the sandbox. In that cool moment I tried to make sense of the place, which stood before me as an expression of the decisions I had made, or as evidence of that impulse I knew only by effects, one of which was the ownership of this building with its shabby paint, its screen door with a hole in it, the clapboards along the foundation that were rotting and needed to be replaced. The impulse, which had produced this place and which was the attempt to realize some fantastical idea of the way things should be, seemed foolish or half baked. The attempt just to make a family and to be someone who was qualified to tell his kids the difference between right and wrong hadn't been anywhere near enough. I stood there, just after dawn, seeing the dim glow of the night-light in the kids' bathroom.

I came into the house like a thief or a burglar and woke the children: they sat up languidly, as though they were being brought to life. They stretched and yawned and rubbed their eyes, and then I made toast and scrambled eggs, made their lunches for school, the warmth and domestic odor of the kitchen having about it a kind of blessing. Faith sat at the table, saying nothing, drinking her coffee. I walked the children to the bus stop, holding each by the hand, listening to the crinkle of the brown paper sacks in which they carried their lunches.

"Dad," said Genny, "you know what the difference between a piano and a fish is?"

"No?" I said. "What?"

"You can't tuna fish."

Then I went to sleep.

One morning Faith came into the bedroom and said, "Ben, there are two policemen here to see you." She stood in front of the window beyond which there was the orchard. The trees were unpruned and there were brush and vines moving into it now. It was fall and the branches were thick and formed a gray fuzz against the hillside. The deer still came at night to look for windfalls or just because they liked the odor.

I sat up now and said, "Tell them I'll be down."

"I'll make some coffee for them," said Faith.

"Good," I said. "Fine."

I put on a robe and a pair of slippers and went into the bathroom. The water was cold on my cheeks, and I stood before the mirror, looking at my face: the eyes there were scared. Then I turned and went out into the hall and into Genny's room. There was a picture of a tiger on the wall, a

Bengalese one with green eyes. Her bed was unmade and there were books and clothes on the floor. Her dresser drawers were open and there were cassettes on the floor around her tape player. Now there seemed to be a new presence here, something that was just approaching the house. I looked around, desperately trying to find some tangible thing that showed its advance or gave me a way to keep it away, but there was only that ominous presence, not attached to anything in particular, but still definite for all that.

They were sitting downstairs, each of them holding one of our best coffee cups. They were large, cream-colored cups with a rose pattern on them and an ornate handle. Wedding presents. Wedgwood.

"Nice cups," said one of the policemen to Faith.

"Thank you," said Faith.

The one who spoke had gray hair and a paunch. He looked tired, and he slowly turned his blue eyes from Faith to me. He wore a pair of slacks and a sport coat, which was unbuttoned. His shoes were black and heavy. Opposite him, on a chair, there was another one, a younger man, tall and blond, thin. He smiled when I came in.

The tall one introduced himself as Detective Frank. The other as Detective May.

"You don't mind if I call you Ben, do you?" said the older one, Detective May. He didn't smile like the other one. His eyes just moved toward me with a slow, fatigued effort.

"No," I said. "That's fine."

"Would you like some coffee, Ben?" said Detective Frank.

"No, thanks," I said. "What can I do for you?"

"We'd like to ask a few questions. That's all," said Frank. "Sorry about waking you up. Your wife said you work at night." He turned to Faith now. "I'm sorry, but I'm afraid we want to talk just to Ben."

"Of course," said Faith. "I understand."

She went out.

"I used to work the graveyard shift, Ben," said May. "You have my sympathy. I could never sleep during the day."

He looked away now, his sleepy eyes going back to his coffee.

Frank opened his notebook.

"Lunn, Ben," he said. "White male. Age?"

"Forty-one," I said.

"Occupation?" he said.

"Meteorologist," I said. "Weatherman."

"Really?" said May. "I've always wanted to meet a weatherman. Is it just predictions you do?"

"Mostly," I said. "It's a little easier with computers and satellite pictures than it used to be. But I have a research project, too."

"What's that?" said May.

"I'm trying to associate weather and earthquakes," I said. "It seems an abrupt drop in barometric pressure . . ."

I stopped now. May turned his tired eyes toward me once again.

"Interesting," he said.

"Very," said Frank.

We all sat quietly for a moment.

"Any identifying marks?" said Frank. "A tattoo, say."

He looked up when he said this, his eyes going over my face. He smiled.

"No," I said. "I broke my collarbone. The bone didn't heal just right and there's a lump in the middle. I guess you could call that an identifying mark."

I slipped my hand under my bathrobe and rubbed it. It ached as it always did at the peak of high pressure, or just as the barometer began to fall.

"Do you know why we're here, Ben?" said Frank.

"No."

"No?" said May.

"What do you mean by that?" I said.

"Nothing," said May. "It was just a manner of speech. You pick it up in my business after a while."

"Ben, do you know a woman by the name of Christine Taylor?" said Frank. May slowly turned his eyes toward me, the effort of it showing in his face.

I shook my head.

"No," I said.

"Maybe you knew her by another name," said May. "Maybe it was Marie Boule?"

"No," I said.

"Maybe something else. Some other name," said Frank. "Do you know anyone who lived at forty-eight Borneo Street?"

"It's a new building, Ben," said May. "Postwar. Next to the alley."

"Not offhand," I said.

"Have you got the picture?" May said to Frank.

He took it from his pocket. It was a snapshot, taken recently, and in it Marie stood at the rail of a sailboat, her face turned toward the camera, her expression cool and aloof, a slight smile on her lips. The wind blew her hair, and she stood next to a heavyset man with gray hair.

"Do you know her?"

I kept looking at the picture.

"No," I said. I looked up now, into May's tired eyes. "Why are you asking me about her?"

"Routine. You had a parking ticket. Were you driving your car about ten days ago?"

"I guess so," I said.

"You haven't lent it to anyone? It wasn't stolen? There was no unauthorized use of it?"

"No," I said.

"Then why did you park about ten days ago, Tuesday before last, in the alley next to forty-two Borneo Street?"

"The summons was given at two fifty-four in the afternoon. We're interested in the time between two and three that afternoon," said Frank.

I reached into my robe again and put my fingers on that constant throb.

"I parked in the alley and took a cable car to a bar at the bottom of the hill, by the bay," I said.

"What's the name of it?" said May.

"The Buena Sierra," I said.

"Why didn't you drive down there?"

"It's hard to find a place to park," I said. "And anyway, I like to take the cable car. I like to get out on my day off."

"The Buena Sierra," said May. "They have a good Irish coffee there, don't they?"

"Yes," I said.

"How long were you there?" said Frank.

"A couple hours," I said.

"Between two and four, then?" said May.

"Right. That's right."

"Did anyone see you?" said Frank.

"No," I said.

We all sat there now, no one saying a word. My shoulder throbbed and I touched it again. Overhead there was the sound of an airplane, a jet. It sounded like distant thunder. Frank went on writing for a while.

"You didn't know this woman by any other name?" said May. He held up the picture again.

"No," I said.

"Well, she knew a lot of men," said May. "There was a list of names and telephone numbers in her apartment. Seventy-eight men. It'll take a while, but we'll get through them."

Frank looked at me now.

"Your number isn't on that list, is it, Ben?" said May.

I shook my head.

"Why should it be?" I said.

"That's right," said May, "why should your number be on a list kept by some slut in San Francisco?"

"I don't know," I said.

Frank looked up from his book. Both of them sat there, watching my face. Frank tapped his pencil against his book.

"Was your number there?" said May.

"How the hell should I know?" I said. "I'd bet it wasn't."

"She was just a slut," he said, looking at me.

"Was she?" I said.

Frank started laughing now.

"Come on," he said to May. "You're barking up the wrong

tree. Can't you see that? Ben's got a wife and kids. Nice house. What is he going into the city for?"

May laughed now, too.

"You pick up habits in this business, you know, Ben?" he said. "Listen. You come around to Costello's some evening. You know Costello's on Geary Street? I'm there some evenings. I'll buy you an Irish coffee. Okay? You can tell me about the whatchamacallit and the earthquakes. Or if you saw anything suspicious around the alley on Borneo Street. Think it over. You can come and talk to me."

They stood up and I did too. Faith came to the door and looked in, hearing the laughter. The meeting broke up, the atmosphere around it like a poker game. Frank and May went to the door, May's tired eyes going over Faith once before turning to me. Then the men went through the door and out to their car, a red one with a short aerial and a shirt hung against the window in the backseat.

The car turned and went down the road, going slowly in the light of midmorning.

I climbed the stairs now and went into Genny's room. From the window you could see the ghostlike hills in the haze. There were clothes, dolls, records, schoolbooks, and some Nancy Drew mysteries on the floor. I sat down there, on the floor, my back against Genny's bed, my forearms on my knees, my head against them. After a few minutes I went down the hall and got into bed, where I slept.

In the afternoon I dressed and came downstairs. Faith sat at the kitchen table. When I came into the room, she said, "Hi. How about a cup of coffee?"

"Please," I said.

She put it on the table in front of me.

"Don't you think it's about time we talked?" she said. "You've been avoiding me."

"Have I?" I said. "It just gets that way when I work nights."

"Does it?" she said. "Well, maybe. I'd like to talk, though."

"There isn't anything to say," I said.

"I can apologize, can't I?" said Faith.

"What's the point?" I said.

"I'm sorry I went to see her," she said. "It wasn't any of my business to go there. It was a mistake. She told you what happened, didn't she?"

"Please," I said. "It's better if we just kept quiet about it."

"No, it isn't," she said. "I was reading in the *Ladies' Home Journal* about marriage. . . ."

I put my head forward now, squeezing the cup.

". . . you've got to keep the avenues of communication open. Don't you see?"

"Do me a favor, will you?" I said. "Let's keep the *Ladies' Home Journal* out of it, all right?"

"Why were those policemen here?" she said.

"I don't know," I said.

"Was someone murdered?" she said.

I took a sip of coffee.

"Was it Christine? If anything happened to her it's what she deserved."

"Please," I said.

"Well, isn't it?"

I squeezed the cup, watching the black surface of the liquid, and in it there was a bright, yellow reflection from the light fixture over the table. Outside the children played in the afternoon, their voices rising out of the orchard.

"Of course, she just had to tell you what happened when I went to see her, didn't she?" Faith said. "Did she make fun of me? Did she talk about the veins on my legs?"

"No," I said, "she didn't. Let's drop it."

"Ben," she said, "you know what?"

She sat across from me, one eye brown, the other brown and gray.

"What?"

"I want to start from scratch. We can get things straightened out. We can go see a marriage counselor. Here."

She put down on the table a bottle of pills from the pharmacy, the capsules in it big and bicolored, half white, half yellow.

"I went to see the doctor," she said. "I won't be sick anymore if I take these. I've already started. Will you give me a chance? Don't be angry, Ben. Don't."

"Don't be angry," I said.

I stood up, listening to the children. In the kitchen there was that cold, greasy sense of something putting the first slimy tendril into the house. Now I strained, wanting to do anything to keep it away.

"We've got a chance," she said. "Please. Don't be angry."

I closed my eyes.

"Will you pick things up and start over?" she said. "Think of the kids."

The children were laughing now, a high, almost contagious giggle.

"All right," I said. "We'll keep things going."

"That's wonderful," she said.

I put my arms around her.

"We'll go see a marriage counselor," said Faith. "We'll keep lines of communication open."

She started crying.

"Hush," I said. "Hush. It'll be all right."

We stood opposite one another, both of us feeling the smoky yellow air outside. It was still. Not a leaf moved. The grass reflected the sun. The children called to each other, their voices sweet, shrieking, the sound having about it a kind of certainty, as though they had been there every fall, in some orchard, for hundreds of years. Their cheerfulness came into the kitchen, and we stood there, hearing it.

"Hush. Hush," I said.

"Tell me we've got a chance," she said. "Tell me."

"We've got a chance," I said.

"You're not just saying that?"

I shook my head

"No," I said. "I'm not just saying that."

She sat down now, her head bent forward, her hands in her lap. The coffee cup sat in front of her, the last thin wisp of steam rising from it.

"Have you seen this?" she said.

She took the afternoon paper from the floor and spread it on the table. On the third page there was a picture of Marie, an innocent one from a high-school yearbook. The headline said, MURDER IN BORNEO STREET.

I sat down now, too, opposite her.

"Tell me we've got a chance," she said. "That's all I want to hear."

I sat there, looking at the picture.

"The police don't suspect you," she said. "You handled them just fine. So tell me. Haven't we got a chance now?"

I read the story and closed the paper. We sat opposite one another, not saying a thing. Faith started crying again.

"Well? Ben? Tell me."

I got up and looked out the window at the hillside. Above it there were some mare's tails. The sky was misty, too: warm front approaching. I put my hand onto that now constant ache in my shoulder. The hillside was the color of a brown hens'-egg. I kept looking at it, hearing the children's voices.

After a few minutes Faith said, "Maybe I should go wash my face."

"Yes," I said. "That's for the best."

"I don't want the kids to see me this way," she said, straightening up now.

She reached for a Kleenex from the box on the table.

"Will you keep them outside for a little?"

She turned and went upstairs, her hand to her face. Outside, the children were at the edge of the orchard, the gray disorder of the limbs above them. There were berry canes there, too, their thorns brownish and beak shaped. The children stood side by side, both in white dresses, both looking at something on the ground. When I came out of the back door of the house, they started running toward me.

"Dad, Dad," said Genny, "come and look. There's a bunch of rotten apples on the ground and the wasps are getting drunk on them. Come look."

"Let's leave them alone," I said. "We don't want to get stung."

"But come and look."

Under the trees there were some cinnamon-colored apples which were fermenting in the warm fall afternoons. The wasps crawled over the surface of them, not staggering exactly, but still having trouble, dragging their black hindparts around. The air was thick with the smell of fermenting apples.

The children watched for a while and then we moved away and stretched out in the grass and looked at the clouds. Genny stretched out on one side and Sarah on the other. I put my arms around them and pulled them next to me, the warmth of their bodies mixing now with the scent of the apples. We picked out the shapes in the clouds.

The sunlight was warm, but the shade of the afternoon approached, the purple-gray sweep of it moving across the yard. The children squirmed against me to get comfortable and the warmth of them came as a steady, infinitely light pressure. The air was filled with dust, which looked golden in the slanting, rayed light. The children pointed out shapes in the sky, pennants, streamers, dragons and running horses, whales, lions and tigers.

On Saturday, when Faith took the kids with her to the market, I was alone in the house. Now I went from one room to another, not hurriedly, but still searching, curious, trying to find something that made sense here, too. In the kitchen I looked at our dishes, the good ones and those for everyday, at the pots and pans, the cookbooks, the shopping lists, all seeming so ordinary, but having now a kind of grief. Upstairs I looked through my closet, taking out the suit I was married in and going through the pockets, hoping that some forgotten thing would appear, some note, some old lost possession that would help me now. I went through Faith's clothes, too, her good serviceable skirts and slacks, all of them arranged there like clothes from the bland, decent-looking womanly manikin at J. C. Penney's. Nothing adventuresome, nothing even that definite. There was some elusive quality here, too, something hiding in that blandness, some cry for help or understanding. I opened the underwear drawer and picked up a pair of briefs and looked at the label: it had come from K mart after all.

Downstairs, in the cool silence of the house, there was

that ominous quality of something waiting just beyond the door or window, as though the house was being watched. I stood quietly, listening for the slightest sound. More than anything else it seemed that if I could just get rid of that presence, of that sense of some waiting thing, I could breathe easily. Now I went from downstairs window to downstairs window, checking the locks, and then I went to the cellar and checked the windows there. I drilled holes through each sash and into the frame and then put a piece of doweling into each hole so that even if the lock was broken the window couldn't be opened. The latch on the screen door to the kitchen had been missing for years and now I took a new hook and a new eye and fastened the door shut, going around to the outside to check it. But when I sat in the living room, that definite quality of something wanting to get in was still there.

In the silence of the house I had an idea about what was watching. In the beginning I stood up and turned away, not wanting to give in to superstition or things like that, but after a while it seemed to have nothing to do with superstition. It just felt like some avenging thing had been unleashed and directed here, not against me so much as against Faith and the children. Now I went around the house, looking for a way to fight it. For a moment, in the loneliness of the place, it seemed that if I got rid of whatever it was, if I could make it go away, why, then, things would be all right: I could get into the car and drive to the city and find Marie at the door of the apartment, saying, "Hi, sugar, where you been?"

They came at night, dark and phantomlike, just as I had imagined, their arrival not accusing so much as just blandly vicious. They were parked in the road, next to the orchard beyond the house, the car having about it a muted quality, like something camouflaged for the desert, but in fact it was just that the paint had lost its sheen. There was a full moon, and the orchard, the trunks and limbs of the trees, the vines that had grown up there, were all seen in black and white. The orchard had about it the disorder of neglected things.

It was Saturday, and I didn't work on Saturday night. At the sound of the first shot Faith and I were in bed, lying side by side, both of us on our backs, both staring at the ceiling, our feet almost but not quite touching. Faith turned now and looked at me, making the sheets rustle. The sound of the shot bled away and disappeared into the landscape.

"Are you awake?" she said.

"Yes," I said. "Did you hear that?"

"Let's not worry about it," she said. "Let's just pretend we didn't hear."

There were about three acres of orchard all together, and even in the brush and vines the neat order of the trees' planting still showed. The shadow of each tree lay around its trunk like a piece of black lace on the moonlighted ground. They were Oregon crab apples. Now, as I stood at the window, the spikes and suckers on the unpruned trees looked white, one branch and limb crossing another, the conglomeration of them looking brushy and impenetrable.

The car was in the road, next to the orchard. It was a station wagon, about ten years old, the entire thing blotchy with primer. From the backseat, on the driver's side, something stuck out of the window, and the sheen on it suggested the bluing of a rifle. There were deer in the orchard, striped with moonlight as they fed on the apples. It was hard to see them since their appearance was almost zebralike in the shadows, but every now and then there was some movement as one of the deer stepped up to another apple. There was a flash from the window of the car and that sound again, too, the *snap* of a .22. It sounded like someone hitting the wall with a flyswatter.

The car didn't move. Faith sat up in bed, one hand to her hair.

"Come on back to bed, Ben," she said. "Let's go to sleep."

I hadn't seen the car before. When men came to kill deer out of season, they went up to the ridge and parked their cars a long way from the house. It happened when the aircraft factories around San José laid men off, but for a while now there had been plenty of jobs.

"Come on, Ben," said Faith. "Please."

"No," I said, "I'm not going to have them so close to the house."

I pulled on my pants with a jerk now.

"They've killed deer here before," said Faith.

"Not next to the house," I said. "This isn't the same as before."

I pulled on my shoes, still feeling the poachers as they waited outside.

"I'm going to get them out of here," I said.

"They never come up here alone," said Faith. "They've got a gun."

"They don't have to come so close," I said.

Outside, in front of the door, my breath rose into the darkness when I looked up the road, trying to make out the car in those lines and shadows, and being certain, too, that these men had been watching the house.

The station wagon began to move. It was facing downhill, and its lights were out, but it was still moving, coasting, and as it came it didn't seem to slink away so much as to suggest some alert, cunning thing. The engine started with a tinny cough and rattle, and then the car moved faster. The lights still hadn't been turned on. There were three men inside, two in the front and one in the back, and as the car passed, the man on the passenger's side in the front lighted a cigarette, the yellow flame showing his face. It was flat, without much of a nose. He had a low forehead, with the hair combed forward, and the cheeks and chin were covered with a thin, dark beard. He had dark brows, too, and his forehead was pocked. The man turned his face toward me, his eyes the color of licorice. Then the lighter went out, leaving behind the small, glowing button of the cigarette.

Faith stood at the front door.

"Please, Ben," she said. "Come back inside."

"No," I said, standing there at the road, turning back to her now. "You know how a poacher works. They kill a deer, and then they go someplace until everyone has forgotten about the shot. Then they come back later. I don't want to lie up there in bed pretending nothing is happening when they come back here."

"Please," said Faith, "I *saw* them."

The keys to the car were in the house, hanging on a hook in the kitchen. There must have been twenty keys on the ring, the locks for some of which I no longer remembered. Faith still stood in the doorway, and when I passed she said, "Look. Why don't we call the police? It's their job, isn't it?"

There was almost no breeze as I turned now.

"Go back inside," I said.

"I'll call them," said Faith.

"No," I said. "Just go back inside."

The road where the poachers had disappeared was silent, the bright, triangular shapes of moonlight in it looking like torn sheets. In the backseat of the car there were some of the kids' toys, a backpack, a doll, a squirt gun, and there were small, empty packages of chips and two empty apple juice bottles.

Downhill from my house there was open land, rolling hills covered with tall grass and scrub brush. There were a few eucalyptus trees, as white as flour in the moonlight. About a quarter of a mile away, though, the land had been divided into lots with string and stakes and surveyor's tape, and in front of each one there was a number. There was a real estate developer's sign, and beyond the sign the first new house emerged from a pile of sand and boards, pails and cement mixers, and around it there were trees in burlap sacks, the name tags from the nursery still hanging from their limbs.

The road forked and I stayed to the right, even though dust and a thin blue cloud of exhaust still swirled in the left fork. Both forks came to the crossroad, and I thought the poachers would turn right there. If I went to the corner and waited, they'd pass.

I stopped the car at the corner of the crossroad. The engine cooled, ticking as it did so, a frail strand of mist rising from the radiator. The plastic of the seat creaked a little. The steering wheel was plastic, too, bright red, smooth to the touch.

The crossroad was quiet, dappled in the moonlight. As I sat there I thought of a form the game warden distributed, one that was to be used in describing poachers: it was supposed to help you make sense of the things you'd seen. On it there was a drawing of a man with arrows pointing at his face, one side of which had a beard, and at his pants, shoes, and clothes, and at an identifying mark. In the black shadows of the trees, I thought of the face I had seen in the car, the pocks, the forehead, the hair combed forward, the lips, all having the maliciousness of a shrunken head. How could I get on a form the sense of that man watching the house and trying to get into it?

After a while I thought of something else. At first I tried to deny it, but even as I shook my head with disbelief, there was the certainty these men were here, so close to the house, because they had been friends of Marie. I looked into the quiet road, trying to think clearly and knowing that it made all the difference in the world if I had brought these men here, that those flat, pocked faces (and worse, the malice behind them) had been produced by that appalling flaw of mine and that the arrival of these men was just one more effect of it. That was the thing I beheld now, the certainty that the safe neighborhood where my children lived had been invaded, and that this had happened because of that flaw, the effects of which were now multiplying. I squeezed the wheel, being certain that this was so and wishing I had brought the pistol my father had given me.

The car still didn't come. In the silence of the evening it seemed possible the car might simply disappear, leaving me to wait for it to come back again some other night when Faith was sleeping. Or worse, when only Faith and the children were in the house. I started the engine and turned into the crossroad, no longer able to wait.

I didn't have to go far though, not more than a half mile. The station wagon appeared, coming over the ridge, its lights still out, its dark silhouette moving toward me. The spring on the rear, right-hand side was broken, and the car seemed to drag itself along, not so much injured as unstoppable. On the front bumper there was a license plate, held there with wire strung through the grill, but the car had been used to push other cars: the plate was bent and flattened, hard to read even in the high beams.

I wanted the license number, if only so I could find them again, on someplace other than these back roads. The glare on the letters and numbers wasn't so bad if I kept my car in the middle of the road. We approached one another, head on for a while, the poacher's car covered with splotches of primer. It came along with that slow, steady rush, neither fast nor slow. Now it began to move closer to the side of the road, although even in the begrudging of each inch there was the hint of some other purpose: it was like watching a snake coiling in front of you, taking its time about it, but still making it clear you'd be taken care of, all in good time.

The station wagon gave more ground. It went into the ditch at the side of the road and over a culvert there, the car rising into the air in a noisy trajectory, the front end first going up, just as though it had gone over one of those bumps put into a driveway to make people drive slowly. When the car came down, tilted forward a little, the men's faces were visible, all of them like brothers or cousins, each with the same flat nose, dark hair and brows, and the same expression. The man in the front, on the passenger's side, held a small-caliber rifle. As the car hung in the air, he swung the barrel across the front seat, the muzzle moving in my direction.

The man in the passenger's seat now put his cheek on the stock and curled a finger around the trigger. The rifle had a sling and the man had slipped his elbow through it and held it expertly, the sling taut, the stock firmly against his shoulder. The man in the backseat leaned forward, putting his head close to the driver, his eyes dark and shiny, too. Then the car moved out of my headlights and came down with a crash and a rattle, as though the hood was only loosely wired shut. But the car still came on, its speed not diminished at all, and then it passed, the interior of it impenetrable now.

There had been no flash from the muzzle, but seeing the rifle, the bore of it dark as a grave, had been enough. I pulled to the side of the road, my suspicions confirmed. They'd come with all the ill will I'd imagined, not to mention the dangerous calculation of people who did their business after dark: the man with the rifle hadn't fired only because he was swinging the barrel across the front seat, toward the man who was driving, and if he had shot, he might have hit the driver, his brother or cousin, in the head. That was what had stopped him.

The headlights of the poacher's car came on, one yellow taillight showing through a broken lens, and as the car disappeared, the yellow light described the long arc of a tracer round. The station wagon went up the slow rise of the next ridge, the headlights of it sweeping over the stars. It had left behind a cloud of blue exhaust.

There was a drive to turn around in, but it was wet, and when I backed in the wheels spun, the mud splattering into the air with a kind of ripping sound. There were pine trees at the side of the drive, but it took a while to break off dry branches and to get them under the wheels. By the time I came to the main road, the one that went to town, the station wagon had been there and had already made the turn.

To the left there was the strip outside of town, a mile or so of road that was filled with Ford, Chevrolet, and Subaru dealerships, a Pizza Hut, McDonald's, and a Wendy's, gas stations, and a Chinese restaurant in a new stucco building.

Against the sky there was the cool glow of the strip, the Ford and Volkswagen signs contributing to the bluish light. In a shopping center there was a supermarket, an ice-cream parlor, a sporting-goods store, all of them closed. It was after midnight. The face of the moon was crossed by telephone wires, which looked like lines for musical notation.

The parking lots had a quiet, late-night air. At the McDonald's, the Pizza Hut, in the dark gas stations I turned off the headlights and waited, looking at the street, at the motels and restaurants, seeing an occasional car, but none was the one I wanted. For a while I parked at the side of a building in the shopping center, a store with a FOR LEASE sign in the window, but around me there were only the empty shadows.

It was hard to believe the men wouldn't appear. The strip had a menace to it, if only because these anonymous buildings provided a temporary home, a partial comfort for people who had been excluded and abandoned and who, in the darkness of the night, so obviously needed to avenge themselves. In front of me there was the main road and beyond it there were more anonymous buildings, the ownership of them disguised in the familiar signs, the overly cheerful colors of which were like those in progressive mental hospitals. I closed my eyes to think, wanting to be clear about what was happening, but only one thing was certain. Faith and the children were alone in the house.

On the way home the light from the moon was buttery, and when I rolled down the window there was the scent of the ground and the grass, of the wet ditches at the side of the road: the barometer was falling. In my shoulder there was the old, comforting ache. It would rain soon.

The road went through a swamp. It was a small one, but it was thick with brush and around the edges of it there were some pines and thorn apples. At the edge of it, by the side of the road, there was a deer. Its coat was silver-gray, and it stood with its head up, its eyes bright with the lights of the car. It twitched its tail. I came closer now. The deer made two dolphinlike jumps, rising into the air almost as far as it went over the ground, and when it landed in the center of the road, not ten feet from the front of the car, I hit it, knocking it down, its eyes bright with the headlights. There was a thump, too, and a tinkling as a headlight broke.

The engine died, and the one headlight shone up the road. When I got out of the car, my breath turned white and trailed away into the air. The deer got up, not limping so much as jumping on one foreleg, letting the other dangle, and when it got to the side of the road, it lay down in the ditch, sticking out its head and pressing its throat into the grass. On the road there were some pieces of mirror, sprayed there from the broken headlight.

The animal's back and side began to steam, the mist there as fine as from a hot bath. There was a light ground fog in the

swamp and in the part of the road that went through it, and it
swept over me and the deer, the tendrils of it twisting back
into themselves. The deer was loose to the touch and warm, its
coat greasy. It breathed, the movement of its ribs labored. The
animal stared into the distance, its eyes wide now and filled
with moonlight. As I knelt there, touching it, feeling the
warmth against my fingers, there was the sense of something
else, too, like a breeze, or a sigh, that streamed past my fingers.
Then I rocked back on my heels, squatting there, feeling the
swamp around me, the stars overhead, the distant bits of them
as bright as the pieces of broken mirror on the ground.

The deer was dead. I put my head down now, feeling
above me the endless glitter of the stars and the darkness of
the sky beyond them. The swamp was cold and damp, and the
ground fog swept along. I reached down and picked up the
deer's head, but I put it down again, feeling the pressure of
the sky, the stars, and the presence of that dead animal. From
the swamp there was an odor of things dark with rotting,
leaves and half-submerged trunks and brush. It was cold, and
at the side of the road there was that impenetrable brush and
the sound of trickling water. The sky was clear, the stars
brighter now, shimmering in the atmosphere, as though reflected in water about to boil.

From the ridge on the other side of the swamp there was a
slight sound, like someone rattling a gate that was wired shut.
I still squatted next to the deer and beneath that sky. The
ground fog blew out of the swamp and across the road, like
smoke from some smoldering fire. That sound continued,
though, getting louder all the time, now appearing to come as
a pounding, like loose things in the bed of a truck going over a
dirt road, and as I looked up, seeing the ground fog and the
dead deer, that station wagon, the one with the men inside,
came over the ridge.

Its lights were on. The car came toward me, and that
hood, which had been wired shut with a coat hanger, made a
continual banging. Its speed was the same as before, not hur-
ried, not slow, just constant. The deer had a furry, coonlike

odor, and I squatted there, not only smelling it, but feeling it, too, on my hands and face.

The station wagon slowed down and stopped. Inside there were those men, the faces of the two of them on my side turned toward me, their expressions seemingly sleepy.

I stood up now, in the gamy odor of the animal, and walked toward the station wagon, reaching out for the door handle.

The driver rolled down the window, his licorice-colored eyes moving from the deer to me. Then he said, "Psst. Hey. Is it dead?"

I stepped up to the window now, leaning forward, my face close to the driver's.

"What are you doing here?" I said.

"It's a free country, isn't it?" said the driver.

He had been holding a can of beer, but now he put it onto the dashboard, where a hole had been cut into the foam for it. There was the sweet smell of hops on his breath.

"You were up by my house earlier, weren't you?" I said.

"We been by a lot of houses tonight, Jack," said the man in the passenger's seat. The rifle was between him and the driver, the barrel pointed downward, toward the hump of the drive shaft.

"Is it dead?" said the man in the backseat.

I still leaned forward, my hand now on the driver's door handle.

"Why are you here?" I said.

"Get your hand off my car," said the driver.

"You looked like you needed help," said the man on the driver's side.

The man in back and the one on the passenger's side got out of the car. They were wearing cheap blue jeans and work shirts. The sleeves of the work shirts were so worn that instead of a cuff there was only the fringe of unraveling cloth.

"Do you want it?" said the first.

"What?" I said.

"Do you want the speed beef?" he said, his eyes set on mine. "That. The deer."

"I thought I told you to stop touching my car," said the driver.

Our faces were close together, and I looked into those dark, shineless eyes, the expression in them now one of constant alertness.

"The speed beef doesn't look so bad," said the second one.

"What good is it going to do you?" said the first.

"He doesn't want it," said the second. "What the hell is he going to do with it?"

"Come on," said the driver. "Put the speed beef in the car. Lets get out of here."

They waited a moment, both of them looking at me.

"I'll make a deal with you," I said, "a friendly one. You take the meat."

"All right," said the driver.

"You stay away from my house," I said. "Understand?"

The driver said nothing.

One of them took a linoleum knife with a curved blade out of his boot, and in a flowing movement he opened the deer up and brought out the paunch, which steamed at the side of the road. Then both of them reached down and picked the animal up, one taking the forefeet, the other taking the hind ones.

"All its ribs are busted," said one. "There's going to be black blood in the meat."

"We'll soak it in saltwater," said the other.

They had opened the gate of the station wagon, and inside there was just the fiberboard that had been under the carpet. It was bloodstained, and the shapes there weren't only black and old, but there were some recent ones, too, and these were reddish brown, the color of terra-cotta. They put the deer in, its hooves rattling on the gate.

"Well?" I said to the driver.

"We never seen your house," he said.

"Up the road," I said. "You were there earlier."

"We were never there," said the second one, now turning to look at me, his eyes set on mine for a moment. "You can't prove anything. You got a witness?"

"You got your deer," I said. "We made a deal. Understand? Don't come back."

"It's a free country," said the driver.

He still sat in the car, but the other two stood next to me now. The ground fog drifted past our legs, about knee deep.

"You aren't very smart," said the first one. "What's to keep me from opening you up and throwing you in the swamp?"

For a moment no one said anything. Above the woods there was the winged, airy movement of some flying thing. I looked from one to the other of them and stepped a little closer, their faces absolutely unmoving.

"Did you know Marie?" I said.

"Marie?" said the driver. "Marie? Sure we knew Marie."

"Fastback Marie?" said the first.

"We used to call her Dirty Dozen Marie, bro," said the second.

"You remember that time in Billy's trailer?" said the first.

"Yeah," said the second. "Too hot to handle. She was a real beauty, when you got her dressed and on her feet."

The driver smiled now.

"You had too much to drink tonight, amigo?" he said. "Is that it?"

"Look," I said, "you got the meat. Don't come back to my house."

"We weren't up at your house," the second one said. "You must be mistaken."

They got back into the car. One got in the front and the other got in the back, where he reached over the seat and picked up that small-caliber rifle. He rolled down the window and said, "Oh, yeah. I know the house you mean. Old one with an orchard. Yeah, I remember. You got a wife and a couple of kids. Girls."

The moon fell over me as I stood in the road.

"Ask him," said the one in the front, "if he's always there."

"Naw," said the one in the back. "I don't have to ask. They'll be alone sometime."

"Until then, amigo," said the one in the front.

Then the car pulled away, the hood beginning to rattle again, the one taillight yellowish, the path of it rising as they approached the ridge. Through the windows and against the headlights there were the silhouettes of the men, and as the car went past the brush and pines, the men sat quietly, not tired or even bored so much as watchful. Every now and then they turned to one side or the other, the motion having about it the air of the quietly methodical. Now the car went at that same unhurried speed, neither too fast nor too slow, the rear end of it sagging on that broken spring as it climbed away from the swamp.

In the morning I made the kids breakfast. Toast, juice, eggs. Genny said, "Dad, do you know what you have with a box filled with ducks?"

"I don't know," I said. "What?"

"A box of quackers!" said Genny.

Sarah giggled.

Outside, that newish red car with the aerial on the top pulled into the driveway. May and Frank were in it, and for a moment they just sat there and talked. Then they got out and looked at the house. They came up the walk to the front door, May in front, Frank behind, one solid and gray, the other tall, blond, and stoop shouldered.

"Listen," I said. "Mom's going to take you kids down to the bus today, okay?"

"But I don't want Mom to do it," said Sarah.

"I'll do it tomorrow," I said.

"Who's that?" said Genny, looking out the window.

"Some old friends," I said.

Genny looked at me now.

"Old friends?" she said. "What are their names?"

"May and Frank," I said as Faith came into the kitchen.

I showed May and Frank into the living room, where they sat down in the same seats as before. The house smelled of toast and coffee.

"Can I get you something?" I said.

May turned his tired eyes toward me, the lids a little heavier than before.

"No, thanks, Ben," he said.

Frank just shook his head.

"What can I do for you?" I said.

"We were just in the neighborhood," said Frank, taking out his book and flipping the pages. "Lunn, Ben. White male. Here it is."

"You got to understand about police work, Ben," said May. "It has its own beauty. It's a procedure. If you got the procedure, you don't make too many mistakes. Every now and then somebody slips away, but . . ." He shrugged now, his tired eyes on mine. "Not that often."

"A lot of it," said Frank, "is just gathering information, y'unnerstand?"

"So we'd like to ask a couple more questions," said May.

"For instance, have you ever been to the Tree Park Cafeteria?" said Frank.

"Where's that?" I said.

"Down on Mission, in the city," said Frank.

"No," I said. "Not that I know of."

"You don't know a man by the name of Kiri, either, do you?" said Frank.

I shook my head. May watched now.

"You see, Ben," said Frank, "we got seventy-eight men to check out, in addition to some others. Kiri said a man, someone who could have been you, used to come into the Tree Park with Marie. He said she seemed pretty happy."

May looked away now, out the window.

"But then, you didn't know her, either, right?"

"No," I said. "But couldn't the man in the cafeteria have been one of the seventy-eight?"

"Sure," said Frank. "Probably was. It would help us, see, if maybe you'd been in there. By yourself sometime. That might explain it. Maybe he'd just seen you some other time."

"No," I said. I shook my head.

May closed his eyes for a moment.

"A waiter at the Buena Sierra says Marie used to go there

with a man who matches the description from Kiri," said Frank.

"That waiter might have seen me," I said. "I used to go to the Buena Sierra."

"Ben," said May, who was still looking at the floor, "what's your blood type?"

"Why?" I said.

"Well, these days there's a lot we can tell from just little things. Like a sample of semen. Or saliva."

"Even dried saliva," said Frank. "Just from what's on a licked stamp, or on the flat of an envelope."

"You never mailed Marie a letter, did you?" said May. "Why would you do that?"

"I said I didn't know her," I said.

"That's right," said May. "I was thinking of some of those other seventy-eight guys. That's right. You said you didn't know her. Well? What about the blood type?"

"O," I said. "Universal donor."

He nodded, looking down.

"All right, Ben," said Frank. "Thanks for your time."

"It's just a matter of procedure," said May, moving his tired eyes from the floor to my face. "But if you're going to leave town, we'd like you to contact us first."

"Sure," I said.

They both stood and looked out the window. That red car was parked in the driveway, the official quality of it seeming faintly out of place. They went out, into the pale sunlight, their figures blending into the dry grass across the street.

After they'd gone Faith and I sat in the kitchen, each of us with an untouched cup of coffee on the table. After a while I got up and said, "I've got to get to work. I'm doing the early-evening broadcast tonight. Some nasty weather in the Pacific."

It was the middle of fall. The children and I had planted pumpkins, and now, on the afternoon when we thought they were ripe, we started picking them and moving them to the side of the garden. The stems were rough and they looked like the skin of a horned toad. The sky was a smoky yellow and the orchard, the hillside, the house, and the garden were bathed in the mild light. The children picked some of the larger pumpkins to make jack-o'-lanterns, and we dragged them to the lawn next to the house. They took black markers and drew faces on the pumpkins so they'd know where to make the cuts. The faces had triangular eyes and a triangular nose, broad grins with jagged teeth and dark eyebrows, the expressions suggesting something both sinister and greedy.

They finished the drawings as that red car came up to the driveway.

"You stay here," I said to Genny and Sarah.

I started walking toward the house. Faith was in the kitchen, peeling apples to make a pie, but when she looked up, she came to the door, drying her hands on her apron. I took my windbreaker, the one I had brought from Marlowe, off of the hook by the door.

"Keep the kids in the backyard," I said.

"What's going on?" she said.

"Please," I said. "Don't ask for explanations now. All right?"

Outside the children were looking at their pumpkins. I started to go around to the front, but May and Frank were walking into the backyard.

"We have a warrant, Ben," said May. "I guess you know that."

May put his hand under his jacket and took out a pair of handcuffs.

"Please," I said. "I'll go with you. But don't do that in front of the kids."

"Ben," said Frank, "I'm going to advise you of your rights. . . ."

"Please," I said.

The children started running now, leaving the pumpkins behind. They came through the pale, yellow light of the fall afternoon, both of them saying, "What are you doing to my dad? Are you hurting him?"

Faith came from the back of the house, too, running now, her hair bouncing in that warm light, and as she came she was crying. I stepped back from May, and Genny put her arms around my leg. Faith came up and said, "Ben, Ben, I'm sorry. Oh, Jesus, I'm sorry. Please . . . let him alone."

"Get the kids off him," said May.

"Don't touch them," I said. "I'll take care of that. I'll get them in the house."

"Get them off," said May.

"No," I said.

Faith had both hands to her face, crying now. The children started crying, too.

"What are you doing to my dad?" said Sarah.

"We're police officers," said Frank.

"Where's your badge, then?" said Sarah.

Frank fumbled for his badge, but May said, "The hell with that. Get the kids off him."

"Don't touch them," I said.

Faith fell down on her knees now.

"Please, please, please. . . ." she said.

"This is getting out of hand," said Frank.

"Don't touch the kids," I said. "Just wait a minute."

"Come on," said May. "Just start walking."

Frank put his hand down and grabbed Genny and pulled her away from me. She screamed and I said, "Let go of her."

Frank pulled again.

I put my hand into the pocket of the jacket and picked up the pistol my father had given me. My hand was still in my pocket. I said. "Just stop. Just stop for a minute."

"What have you got there, Ben?" said May.

"Don't touch the kids," I said.

Frank reached under his coat, and I took the pistol out of my pocket, saying, "Just stop. Let the kids get away. . . ."

The sound of the shot rolled across the orchard, through the brush of it and up to the ridge, the sound of it like thunder. Frank stood with his gun out now, both hands on it, and I lay on the ground, saying, "Ah. Ah. Ah." Faith grabbed the kids and pulled them back, toward the house, both of them no longer even crying. The shot, the impact of it, had come like someone slamming a door, and now I put my hand under my shirt, over the numb but still hot and wet place. I took my hand away from a rib, which was broken into the texture of coarse salt. Now I looked at the pumpkins, the segmented, orange things at the back of the lawn, both of which had those black faces with those enormous, grinning mouths, the teeth stumpy and somehow voracious. I had thrown the pistol away and May picked it up and said to Frank, "For Christ's sake, get an ambulance up here."

"I didn't mean to do it," said Frank.

"Just get the ambulance," said May.

I was sleepy when it came. The sheets were clean and fresh. The medic leaned over me and the driver turned on the siren. We went fast past those new lots and that new house.

"Is he going to make it?" said the driver.

"No," said the medic. "With vital signs like this, you got to bend over and kiss your ass good-bye."

The siren wasn't so loud after a while, and there was the reassuring odor of the sheets and the stiffness of them, which wasn't like those in a good hotel so much as like sheets in a cabin my father and I used to rent. It was in the Sierras, and we took a trip up there in the summertime.

In those days, after my mother left, my father insisted we go on as before and act like a family even though there were only two of us. So we did the things we had always done, like taking vacations together, but now when we went we took with us an odd emptiness, which, if nothing else, made our mutual awkwardness that much more apparent. We packed our things and got into the Willys, my father wearing his white shirt and bow tie, and I sat next to him, wearing a white shirt, too, and a pair of khaki-colored trousers my father ordered through the mail from Brooks Brothers, the cuffs of which he finished himself, sitting under the Tiffany lamp in the dining room, the stitches resembling the ones he used to close the wounds of his patients. He finished the cuffs off with a surgeon's knot.

Both of us got into the car not with the air of a man and a boy who thought they were going to get anywhere so much as like a man and a boy who were sitting in a clean, deserted train station where the trains didn't stop anymore: we weren't expecting an awful lot. He started the engine, but before he backed out of the driveway (away from the veranda outside his office), he took a list from his jacket pocket and carefully read through it, checking off the things written there, underwear, socks, bathing suits, insect repellent, mosquito netting, sweaters, and pen (to write a postcard to Anthony Bompasino). Then we drove out of town, toward the Sierras, where we stayed in that real log cabin by a lake.

Up there, in the winter, men went out on the frozen lake and cut blocks of ice, using chain saws to do so, and then they stacked them on a sled, the blocks having the color of paraffin and suggesting a short, milky wall. The icehouse where the blocks were stored was a large building, the size of a small hangar, although it was made from wood, the posts at each corner still having the taper of a pine tree, not to mention knots where the branches had been cut off. The roof and sides were covered with shingles, which had long since turned gray.

It was hot and muggy one afternoon when my father and I were staying at the cabin, and in the distance there was the thump and roll of thunder, but even so we began our afternoon walk, crossing the porch and then going down the steps, both of us bent forward a little, hands in pockets, going fast. We wore white pants and cotton sweaters, the patterns of them identical (a red V around the neck), and both of us appearing, as I imagined then, anyway, very British, if only because we so obviously were getting through yet another vacation without so much as batting an eye. In fact, we probably looked like we were training for an event in speed walking: we came down the steps, all elbows and knees. On this afternoon, with the air wet and heavy, we went into the icehouse, the door closing behind us, and then we stood in the dim light and smelled the sawdust the ice was packed in. It was cold there and above us there was that dark, empty space, brown as the old wood of the ceiling. At one end of the building there was a small window, which let air in and kept the beams from rotting. My father and I stood there, heads back, eyes on the window, through which air came and turned white, forming a cloud inside the building. Outside there was the sound of thunder. The cloud got larger, now spreading over the blocks of ice, the edges of some of which were turning clear where they had melted a little.

The cloud had the same paraffin color as the ice, and as it spread, as it filled the icehouse from one end to another, snow began to fall from it. The flakes were small, but they were still cool, and they fell in lines straight as strings used to lay out a vegetable garden. I opened my mouth, and my father opened his, both of us hot and thirsty and wanting something to drink, and as we snapped at them, we tasted the pine rosin of the sawdust the ice was packed in. We still were panting a little as the flakes made a thin dust around us, and my father turned to me, his face coming out of the darkness beyond him as he said, "It's just like love, isn't it, Ben?"

"How so?" I said.

"Well, love is about the only thing that could make you feel like it had snowed in August," said my father. "Come on. Let's finish our walk and then take a swim." Then we went into the heat, both of us going quickly, perfectly in step, our movements seeming to be all elbows and knees as we went outside, into the bright sunlight.

Now, when the door of the ambulance was opened, the light seemed speckled. Another attendant got into the back and helped lift the stretcher, the thing now swaying in the air (the sensation just like being on a glider on a front porch), and as the attendant looked down on me he said, "Hey, amigo, we been waiting for you. We're all ready."